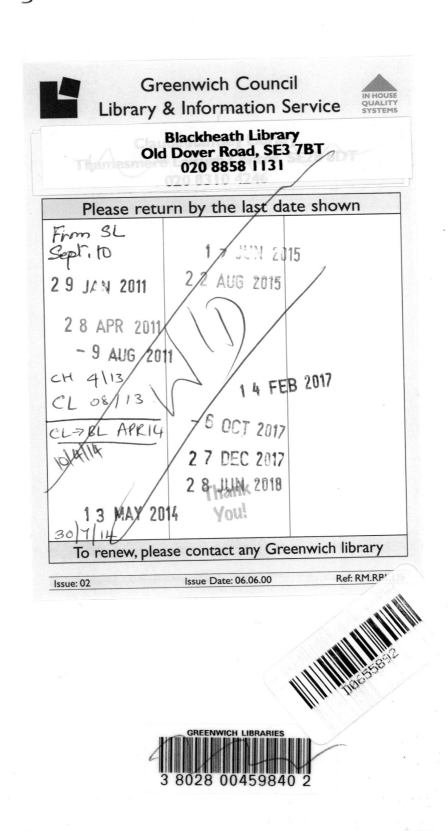

SUMMERTIME

When Trilby meets Lewis, the powerful proprietor of a newspaper group, she suspects that her life might be about to change, for not only does Lewis wish to acquire her cartoon strip, but Trilby herself. She is inevitably drawn to this handsome, older, and far more sophisticated personality, just as Lewis is, from the first, determined to marry the insouciant Trilby, despite the opposition of her friends and family. But having won her, Lewis reveals himself to be irrationally possessive. It is not long before she realises that Lewis is prepared to go to extraordinary lengths to keep her to himself. Quite by chance, she discovers the real reason for her husband's unforgivable behaviour. Trilby must come to terms with the truth about Lewis, and, more importantly, herself, before she can experience the kind of carefree happiness she once knew before her marriage.

SUMMERTIME

Charlotte Bingham

CHIVERS PRESS
BATH

First published 2001
by
Doubleday
This Large Print edition published by
Chivers Press
by arrangement with
Transworld Publishers Ltd
2001

ISBN 0 7540 1665 X

British Library Cataloguing in Publication Data available

Printed and bound in Great Britain by
BOOKCRAFT, Midsomer Norton, Somerset

This book is dedicated to my editor,
Francesca Liversidge, in gratitude for
her unswerving loyalty through many
long and difficult times.

Acknowledgements

My grateful thanks to Dick and Betty Hunt who entertained me to a sumptuous tea while enchanting me with stories about farming in 1950s England, and tales of what were indeed the good old days.

Also to my neighbours, Avril and Robert Jackson, for inviting me to their milking sheds and instructing me on the terminology of milking.

Hardway, 2001

ENGLAND IN THE NINETEEN FIFTIES

People say never go back, not to the past, but it's not as easy as that, is it? Certainly Trilby did not find it so. She had only to close her eyes and it seemed to her that she was back in the house in Chelsea and she was eighteen again, and she could hear the laughter, and with her eyes still closed she could feel the thick velvet of her black dressing gown and wonder at its large sleeves and ruffled cuffs as she crossed the street to have ten o'clock breakfast or midnight Ovaltine with all her friends who lived opposite.

Never mind that the King's Road was only down the way, everyone in Glebe Street crossed and re-crossed it as if it was not a road in London, but a communal garden. They crossed it with jugs of borrowed milk and dresses on loan for a special occasion. They crossed it with clippings from a newspaper or a rose bush, with last night's casserole for someone else to dine from, or last night's gossip with which someone else could be entertained.

And no-one minded the time that anyone went to bed, or the time that the rest of the world was prone to rise. They kept their own hours in Glebe Street, priding themselves on going to bed with the owls that still haunted the trees in their small gardens and getting up long after the rest of the richer, smarter world only a few streets away had left for their offices.

It was to all of them that Trilby found herself looking back, closing her eyes and allowing the colours and the music, but most of all the voices, to return, echoes of what seemed to her now, in her isolation, to be a warmer, kinder world.

PART ONE

Inside the doll's house everything was quite, quite perfect, but it was awfully quiet; so quiet that you could have heard a pin drop.

CHAPTER ONE

There was a place where Trilby could go where her stepmother could not find her. It was a beautiful place and full of colour, not magical but real and funny. In this place her stepmother's dissonant tones, her endless carping, could not be heard.

Here too Trilby could not be touched by her father's unhappiness, his aura of loneliness and loss.

It was to this imaginary place that Trilby would look forward to retreating when she returned from typing at the Lifetime Assurance Company, just a few streets away from Glebe Street where they all lived.

Trilby's daytime occupation was always decorously referred to by her stepmother, Agnes, as 'Trilby's pin money job'. Since none of the wages that she dutifully surrendered to her stepmother each week seemed to be spent on anything remotely resembling pins, this way of referring to her earnings puzzled and, occasionally, irritated Trilby.

'You must pay your way, Trilby, the same as the rest of us,' her stepmother was in the habit of saying. 'We all have to put our shoulders to the wheel and contribute to the housekeeping, you know.'

Trilby could see the reasoning behind this, but she could not see the fairness, since Agnes herself contributed nothing at all to the house. As it was, from the first week that Trilby started earning, her stepmother seemed all too eager to take her wages, leaving Trilby with only enough to buy herself small items and to pay for her hair to be cut by a fashionable stylist at a nearby salon.

'Girls like you do not need to have their hair styled, Trilby,' her stepmother insisted. 'You are best left *au naturel*. No amount of cutting and styling can alter what nature has given you, believe me. So much better to have left it alone instead of wasting money on it.'

This was a point that always seemed to come up when Trilby was about to leave the house for what she secretly thought of as her monthly appointment with glamour. There was no denying that she loved to go to the hairdresser, loved to enter the palely painted salon with its French proprietor, and its lady clients discreetly hidden behind cubicle curtains, all with their own facilities.

In this discreet haven women could enter the salon a certain shade of grey and leave it a rather uncertain shade of blue. Here too perming and cutting were a way of life, and while Trilby was determined never to have her hair permed, hating even the smell of the lotion, cutting was a must for anyone determined, as she was, to at least try to be fashionable. Besides, the new shorter cut suited her heart-shaped face, the lightly feathered fringe making a little curtain above her large dark eyes.

'I have no idea why Trilby should have had her hair cut off. When I married you she had such nice long hair, Michael, really she did. It would not be so bad if she had it permed, but she will insist on this feathering or whatever it is that she is so fascinated by, and really, it does nothing for her.'

This speech of Agnes's was inevitably made as Trilby was preparing to leave the house for the

4

salon, and it always seemed to follow Trilby, halfway down the road, sometimes even round the corner into the King's Road where finally, and thankfully, it was drowned out by the sound of the traffic. And even as Trilby quietly closed the front door behind her, she knew, although she could not hear, her father would be saying in his gentle tones, 'As a matter of fact I think short hair suits Trilby.'

'She is just not right for short hair—'

'She has beautiful eyes, and the short hair does show that up.'

'If she had your looks it would be different, Michael.'

Michael looked across at his second wife. He was well aware that Agnes must feel jealous of her stepdaughter, and that a pretty, younger woman in the house posed a threat to her, but he was also aware that, whatever happened, he had to stay on Agnes's side, because after all she was younger by some years than himself, and although he was tall and handsome it was a recurring nightmare that he might lose her to a more youthful, perhaps more virile man. The truth was that he was grateful to Agnes for marrying him when she had, and, most unfortunately, she knew it.

'I think you will find that Trilby just wants to follow fashion, just her age, you know, darling? I expect we were all like Trilby at her age, but we have just forgotten.'

Often as Trilby had heard this conversation, often as she knew it would be carrying on even as she swung through the doors of André's salon, at the same time she could not help feeling depressed by it.

Despite her father's defence of her hairstyle, his

5

insistence on the fact that she had beautiful eyes, though loyal, finally made her feel as if she *only* had eyes, and nothing else. So when she stationed herself in front of the hairdressing mirror preparatory to submitting herself to the undoubted art of André's cutting scissors, it seemed to Trilby that her nose, mouth and chin must be a complete waste of time, with the result that when she stared into the mirror at herself she looked only at her eyes, ignoring the rest of her face, even hoping that it would go away.

'I shouldn't take much notice of Agnes. Women always cling to the fashions of their own eras,' Michael would sometimes murmur to Trilby when they were alone in the house, and out of reach of Agnes and her opinions. 'The most important thing about you, Trilby, is that you are an original. That is as important, believe me, as being pretty. Be yourself, like Shakespeare says, that's the ticket. Be yourself, whatever happens.'

It was kind of her father to say so, but Trilby certainly did not feel very original. She felt most particularly unoriginal when she was at the insurance company. Working in a typing pool, even if you lived at home in genteel circumstances, was a soul-destroying business. The supervisor, who sat at the top of the room at a raised desk, was a beady-eyed high priestess of time and motion. Once seated, and having hit her wooden gavel on the desk in front of her as a signal for the luckless girls in the typing pool to start work, she would sit motionless, staring, always staring.

The sound that the old-fashioned typewriters made was almost insupportable, but the supervisor appeared to be untouched by it. Instead, as the din began, her eyes would start to move down the rows of girls, and she would examine them one by one with sadistic interest, searching for the slightest pause in production, the slightest indication that someone's fingers had ceased to operate in the interests of the Lifetime Assurance Company.

Even a small pause to sneeze or unwrap a cough sweet would secure the immediate and overt interest of the supervisor, and she would stare at the lozenge or the offending handkerchief as if they were the evil instruments of the work-shy. With narrowed eyes she would wait, hoping to witness something untoward, something that she could report, or, worse, note in her records.

Sometimes Trilby fantasised about what the supervisor would do if she, say, blew her nose twice or sucked a cough sweet for five minutes, which would mean, horror of horrors, that she would have left the Lifetime Assurance Company short of a page of its endless, and sometimes, it seemed to her, quite pointless reports.

The small wooden gavel was also used to point to any individual who was due to take her fifteen-minute coffee break. The moment it was pointed at Trilby she would spring up, and hurry off, not to the refreshment room, but to the outside world where, if it was a fine day, for a blissful fifteen minutes she would take out her drawing pad and pencil and sit on a pavement bench in a side street furnishing the secret world she was so anxious to create. What she drew was meant for her own amusement, longing only as she did to create a world where lives were not grey and brown, where there were no supervisors with wooden gavels but only fascinating and colourful people who were

7

tolerant and kind and never died, as her own mother had done.

Trilby called her cartoon strip *The Popposites*, because ever since her father and stepmother and herself had come to live in Glebe Street it had seemed to Trilby that the people opposite them, and on either side of them, lived far more glamorous lives than the Smythsons, who pursued regularity of meals and appointments with a near-religious fervour. These people were quite different, always arriving back at odd moments of the day and night. They seemed to Trilby to openly despise any regularity of existence, any kind of security.

Yet it soon became clear to Trilby that her father and stepmother, while tolerating their neighbours, did not in fact like them as much as Trilby did. In fact they seemed to pride themselves on not being 'that kind of person'. The Smythsons were respectable. The people opposite and on either side lived in brightly painted houses, and were anything but respectable. Indeed, they were, and did not mind being, complicated and glamorous.

They lived for the day, which was probably why they were always out at night. They cooked strange French dishes whose smells tantalised the senses on a hot summer London evening, and they did up their gardens with fountains and mirrors and planted their flower pots with colourful flowers. They were not tasteful like the Smythsons, who had old furniture and nineteenth-century flower paintings, and only liked pale pink roses and lavender. But even if their chairs and wallpapers, their curtaining and furnishings were bought from Liberty and Heal's, and not inherited from an aunt

8

or a great-uncle, it always seemed to Trilby that their neighbours smiled more, and laughed more, and that music came from their houses at odd times of day, and there were no routines or supervisors, and 'pin money' was certainly not a phrase that you would ever hear them use.

The worst thing about living with her father and stepmother was the food. The food at the Smythsons' house was not influenced by Paris or Rome, it was stolidly post-war British. It did not smell tantalising, or look colourful. It knew nothing of bright peppers, or Spanish oil. Rather, it looked grey and sometimes deep brown, and, worse than that, it always had to be 'finished'.

The Smythsons' 'cook' was Mrs Bartlett, Agnes's daily maid, who came in and cleaned and cooked for them every day except Saturday, when she only came in for the morning. It sometimes seemed to Trilby that while she worked at the insurance company a few streets away, and her father worked at the Foreign Office a taxi ride away, her father and herself were working long hours so that Agnes need not work at all.

Of course Agnes would not clean—she often said that she would not know how to—and she certainly did not know how to cook, but she did insist that Trilby 'finished up'. From the moment that she had married Michael Smythson, and brought him back from the country to London, from the moment she had taken on Trilby's upbringing, the one thing that Agnes had insisted on was a clean plate. Not from her—she herself hardly ate at all—but from Trilby.

Sometimes it was possible, when, thank God, the telephone rang for Agnes, for Trilby to smuggle

9

Mrs Bartlett's utterly inedible cooking into a handkerchief and conceal it in her handbag. At other times, when her father and stepmother were out, the food was left for her on the mahogany sideboard and she was able to throw it into a shopping bag and, her heart in her mouth at the idea that she might be discovered, smuggle it out to a dustbin by the back door.

Once she was nearly caught by Agnes as the latter returned home early from a party.

'What's in that bag, Trilby?'

'Nothing that you would want to find, Agnes,' Trilby answered truthfully, and she eyed her stepmother, who was a great deal taller than herself, with as much humour as she could muster, considering the situation.

'What do you mean by that, Trilby?'

'We-ell, put it this way, Agnes. What is in this bag is for you, but not now, later. It's a surprise.'

It was always easy to flatter Agnes. She stared down into Trilby's large, dark eyes preparing to be moderately flattered, although for a second Trilby could see that she did not believe her.

'Surprise, for me? When?'

'Guess.' Trilby's expression was now droll, and she rolled her eyes.

'Oh, I see. Yes, of course.' Happily Agnes had a birthday coming up. 'But in that case why are you going out?'

'Put it this way, Agnes. Aphrodite has a sewing machine, remember?'

At that moment Agnes's best friend the telephone rang, and she hurried away from Trilby, who then fairly sprang out of the door and ran across the road to Aphrodite Billington's house, where Aphrodite, already a staunch ally of long standing, opened the door to her. Trilby hurried in and down to her dustbin, into which she thankfully flung her wretched shopping bag, leaving the wondrously exotic Aphrodite to gaze after her and sigh, 'Not more of Mrs Bartlett's stodge, you poor love?'

For the fact was that everyone in Glebe Street was on Trilby's side in her war against Agnes, and not least of these was tall, raven-haired Aphrodite, who, with her svelte figure and artistic leanings, wanted nothing more than that Trilby should stay as slender as Aphrodite herself.

Aphrodite loved clothes, and clothes, as both she and Trilby were well aware, never looked so good as on a slender silhouette. Sometimes Aphrodite would lend Trilby dresses to try on, but only in her house. Trilby always had to change back into her own dowdy office clothes to go back home.

It was both glamourous and exciting to waft about Aphrodite's house in borrowed clothes, pretending to be someone else. Trilby would look forward to such moments with an almost passionate intensity, an intensity made more piquant by the fact that she knew that both her father and Agnes would not approve. They would not only disapprove, they would be appalled.

Following the incident of the carrier bag, however, both Trilby and Aphrodite nearly had their comeuppance, for when Agnes's birthday did eventually arrive she opened Trilby's present to her in puzzled silence.

'I fail to see why this needed *altering*,' she said at last, frowning across the breakfast table at Trilby, as she folded the silk scarf that her stepdaughter had given her.

Trilby smiled, her expression assuming what she hoped was a mysterious air, while she did not venture to say anything. Her smile, she hoped, indicated that she had made the scarf for Agnes, when in fact she had, with Aphrodite's assistance, merely removed the manufacturer's label.

Sometimes, as she was growing up, the awful ways that she contrived to deceive Agnes made Trilby feel guilty, but only for a few seconds, because, finally, she knew that whatever Agnes did for her was not for Trilby's happiness, or even her own, but to Trilby's detriment. And occasionally, in the middle of the night if she was feeling low, Trilby did sometimes make herself face the fact that her own unhappiness, or discomfort, could be a source of some great content to her stepmother.

However it was, it certainly took a long time for the penny to drop, but when it did at last, Trilby realised that the reality of 'finishing up' was that Agnes did not want Trilby to be slender and pretty, she wanted her to be fat and plain.

For a few years she definitely succeeded. Following her mother's sudden and awful death in a car accident in the country, where they were then living, with Agnes's help Trilby did actually, and perhaps inevitably, become incredibly fat and plain—so much so that Agnes felt quite able to be nice to her.

After the death of her lovely, lively, life-loving mother, Trilby's existence had become a matter of total despair. She had moved slowly and sadly from one day to the next, not looking forward to anything except the dullness of another day, when, of a sudden, her newly remarried father had turned to her and said, I have made arrangements for you to go to Switzerland. There's a friend of mine there you can lodge with, teach you skiing, that sort of thing.'

Away from Agnes in the cold mountain air, Trilby did not just learn to ski and speak French, she lost weight, pounds and pounds of it, so that it felt to her as if she was leaving it on the mountain slopes as she skied by. When she returned home, she was, it seemed to her, and to the rest of the street, a different person.

Seeing her stepdaughter, glowing and fit, Agnes simply made her *hmm* noise and turned away, back to the telephone and her engagement diary.

However, when Trilby crossed the street to see Aphrodite, her reaction had been quite different.

'But you've become beautiful!' she said, pulling Trilby into her house. 'Slim and grown up and beautiful. Well done *you!*'

It might have been possible for Trilby to have remained beautiful if she had not had to go back to living with her father and stepmother. Gradually, as day after wretched day she had to sit opposite her stepmother at breakfast and dinner and eat up everything on her plate as if she was a girl of seven, not seventeen, it became clear to Trilby that if she did not take decided steps to protect herself from her stepmother the plainness would return.

Sometimes she would pretend that she had already eaten, at other times she would insist that she felt sick. In fact avoiding meals at home became a hobby with her, and playing cat and mouse with Agnes a sort of long protracted game with Trilby slipping in and out of the house at determinedly odd times. Occasionally she would let herself into the basement to make sure that the house was utterly quiet, which would mean that her stepmother was out. Or she would let herself in the back door and wait until she heard Agnes leave the house for some new social engagement before zipping up to her room, and locking the door.

To make up for all this avoidance of meals, Trilby often ate, and always with pleasure, in the houses opposite, or on either side. She ate homemade croissants, and pâtés, making deeply appreciative noises. She hung around their kitchens testing their casseroles and pronouncing on their mousses, she even, on occasions, drank wine, but she made sure that she never again put on weight as she had done after her mother's death.

Often when she was in the kitchen helping Aphrodite or Mrs Johnson Johnson prepare for some dinner party, Trilby would show them some new set of drawings, some new episode of *The Popposites*, and they would laugh, and murmur, 'You naughty girl, you've got me to a T.'

*   *   *

Trilby had captured Aphrodite's next-door neighbour Mrs Johnson Johnson most particularly: her tall, angular figure, her large red lips, her habit of wearing turbans and exotic eastern garments at all times. As a widow she revelled quite overtly in her freedom to wear what she liked when she liked, unhampered by the embarrassment of a disapproving spouse. A cigarette holder always to her lips, a gin and tonic comfortingly close, Mrs Johnson Johnson had made Trilby her hobby. She liked Trilby, and Trilby knew it from the approving

14

expression in her eyes, just as she knew from the same set of eyes that Mrs Johnson Johnson disliked Agnes Smythson.

'You're a talented little sausage,' she would tell Trilby, fitting yet another cigarette into her holder. 'Should go far, I would say, wouldn't you, Aphrodite?'

At which Aphrodite would look up from some casserole that she was cooking and nod vaguely, saying of *The Popposites*, 'Don't you love them, though, Melanie, I mean to say, don't you just love the way she's got us all, really?'

It was different at home. At home, Agnes would sometimes, most unfortunately, catch sight of Trilby's drawings, and say disapprovingly, 'Wasting your time and energy on your silly drawings as usual, Lydia,' and push them away from her as if they were dirty tea towels she had come across in the kitchen.

For this was another aspect of her stepmother which had, over the years, proved most upsetting to Trilby. Agnes hated her name. She thought it was silly. Time and time again she remarked on the ugliness of Trilby's name, most especially in the early days after she had married the besotted Michael Smythson.

She did not like 'Trilby' as a name, *she* preferred 'Lydia', she said, and so, every now and then, when she was in a particularly vile mood, and despite Trilby's having finally, as she grew older, insisted on retaining her own name, she would address Trilby as 'Lydia', and Trilby would take it. But however hard she tried to accept it, it always acted like a slap in the face, which was, she thought, how it was meant to act.

'Your poor mother. Why on earth she should saddle you with a silly name like *Treel-bee*, I wouldn't know.'

When they moved back from the country to London, Agnes took ruthless advantage of Trilby's new school, and on her insistence Trilby's name was put down as 'Lydia Smythson'. It was by this name that the teachers knew her for her remaining years at the school. Trilby was able to counter this stepmotherly manoeuvre, however, by insisting that her classmates called her 'Trilby', pretending to them that it was, in fact, her nickname.

So finally, in a kind of way, Trilby did win.

Except with Agnes you never really won, you just waited until the next time, when she tried it on again, and you never really knew when it was going to happen, when some new little sadistic ploy would come into play, when some new idea that would add to the discomfort of another might suddenly occur to her.

Yet, despite all this, Trilby did not hate Agnes. She was too like her tall, handsome if diffident father in temperament to hate her stepmother. She always thought that to hate Agnes would be like hating a mountain for its crags, or snow because it was cold, or rain because it was wet. Agnes could not help how she was. Trilby had known that from the moment that she came into their lives. Agnes was Agnes, and there was nothing to be done about it.

Of course, after a few years, both her father and herself had quite separately come to the realisation that Agnes had not perhaps fallen in love with Michael Smythson, despite his good looks and sweet ways, in the same way that Michael had fallen, head over heels, in love with Agnes.

Agnes had been a divorcee, which meant that socially, until she married Michael, she was far beyond the pale as far as Society was concerned. So, besides falling passionately in love with her, Michael had felt sorry for her. Not that it was difficult to fall in love with Agnes, if you were a man. She was tall, dark-haired and very beautiful, in aspect not unlike the fashionable and elegant Duchess of Fife whom Agnes always admired and liked to read about. Not only that, but she had beautiful limbs, and a fascinating manner, when she wished. What she did not have, however, was that final requisite, so seldom found in people who have always known that they are beautiful, namely—kindness.

If Trilby had wished to hate Agnes, she would have hated her, but she did not wish to hate her. She wished simply and solely that she would be nicer to her father, but that too, she came to realise, was a silly waste of time.

Agnes had no more wish to love anyone except herself than she had to live in the country with Michael, or to allow Trilby to have a dog or use her real name, or for any other thing that involved another human being. Agnes only wished things for herself, whatever those things happened to be.

Michael had sold his eighteenth-century rectory and bought the house in Chelsea, for Agnes. He lived a life which, under torture, he would have had to admit he loathed, but he did it for Agnes. Just as he had taken Trilby's dog, when they were leaving the country, to be put down, for Agnes's sake. She did not like dogs. The dog had been taken to be put down, but not by Agnes, by Michael, because

Michael loved Agnes. Besides, he was so grateful to her for marrying him, and rescuing him and Trilby from their numbed loneliness, their bewilderment and grief. That was how much Michael had fallen passionately in love with Agnes, enough to not mind hurting Trilby by having her dog put down.

Finally too he had loved her enough to not mind hurting himself, ruining his own life, making himself miserable, if it meant that Agnes would be happy. That was all he wanted, for Agnes, this beautiful and fascinating woman, to be happy. So that was what he did. He made himself violently unhappy in order to make her happy.

Except Agnes was never happy, not with anything or anyone. She was always restless and dissatisfied. She was always waiting for something better to happen, tomorrow. Today was always a burden, or a nuisance. If she did remember anything good for which she could be thankful, it was always in retrospect, and it had always happened some years, sometimes many years, before. Sometimes these idyllic occasions had happened before the war. Other times, strangely, during the war.

'I had a really good war.'

Agnes often said that, and it puzzled Trilby dreadfully, because she could not imagine anyone having anything called a 'good war'. War, it seemed to her, must be terrible: people dying, buildings on fire, sadness, grief, sorrow—most of all sorrow. But none of this grief or sorrow had, apparently, affected Agnes, who had thoroughly enjoyed *her* war.

Of course she blamed the war for her divorce.

It seemed that her first husband and herself had

18

remet as total strangers after Agnes had finished enjoying her really good war. The first husband, Trilby heard frequently, had been 'tiresome' to live with. He had suffered from depressions and frequently disturbed *her* sleep in the night with his crying and sudden yelling. The end result was that Agnes had to be shot of him. He had proved intolerable as a husband, and a disaster at his job. Finally, and, it sometimes seemed to Trilby, to her stepmother's ill-concealed satisfaction, he had committed suicide, which meant that Agnes could once again be admitted to the Royal Enclosure at Ascot and was no longer a 'second class citizen', something about which she had moaned to Michael and Trilby at some length during the first years of her second marriage.

Back in London, and with her stepdaughter and second husband safely out of the way during the day, Agnes could pursue the kind of life for which she had always longed. Of course she was not as rich as she wished, and of course they did not live in Mayfair, but they were none the less respectable, and Michael was certainly a leg-up socially, after the failure of her first marriage.

Not that this made her feel in the least bit grateful to him. On the contrary Trilby often felt it made her resentful. For the kinder that her father was to Agnes, and the more tolerant, the less she seemed to love and respect him.

It was to escape the frequent spectacle of his humiliation at her stepmother's hands that Trilby bolted across the road to visit Mrs Johnson Johnson or Aphrodite, or let herself out of their back garden gate only to sidle along the path and visit Berry Nichols and his wife Molly, who were

19

always kind enough to be, or pretend to be, amused and interested by *The Popposites*.

Molly Nichols would read the latest set of drawings rocking with gentle laughter, and saying occasionally, in between taking deep, appreciative puffs of her cigarette, 'Oh, Trilb, you are naughty, you've captured us all so well. Oh, look, Berry, she has put us in this week, it's all about your exploding steak and kidney pie! And Mrs Johnson Johnson, look, Berry, do, it is so killingly funny. So funny.'

Berry, who always did the cooking at their house, did not look up from the sauce he was preparing over a *bain-marie*. Molly poured them all a glass of champagne and said, with some diffidence, 'I say, Trilb, would you mind terribly if I gave your *Popposites* to a friend of mine to look over? I mean, he might not like them, but he has, as they say in Fleet Street, friends at court, and really, we all, everyone in the street, we all think it is so amusing, you might get a sale, and, well—you *might*, you know, and that would be quite something, wouldn't it?'

Trilby nodded, not really listening. It was always the same when she was involved with a new set of drawings, making herself laugh deep down, but holding it back while getting it all down before the laughter burst out of her, and stood in the way of her caricatures.

Yet she could not help delighting in seeing Berry and Molly, Aphrodite and Mrs Johnson Johnson laughing too.

The fact was, and it could not be denied, making other people laugh was something that Trilby found not just satisfactory, but thrilling. For a few minutes, or even seconds, when people laughed she could see that they had been forced to stop worrying about the Bomb, or bills, or in Berry's case some new portrait that was not pleasing some new client.

'Yes,' Molly continued. 'Yes, if you thought you wouldn't mind, Trilby, I could show your last set of drawings to this man we know, and see what he *thought*. I mean, it just might be that your drawings are amusing only to all of us, love, you know, because we are all in them. But, on the other hand, it might mean that if he finds them funny, he could show them to his boss, and he might buy them.'

Trilby frowned. She could not imagine, not in a thousand years, actually selling what she had drawn. It had never occurred to her. Indeed, it had to be faced, she often drew just for the amusement of their neighbours, an amusement which, she had to admit, meant that she gained a great deal of popularity with them all, not to mention a taste of their fresh croissants and home-made pâtés and casseroles. The drawings were, in their way, her meal ticket.

Not that amusing the neighbours was the only reason for her escape into a world of her own. It was also a relief, for it never seemed to matter to her, once she started to draw, what happened in the outside world. Nothing mattered once she took her pencil in her hand. Not the typing pool, not Agnes, not her father's lonely, unhappy life; none of that mattered once she was busy with her pencil and drawing pad. So now that Molly mentioned the possibility of trying to sell what Trilby did, of being paid money for *The Popposites*, it seemed somehow almost greedy, such was the fulfilment that she gained from her observations of the little world of

Glebe Street.

Nevertheless, she gave Molly and Berry a set of the latest drawings and, having done so, put the whole matter out of her mind.

Happily Agnes was out when Molly rang one evening the following week.

'Come round, at once. You must, really. Such excitement. We are popping several corks.'

By now, as was her habit, Trilby had changed into her black velvet dressing gown, but knowing that Berry and Molly would not care how she was dressed she did not bother to change but sauntered out into the back garden, let herself out of the bottom gate and into their garden and drifted up to their French windows, not really thinking very much about anything other than that it was a fine night and that despite its being a London night sky above them she could see a great many stars, which to Trilby was always and eternally magical.

'Molly!' Berry, tall, bespectacled and always, it seemed to Trilby, in an apron and gym shoes, and faded jeans, called out to his wife. 'She's here! Trilby's here!'

Molly, always elegant and still pretty, came into the room with both her hands outstretched towards Trilby.

'My dear Trilby, guess what?'

'I can't.'

Standing in her black velvet dressing gown Trilby tried to look soignée and grown up, cool and even a little off-beat all at the same time, while also trying to ignore the very real fact that she could see at once from Molly's glowing expression that something exciting had happened.

'My dear, guess what?' she said again. 'He *loves*

22

it!'

Trilby looked at her, straight-faced. Her habit of not being entirely present in her life sometimes caught up with her, and not just when she was in the typing pool. She knew she could not say 'Who likes it?', it would sound too rude, so she settled instead for something suitably vague.

'Oh, so that is good, I suppose?' She smiled and raised her eyebrows questioningly, her head on one side.

'*Good!*' The word burst out of Berry, and he hurried off to his kitchen. 'Tell her, Moll, tell her. Go on, tell her how *good* this *is*.'

'Sit down while I get us both some champagne,' Molly commanded, and she opened the drink cupboard where they kept what sometimes seemed to Trilby a thousand glasses of all different shapes, and a hundred different types of wine bottles the same. 'There.'

Molly sat down opposite Trilby, and Trilby sipped at the champagne, while Molly stared at her, and Trilby looked around the Nichols' sitting room, which she liked so much, being such a mixture, as it was, of the old and the new, the beautiful and the strange. African masks placed on a Chinese Chippendale sideboard, a white leather sofa beside a chintz chair. It was all endlessly interesting, and, to Trilby, somehow stimulating.

Molly began again, after a long pause, obviously trying to marshal all her strength not to sound too excited.

'Well. Trilby. You know how I said we had a friend who had friends at court? Well. It has turned out that he has indeed, but what he has too—that doesn't sound very grammatical, does it? But you

23

know what I mean. To cut a long story short, what he has done is show your drawings to his proprietor, the man who *owns* the newspaper group that he works for on the management side, and guess what?'

Trilby shook her head, still too happy about being in the Nichols' sitting room to take much notice of what Molly was talking about.

'I don't know,' she said, cheerfully.

'He wants to buy your drawings. He wants to buy your cartoons, Trilby. He wants to buy *The Popposites.*'

Trilby frowned. 'I see,' she said in a shocked voice, not really understanding what was being said, or the actual import of what might be about to change her life for ever, which meant that, after a pause, she asked, tentatively, 'but I mean, what for?'

'What for!' Molly laughed delightedly. 'Why, for his *newspapers*, Trilby. For his newspapers, and for himself too. He fell in love with them. He said so to David Micklethwaite, this friend, well, acquaintance really, this acquaintance of ours, he said he had fallen in love with *The Popposites.*'

'What will he do with them?'

'Do with them? Why, he will publish them in one of his newspapers, and he will pay you money for them, too. He might pay you quite a lot of money.'

Trilby stared. Money. She had never thought of being paid to draw. The whole idea seemed too fantastic to believe. After all, as everyone knew, cartoons were completely a male preserve, as her stepmother had always taken such great delight in telling her.

'You'll never sell those silly drawings of yours,

24

Lydia, not in a million years, will she, Michael?'

But Michael would always manage to avoid replying to this kind of challenge, instead waiting until Agnes had gone out before searching Trilby out and saying with his kind smile, 'I think they're jolly funny, I should carry on if I were you.' Then he would wander off in search of something to do, which seemed to be his lot whenever Agnes was out for the evening, and he was left to do the crossword and listen to music.

Once Agnes had a bee in her bonnet about something, however, it would take another war to stop her, and she would return to the subject of Trilby's drawings again and again, and again.

'You're just wasting your time, really you are. You would do far better to take up fashion drawings. Now there really *is* a place you could find a niche, drawing dresses and so on, and it would get you into all the fashion shows. You could *sell* those, I should think.'

But Trilby had never wanted to draw dresses and hats. She did not want to dwell in the ephemeral and ever-changing world of the wasp waist, the New Look, or the little black cocktail dress. She loved human beings, not what covered them, and, more than that, human beings made her laugh. For her there could not be a moment's enjoyment in just drawing a hat or a shoe, but put the right, or rather the wrong, face under the hat, and the wrong pair of shoes on the wrong legs, and she was away.

'Now listen, Trilby, we have a problem, because you know you are at the office all day long, at your job? Well, this chap is going to telephone here, tomorrow, so really you should be here, because I gave this as your number, because, you know, I know how it is with *you know who.* She won't really like this at all, will she?' Molly stared at Trilby.

They both knew what or rather *you know who* was, and how she was about Trilby's drawings. They both knew how much she had mocked Trilby's hobby, and how she had, on occasion, even accused her of making fun of people who were fond of her, people who had brought her up, suspecting perhaps, Molly had once suggested to Trilby, that somewhere among the ladies that peopled Trilby's cartoon Agnes herself lurked. This was far from being the case, for Trilby, having no affection for Agnes, could not find anything about her in the least bit amusing, and that being so would not have been able to draw her even should she have wanted to do so. It was just a fact. She had to be fond of people to caricature them.

'We will have to make a plan.'

Molly, and Berry, always said this when they were hatching something.

'Yes, we will.' Trilby had put down her champagne glass, and was now sitting up really very straight, thoughts whizzing through her brain in a way that she had not thought possible.

'I could ring up Lifetime Assurance and tell them you were ill.'

'Yes, you could.'

'I could ring them up and say that you were sick, and if it is only one day, well, you won't need a doctor's certificate, will you?'

Trilby shook her head. 'What about you know who, though?'

Molly nodded. They both knew that you know who would see everything and anything unusual in

26

the street, and that being so, Trilby would have to leave for the typing pool as usual, and slip back to the Nichols' house when Molly or Berry had created some kind of distraction.

'I'll send Berry to borrow flour from her, or something, that will distract her all right. And I'll give you a front door key, so you can double back and quickly let yourself in here and hide up until the telephone call comes through.'

Trilby nodded. 'That's a good idea.'

They looked at each other directly, suddenly serious. Molly finished by sighing, for both of them.

'Gracious, what a palaver, duck, to have to go through all this in order for you to take a very exciting telephone call. It doesn't seem right somehow, but what else can you do?'

'Nothing,' Trilby agreed. 'After all we both know that Agnes hates *The Popposites*. She wants me to do fashion drawing, that kind of thing, you know? I mean, she really, really hates *The Popposites*, worse than sin. I always have to hide my things when she comes into my room. Nowadays, I lock my door, because sometimes she used to creep up the stairs and burst in, trying to, you know, trying to catch me *at* it.'

'Personally, I think she is quite dotty. I know I shouldn't say it to you, but I do really. And honest to God, duck, why your beloved father doesn't give her a good clip around the head, I don't know.'

This was from Berry, who had overheard the last part of their conversation and now strode past them to the drink cupboard.

'Now Berry, darling boy, that is no way to talk. Besides, it has nothing to do with anything, as it happens, because Trilby and I have devised a plan,

27

and as it happens we are going to need you to borrow something.'

Berry groaned, half mockingly. 'Not a "borrowing something" plan, please!'

'Yup, Berry darling. You are going to go next door tomorrow morning and borrow from Agnes, while I keep watch, and Trilby leaves as usual, except she won't. She will not leave for work, she will come here and take David's call about Mr James.'

'Sounds frightfully complicated to me. Bound to go wrong.'

'Nevertheless, that is what we shall do.'

*   *   *

Deceit had not come naturally to Trilby until Agnes entered her life, and then she had never thought of it as deceiving Agnes, merely as avoiding her persecution. Nevertheless, Molly and herself had undoubtedly hatched a plan to deceive her stepmother, and Trilby could not help feeling guilty as she called goodbye to her the following morning.

'Goodbye, Agnes.'

'What time will you be back?'

'The same time, around six o'clock, if there are no retypes at work.'

'Very well. Supper will be at seven. Try not to be late.'

This was their usual conversation. It was so usual that Trilby could hardly bring herself to hold it, although she nevertheless always did. Today she walked out of the house convinced that her stepmother was watching her. Perhaps it was the guilt of knowing that Molly was going to lie for her to the Lifetime Assurance Company, but Trilby had the feeling that Agnes had removed herself from her usual station in front of her dressing table mirror and was watching Trilby from her first floor window. Watching her walking down the garden path and turning right, as if to go to the Lifetime Assurance Company, instead of which, after duly passing an aproned Berry leaving his house for theirs with an empty flour bin, she quickly doubled back, and let herself into the Nichols' house with Molly's front door key.

'Phew!' Trilby collapsed dramatically against Molly's hall wall, and they both laughed. 'I don't know why, but I had the feeling that she was watching me today.'

'Oh, I dare say she was. Agnes is most peculiar, really she is. Too little to do, Berry always says. Coffee?'

At home the coffee was always part chicory. At Molly's house it was quite different, resoundingly French and delicious, and always served with a swirl of cream. Molly was a great believer in swirls of cream, delighting in post-war produce and its availability, enjoying everything that now came their way where once even a piece of four-day-old fish had been a treat.

They both sipped their coffee without saying anything, and their eyes strayed to the old black telephone with its Chelsea number, now so faded that anyone who did not know it would have been hard pushed to read it on the old, round label.

'Just like a watched kettle not boiling, a watched telephone will not ring. Let's go upstairs and try on hats, that will make it ring. He did say, David

29

Micklethwaite did say that he would ring here this morning.'

They both tried on Molly's old hats, and then Molly's new hats, and they did prove to be a complete distraction, but it did not do the trick, still the telephone did not ring.

'He is a very busy man.'

Trilby nodded, not really paying much attention, because she was now trying to remember if a day missed, even through illness, meant that she would have a day's pay docked from her wages at the end of the month.

If so she would be in trouble with Agnes, who always took her pay packet from Trilby with a peeved look, the expression on her face implying that if only Trilby, not to mention Trilby's father, would work a little harder they would bring more home for Agnes to spend.

Just as the excitement brought about by simply the idea of good luck coming your way raises the temperature of everything around you, now, Trilby discovered, despite the warm autumnal weather, her temperature was being unnaturally lowered by the non-ringing of the telephone.

She felt almost damp with despair, and bewildered too, because, really, when all was said and done, none of the excitement, the deceit, or the probably impending disappointment had been caused by her.

'I feel awful. Perhaps David Micklethwaite was having me on?' Molly stared at her watch. It was twenty past twelve, well past what she herself considered to be morning. 'I really do feel awful, Trilby. I mean, if that was just tinky tonky talk, I will go round and personally berate him, really I

30

will. I mean, to raise all our hopes this way, and then not even bother to ring when you say you will. It's the way the world is going now, believe me, it really, really is. Nothing but hard, cold, commercial people, post-war spies who do nothing but think of themselves and their wretched bank balances—'

'Molly—'

'I always thought that David Micklethwaite was a bit of a spiv, and now I know that he is. I really, really would not credit it. It's not as if he is not on the management side, it's not as if he—'

'Molly—'

'I promise you, Trilb, I feel like going round and boxing his ears, really I do.'

'Molly, the telephone is ringing!'

They ran downstairs to the sitting room, and Molly fairly plucked the receiver from the telephone in a movement that suggested a red-hot plate being removed from an oven. Then, her lips firmly closed, her eyes wearing their most startled expression, she handed the receiver to Trilby, who heard herself saying in a low voice 'Hallo?' and then, not being able to remember Molly and Berry's number, she said 'Hallo' again.

'Hallo, yes. This is Trilby Smythson. Good morning, or rather good afternoon. Oh, I see.' She covered the telephone and whispered, 'It's not Mr Micklethwaite, it's a secretary asking for me, on behalf of a Mr Lewis James?'

Molly's hand went round her throat and she fell against her sitting room wall and slid down it.

'That's *him*!' she hissed. 'That's, you know, the man who owns everything, all the papers.'

Trilby felt herself losing all colour, until she knew that she must have turned a very, very

31

delicate shade of green. Her mouth went dry and she breathed in and out as slowly and carefully as she could as she heard the secretary saying, 'Mr James? I have Trilby Smythson on the line for you.'

'Hallo, Miss Smythson?'

'Mr James.'

'I wanted you to know that I so enjoyed your cartoon series, what's it called, yes, *The Popposites*. So enjoyed it, wonder if you would care to meet for luncheon, at my house. Perhaps tomorrow? I don't want anyone else to buy it, Miss Smythson, really I don't.'

He had a deep voice, mellifluous, beguiling, so much so that Trilby felt her colour changing from white to pink as she realised in a second that he must be very attractive.

'Meet you for luncheon? Tomorrow? Yes. Of course. At your house, did you say?'

'If you don't mind? It's much quieter than a restaurant, I always think.'

'Yes, of course. Thank you.' Trilby nodded at the telephone receiver as if she was nodding at the man himself, and then realising suddenly she quickly added, 'Except I don't know your address.'

Out of the corner of her eye she saw Molly darting off to her telephone pad and waiting, poised with a pencil. She slowly repeated the address in Holland Park, and Molly scribbled it down.

'Thank you, Mr James.'

'On the contrary, thank *you*, Miss Smythson.'

'Goodbye, Mr James.'

'Goodbye, Miss Smythson.'

Trilby put down the telephone and turning to Molly she heard herself saying in a shocked voice,

'Lewis James wants me to have luncheon with him tomorrow. He just said that he wants to buy *The Popposites*, for one of his newspapers, before someone else does!'

Molly bounced forward and shook both Trilby's hands at once.

'I told you, darling Trilby, I told you! Your cartoon is most amusing, we all think so. Even Aphrodite thinks so, and she really has no sense of humour at all, so that *is* a compliment, if it makes *her* laugh!'

There was a Strauss waltz playing on Molly's wireless, which she left on at all times for some reason. Downstairs Trilby could hear Berry singing in tune with what he could hear, through the open windows, was playing on the floor above him. Trilby looked at Molly. She was wearing a blue cardigan, and a white blouse with lace edging around the collar, and she was smiling so widely that she could have been an advertisement on the Underground.

'Well, now, darling, in that case we had better think about the all-important question. What will you *wear* to your luncheon?'

Trilby started to laugh. 'I thought maybe I should go like this?'

There was a small silence as they both stared down at Trilby's office clothes. A pleated navy blue skirt, a white blouse, a navy blue cardigan, dark stockings, and black shoes with a small heel.

'I think the spinster look will not be *quite* right, duck! But I tell you what, Aphrodite might have something for you, I know. Pop across and tell her the good news and she'll be sure to fish something out of somewhere for you. Geoffrey, her lover, he's always going to America, and you know how it is there, you can get just anything in America.'

The reference to Geoffrey as Aphrodite's lover, while not being new, was nevertheless always exciting. In the Smythson household people did not have lovers, or if they did they were never, ever referred to as such. People had friends, or they were married, or confirmed bachelors, and that was most definitely that.

'I can't pop across to Aphrodite, *you know who* might see me.'

'Oh yes, of course. Can't send Berry to borrow anything more, can we?'

'Nope, don't think so. I say, Molly . . .' Trilby stretched out her arm and they both looked at her shaking hand with detached interest. 'I'm shaking, look, I'm shaking.'

'You would be, love. It is very shaky-making being rung by someone like Lewis James, really it is. Anyone *would* shake. So. Look. Tomorrow, the plan will be, the two of us will just have to wait for the proper moment when you would normally come back from work, which should be all right. Now, at this moment, straight away, and without more ado, I will call you know who and say that you are having supper with me tonight. So then *you* can go to Aphrodite's house and sort through and try and find what she will be prepared to lend you for tomorrow. I'd lend you something but we are not the same size, duck. Oh, dear. It's all so exciting.'

'I know, but, Molly, I've suddenly realised that I will have to be sick tomorrow too, won't I? I will have to tell Lifetime Assurance that I am ill on two days. The supervisor will go mad, she will, really.'

'Listen.' Molly patted Trilby on the arm. 'If

Lewis James is after your drawings you are not going to need the Lifetime Assurance Company. In fact, you won't have to go back to that wretched typing pool ever, ever again. Think of that!'

*　　　*　　　*

At six o'clock, having spent a very pleasant day with the Nichols, helping Berry in the kitchen, and Molly in the house, Trilby opened the front door and paused for a second on the top step. Outside the sun was still shining and the sky was still blue, although whether they really were or not she could not have told, for, with Lewis James interested in her drawing, it seemed to her that from now on they always would be.

Molly had duly telephoned Agnes, as planned, and while Agnes sounded mildly disapproving of Molly's inviting Trilby to supper, on the other hand she sounded vaguely uninterested too, so that Trilby knew that she herself must be going out to dinner.

Trilby skipped across the road to Aphrodite's house. She knew that the moment she arrived on Aphrodite's doorstep tantalising smells would be wafting up from the basement kitchen, because, like Berry, Aphrodite seemed to be able to make even the most awful ingredients, ingredients that completely defeated Mrs Bartlett, into perfectly delicious meals, meals which Aphrodite's lover Geoffrey Hill, so artlessly referred to by Molly, had become convinced that Aphrodite had delivered from some secret address in Paris when no-one was looking.

Aphrodite opened the door looking beautiful

and depressed. Trilby was unimpressed, because this was Aphrodite's ordinary day-to-day mien, a potent mixture of elegance and sadness. She never bothered to conceal her gloom from the world, and somehow, in view of both her elegance and her depressive aura, Trilby always found it surprising that Aphrodite was such a sensational cook, because cooking seemed to Trilby, who had never really attempted the art, such a tremendous act of optimism.

'Oh, do come in, do, Trilby. I will make you a coffee. I have just made some *mousses au chocolat*. You like *mousses au chocolat*, don't you? I hope you do, I have made far too many. Something must be done with them, really. You must take some back for Molly and Berry for their supper. Really, I have made far, far too many. Geoffrey will be furious.'

Aphrodite's lover, according to Aphrodite, was always going to be furious. His fury never seemed to be evident to anyone but Aphrodite. In fact in all the time that they had pursued their uneven romance no-one but Aphrodite had ever known Geoffrey to be anything except mild-mannered and vaguely defeated. Of course, it went without saying that Trilby had translated more than a little of their relationship into two of the characters in *The Popposites*, but this did not stop Aphrodite from pursuing the fable that Geoffrey was a man just about to explode, and at any moment, into a quite ungovernable rage.

There were still memories of the war lurking around every English woman's larder, and yet when Trilby obligingly sat down on the banquette under the window and Aphrodite, ignoring as she always did the general rules of mealtimes, placed a small almond-filled pastry in front of her on a blue and white plate, and Trilby saw the golden-crusted confection and her fingers closed around its still warm surface, she knew that the moment she took her first bite her whole body would have to surrender to the sensation of eating such a delightfully unexpected creation.

And that was all before she drank Aphrodite's proper coffee, which like Molly's was unendingly satisfying, with the cream swirling across its dark brown surface until the brown sugar was sprinkled on top and the two sank together, at last becoming one with the coffee. For, despite Trilby's having already eaten and drunk at the Nichols' house, they both knew that not to eat at Aphrodite's house too would have been an insult to her.

'Molly says to tell you that I have to borrow something from you to wear tomorrow, because none of her things would fit me. I have been asked to lunch with this man who owns all these newspapers, d'you see, and she thinks that I am too *dull*, that my own clothes are too *dull* for luncheon. Although I should have thought that my pleated skirt and cardigan would do. I mean, I am no fashion model, am I?' Trilby sighed. 'But apparently they will *not*. Molly says I must not go for my luncheon with this Lewis James man looking *poor*. She says that would be all wrong. Which is why I am here with my best spaniel's eyes begging to borrow from you some little piece of elegance which will stun this Lewis James person.'

Trilby did a mock imitation of doe eyes and a pleading look and barked like a dog, but of course Aphrodite did not laugh.

'Who is he exactly, pet?'

'I told you, he owns all these newspapers and he thinks *The Popposites* is funny, so he must be warped!'

'Oh, nonsense. It is very funny. Of course you will sell him your cartoony thing, Trilby. And you know, Molly was quite right to send you across.'

Aphrodite gave a small sigh of approval and nodded, and her hair, piled on top of her head in thick curls the colour of autumn leaves, appeared to be agreeing with her quite vehemently as the curls momentarily tumbled towards her forehead, before at a small toss of her pretty head they resumed their more stately position.

'Why was she quite right, Aphro?'

Aphrodite sighed. 'Why, because Geoffrey has just bought me a coat and skirt with a blouse in pale blue, the collar cut to make not one but two bows. The back of the suit is a sort of sling of curved folds—quite pretty, but not me at all. I so dislike Geoffrey's taste. I think *he* thinks that once he has filled my wardrobe with his choice of clothes I will, for some ridiculous reason, marry him, which is absurd.' She paused and frowned heavily as if the very thought of both Geoffrey and marriage was too awful for words. 'Geoffrey has such old taste. But what can I do? He gets simply livid if I don't wear the clothes he buys for me.'

Aphrodite looked across her immaculately kept kitchen with its wooden cupboards and floors towards the back garden and sighed as if Geoffrey, like some wild beast, was concealed there ready to spring out with a mighty roar from behind the small ornamental fountain.

'But you know how it can be with men, Trilby. At

least you don't, happily for you. Men always want to love women who don't want them. Molly, I am sure, would love Geoffrey, if she didn't already have Berry. In fact I know that she *does* love Geoffrey, but I don't think Geoffrey would be interested, simply because she thinks he is such a dish, do you see?'

Trilby, her mouth full, looked across at Aphrodite and nodded, although she did not see at all, but then she rarely was able to quite follow Aphrodite's conversation, except at a distance. All she knew of Geoffrey was that he was in the diplomatic service, always abroad on some mission or another. Trilby looked across the road at what she could see of the Nichols' house from where she was seated, trying to imagine Molly and Geoffrey together, and finally failing.

'Molly can't cook, Geoffrey wouldn't like that,' she reminded Aphrodite. 'Berry does all the cooking at their house.'

Aphrodite considered this for a moment, and then nodded as if it finally put the whole matter to bed.

'Well, no, then that would never do, if Molly can't cook,' she agreed. 'Oxtail stew tonight, I am afraid,' she announced sadly, as if the tail she was to cook had once belonged to a dear departed friend. 'And then of course Geoffrey would like to take me to the Arts Club, but really—' She stopped. 'Last time we were there it was so awful, all jolly and merry and full of men in berets. How people can be so cheerful when we live in the shadow of the Bomb I have no idea. Have you read this . . . ?'

She placed two thumbs in her belt and walking

39

in a strangely ostrich-like way swooped towards a table placed near the French windows leading on to the garden. Trilby watched her in some dread. Aphrodite's idea of what was interesting to read was hardly ever her own.

'I haven't read much, Aphro, you know me!' Even to her own ears Trilby's laugh sounded false. 'All I do is type all day and draw all night, often well into the night. I just draw.'

'*Deep Into Darkness*—a book of poems—you know, about being in the shadow of the Bomb.'

Before going upstairs Trilby glanced into the book. 'I say, Aphro, none of these poems rhyme,' she said, once again assuming her most innocent expression as she jumped up the stairs behind Aphrodite.

'Only philistines expect poems to rhyme, Trilby dear.'

Aphrodite's bedroom was a great grand sweep of a room and unlike Agnes's or Molly's furnished in a tremendously luxurious style. Thick white velvet curtains vied with modern furniture purchased from Heal's, although the fronts of cupboards and her dressing table mirror were all vaguely pink and reminiscent of the 1930s, so that when Trilby eventually stood in the rose pom-pom printed chiffon dress that Aphrodite had taken from one of the wardrobes, it seemed to her at that moment that, along with the dress, the whole world had indeed taken on a rose-coloured tint. 'It's the only dress that I have with *any* kind of youthful feel to it, Trilby dear,' Aphrodite had said sadly, 'and yet still, it has to be faced, really quite, quite old. Geoffrey again, I am afraid, and hardly worn, just the once, because otherwise he would have been

40

simply livid.'

But Trilby had hardly heard her for the good reason that she had never thought, ever, to be standing in Aphrodite's bedroom trying on dresses preparatory to going to luncheon with one of the most powerful men in London.

She gazed at her reflection in the rose-tinted mirror. The dress had a swathed collar ending in a bow above the bust, below which were tiny pleats. A narrow belt around the waist emphasised a skirt that was gathered, but not full. Long sleeves and a coat lined with the same rose pom-pom chiffon completed the whole unmistakable couturier effect.

'Dark stockings with this dress, Trilby dear, and take your pick of my shoes—what a blessing we are both so much the same size, five foot four and size five shoes—it is a blessing, most particularly if one's figure is thirty-four, twenty-four, thirty-four. If it was not, it would not be a blessing, but a total bore. But since we are both such normal sizes, one can just walk into anything, that is, if one really wants to,' she added gloomily.

A ring at the bell downstairs prompted Aphrodite to call from the bedroom, 'Just push the door, I am upstairs!'

'My dear! But how glamorous! My dear! Too too!' The visitor paused in the doorway as she took in Trilby wearing Aphrodite's couturier clothes.

It was Mrs Johnson Johnson, sporting as usual one of her exotic Chinese gowns, and it being evening she had placed a jewel in the turban she was wearing. She was smoking a Turkish cigarette which smelled pleasantly decadent. As soon as she saw Trilby wearing the chiffon dress with the mass of tiny pleats, she smiled at her in the full-length

41

mirror.

'My dear! I have just heard the *news* from Moll.
Although I gather we must not tell you know who!
You know that, don't you, Aphrodite, you know we
must not tell you know who? Agnes must not be
told.'

'Oh, tell her! For goodness' sake tell her! Agnes
is a first rate bore,' Aphrodite announced from the
depths of her shoe cupboard. 'If I were you, Trilby
dear, I would go and tell the silly woman and be
done with it.'

'I can't.'

Trilby said this so emphatically that both the
older women stopped doing what they were doing,
and stared at her.

'She will make my father's life hell,' Trilby
explained. 'And supposing he—you know, this Mr
Lewis James—supposing he does not buy the
drawings then it will have been made hell for
nothing, nothing at all.'

Mrs Johnson Johnson lit up her cigarette and
snorted lightly. 'Of course he will buy your
cartoony thing, Trilby, of course he will. If this Mr
Lewis James man knows what's good for him, he
will buy it, of course he will. Do you really think
that a man like that can afford to waste his time
asking someone like you into his office and not —'

'To his house.'

'To his house. Exactly, and not be really
interested? I believe he spends most of his time
with the Prime Minister and the head of the Bank
of England. That kind of person can't have his time
wasted, whatever you might think. If I was him, I
would buy it. Newspaper proprietor, isn't he, he
owns the paper, doesn't he? I think that is what

Moll told me. It's not as if he's not the owner. But to *ask* for you, personally. Mind you, if it wasn't for Molly knowing him during the war—but there. If he buys your strip thing you must take old Moll out to dinner, really you must, but then, that's not up to me, is it? But Trilby . . .' She stared ever more deeply at the unmoving Trilby, still seemingly frozen in front of the mirror. 'I say, my dear. You'll sweep the board in that! Really, you will.'

She leaned towards Trilby, smiling, and caught her arm and squeezed it, and Trilby jiggled a little up and down on the spot, laughing at both their images in the mirror.

'It is so exciting,' she agreed, 'and now Aphrodite has loaned me this dress for luncheon tomorrow, isn't that just *too too*—' She stopped, the look in her eyes half mocking, half humorous.

'If not *three three*,' Aphrodite put in, which from anyone else would have been a joke, but somehow even when Aphrodite managed to think of a joke she always made it sound more like a fatal diagnosis.

'As a matter of fact, I must tell Molly, now I come to think of it, that I am not at all sure about Trilby having luncheon alone with this fellow,' Mrs Johnson Johnson went on, frowning suddenly. 'How say you, Aphrodite?' Since Aphrodite only shrugged her shoulders and sighed a little hopelessly, she continued, 'I mean, all alone, and only eighteen? Surely one of us should go with her—go with Trilby?'

'I can take care of myself!'

'No young girl can take care of herself, Trilby dear, it has never, ever been known.'

'Yes, but I am not going as a girl, Mrs J.J. I am

43

going as a cartoonist, just a pencil for hire, so that is not at all the same thing, after all, is it?'

'Not to you, maybe, but to a man like Lewis James, dear, you will probably be like the mice with their parcels coming in and out of the little shop in *The Tale of Ginger and Pickles*—so tempting, so mouthwatering—so difficult not to make a meal of.'

'Not in these clothes,' Trilby replied blithely. 'I look at least twenty-five in these clothes of Aphrodite's, don't I, Aphro?'

Aphrodite nodded, and then sighed. 'I should imagine that you must, I know I look at least forty in them.' Aphrodite sighed again, the weight of the world once more settled securely around her shoulders.

'I really think either Molly or myself, or *someone* should go with Trilby, Aphro darling, really I do. I mean no-one in Glebe Street knows much about him, do they? None of us knows anything about this Lewis James man.'

'I am only having lunch with him, Mrs J.J.,' Trilby said, seeking to reassure her. 'Really. Only having lunch.' She peered from under a hat that Aphrodite had just found on one of the lit shelves near her dressing table and laughed up at her. 'Only luncheon, nothing else!'

'Don't you believe it, dear,' Mrs Johnson Johnson assured her. 'Luncheon is *never* nothing else!'

And of course, the following day, with Agnes safely out of the way visiting a friend, dark-stockinged, high-heeled, and having rehearsed her clothes for what now seemed hours, Trilby stepped into the taxi cab ordered by Molly feeling nervous

44

to the point of sickness.

Despite living so very near to everything in Chelsea, as she had since the war ended, she had never before been to a proper luncheon, and certainly not with a powerful mogul in a large house just off Holland Park.

Now it seemed to her, as the taxi pulled up the hill towards Lewis James's mansion, that it might just as well be set in another country, so different were the houses, their exteriors so broad and impressive, from those in Glebe Street. And unlike where she lived, there were no pubs or shops to give it a feeling of being cosmopolitan and artistic. For this reason she knew that she must be dressed really rather right in Aphrodite's couture dress and coat, and at the same time she felt quite wrong, for she failed to see how she could be herself in the clothes chosen for her by the older women in her life.

'Stop!'

The taxi driver turned round and stared at her. Trilby stared back at him, but it was too late to go back and change into her office clothes, into safe old navy blue pleats and cardigans.

'No, go on.'

The taxi driver stared at her in his mirror, and smiled. 'Nervous, miss?'

Trilby nodded, swallowing hard. 'You bet. I am having kittens, actually.'

'Just imagine them all with their clothes off.'

Trilby paid him and waved at the change, indicating that he should keep it. 'I'll try.'

She forgot the taxi driver's advice as soon as the butler opened the door to her. It was, after all, a little impossible to imagine anyone with his clothes off when you were wearing a large black straw hat and could hardly see him from under it. She smiled up at him with some difficulty, because both Aphrodite and Mrs Johnson Johnson had insisted that she wore the hat, straight across and sitting flatly on her dark hair, *au cardinal.*

'Mr James is in the library waiting for you, miss.'

Trilby thought *Crikey, a library in London!* but out loud she said, 'Shall I leave my coat?'

The butler stared at the eighteen-year-old. The anxiety on her face was so visible that he instantly felt sorry for her.

'It is very much part of your *ensemble*, miss, if you don't mind my saying so. I should take it in, if I was you, that is.'

They both stared at the rose chiffon lining of the coat, which exactly matched the dress. It was indeed, quite obviously, very much part of Trilby's *ensemble.*

'I suppose it would be a pity to leave it in the cloakroom where no-one will see it, wouldn't it?' Trilby conceded.

'I should drape it round your shoulders and then leave it on your chair when you go in to luncheon, miss, if I was you, that is.'

Trilby could have kissed the butler. She saw exactly what he meant as he carefully put the coat back around her slim shoulders.

'I say, thank you! I am not very good at this sort of thing, as you can imagine. As a matter of fact, all this, well, I am not used to it at all.'

The butler smiled and leaning forward he whispered, 'You'll do very well indeed, miss, really you will.'

He opened the library door and, with a

reassuring smile which seemed of a sudden to Trilby to be extraordinarily warm, announced, 'Miss Smythson, Mr James.'

Lewis James stood in front of an ornate marble chimneypiece. Behind him was a large portrait of a gentleman with an old-fashioned look to him, not just moustached, but bearded, leaning on a book, and staring out at the painter as if he knew the truth of the world. Perhaps there might have been a resemblance to the man who stood beneath it if the sitter in the painting had not had a beard, but as it was it seemed to Trilby that Mr James was standing beneath a portrait of someone whom he might once have at least known. He himself was clean shaven, however, and his suit and styling were formal to a discreet degree, the pale grey of the suiting very much of the moment, the pattern in the cloth hardly noticeable, unlike the white of his shirt which set off his tan. His hair was dark, greying slightly at the sides, and combed back with a side parting; his features were handsome and manly, but almost too even, something which was compensated for by a small scar to the side of his mouth.

His whole aura was of a man who had power, and money, and had been turned out to the point of perfection by his valet. He was, in short, a hothouse flower of a man, and as he raised a cigarette to his lips the signet ring on his smallest finger caught the light coming through the tall windows so that it seemed to Trilby that even the elements approved of his perfection.

Throwing the cigarette into the fire he walked forward, lithe, practised at greeting, completely in command of his manners, the manners not in control of him.

'Miss Smythson, how nice that you could come to luncheon so soon.'

Trilby shook his hand and smiled up at him from under her hat. His self-possession was so obvious that she almost felt cowed. Almost, but not quite, for Trilby, having hated her days at school and having made few real friends, had as a consequence spent most of her free time with grown-ups, and she knew from them all that in Society shyness was the first sin, and to allow it to show meant that you were only thinking of yourself.

One must be seen to try, Trilby duck, even if one falls on one's backside one must try, it's just a fact I'm afraid.

Molly had often said that. Now, remembering this exhortation, Trilby smiled up as confidently as she could at Lewis James.

'It was very nice of you to ask me, Mr James.'

He indicated that she should sit down and, remembering the butler's advice, as she did so Trilby casually flicked Aphrodite's coat over the back of a Louise Quinze chair and seated herself against it, remembering to keep her feet together and ankles uncrossed as Mrs Johnson Johnson had most particularly advised as she had finally left Aphrodite's house.

'What would you like to drink?'

'I would like a lemonade, please.'

The butler brought in a lemonade on a small silver tray, and as he poured it from a small cut-glass jug into a matching glass it seemed to Trilby, in the silence that surrounded this small ceremony, that the lemonade was being handed to her as if it was a medicine, and she might even be expected to

48

hold her nose as she drank it.

'I would like to buy your cartoon strip, Miss Smythson.'

It was good that Mr James was prepared to go straight to the point, and when he did, and she heard telephones ringing seemingly all over the house, Trilby thought that a man as busy and powerful as Lewis James must after all have to always get to the point straight away, because there would really be no time for anything else. A thousand demands on his time must mean that something like buying *The Popposites* would be so far down his list that it would hardly register at all.

'Yes, I would like to buy your strip cartoon for the paper. We need something young in flavour for the back page. Tell me, where do your characters, where do *The Popposites*, come from?'

Trilby looked up at him and smiled, expecting this. 'Oh, from where I live, of course, in Chelsea. You see, where I live everyone is always borrowing from someone else, so I nicknamed the people opposite the Popposites, just as a joke, because they were always popping in and out of each other's houses. And the people our side of the street, well, I called them the Have-You-Anys, and it all grew from there, really. You know.'

'Charming, charming. They're all so real I feel as if I have always known them, and they are so wonderfully—eccentric. Does Miss Golly Gosh really exist? Does she?'

'Of course.'

He looked across at Trilby, himself now seated on an uncomfortably elegant chair, and he laughed. 'Really? She really exists? What will she say, when she sees the cartoon in the paper, do you think?'

49

'Oh, they have all seen it, and they love it. They know they're all in it.'

'What about Lady Droopy? And Mrs Smokey Smokey?'

'Oh, yes, that's our neighbour Mrs Johnson Johnson. She made me alter her Turkish cigarettes to a cigar. She wanted me to make her character even more bohemian-looking. And Lady Droopy's Aphrodite. She, er, well, she's opposite too—at number fifteen, actually.'

'What a remarkable set of acquaintances you must have, not to mind you amusing yourself at their expense. You must have a very jolly life in . . .'

'Chelsea. Oh, I do.' Trilby leaned forward, suddenly thinking how far away Glebe Street with all its informal delights seemed now that she was seated in this palace of a house with its aura of quiet, and almost overpowering sense of luxury. 'Yes, they are all remarkable. We have such fun really, and that's why I drew them all, and, you know, did it, did *The Popposites*, because I wanted to get them all down on paper before I grew too old, or they did. You know how it is.'

He looked at her and for a second she thought he looked surprised at her sudden intensity, but then he shook his head and instead of looking surprised, he laughed. 'No, I am afraid I don't. But, never mind. We must go in to luncheon or else we shall be in trouble with my cook, the soufflé, you know. It is always a soufflé at lunch nowadays, I am afraid. I can never think of anything else more pleasant to start with.'

Trilby smiled, mentally thanking God for her continual plaguing of everyone in Glebe Street, as a result of which she had not only eaten a soufflé

50

before, but had even helped Berry to make one, and only last week.

'I love soufflés, particularly cheese soufflés.'

'This I am very much afraid is fish. I hope you like fish?'

Trilby liked anything outside her own home.

'Remember the Charlie Chaplin scene, when he eats the shoe as if it was fish? Takes the nails out of the shoe, one by one, as if they are fish bones? That is very, very funny, don't you think?'

Again thanks to her neighbours Trilby knew a great many old films and books. She also knew how to laugh obligingly, and in a way that made people think that she was exactly the same age as them. She therefore both laughed and nodded appreciatively as one of the maids attending them at luncheon pulled out her chair and she sat down on it.

'Yes. That is so funny. I love Charlie Chaplin.'

'But not more than Buster Keaton?'

'No, not more, but as much.' She felt quite firm on this point, and for a second she saw the expression in Mr James's eyes turn from amusement to surprise at her decided tone.

He unpicked his stiff, white linen napkin, and as he did so he said, 'You know your own mind, don't you, Miss Smythson?'

Trilby smiled across at him from under her cardinal-style hat. 'I know what I think is funny, if that is what you mean, but that is hardly a guide, is it? I mean when it comes to making people laugh how do we know?'

'Only by trying.'

'How do you know what to put into your newspapers?'

51

'I don't. I have editors who, as you say, put things in my newspapers, and then I read them and I find that I feel just as ordinary or extraordinary as the next man. In other words I go by my instinct. Isn't that the only way?'

'I thought newspapers had policies, like governments.'

'Quite right, Miss Smythson, they do, but they try not to let it show too much. They try to let the readers guess at what their, as you put it, policies could be.'

'It must be so exciting.'

Without her realising it Trilby's tone had taken on a dreamy quality, not actually because she was really very interested in newspapers and their policies, but because the fish soufflé was so delicious.

'Like everything, Miss Smythson, it is only as exciting as you make it. There are times when I wish I had inherited anything but newspapers. A cattle ranch, or a chain of hotels, something less, if you like, opinionated.'

Trilby put her fish knife and fork together and nodded. 'Inheriting things is difficult, apparently. Because it's not you that's done it, and you can't really value it the same as if you work for it, can you?'

For a second Trilby thought she had offended him as he stared across the table at her and a dull red flush appeared across his forehead.

'Out of the mouths of babes and sucklings, Miss Smythson,' he murmured finally, and laughed. 'You are quite right, and do you know no-one has ever dared to say that to me before?' He smiled. 'You're a very truthful person, aren't you, Miss Smythson?'

After that luncheon seemed to fly past, and when the delicious pudding had been presented and duly relished by Trilby, it seemed hardly minutes after she had put down her spoon that they were both leaving the house, he to step into his Rolls-Royce, waving and kissing his fingertips to her, and she, in her turn, to wave not at him but at a taxi cab from which ten minutes later she quickly decanted herself outside Aphrodite's door in a flurry of excitement, running up the steps so quickly that not even her stepmother could have caught sight of her.

'How was it?'

Molly seemed to spring out from behind Aphrodite's front door, giving Trilby the impression that she and Aphrodite had been waiting for her ever since she went out. Trilby smiled up at her from under Aphrodite's hat.

'He was really very nice.'

'Yes, but—will he buy *The Popposites*, Trilb?'

'Yes, he wants to buy the cartoon strip. Actually, I can hardly believe it.'

'But my dear girl, that is so exciting and wonderful!'

Trilby's eyes drifted past her. 'Yes, it is, isn't it?'

'What's he like, my dear? Tell, do.'

'Like? Oh, he's terribly tall, and he has such a nice voice.'

Molly stared at her. 'Oh dear. Not smitten are you, Trilb?'

'Goodness no. No, but I must say I thought such a rich and powerful man might be dull and have no sense of humour, but he laughed and talked just like we do here, really.'

'That is good.'

'But just remember he is buying the cartoon strip, not you. You are not thrown in.' Mrs Johnson Johnson had suddenly appeared from Aphrodite's basement, as usual smoking a Turkish cigarette and looking regal.

'Oh, Melanie, do stop saying that. It's not as if Trilby has any interest in him. She has more sense.' Molly patted Trilby on the arm, and they all smiled at her.

As for Trilby, she was suddenly very glad that she was wearing the cardinal-style hat, so comforting to hide behind.

CHAPTER TWO

There was a long and terrible silence, and Trilby knew at once that if she lived to be a hundred, she would never forget it. She felt as if she was confessing to a robbery, or had been found planning to murder one of them.

'You what?'

It was her father who spoke, not Agnes, for once.

'I have sold my drawings to a newspaper, to a man who owns them.'

She had always known that it was going to be a difficult moment, that her father and stepmother might not approve of selling something to a newspaper. Thinking of themselves as they did as being extremely respectable, the Smythsons had little or no respect for Fleet Street, so that Trilby had wrestled with the idea of not telling them at all, of publishing the whole series under a different name, but because she was still a minor this was not possible.

Molly had explained all this to her, and they had all, Molly and Berry and Aphrodite and Mrs Johnson Johnson, tried to find a way round it, but the fact was that there was none, she had to tell the truth.

Trilby was only just eighteen. There would be three long years before she was twenty-one and able to do as she wished. Besides, the contract with the newspaper, as Berry had explained, was bound to be long and complicated and cover all kinds of agreements, so it was not practical either. Trilby would need someone to advise her, someone like Geoffrey, or her father.

'I told you she was up to something!' Agnes looked across at Trilby's father with a smug expression on her face. 'I told you she was up to no good. I just had this feeling these last days,' she addressed herself to Trilby now, 'I just had this feeling that you were up to something, going behind our backs about something.'

'I didn't want to raise your hopes,' Trilby lied, but her feet wriggled in her shoes, and she knew that her father could see this, and that he had always said that shifty feet meant a lie was being told, so she stopped them wriggling, only she could see that it was a little too late and he had noticed.

'How did this come about?'

'Er. Well. You see, what happened was this.' Trilby stopped, aware that her voice sounded nervous. 'I, er, I, er, had the newest set of drawings, and one day I was in Molly's kitchen talking to her and Berry.'

'You go round to their house *far* too often. I told

you she goes round to their house *far* too often, Michael.'

Michael Smythson nodded but remained silent for a moment, staring across at Trilby. He often stared at her as if he was not quite sure how she had come about, as if he had not really expected her to grow up, change from child to teenager, and since she had it was necessary for him to examine her very closely.

'Yes, you do, Agnes is right. You go round to their house too often,' he agreed. 'But please, go on. Tell us how this all came about?'

'As I said, I was in the kitchen with Molly and Berry, and they were laughing at the latest set, you know? I mean I always show them all what I am drawing, because, well, because I wouldn't want them to be upset or anything.'

'A bit too late to think of that if you have sold them. Much too late, I should have thought.'

'Go on.'

'And, well, Molly came out with . . . well, she came up with this idea, rather, that I should, that she should send them to this friend of theirs, a Mr Micklethwaite or someone.'

'David Micklethwaite, yes, I know him. We have met him at their house.'

'So she did.' Trilby swallowed hard, knowing that there were rough waters ahead. 'She sent them to Mr Micklethwaite, and he showed them to his boss, Lewis James, who owns all these newspapers.'

'We know who Lewis James is, thank you very much!' Agnes lit a cigarette and went to the sitting room window where she stared out at the houses opposite as if they were offending her.

'And?'

56

'And. And, well, he bought them.'

Trilby had to miss out the luncheon bit. They had all agreed that she must, Aphrodite, Molly and Berry, all of them had agreed that it was the only way. One whiff of deception, they had all agreed this too, and Michael and Agnes would put a stop to the whole deal, and she would never be allowed to sell *The Popposites* to anyone.

'Just like that.'

'Yes, he apparently finds them very funny.'

'Does he.'

'Yes.'

'So. Where from here, Trilby?'

'I don't know, that is why I came and asked you.'

Her feet had stopped wiggling and for a minute or so it seemed to Trilby that the waters ahead might be going to be a little calmer than she had anticipated.

'Anyway, that at any rate is good, that you came and asked us,' her father said, and approval suddenly registered in his gentle smile as Agnes turned back from the window.

'I fail to see what is good about it, Michael. I do really fail to see that. All I can see ahead is trouble.'

Michael Smythson turned and contemplated his wife with a bland look in his eyes as if he had only just realised that she was in the room.

'How is that, Agnes?'

'All the people in the street, they will all sue her. You will see, and *we* will be left with all the pieces. I mean Trilby has spent weeks and months showing these wretched drawings of hers to everyone and anyone, which is one thing, but as soon as they see themselves depicted in a newspaper, you wait.

They will change their tune all right. You'll see.'

There was a small silence which crept into a long silence during which Agnes finished smoking her cigarette and stubbed it out in a silver ashtray, while at the same time allowing a look of triumph to creep into her dark eyes.

'Oh, I think we can cope with that, Agnes,' Michael said. 'We can ask them all to sign away any . . . you know, make them agree to not suing, as you put it. And that being so, it would be very difficult for any of our friends to sue Trilby, I should have thought.'

'So foolish of you to show them your drawings, though, you must admit, Trilby; it was really very foolish.' The triumph in Agnes's eyes was now reflected in her voice.

'Oh no.' Trilby's own tone had changed. She so hated Agnes in her sadistic mood. When she was younger she had dreamed of killing her, but now that she was older she just settled for hating her. 'Oh no, I should always have shown them what I was doing. It simply would not have been fair not to have shown them as I went along. And, after all, when you think of it, without them having seen the drawings, Mr James would not have been interested in them, would he?'

'She's quite right, Agnes.' Michael closed the door on that particular line of conversation with a look. 'Well, now, young lady,' he went on, his face devoid of emotion as it always was, even when he was feeling emotional. 'We had better hire you a lawyer, or someone who knows about negotiating with a newspaper over rights and so on. You don't want to go signing away something that you should own, do you?'

Trilby shook her head, silent. She could hardly believe her father's tacit acceptance of her new situation. It did not seem possible that, starting off as he had in a kind of silent fury, he had finally ended up on her side.

For a second she found herself wondering why, and then a possible answer came to her. Agnes must have gone too far. She did sometimes. Sometimes her cruelty and mockery, her sadism and domineering ways came to Michael's notice, at which point he would side with Trilby. But for how long?

Agnes never let a matter she wanted to win rest for any length of time. She always returned to it. If not today, tomorrow. Trilby knew that ultimately her freedom rested on one thing and one thing alone, and that was on everyone in the street keeping their mouths shut about the luncheon. If Michael found out about the luncheon, Trilby would, as Aphrodite would put it, 'have well and truly had it'.

'I will let you know if I hear about anyone, as soon as I can,' Michael told his daughter.

Not long after this, Trilby bolted across the road to Aphrodite's house.

'I need a lawyer, and very quickly,' she told the startled Aphrodite, who was lying on a Victorian chaise longue frowning at a book of poetry entitled *Les Fleurs du Mal.*

'The French really have such a good eye on life,' Aphrodite sighed, replacing the book on her coffee table with ill-concealed relief. 'Now, Trilby, you want a lawyer. Of course you want a lawyer, for your contract with this newspaper man, but why quickly?'

'It's you know who. She is completely against the whole thing, the whole newspaper thing, I am sure of it. If I don't get a contract tidied up quickly it will be hell to pay, you know? And she might discover about the luncheon, and borrowing your clothes and all that, and then my father will not let it all go ahead.'

'She will not discover anything, Trilby, for the simple reason that we will not let her.'

Aphrodite, as was her habit, stuck her thumbs in her belt, and with her strange bird-like walk went to the window to stare across the road at the Smythsons' house, as if by doing so she might see *you know who* staring back at her, and outstare her.

'Your stepmother is such a nuisance, Trilby.' She turned, sighing, from the window. 'Never mind, though. We will get Geoffrey to look over the contract for you. He is very good at small print. I will tell him to suggest it to your father when he gets back in an hour or so.'

Trilby looked at Aphrodite for a second. Thank heavens for her. 'Thank you so much.'

She must have sounded unnaturally emotional because Aphrodite leaned across and hugged her suddenly, which was not at all Aphrodite, really, and Trilby crossed back to her own house, stopping at the door and waving to her, knowing that she would be watching. Aphrodite waved back, knowing that Trilby could not see her, but also knowing that, in so many ways, she could.

*   *   *

Back at the Lifetime Assurance Company, after two days' absence, Trilby could hardly believe what

60

had just happened to her. The whole world of Lewis James, his vast house, his exquisite food, his butler, her borrowed clothes, seemed not just a lifetime away, it seemed a world away. Much as she tried to concentrate on her work she kept seeing Lewis James in his perfect suit, with his perfect tan, and remembering him watching her, and laughing at her jokes. What a different life from the one that she normally led, facing the supervisor and her gavel, watching the clock out of the corner of her eye, waiting, always waiting, to be let free.

As a child, living with Agnes in London, she had often thought that she knew how a caged animal felt, shut up in a place that was so alien to it that there was no longer any meaning to life. When she was at the Lifetime Assurance Company she thought of herself as a single canary, bright-feathered, but quite alone, singing and singing from behind bars and yet never, ever having any hope of being released to find another of its own kind.

Now she could look back on that hour and a half spent with Lewis James as a time when she had been released from her cage, when she had, however temporarily, found someone else with the same brightly coloured plumage, someone who found people as funny as she did, and life as amusing and diverse as she found it.

But Lewis James was a proprietor of a newspaper, as everyone said, used to spending his time with prime ministers or governors of banks. He would, she was sure, buy her cartoon series and forget about her for ever, because for someone like him Trilby Smythson would be just one of a thousand writers or illustrators, journalists or

61

cartoonists. It was not false modesty, it was just a fact.

As Trilby's days returned to their usual dreary grey normality, Michael Smythson called on all their neighbours and asked them to sign away any kind of possibility that they would, as he put it, 'take exception' to *The Popposites*. Since they were all part of the same conspiracy, they all quickly did this, while Michael agreed to let Aphrodite's lover Geoffrey run his eyes over the agreement sent with such surprising haste by Amalgamated Newspapers.

It was therefore only a very short time later when Michael signed Trilby's first contract on her behalf, watched by a silently furious and inwardly raging Agnes.

Perhaps because of her inner fury Agnes now spent a great deal of time away from the house. More than she had ever spent in all the time that Trilby had known her.

Trilby imagined that she must be having a great many dresses made, and visiting a great many girlfriends, of whom Agnes seemed to have an endless supply. Whatever it was that was keeping her away from the house from just after Michael had left for the Foreign Office until just before he came home was of no interest to Trilby. She herself had resigned from her job, to the astonishment of the Lifetime Assurance Company. Worse than that, she had exulted in her resignation.

'I have sold my work to a newspaper which is going to pay me a great deal of money,' she told the supervisor, who looked suddenly so wan at the idea that Trilby would no longer be one of her victims that Trilby almost felt sorry for her.

However, all was not quite as rosy as Trilby had boasted to the supervisor as she sashayed out of her life for ever. Most unfortunately, the agreement that Geoffrey had negotiated for her was soon discovered to be for much, much less than Trilby had hoped. Naturally this made Agnes very happy. So happy that she crowed about it to Michael, often, and loudly.

It seemed that the 'money boys', as Geoffrey called them, had considerably altered everything after Geoffrey had agreed to it, and that Michael had gone ahead and signed it on Trilby's behalf without reading the contract through again. Now it was all too late, and Trilby was going to have to work far too fast for far too little, and not only that, but because she was a girl she could not put her name to it, because it seemed that male readers might be offended by the idea of a female cartoonist.

'I am sorry, my dear. These money boys seem to be such sharks nowadays. Geoffrey and I thought we had managed everything so well, really we did. We never thought they would alter everything that he agreed with the way they have, and to such disadvantage to you. I suppose we should have read through the contract again, really, before I signed it and sent it off?' Her father looked sad, but not particularly surprised.

'Doesn't matter, really it doesn't,' Trilby told him. 'After all, they're still going to do it. I didn't do it for the money. It will be great to see it in print, that's all.'

'I suppose living here with me—well, I mean you won't ever starve, will you, Trilby? And, well, I suppose male readers would prefer a man's name

63

to the thing, so perhaps that will be better too, in the long run.'

Trilby nodded her head in agreement. No, she would never starve, that was true. It was just that she *had* hoped to be paid more so that she could buy a small second-hand motor car, and perhaps a better drawing board, things like that. Not a great deal really, not compared with Lewis James's wealth, but she had hoped for a little more than she now knew that she was going to receive. And as to putting 'Jerry' instead of 'Trilby', well, it only went to show something, but what, she was not, as yet, quite sure.

'Oh well, no matter.'

'Where are you going, Trilby?'

Trilby turned at the entrance to the small dining room, still in her black velvet dressing gown. 'To have breakfast with Berry, you know?'

'Jolly good idea,' said Michael, turning back to his newspaper. 'Not seen Agnes anywhere, by the way, have you?'

Trilby had not seen Agnes, which somehow made it easier for both of them to relax, and since it was Saturday and neither of them had to go anywhere Michael watched Trilby going down the garden in her black velvet dressing gown, carrying a breakfast tray, with some pride. She was a good girl, really, even if she did get on Agnes's nerves. Not that getting on Agnes's nerves was difficult; almost everyone did.

Berry peered round the door at Trilby and her tray.

'Here for brekker, that's my girl! Oh, and brought some *pains au chocolat* too!'

'Bought them at the patisserie yesterday

64

evening.'

'Come on. Coffee's brewing and bubbling, and your life the same, I hear, although I have to tell you that the postman is very unhappy that *he* is not in *The Popposites*. He just told me so in no uncertain terms.'

Trilby followed Berry into his studio, a place where she always loved to be.

'I am not telling anyone in the cartoon who anyone is any more,' she said firmly as Berry returned with hot coffee. 'It is just going to have to be a surprise from now on. It is, it's going to have to be a surprise.'

'Exciting, though, isn't it, lovey?'

'I know.'

Trilby sighed suddenly with total pleasure. There was no getting away from it, even if she was being paid less than she had thought, it did not matter in the least. She was being paid to do something she really liked, and what was more she was now free of the Lifetime Assurance Company. It was unbelievable to think that she would never again have to go back to sitting in a row of girls pounding ancient machines and being stared at by a narrow-eyed supervisor.

As Trilby finished her breakfast and her face assumed a dreamy expression of intense contentment Berry stared across their mutual breakfast table at her, his expression suddenly serious. Quickly finishing his roll and butter he stood up, at the same time reaching for his sketch pad and pencil.

'I think I will just sketch you like that, Trilb, if you don't mind. Sit still, don't move, no, really, but don't move. No, tell you what—you can pick up

65

Monty and cuddle him.'

Trilby was quite used to being told *not to move*, or *to pick up the cat*, or *to stay just where you are*, which was what she did for the next half an hour, in between sipping coffee and allowing Berry to tell her about his youthful, and quite hopeless, love for an older woman whose portrait, it just so happened, he had, by chance, just finished painting.

Trilby stared at the painting. The woman was older but very beautiful. She was also staring out at the world as if she had not been pleased by it.

'Molly always says never trust a woman with a Pekinese.'

'I didn't know Molly then, but Molly is quite right, but it is not trust that I wanted from her when I was a young man, dear heart, but *love*.'

Trilby sighed inwardly, while remaining as still as any sitter can who is trying to hold a cat on her knee. Love! People were always talking about love, and yet what was love about, at the end of the day? She had no idea and sometimes felt that she cared less. On the other hand, when she had lunched with Lewis James she had definitely thought that she had suddenly known at least what attraction was, or thought she might.

'I don't really think I ever want someone to be in love with me,' she said finally, after sitting through yet another half an hour of Berry's eulogies on his long past amour.

'Why is that?'

'Because it makes people so sad. Every time Aphrodite talks about someone who was in love with her, or whom she once loved, she becomes more and more sad, until, in the end, I think she will be taken to heaven.'

66

'Oh, Aphrodite is yards better now than she was, whatever she might tell you. I know that she grumbles about Geoffrey, but before him she was in love with an absolute so-and-so. You never knew him, before your time, and just as well. In the end she had to go to that place in Ascot, and that was not nice. Darling Molly always thinks that she has not been quite the same since, not really.' Berry's dark brown eyes stared down into Trilby's large grey ones, and the pencil in his hand momentarily ceased its activity. 'No, that was not nice at all. Not at all, but then that is what happens when they put those electrode things on your head, you're never quite the same, at least I don't think so. Now, tell me about Lewis James—'

Trilby was frowning. '*What* things? Do tell.'

'They clamp things on your head and send bolts and bolts of electricity through you, and then they expect you to be quite the same afterwards. I mean to say, I mean with such insanity coming from the doctors it's quite enough to make the rest of us mad. But you were going to tell me about Lewis James. Dull as the proverbial ditch water, is he? Like most rich men?'

'No. As a matter of fact, he is not at all dull, and quite easy to talk to, really.'

'If you had to draw him, how would he be?'

Berry took the cat and handed Trilby his sketch pad and pencil. A minute went by as Trilby thought about the tall, urbane, undoubtedly handsome, dark-haired, brown-eyed, cleft-chinned Lewis James in his impeccable tailoring, his white shirt that set off his even tan, and his grey suiting and grey tie, and then she drew.

Berry took the pad from her and stared down at

67

it.

'I say, ducks. He is quite a dish, isn't he?'

*   *   *

Just for a moment, following the signing of her contract, Trilby was suddenly afraid that the magic had quite gone from *The Popposites.* What with its not going to have her own name on it, and not being paid enough for it, all of a sudden it seemed to be a bit of a blinking disappointment. Sometimes she found herself wishing that she had kept it to herself. Just kept it all as a Glebe Street joke, something which made them all laugh at each other, and left it at that. And of course, not being used to the ways of newspapers, when she did not hear from anyone she began to imagine that Lewis James had lost interest in it.

She had just begun to be quite sure that she would never ever see the strip published, and in some strange way even to be glad that she would not, when a vast floral display—it certainly could not be called a bunch of flowers—arrived at their house.

Agnes was disgusted by its size and undoubted cost.

'It does seem a little bit much, really it does,' she protested loudly. 'To send such a very big basket, so vulgar, really. Why, it's as tall as you and twice as wide.'

They stood back and stared at it, knowing at once that it must have come from Lewis James, even before Trilby opened the small white envelope and read out the message, *'Look in the paper tomorrow!* The card's unsigned.'

Agnes snorted lightly. 'It's too big, even for the sitting room. Really, far too big for the drawing room. I don't know where we will put it.'

Trilby looked rueful, and felt guilty. It was true, it was really far too big for the house.

'I suppose that is rich people,' she said eventually, looking from her stepmother to the vast floral display and back again. 'They send you things that fit into *their* houses but not into *your* house, because they think that you have a house the same size as theirs. It's just human error, really. Nothing more and nothing less.'

Trilby looked so droll and yet so apologetic when she repeated the story a few minutes later to Berry that Molly started to laugh.

'It *is* just human error on the part of the rich, Trilby, you are quite right. But oh, do tell, do, what did Agnes, what did you know who, do with this human error?'

'She says she is going to take all the flowers out and put them in individual smaller vases everywhere.'

There was a brief pause.

'That does seem a pity.'

Molly said this a few times, and having, finally, persuaded herself of the pity of it all she went round to the Smythsons' house, and persuaded Agnes to bring the flower basket to their house where they placed the vast arrangement at the back of the small garden where it looked really very pretty. After which act of floral preservation Molly asked everyone in the street to come to number eighteen for drinks to celebrate the printing of Trilby's first cartoon in the paper.

Berry, who was always quite happy to be a

69

busybody, took Trilby down the garden.

'Did the great man telephone?'

'No.' Trilby avoided looking at Berry and plucked a rose from the arrangement in the basket instead and placed it in his buttonhole.

'In that case I should think that he is busy. But still thinking about you.' Berry nodded at the basket. 'Believe you me, and I know, that is a *too busy to see you but can't stop thinking about you* floral tribute.'

'Agnes says it looks more like the sort of display that you see on old newsreels behind gangsters' funeral cars in Chicago.'

Berry stood back and stared at the immense arrangement. 'I am awfully sorry to say that in this instance Agnes is absolutely right.'

They both started to laugh, but the following day it was Berry who was proved to be right. Lewis James telephoned Trilby and asked her out to a celebration dinner.

Back in Aphrodite's bedroom Trilby stood as still as she could while Aphrodite and Mrs Johnson Johnson held up evening dresses against her.

'They are all so dated, Trilby dear, I keep telling you, so dated, really, dear, they are so dated,' Aphrodite kept moaning. 'I mean—this is, well, this is, this must be from 1948, would you believe? A man like that, like Lewis James, a newspaper person, he will spot it straight away, he will say Dior 1948, straight away, men like that *know*. I've been out with so many of them.'

'Yes, I know, Aphrodite dear, but really they can't be blamed, not really. When men have *things* about you, about women, they always love to buy us clothes, and let's face it, a little adjustment here,

70

and a little adjustment there, and I don't think Lewis James is going to rock back on his heels and think less of Trilby because she is not right up to the minute, as long as she looks decorative, that is, and not tarty or anything. I mean to say, it is just a fact, they expect less of one when one is young, surely?'

In the end they settled on a white organdie kimono blouse with a wide turnback cuff teamed with a satin evening skirt and matching coat of the same material, which fell to the floor and was distinguished by its stand-up collar.

'All so *old*, Trilby dear. I mean, are you sure? I mean—really, these are at least—oh, I don't know, they are so out of date, like the men who gave them to me,' moaned Aphrodite again, but Mrs Johnson Johnson would have none of it.

'Classic, quite classic,' she asserted, patting Trilby on the arm approvingly. 'And really, Aphrodite, really, you are only thinking like that because you have gone off the man who gave it to you.'

'I certainly have gone off him.' Aphrodite frowned. 'As a matter of fact I have so far gone off him that I can't even remember his name, Melanie, I can't really.'

Mrs Johnson Johnson mouthed, 'Not since the electrodes on her head,' at Trilby behind Aphrodite's back.

Trilby nodded briefly, understanding what she was saying, but not wanting Aphrodite to see.

Poor Aphrodite never did seem to remember anything nowadays except Geoffrey's being annoying and, occasionally, a recipe which she happened to have made a few hours earlier.

Otherwise, nothing.

Once dressed Trilby felt overpoweringly smart, which made her hold her head rather stiffly and walk in a funny way, she thought, but Molly insisted that if Trilby was being asked out to the Savoy by such a powerful figure as Lewis James she must not be seen to let the side down. She must look as if she came from not Glebe Street but Knightsbridge, which although only ten minutes' walk from their houses might as well have been Paris, as far as they were all concerned.

To get herself used to how she looked, to become accustomed to this new sophisticated image, Trilby walked up and down the street for a little while, and so, eventually, to Berry and Molly's house. Molly opened the door to her.

'This is terribly exciting really.' Berry handed Trilby a glass of sherry while noting that she was looking really awfully pale. 'I mean he probably wants to syndicate *The Popposites*, duck, hence all the floral adulation, wouldn't you say? Imagine that! And then we shall probably see *The Popposites* in the *Herald Tribune*, and heaven only knows what other places.'

Trilby knew that the Nichols were trying to calm her nerves, that they were both aware that an invitation to dinner might not just be for business reasons, and that being so things could get complicated, or awkward, or at the very least confusing and unreal.

'Make sure to tell Mr James that you have promised me to be back by midnight, Trilby,' Molly said as Trilby, seeing the chauffeur-driven car drawing up outside the Smythsons' house, put her glass down on the side table beside the old faded chintz armchair with its old faded satin cushion collapsed in its centre and hurried off back into the street.

'Yes, of course, but we are not going to be alone, so don't worry, Molly, really.'

Trilby pulled on short white evening gloves and walked towards the gleaming, polished motor car. She felt so odd in her floor-length satin evening coat, and her satin evening skirt and white organdie blouse, just as if she was in a play, not herself at all, more like some actress walking onto a stage somewhere in the West End—or 'London's Theatreland', as they always called it on the wireless.

The chauffeur opened the door for Trilby and as he did so she turned and waved back to Berry and Molly, who were standing at their window, unmoving, more like figureheads on the prows of ships than people, like children playing statues. Too late, as the chauffeur heaped her skirt in beside her Trilby noticed her father standing at his window and looking out. She waved at him but she was not sure that he had seen her. If he had, he did not wave back, but turned away, into the room, probably pacifying Agnes who, unlike her father, had not approved of her accepting the invitation to dinner with Lewis James.

'I think my father's going to stand there all evening until I get back,' Trilby joked to the chauffeur, who did not smile.

'Mr James will be waiting for you in the foyer at the Savoy, Miss Smythson.'

Trilby had the feeling that the chauffeur had said this sentence many times before, and to many other women. Perhaps he realised that his words must have sounded too well rehearsed, because he quickly glanced at her in the mirror and said in a more normal voice, 'Have you been to the Savoy before, Miss Smythson?'

Trilby shook her head. 'I have hardly been anywhere, I am afraid. I shall probably use all the wrong knives and forks.'

The chauffeur smiled, understanding. 'In that case the Savoy is the best place to start learning, miss, if that's any help. Start as you mean to go on, with the best.'

Lewis James was standing in the foyer. He was in evening dress, immaculate, tanned, and perfectly turned out from his shining evening pumps to his beautifully cut hair. Trilby felt at once that she must be going to let him down. But he did not seem to notice, or mind, that her clothes were seasons old, for he came towards her with the most delighted smile and immediately led her upstairs to a private room.

'This is your first print dinner, Miss Smythson,' he said, taking her coat from her, and moving her round the guests, all of whom were smiling in such a way that Trilby had the feeling that they had been told to be there well in advance of Trilby herself.

'Congratulations,' they murmured, each in turn, as they shook Trilby's hand.

Lewis moved her from one small group of his chattering guests to another with the expertise of an accomplished and experienced host, and, having given Trilby a glass of champagne, took one himself and raised it to her.

She looked everything that he had hoped she would look. Young, beautiful, her short dark brown hair combed back from her forehead, pearls

74

around her neck, large dark brown eyes, perfectly arched dark eyebrows, the white organdie blouse showing off her perfect complexion, the full-skirted, dark blue satin evening skirt emphasising her youthful figure.

'She is beautiful, sir, congratulations, not only talented but beautiful. What a discovery! I mean she truly is not just talented, but beautiful.'

Lewis turned and, seeing his second in command David Micklethwaite, smiled in a proprietary sort of way.

'Yes, I am very grateful to your friend, David,'

Lewis agreed, still not taking his eyes off Trilby, who had fallen into conversation with his old friends Henri and Lola de Ribes and, judging from the way that they were smiling, was enchanting them as much as she had already enchanted him. 'Believe me, I asked her to luncheon only out of curiosity, but you can imagine, when she came into the room . . .' He shrugged his shoulders. 'I was captivated at once. The thing is, she is such an original.'

'What I like about her, and her work, is that she is so fresh, so innocent, and insouciant, I think that is the word I would use.'

'Insouciant. Yes, I would say that is just the right word for her work, Micklethwaite, insouciant.'

Lewis moved off and David Micklethwaite watched him for a few seconds, making his way towards Trilby Smythson. He had not worked very long for Lewis James, but long enough to know all about his numerous affairs. He imagined that there could be little hope for Miss Smythson, really. She would never be able to hold the attentions of a man as attractive, handsome and powerful as Lewis

75

James. It would be surprising if she was able to interest him for more than a few weeks.

Lewis James was literally irresistible to women. Perhaps his fascination for them was that he did not seem to have ever cared over much for any one of them. Perhaps he was too much of a challenge. Love came too easily to him in the form of willing, beautiful women, and so he had never learned to respect it; or perhaps he had not wanted to make mistakes. He had remained resolutely single for many reasons.

'She's enchanting,' Lola de Ribes whispered to Lewis as they all took their seats for dinner. 'Quite enchanting.'

Lewis did not reply, but only stared down the candlelit dinner table at Trilby, who, of a sudden, looked directly at him, and smiled. She did not know it at the time, but that mischievous smile sealed her fate.

From now on, as Lola de Ribes remarked later to her husband, 'she has not a chance!'

*   *   *

'Oh, not more flowers,' Agnes moaned as a smart dark trade van with discreet gold writing drew up outside the house. 'Oh, please, not more flowers.' She went from her small chintz-curtained drawing room through to the pale yellow-painted hall where she called up the stairs, 'Trilbee! Flowers! More flowers!'

She had to shout for Trilby, because if she called for Lydia she knew Trilby would never answer.

Trilby sprang down the stairs, a pencil stuck behind her ear like a bus conductor. Agnes at once

76

reached forward and removed it, as if even the delivery boy might be shocked by the sight of it.

'Sorry, Agnes.' Trilby straightened her hair where the pencil had been. 'Sorry, I mean about the flowers again, but goodness, what can I do? I mean I can't very well tell Mr James to stop sending me flowers, I mean to say—he might sack me!'

They both now smiled a little wanly back at the professionally smiling delivery boy, and Trilby reached out and took in yet another over-tall flower arrangement. The front door closed and they were left staring at the heavily scented, multi-flowered offering. A minute or two later, as if on cue, Agnes started to sneeze.

This time the message when Trilby opened the little white envelope read *As brilliant as ever! L.*

'Down the garden! Down the garden with it! Or take it to Molly!' Agnes pointed towards the garden door as if the flower arrangement were a dog who was about to have an accident in her hall. 'If Lewis James goes on sending you these floral displays for the rest of your life, I shall have hay fever all the year round,' she told Trilby, her voice tailing off as she noticed that the card was signed only 'L'.

This was a significant fact that was not lost on Agnes. Trilby had already been out with Lewis James twice, so she supposed it was not *that* extraordinary to sign himself in that way. On the other hand, she could not approve of L, as he was happy to call himself. She would not approve of anyone who thought Trilby attractive.

As a matter of fact, as she kept telling Michael, she could not understand someone like Trilby being attracted to a man like that. She herself had never been able to get on with anyone as rich as Lewis James. They were always so suspicious. Too much money was like everything too much—it was too much. She wished that Michael would *stop* it. But Michael would not stop Trilby going out with Lewis James.

Michael saw it differently, it seemed. He saw that the situation between Trilby and this Lewis man was even more difficult than it usually was with the terribly, terribly rich, because Lewis James was his daughter's boss, her employer, the owner of the magic wand, the person who could make or break his daughter's burgeoning career.

'Oh dear!'

'Something the matter, Agnes?'

'No. Just my sinuses, brought on by hot-house flowers, most likely.'

Trilby stared after her departing stepmother for a second. The now twice weekly flowers *were* becoming a nuisance, she could quite see that, and then again the telephone ringing all the time, that too was annoying, but still, it was not the Bomb, it was just *flowers* for goodness' sake, nothing lethal.

'Trilbee! Lewis *James*!' Agnes called up the stairs, accusingly, a few hours later.

Agnes stared malevolently at Trilby while holding out the telephone. Trilby took the receiver without looking at her. Somehow it was so embarrassing, Agnes always saying Lewis's name like that—Lewis *James*!

It would be so much easier, too, if Trilby was able to take telephone calls anywhere except in the hall with Agnes standing so close to her that she could say nothing to Lewis except 'Yes' or 'No' and

78

occasionally 'I quite understand.'

'Are you one of these people who hate the telephone?' Lewis asked her that evening when his chauffeur, himself and of course his Rolls-Royce picked Trilby up from Glebe Street.

'Oh, yes, absolutely,' Trilby lied, because she could not very well tell him that there was only one telephone in their house, in the hall, and that it was always listened in to by Agnes.

'To the theatre tonight to see *An Unusual Woman*, and then I thought a quiet supper afterwards at the Savoy.'

Trilby turned and smiled at Lewis. 'Thank you so much for the flowers. They are beautiful.'

'Did they send you something beautifully scented? I always ask for something heavily scented.'

'Oh yes, they were very heavily scented,' Trilby agreed, remembering with some guilt how often Agnes had sneezed once they had entered the house. 'And they are truly beautiful.'

In fact far from making the house look beautiful Agnes had now decided that the garden was beginning to look 'positively idiotic' with vast floral arrangements standing about it like guards outside Buckingham Palace, but of course Trilby could not tell Lewis that, any more than she could tell him what her stepmother thought of his asking her out not once but now three times in less than two weeks.

She had kept saying, in a rather low, almost guttural voice, a voice not at all like her normal tones, 'He's after his oats, that's all. Just after his oats.' She had said it so often, before she left the house, or when she came back, that the previous night Trilby had dreamed that Lewis was a horse and she was feeding him.

The dress that the long-suffering and ever more depressed Aphrodite had loaned Trilby this particular night was strapless but had a dark stole, which Trilby had been forced to rehearse many times in order not to look, as Mrs Johnson Johnson said, 'as if you're pulling a curtain across you, my dear. Never make a stole look like that.'

The bodice, like the stole, was black and made of hand-knitted stocking, very tight. A grey belt circled her waist and emphasised the lilac satin skirt, which was tulip-shaped and ankle length. With this she wore no evening hat, but her hair brushed back and tucked behind her ears.

It seemed that tonight's dress had been yet another gift to Aphrodite from yet another lover, the one before Geoffrey: 'Don't ask me why, Trilby, but men always seem to feel the need to give one *clothes*!'

As the car arrived outside the theatre, a small crowd gathered, ten or twelve vaguely curious people with nothing better to do than to peer into the Rolls-Royce as it drew up. The chauffeur jumped out of the front and opened the door for Trilby. She stepped out onto the pavement and heard several women sigh, and amid the small flurry of interest a voice was heard saying, 'I say, who *is* she? Must be a film star surely?'

Since it was a warm evening Trilby let her stole fall a little, revealing bare shoulders, and a slight tan from sitting in Berry's garden of an afternoon. She knew she looked beautiful. She smiled back at Lewis, the architect of the moment, and as she did she saw something in his eyes that was gratifyingly proud, and protective. He put out his arm and guided her into the theatre, and up to their box. Older man, younger woman, Rolls-Royce motor car, chauffeur in uniform, it all fitted. The front of theatre staff and the other members of the audience knew it, as Trilby did, and she realised as Lewis showed her to her seat that he did too. Of a sudden they looked a couple. Thanks to Aphrodite's clothes Trilby looked older than she was, and, more than that, she felt older, and sophisticated, and when they discussed the play over drinks in a little ante-room at the back of the box during the interval she realised that she had started to sound older too.

She was grown up at last, and on this third evening together she realised that she no longer thought of Lewis as her boss, or even a newspaper proprietor, so it was no surprise when at the end of the evening, as he saw her to her door, pausing under the light of a street lamp, he kissed her long and tenderly, and of a sudden Trilby found that kissing a man was quite, quite beautiful, and not at all what she had dreaded it might be, awkward or uncomfortable, or even a little silly.

'Did you mind my kissing you, Trilby?'

'No, it was what I wanted.'

'You know I am falling in love with you?'

'Of course.' Trilby smiled up at him, and, as she did so, unbeknownst to her Lewis felt his heart was about to explode in his chest. He leaned forward to kiss her again, and again, but he leaned towards nothing, because a second later Trilby had darted away, up the steps to her house, pausing only to kiss her fingers to him, and it seemed to him that he had been dreaming, that the moment had never really happened.

It was only when she had opened the front door with her key and found Agnes standing in her dressing gown with her father behind her that Trilby realised they must have witnessed everything.

'No good will come of this, Trilby,' Agnes said, turning on her heel.

'If you are going to make a display of yourself it would be better if it were not in the street.' Michael too turned on his heel.

Trilby stared up the stairs after them, feeling ashamed.

She waited, calming herself, until she heard their bedroom door shut and Agnes's voice raised, as usual in awful protest against her, then she slipped into the drawing room to stare down the street after the Rolls-Royce, which was still outside, the smoke from its exhaust making a stream of white-grey as it filtered past the street lamp.

Eventually it moved off, but so slowly it was as if Lewis had told his chauffeur not to drive off too quickly, as if he too was staring out of a window, back to Trilby, who waved even though she knew that he could not see her any more.

*   *   *

Lewis was not someone even his best friends would have called patient, but when all was said and done, this was not so very surprising. If you were as rich as he was, there was no real reason to wait for anything. His least whim could be satisfied, and was, at every turn. Now to his horror he discovered that he was being made to wait, and by a slip of a girl who seemed to him to be forever out of reach.

'My father and stepmother think that I am too young for you.'

This was Trilby's tactful way of saying that they thought Lewis was too old for her, and they both knew it.

Lewis stared into Trilby's dark brown eyes. It helped that he was holding one of her small white hands, and that she was wearing a dark dress with white gardenias pinned on the shoulder, and that they were in the garden of his house, and that he felt that she belonged there now, beside him, in his garden.

'I suppose I will have to ask for your hand, from your father, I mean? Is he very stern?'

Trilby laughed gaily. It was all so old-fashioned and formal. She held up both hands in front of Lewis's face.

'Which hand will you ask for, Lewis? This one— or that one?'

Lewis sighed. Trilby had a way of making him feel even older than he was. Very well, he was thirty-five, very, very rich, and very, very powerful, and had enjoyed many, many women, but he wanted this girl, Trilby, so much that she made him forget all the others.

'What is it really that your father and stepmother so dislike about me?'

Trilby looked serious for a moment. She stared ahead to something that Lewis could not see in the distance.

'I had rather not tell you, really, Lewis. I mean, I think you would rather not know.'

'I would not have asked you if I did not want to know, Trilby.'

'Very well, I will tell you.' Trilby faced him, her face grave, her expression for once sad. 'No, I don't think I can, not really. It would hurt your feelings. No, I won't.'

'Yes, you must.'

'For a start, and I know you won't understand this, but my stepmother does not like rich people. And what is more, I am dreadfully afraid that she thinks that you are just too, too rich. She thinks that you have too much money and too much power, and that you will not be able to interest me, when you are older. I mean,' Trilby continued artlessly, 'you know when you are *much* older, even though I will be older too. And my father thinks you will spoil me, and it will be bad for my character. And, well. That's all, really.'

Lewis stared at Trilby, and without his realising it his forehead started to redden. He had wanted the truth, of course, but he was not sure that he wanted so much truth, at least not all at once.

'Go on. Continue, please.'

He did not want her to continue. As a matter of fact he suddenly felt as if Trilby was one of his editors giving him hard facts, or someone coming in from abroad with the latest news from some far-flung part of the world. Of a sudden, too, the occupants of this street in Chelsea were less like anything he had ever known, less like anything he could ever imagine. More like the inhabitants of one of those far-flung foreign posts to which he sent his men.

How could anyone possibly object to him on the grounds of his *money*? Or his power? It did not seem possible. He had everything that everyone else wanted. More than that, he could have

84

anything he wanted, whenever he wanted it, and now he was willing to share it all with little Trilby Smythson, which would be wonderful for her, after all, wouldn't it? So how could these people who lived in downtown Chelsea object to him? If Trilby married Lewis James she would have the best of everything for the rest of her life. It was just a fact.

'I can't go on—not really. The thing is, well, I have to admit, Agnes is pretty peculiar of course, but I am afraid she is not alone. The others, in the street, they don't really approve of you either. Not because of your age—no, they just think that you're too rich. But I mean to say, I said to them—you can't be expected to give away all your money, after all, can you? Also, I said, well, I said it was not your *fault* that you inherited all these newspapers and so on. And I mean, it isn't, is it?'

Trilby put up a hand to Lewis's tanned face. He was looking so helpless and worried that she felt quite protective of him.

'What shall I do, then? To convince all these neighbours, all these friends of yours, that I can make you happy?'

'I don't know, really. But if you think about it, it will be over two years until I reach my majority and by that time you will probably have grown tired of me anyway.'

'Never!'

Lewis started to stride about the immaculately kept lawn, loosening his evening tie from around his stiff white collar and lighting a cigarette, in other words giving every possible outward display of impatience and frustration. Inside himself, however, he felt no frustration, only a breathless amazement that he, Lewis James, proprietor of a

85

whole world of communication, was being turned away on account of the very thing that the rest of the world admired him for—his wealth. It did not seem possible, and yet it was possible! And it was happening, and to him.

However, he was not so stupid as not to know that fathers and stepmothers, however eccentric, could be most influential with their daughters. How could he prove to Trilby, to this innocent beauty, that he would and could make her happy for ever and ever? He was so used to being offered ideas that he now found he could not think of one for himself, but seconds later a thought of his own did occur.

He would ask Micklethwaite. He would ask David Micklethwaite what he should do. David Micklethwaite would know.

'Let's go in to dinner.'

Lewis stared across the lawn to the windows of the dining room. There were beautiful flowers on every surface in the room, and he could see them from where he stood. He could also see the great displays of candles on the sideboards, and knew that his collection of French paintings, Impressionist and Post-Impressionist, and some English modern art was all about his house, hanging in place on his silk-lined walls, waiting for him to stand in front of it and admire it.

From where he stood he could also see two of the maids checking his dining room table, their black and white uniforms standing out starkly against the dark oak-panelled walls of the room.

He wished of a sudden that his life could be like the maids in their uniforms, black and white, and capable of being ordered the way he wished. But it was never as easy as that. At least, it *was* as easy as that when it came to the running of his newspapers. He could have whatever he wanted there and in any way he liked it, but not now he was in love again. Now he was in love again, nothing was easy. He did not want one moment of this intensity, this frightening passion of his for this young girl, to go, or disappear, or to be thwarted in any way.

He put his arm round Trilby, and as she leaned her head against his shoulder her hair momentarily brushed his face and he could not avoid breathing in her youthful scent.

Something terrible but familiar ran through him as the perfume of her innocence enveloped him, and not wanting to frighten her he quickly let her go, saying, 'I love the smell of gardenias—don't you?'

They walked towards the house, up the steps, and so to the dining room, where they dined opposite each other, each staring down what now seemed to Lewis to be a vast distance. A distance that he had to shorten, and quickly.

*   *   *

David Micklethwaite, small-eyed, small-boned, and with the look of a man who had too much to hide, could see the problem at once.

Lewis had known that he would, but nevertheless was shocked that his right-hand man was not more surprised by the objections that had been put up.

'Trilby Smythson is so young, and you are, from her point of view, of course, some sort of mogul. Coming from her background—I mean, I know her father and stepmother and they are not the kind of folk who like rich, powerful men, I am afraid, sir.'

Lewis shrugged his shoulders. 'I own newspapers. I am not a dragon.'

'Exactly, but she is not to know that, if you don't mind me saying, Mr James. What you want to do is to take them all down to the seaside, some nice quiet place, some ordinary place—Bognor, say, or Brighton, or Seaford, anywhere like that, and show them a good time. But not your kind of good time. Show them that at heart you are just a simple man who likes simple things. That is what will go down well with them, if you convince them that you like walks on the beach and simple fare, all that kind of thing; convince them that you are as old-fashioned and full of the right kind of values as they imagine themselves to be. Be at pains to be ordinary, a nice sort of chap who can be forgiven for being what he is.'

Lewis stared at Micklethwaite. He had not had that kind of seaside holiday since he was a child. Moreover, he had not quite liked the nostalgic tone that had crept into Micklethwaite's voice when he described this type of holiday. He himself had twice, if he remembered rightly—yes, twice, in the past two years taken Micklethwaite with him to the West Indies in the winter, and on his yacht in the summer.

Not only that, but Micklethwaite had accompanied Lewis to Scotland for shooting and to Norfolk for more of the same. Why on earth would Micklethwaite like to go to Seaford or Bognor and enjoy walks along the beach when he did so many other more exciting things with Lewis? Exciting and expensive things, things that Micklethwaite could never afford on his own, not in a million years.

'Very well, Micklethwaite. I will do as you say, but it had better work, because quite frankly it sounds to me as if it is going to be hell.'

*　　　*　　　*

'Bognor? We have been invited to Bognor Regis, did you say?'

'Lewis has hired a house on a private estate and he wants all of us to go with him. It sounds an awful lot of fun. He has a beach hut, and we can bicycle everywhere, which will be good, don't you think?'

Trilby could hear her pleading tones and heartily despised herself for it.

Her father took out his diary and studied it. 'I can't possibly go, I'm afraid, Trilby. I can't do anything until well after Christmas, so much on at the office. Agnes could go, though, couldn't you, Agnes, as a chaperone, and so on?'

'Oh joy! Thank you very much, Michael, just what I could do with.' She glowered at her husband, who fingered his tie and stared into the middle distance.

'Oh, you don't want to go, do you, Agnes?'

Even Trilby felt sorry for her.

Agnes sighed heavily. 'I shall have to do it, if Michael can't, I shall have to go.'

'He is only bringing his right-hand man, his assistant, with him, no-one else, although there will be someone coming in to do some cooking from time to time. But otherwise it will be just us, and Lewis, and David Micklethwaite, you know, his right-hand man person. Everything will be quite informal. It could be nice.'

'It could also be ghastly. You do realise that, don't you?'

Michael carefully folded the *Daily Telegraph* into a small square so only the crossword was showing.

'I am sure you will like them, when you get to know them, my dear,' he murmured quietly.

'Very well, I suppose we will have to say yes to this invitation. I suppose we will have to say yes! As a matter of fact I can't very well see what else we *can* do, seeing that he is your boss and pays you and so on.' Agnes lit a cigarette, and stalked off towards the garden.

Trilby smiled. She was not going to be such a blithering idiot as to say '*I know you will like Lewis, Agnes.*' Agnes was not the kind of person who responded to that kind of persuasion.

'With any luck,' Agnes called back, 'with any luck I shall fall ill before the dreaded day.'

Unfortunately for Agnes neither of them fell ill, and so, the packing done, which in both their cases was hardly considerable, the chauffeur called to collect them in a Rover in which he drove them down to Sussex at a steady speed. They stopped on the way at a pleasant hotel for what Agnes called 'a typical hotel lunch' with soup and cold cuts and all sorts of salads.

Privately Trilby thought it was all very agreeable, so agreeable, in fact, that by the time Agnes was climbing out of the car, the chauffeur holding open the door for her and Trilby, and Lewis was stepping forward to greet her at the door of Shell Bourne— the garden of which actually had palm trees growing in it and a swing seat overlooking the Sussex sea—Trilby, ignoring the woman beside her, found that she was brimming over with happiness.

The house was quite unassuming, 1920s and a nice double oak door, and mock Tudor windows, which she always found quite charming by the seaside. Inside it was large but modestly furnished, at any rate to Lewis's eyes, but to Trilby it seemed really very luxurious in the way that Aphrodite's house was luxurious. It had obviously been quite recently done up, because it sported the newest in turquoise colours, and glowing paints. And the wooden floors had large fur rugs, and there was something that Lewis called a 'rumpus room', which sounded really rather American but turned out to be a room with a television and a ping-pong table. All in all the house positively beamed a welcome to them, and at the same time glowed with quiet wealth.

To Trilby, newly in love with Lewis, Shell Bourne was everything that anyone would wish for in a holiday house, and what with the sun shining outside, and a bedroom and bathroom each with a balcony overlooking the garden and unimaginable luxuries such as bowls of fruit in their bedrooms and extra-large bars of soap and piles of towels in the bathrooms, she felt she was in a small corner of paradise.

Agnes thought quite differently.

'What a time to come to the seaside! Really. The weather feels positively autumnal.'

'Lewis thought we would enjoy it being so quiet, and the weather forecast is good.'

Having hung up some coats and skirts and jumpers in the large cupboard, where they looked really rather shabby, Trilby followed Agnes into her room to help her unpack, only to find her feeling about in the bottom of her suitcase until she produced a flat half-bottle of Gordons gin, which she promptly put into the drawer of her bedside table.

'I always travel with my own drink,' she told Trilby, adding for no reason, 'after all, you never know, do you?'

Trilby took care not to say anything, but only turned towards the windows and the view of the sea. 'Your view's the same as mine.'

'Well, it would be, since both rooms face the same way.'

Trilby nodded absently, and continued to stare out of Agnes's floor-length windows for a second before bending down and promptly standing on her head, a favourite pastime of hers when she was in a happy mood.

She held her position on the floor steadily, while pursuing the conversation with, 'I love all that turquoise colour downstairs, don't you?'

'Really?' Agnes continued with her unpacking, ignoring her stepdaughter's unconventional pose. 'I think it is perfectly frightful.'

'I love colour. Daddy was saying that he could do with more colour at home, only yesterday, as a matter of fact.'

'Where exactly? Where did Michael say that?'

'Oh, you know, in the drawing room, or perhaps upstairs in my room. It's so jolly, colour is so cheering.'

Agnes stared out to sea and for a second there was a look on her face that Trilby could not translate. 'Your father never tells *me* anything.'

Trilby stood upright again. She wanted to say, *'That's probably because you never ask him, Agnes.'*

Instead she fell silent, and all they could hear for a few seconds was the sound of the sea outside, until Agnes said in a dull voice, after a small sigh, 'I suppose we had better go downstairs. No-one's changing, I understand, so we might as well go downstairs.'

*   *   *

The following day, after a surprisingly jolly supper, Lewis looked out of his window to see Trilby in a bright red bathing costume stepping gingerly down the short pebble-strewn beach to the sea, now at high tide. Despite great inward gasps at the cold of the water, swimming backwards and forwards, her bright red swimming hat bobbed about, at times looking more like a beach ball than a swimming hat with a head in it.

Trilby was the only one to swim that morning, not surprisingly, for when she returned to the house her teeth were chattering, and her hands and feet vaguely blue in colour. Not that she cared a threepenny damn. She was determined to swim every day. She loved the sea, was mesmerised by it, and living in London seldom saw it, but always dreamed of its magic, its splendour, its compulsion.

Lunch was laid out on the terrace, an informal affair, red napkins, checked tablecloth, and a large beach umbrella. Here Lewis took care to command the drinks trolley, while David Micklethwaite supervised the daily maid who had come in to cook and shop for them, because in the end it seemed that neither of the men could quite run to that.

'No, can't run to cooking, David, really I can't, not even for Trilby Smythson, not even for a

93

second. And I refuse to be by the seaside eating your burned toast and watery vegetables. No, you will at least have to hire us a maid who can cook and shop and clean, and that sort of thing, never mind the lack of grandeur.'

'We really will have to do tea in the beach hut though, sir. We can't ask the maid out there, or she really will think we're complete phonies.'

Even as Lewis mixed some really quite startling martinis for the three of them, and a less potent cocktail of orange juice and a thimbleful of gin for Trilby, he knew that the beach hut test was at last looming, and before he had even downed his first martini he thought he could see the awfulness of the sandwiches, and taste the weakness of the tea that he and Micklethwaite would attempt to make them all, after a jolly game of beach cricket, and yet another swim for Trilby. Never mind, it had to be got through. It was part of his proving to Trilby and her sour if beautiful stepmother that he was not just some rich and powerful man who thought he could buy everything and anything at whim, part of proving that he was worthy of a penniless girl. How perverse could people be, he thought, suddenly feeling petulant, and yet somehow how very *English*, to not want someone to be rich and powerful.

A few hours later Trilby thought that she had never seen a man look so embarrassed as when Agnes stared down into the cup Lewis was holding out to her, and from the cup to his face, and then back to the cup again.

'What is this?' she asked in a voice not very far from reaching its highest note, which happily in her case was not very high.

'This is a cup of tea, Mrs Smythson.'

'If that is a cup of tea, Mr James, then I have seven children. Can't you even make a cup of tea for yourself?'

There was one second of horrified silence as both David and Trilby saw Lewis's mouth tighten and a small patch of red gradually appear across his forehead. He was quite obviously not used to being made fun of, and certainly not to being told off. Following this moment of tension David Micklethwaite fairly leaped forward and seized the cup and saucer.

'Oh dear.' He could not help starting to laugh. 'Dishwater with leaves.'

'I thought it did not seem quite right,' Lewis stammered, looking suddenly to Trilby more like a boy than a man. 'I know. I must say, I did think, I thought—it's a bit of a mess.'

The wind whipped through the small patch of sand that surrounded the beach hut, and reversing back sprayed sand into everything as Trilby joined Micklethwaite, staring into the tea cup for all the world as though they were both gypsies reading fortunes. As Micklethwaite had said, there was liquid in the cup, milky water, and there were tea leaves floating at the top.

'Perhaps I should have put it in a pot? Yes, I think that is what I should have done, put it in a pot and then stirred, is that it?'

Lewis started to laugh at himself now, which was just as well since everyone was laughing at him, but as Micklethwaite stopped laughing he caught sight of the look in his employer's eyes, and it seemed to him that Lewis was not really finding the situation at all funny.

'We should never have taken on making the tea,' he muttered, as Trilby stepped forward and, having given him a sympathetic look, took charge. 'I said it would be a disaster, if we made the tea.'

'Have you never made a cup of tea before, sir?'

'Never had cause to,' Lewis told him, turning away. 'Why should I keep dogs and bark myself? You know how it is, Micklethwaite. I was always pampered as a child, and now, well, now there is no time for such things. You know how it is,' he ended lamely.

With anyone else David Micklethwaite would have put out an arm and placed it round his shoulders, but since it was Lewis James, and he was his employer, Micklethwaite merely remarked in a kindly tone, 'The rule of thumb with tea and coffee, sir, is that the tea or coffee goes in first, and the water, having boiled, goes in second.'

'And *I* would like to go in *soon*.' Lewis sighed, but because the red patch on his forehead had died away Micklethwaite only nodded in an acquiescent, unhurried manner while staring out to sea in a diplomatic fashion.

'Quite right, sir, we have had the best of the afternoon, but now the ladies have gone to the trouble of making tea for us, I think we should at least join them for that, don't you, sir?'

They turned towards the hut which the women had now organised for tea, placing small chairs around a picnic table, and spreading buttered bread with Marmite or jam, and as they did so it seemed to Lewis, throwing a petulant stone towards the incoming sea, that, of a sudden, Micklethwaite really got on his nerves.

He was so dull, always saying 'sir', more of a

creep than a right-hand man. Now Lewis came to think about it he really thought that when they returned to London he might send Micklethwaite to America on some mission or other. He thought he might be quite tired of taking Micklethwaite around all the time. Of course Lewis knew how to make tea, he had just been *confused* that was all. It was ridiculous to be inside a beach hut sipping tea from plastic mugs when he could be drinking martinis or Italian coffee on the deck of his own private yacht. What was more, judging from the way the stepmother had downed her lunchtime martini she would very probably have been more impressed and gratified by a week on his yacht than footling about on an English beach with the wind blowing sand into the bread and butter.

'There really is nothing quite like British beach hols, is there, Mr James?' All of a sudden Agnes smiled across at David Micklethwaite and Lewis. 'What fun it has been today, wouldn't you say? More fun than I care to remember. Like a day before the war, like a day when I was a child, all fun and merriment, tea and sandwiches, sand in the butter. Dear me, takes us all back, doesn't it?'

Lewis too smiled, and a second later he had quite forgotten that Micklethwaite was getting on his nerves. 'Yes, it is quite my favourite sort of holiday,' he agreed, lying. 'Quite my favourite.'

Agnes nodded, at ease with herself for once. She thought she could grow to like a chap who did not mind being teased, who enjoyed his beach holidays like a good Englishman. More than that, she realised that Trilby might be right: despite being so rich and powerful Lewis James was quite able to come off it. After all he had joined in the laughter

97

against himself, hadn't he? He had generally mucked in. He therefore surely could not be quite such a mogul as she had first thought. Not that it mattered really, not to her, whom Trilby married, it was only Michael who disapproved really, but then Michael would. When all was said and done there was no doubting the fact that he was wild about Trilby.

Agnes looked thoughtfully over at Lewis. He might, after all, be very useful to her, and to Michael. She had no real idea how he could be useful, but she had a feeling that no man as rich and powerful as Lewis James could not be useful, in some way or another. And then, too, he was handsome, he was stylish, he was solicitous—always asking Agnes if she was quite comfortable, seeing to her needs at every turn, that kind of thing.

No, all in all, it seemed to her that provided this Lewis James man did not reveal something appalling about himself, she might now consider telling Michael to come round to the idea, and give his consent to whatever it was that Lewis had in mind for Trilby and her future.

Always providing it was marriage, of course. Michael would never consent to anything else. The Smythsons never lived in sin. It had never been known. She smiled across at Lewis, who had just come back from a short walk along the beach with David Micklethwaite, who was now smiling down at Agnes. She smiled brilliantly back at him. Happy for once, and in her own way even carefree.

*   *   *

'Seduce the stepmother—she is quite a beauty,

after all, David,' Lewis had said, impatient as ever. 'I can't stand another day of this sand and Marmite nonsense, just seduce the wretched woman for God's sake. Judging from the way that she keeps looking at you she's obviously dying for it, and that will soon put an end to her stupid objections.'

'I can't do that, sir.'

'Why ever not?'

'Well, you know how it is, we know so many of the same people!'

'Don't be ridiculous, Micklethwaite, whenever has that ever stopped you before?'

CHAPTER THREE

For luncheon that day Trilby wore the latest Chanel navy blue suit with square, slightly padded shoulders, comfortable uncinched waistband, and a sailor hat. A white shirt with bow tie and a gardenia in her buttonhole completed her new look. She felt at ease, happy, and satisfied that she looked as she should for such a smart place as the Caprice.

Of course everyone smiled at Lewis and Trilby as they moved down the restaurant. Despite their engagement's having been announced some few weeks before, and the wedding's being about to follow some few weeks later, the whole of London had stayed interested in this particular couple, one of whom had, in the best tradition, youth and beauty, and the other of whom had not just power and wealth but, most unusually, the good looks and charisma to go with them.

'Agnes says it's bad luck for the bridegroom to

see the dress before the wedding day, and that Hartnell is far too expensive and swanky for a girl of my age.'

As far as Lewis was concerned, Agnes, having been duly seduced over large brandies and a great deal of sympathy by David Micklethwaite, was now yesterday's fish. In fact any mention of her name nowadays was beginning to grate on his pre-wedding nerves, but he managed to smile and look interested nevertheless.

'I have, in the past, invested enough money in the house of Hartnell to give me a quite different angle on the story.' Lewis raised his glass of ice cold champagne to Trilby, and she raised hers to him, and smiled.

'Of course, all your *other* women, you took them all to Hartnell, didn't you? Whereas I myself actually prefer Chanel,' she added, impishly.

'Besides,' Lewis went on, ignoring her, 'your stepmother must know that the paper has first call on the design of the dress. They are, technically speaking, paying for it. My fashion editors must therefore advise. Let's face it, darling, if it was left to your parents you would be marrying me in a utility suit holding a bunch of daisies from the park.'

Trilby laughed. It was all too true. Inevitably Michael and Agnes both did still have a wartime complex.

'If I explain to you what *I* think you should look like, if you don't mind, and after that I will leave all the rest up to Marion Holton!

Trilby frowned, not knowing who 'Marion Holton' was, and why she should be handed over to her.

'Marion Holton is the real name of Lauren Ashton, our so-famous fashion writer.'

'Oh, good, that is a good idea. What do you think I should wear? Mrs Johnson Johnson says that left to themselves men only want to see women in black stockings and suspenders. Do you think that is what you would like?'

Lewis laughed. He felt quite able to laugh, for he had already instructed Miss Holton on exactly what he expected his bride to look like, and black stockings and suspenders were definitely not on the menu, at least not until the honeymoon. More than that, detailed sketches of every single item in his bride's trousseau had been handed over to Marion with precise instructions.

When she saw them Marion had thought, *Gracious, a bit old-fashioned, aren't they?* while saying out loud, 'Yes, yes, of course, Mr James, I will have all these copied for your bride.'

It went unsaid, but they both knew of course that if Marion wanted to stay on as Lauren Ashton the columnist she would make utterly sure that everything was done as her employer wished, even if, privately, she thought his taste must have petrified some few years before, as it so often did with men, with Dior and the New Look, or even before that.

*　　*　　*

Marion Holton chain-smoked, but not in the salon, of course. In the salon of the house of Hartnell she behaved herself. Trilby could not believe, looking as she did, so unlike the photograph at the top of her Sunday fashion column, that Miss Holton would have any taste at all. However, within a few minutes of their meeting Trilby quickly came to realise just why it was that Marion was the most feared fashion editor in England.

Miss Holton had taste from the top of her tangerine-coloured hat to the bottom of her polished Rayne shoes. She was It as far as England's fashion trade went, and although she could never have any influence with the house of Hartnell, she could, when all was said and done, create yet more interest.

If the future Mrs Lewis James was married in a Hartnell dress it would certainly attract enough press interest, even for Norman Hartnell, to keep his adoring clientele bubbling along in the happy conviction that they were buying their evening gowns and wedding dresses from the right place.

'Nothing white, nothing tulle,' Miss Holton had stated in the taxi on the way to the salon, quoting her employer, and Trilby had agreed. 'Something cream, satin, stately, just a hint of the Coronation dresses they did last year. But not so intricate, you understand.'

She was still quoting Lewis James chapter and verse, but she knew that Trilby would not know this. As a matter of fact, looking at the young, slender girl seated beside her with her large dark eyes and short dark hair, Marion could not help pitying her. Marrying a man of thirty-five was no walkover, poor kid, but marrying Lewis James! Inwardly she sighed for her in her innocence. But there it was, he was very rich, she would have anything she wanted, which, so long as she knew what she wanted, was after all not nothing.

The dress, after many, many fittings and what

finally seemed to Trilby to be endless months of preparation, turned out to be exactly as Lewis had described to Marion and she in turn had described to Trilby.

Made of cream satin, it looked very stately from the back, with an embroidered train falling from a waistband of barely half an inch. The train was sewn for twelve inches with the most intricate knots and beads, and small heads of flowers, each one outlined in tiny diamonds and pearls, and the whole banded either end by a two-inch width of satin. The bodice too was embroidered, the embroidered piece shaped as a collar beneath which could be seen two small classically cut sleeves with edges picked out in the same detail. All in all it was a magnificent dress, but it was not all Trilby wore on that famous day. She also wore a modern tiara, the centre of which was a flower which Lewis had ordered to be designed as nearly as possible, because she so loved them, to look like a gardenia.

The tiara was a new piece, commissioned especially for her as a wedding present by Lewis, and a great deal more simple than the old-fashioned, more traditional tiaras. It looked beautiful, because Lewis had been careful to have the jeweller match the diamonds to the cream of the dress. There was to be no blue in the gems, 'only rose'.

*　　　*　　　*

As a rule no-one remembers much of their own wedding, but Trilby remembered every little detail of hers.

103

First of all she remembered her father standing waiting for her at the bottom of the stairs, once Marion Holton, the hairdresser and most of Glebe Street had finished with her. Trilby was no hopeless romantic, but neither was she entirely devoid of sentiment. She had hoped that on seeing her Michael would look at the very least pleased, even perhaps a little overcome, because this was after all, to all intents and purposes, meant to be her big day. What she had not expected was that he would be staring at his shoes, smelling slightly of alcohol, and swaying. It was not something that she had thought would happen. As she reached the bottom of the stairs she looked directly at him, but he seemed intent on avoiding her eyes, as if she had come downstairs dressed in something outrageous, not a beautiful satin gown and a tiara.

'The court photographer is waiting for you in there,' he said baldly, nodding towards the drawing room door, and he stood stock still as she walked past him to join the myriad bridal attendants who were hopping and jumping around the room like so many dressed-up dolls while Mrs Johnson Johnson stood in the middle smoking and saying every now and then, 'Now come on, darlings, be still, just for a few minutes, just for the photies, please, be still.'

As she stood still as a marble statue for the old-fashioned photographer Trilby felt swamped with disappointment. She had always imagined that her father would be grateful for her getting married. After all at long, long last he would be alone with Agnes, and could give his second wife the sole attention that she so obviously craved. She had imagined that he would be proud of her, that he would think that she was doing well, that somehow she was making up for his being so unhappy, for his sense of not having ever had quite what he wanted.

Moreover, by marrying Lewis and going to live elsewhere Trilby had fondly imagined that she was removing one helluva obstacle from her father's marriage. Try as she would to absent herself from the house, spending more time with her neighbours than at home, Trilby knew herself to have been a constant source of irritation to her stepmother. Now she would be gone. Agnes would no longer have to grumble either about Trilby or to Trilby; she would be free of her stepdaughter. She would be free of her at long, long last after what must have been for her, poor woman, nine endless, tedious years.

Later, walking down the aisle on her father's arm, Trilby tried to remember all his many kindnesses to her, all his little comforting asides when Agnes went too far with one of her destructive remarks. His habit of leaving little sweetmeats by her bedside when he came back late from a restaurant, his defence of her looks. All this came to her as they walked slowly up the aisle, but even so, she could not prevent the overwhelming sense of relief that washed over her when the moment came when Michael placed her hand in Lewis's and stepped back into his pew again.

After that Trilby remembered only the trumpets, the faces, the flashlights, the sounds of the voices in the crowds outside *ooh*ing and *aah*ing. She remembered Lewis stumbling over his second name when they took their vows, which made her smile reassuringly up at him, and press his hand. She remembered the smell of the arum lilies, which for one awful moment seemed so overpowering that she thought she might faint, which would have been particularly terrible because she knew that Lewis had flown in several hundred of them from somewhere very far away, and for no better reason than that Agnes had said that she liked them.

And then, as always happens at weddings, events moved terribly quickly, and the wedding luncheon that had looked from the size of the menu to be going to take for ever was over, and Trilby's tiara and veil were removed and she was being prepared by her new Chinese maid to change into her going away suit, a tightly buttoned coat and skirt, the latter long, nearly to her ankle, and the jacket distinguished by its large piqué collar and matching hat which gave her heartshaped face a gamine look, since the hat was shaped in the form of a petal.

She threw her bouquet towards the crowd below the staircase upon which they both stood before departing and Marion Holton, who was proudly unmarried, caught it quite by chance, and within a few seconds Trilby was kissing her goodbye, and kissing all the children who had made up her twelve attendants, and then, in the back of the limousine, kissing Lewis himself, which was the best kiss of all, naturally, while behind them followed another motor car bearing his valet, her maid, and all their luggage.

Trilby had not wanted to go abroad for their honeymoon, and so Lewis, once more bowing to his young bride's modest wishes, had taken over a small hotel in Cornwall, set right on the water. It was September, still a warm time of year in Cornwall, but by the time they reached the place, driving through the afternoon and evening, and stopping only for a drink and a sandwich, it was nearly midnight, and they were both tired.

Lewis at once demonstrated how thoughtful he was, for, on seeing Trilby at the door of their bedroom barely able to keep her eyes open, he smiled, and kissing her hand, and then her lips, said tenderly, 'I will leave you to your maid, darling, and see you in the morning.'

In the morning Lewis knocked at her door, and Trilby, who was wide awake, called, 'Come in!' and no sooner had Lewis walked into the room than she ran across the room and flung her arms around his neck.

'Look at the blue sky, look at the sea, right outside the window. As always when I am by the sea, I am in heaven!'

A few minutes later it seemed that they both were.

*　　　*　　　*

'Welcome home, Mrs James.'

Their honeymoon had been filled with happiness, but even so Trilby was glad to be home, not for herself, but for Lewis, who she had sensed, after the first ten days, was beginning to turn his face towards London again.

In fact Lewis had enjoyed his honeymoon more than he could have thought possible. After the disasters of Bognor Regis and having to try so hard to earn the wretched stepmother's—and therefore the father's—approval, to his amazement Cornwall had answered every honeymoon need. Long breakfasts in bed, followed by day trips on a small sailing vessel that he had hired for their use. Luncheons overlooking the sea, dinner followed by a game of cards, or dominoes. For Lewis it had all been inescapably, but delightfully, ordinary, whereas for Trilby, trying to become used to the luxuries that he had spread before her, it had been precisely the opposite.

Naturally Lewis had photographed Trilby at every possible opportunity, but there were some moments, moments that he could not snap, that he would always hold to him, that just the mention of her name would for ever conjure.

Trilby looking for shells on the beach, hop-scotching on the sand. Trilby hanging up seaweed in the hall of the hotel in order to forecast the weather the next day. Trilby lying on her pillows after he had made love to her with an enraptured look on her face, staring ahead of her wordlessly. Those were the images that he held close to him, moments that made him wonder, over and over again, if he would be able to hold on to her, asking himself endlessly and unnecessarily if she would always love him as she did now, unable to contemplate the thought that she might not, that she might fall for someone else, some younger man.

Now he stared at her dark head on the pillow and found himself wishing suddenly that it was greying a little, as his was, wishing that they were equal, that she did not have such power over him. They had just made love for the first time in his house and he was, as he had been for the past fortnight, overcome with happiness.

She was, she had to be, perfect, this one at last; this woman was going to be perfect for him in every way. He was sure of it—quite, quite sure. She would not let him down. She was a sublime gift that only he had received. All his life he had been searching for such perfection and now he had found it in little Trilby Smythson. Most of all she was an original. She was not like other women, the other women he had known, the other women who had let him down.

As if to prove him right she turned to him, and where other women might have said something trite after lovemaking, words that immediately lowered the temperature such as 'That was perfect' or 'Wasn't that wonderful, darling?' Trilby now said, 'I was thinking—isn't it funny, afterwards— you know—after you've made love, you can't really remember much about it, can you? I mean not the exact sequence of events. At least, I can't, can you?'

Lewis laughed hugely, because just hearing her voice, knowing that she had not of a sudden changed, even in the last minute, was as always a gigantic relief.

He drew her closer to him. It was true. It *was* difficult to remember making love after it was all over; in a matter of minutes you could hardly recall the sequence of events that you had just lived through. He smiled. 'I agree. It's the feeling that you remember, not a great deal more.'

What a strange creature she was. He never quite knew what she was thinking. However much he wanted to, so far he had never been able to guess where her mind might be straying, into what light or dark areas. In this way too she was not at all like the other women he had known and enjoyed. Lewis knew that if he said *'A penny for your thoughts'* to Trilby she was quite capable of replying anything from *'Mongolian goats'* to *'I was just wondering how long it would take to learn the double bass.'*

As if sensing Lewis's overpowering feelings of possession Trilby moved away from him, rearranging herself on her own pillows, and giving a small contented sigh. Lewis watched her, as always after lovemaking feeling once more objective, studying her closely as if she was an editor he was considering employing, someone quite detached from him. Unlike an editor, however, he truly wanted to know everything about her. He did not want her to surprise him, yet at the same time he did not want to cease appreciating her for her individuality, for the fact that she was bringing something new and quite different into his life, just as a new editor had to be seen to be introducing something original into one of his papers. Besides, he was all too aware that it was vital that he remain undeceived. This time he really did not want any surprises.

He had always appreciated, from the moment that Trilby had walked into his drawing room wearing a black matador hat and clothes that were a tiny bit dated, that she was independent, and spirited. In fact Trilby's independence was something that Lewis had particularly liked about her from the start. He remembered her standing in his drawing room downstairs looking as if she was about to whip off her modish hat, throw it on a chair, and sit and draw what she could see around her, so much did she look fascinated by her surroundings.

Added to this sense of independence, she seemed to have no sentimentality. Of course she liked to laugh with him, she liked to make love, but she was not suffocating, as so many of his former girlfriends had been, she did not cling, she did not chatter. Perhaps it was because of this that Lewis sensed that there was something deep inside her that he could not reach, that stayed aloof from him, some inner pair of eyes that he instinctively knew were staring out, but not at him, at other things, at other people. And this again was different from any other woman he had known.

The thought suddenly occurred to Lewis, and it was intoxicating and exciting, that if only he could reach those inner eyes, he could put his hand over them. He could blindfold them. He could make her tell him what they saw. Silently he vowed that one day, he would. Normally the idea would have excited him so much that he would have stayed to dally, but today business called and he had to get on.

Trilby watched Lewis climbing out of bed and walking across the room. He was very well made. His legs were long. He had a fashionable tan, no white strips in places which might have made him look slightly silly when he was naked. Of course she had no-one to whom she could compare him. She knew nothing of what or how he could be as far as other women were concerned, and frankly she cared less. He was a wonderful lover, thoughtful, attentive, tender and imaginative. She did not know, but she assumed that it must be rare in a man, and therefore she must be very lucky. More than that, she was happier than she could have ever dreamed was possible.

' 'Bye, darling. See you at lunch.'

Trilby had fallen asleep and now Lewis, immaculately dressed for business in a pale grey suit and pale grey tie, was kissing her goodbye. She smiled up at him from her pillows.

111

'Is oo going to telephone me from the office when oo has arrived safely?'

He stared down into her large dark eyes, knowing that she was teasing him, making fun of lovers' talk and despite the inherent mockery in her tone, which made him feel uneasy, he laughed.

'No, I am not, *oo* will be happy to hear.' He walked to the door, and then he stopped and turned. 'Yes, I am.' He turned back to the door. 'I am going to telephone to *oo*.'

He hurried down the wide staircase to the spacious hall below, where he knew that Paine would be waiting to hand him his hat and his umbrella. It would be best if he telephoned her. After all, she had said earlier that she was going to stay in all morning.

'Madame?' Mrs Woo, Trilby's personal maid, scratched at the door, and her small, dark head appeared at about the same height as the door handle.

'Oh, Mrs Woo, will you lay me out something beautiful to wear for lunch at home?'

'Yes, Mrs James. Of course.'

Trilby lay back against her pillows once more. It was incredible to think that she, Trilby Smythson, was *Mrs James*, and that she was now lying in a vast bedroom with a great satin bedspread and contemplating being called to a bath drawn by her own maid. From now on she knew that, as Mrs Lewis James, she would always be expected to take her maid with her everywhere.

Lewis had explained this to her. It was just a fact. At the time the very idea of it had made Trilby laugh disbelievingly, although of course she had accepted what he had said as the truth, because after all Lewis moved among such different people, people who had always had their personal servants, people who would not understand a man and wife arriving without a valet and a maid. People who would think that you were *not one of them* if you should do so. What was involved, it seemed, was prestige and status, and that was more than important for Mr and Mrs Lewis James—it was vital.

Trilby, tongue in cheek, had pretended to search for a comparison.

'Would it be like the Queen opening parliament wearing a feather in her hair instead of a crown?'

'Precisely the same,' Lewis had agreed. 'I am expected to be a certain kind of person, and for the sake of the newspapers that I own, it is vital that I am also *seen* to be that kind of person. I cannot go to the office on a bicycle, or eat my lunch from a paper bag on a park bench. It is just a fact. And now, darling, as my wife, I am very afraid, nor can you.'

After her bath Trilby allowed Mrs Woo to lay out her clothes, but yet again indicated that she had no intention of letting the small, light-boned Chinese woman in her black and white frock dress her.

'No, really, I would hate to be dressed.'

It had been a battle that had been going on for some time, a good-natured battle but a battle nevertheless, with Trilby racing to dress herself every morning before the maid could help her.

'Madame! I must beg you. Monsieur will be velly cross with me, madame. My other mistress she always lay on the bed and Mrs Woo dressed her. She never, never dress herself.'

113

'Yes, Mrs Woo, but from what you have told me she was eight hundred and nine, and not used to lifting even her own little finger by herself. I can do up my own suspenders and step into my own coat and skirt, thank you very much, really I can. Besides which, it's not fair on you, to have to dress me. Really, it isn't.'

At this the wretchedness on Mrs Woo's face was so palpable, and she looked so bereft, that Trilby herself felt quite torn up and guilty.

'I am sorry, I didn't mean to sound horrid. I did sound horrid, didn't I? But you see, I am not quite, yet, used—to—to having a maid.'

Mrs Woo turned away. 'No, madame. Maybe this evening I will be allowed to dress madame, if you please, madame?'

'Of course, this evening.'

Trilby found herself swallowing hard at the prospect of being dressed by Mrs Woo every morning and every evening. It would take hours!

Putting the thought out of her mind, she skipped downstairs to the library dutifully wearing Mrs Woo's choice for her, a black and white knitted wool jacket and matching dress, the jacket cut so tight it was more like a jumper. She felt strangely grown up in it, and yet also chic; also very much *Mrs Lewis James*.

'Allow me, Mrs James.'

The butler stepped forward, out of the shadows of the dark-panelled hall.

'Oh, Paine, goodness! Heavens, you gave me a bit of a fright, I can tell you!' Trilby laughed. 'I didn't see you standing there. You're a bit like the white rabbit, now I see you, now I don't, as it were.'

They smiled at each other as Trilby walked into

the library, and over to the fire that was burning in the large marble fireplace. She sat down. Paine closed the door. As soon as the door was shut, Trilby, already at a loss as to what to do with herself until lunchtime, stood up again, her beautifully shod feet in their Rayne shoes still looking, to her eyes, as if they belonged to someone else.

Now was obviously a good time to start discovering what there was in the room. While the servants played at dusting and mopping, the mistress could make time to explore. She had married Lewis in such a hurry that she had never had time to ask him about any of his possessions, least of all the history of his house, its paintings and its objects.

As she had thought, the man over the fireplace was called William Barnaby James and was obviously a grandfather. He still looked as solemn as the day she had first lunched with Lewis. Very straight-faced, almost biblical, more like a religious leader than a founder of a newspaper, it seemed to her, as she stared up at him.

She straightened the painting, and walked on to a table filled with objects and photographs, some of which she picked up and examined. Babies on fur rugs, women in Victorian dress, very solemn, full of the look of people who would never miss church of a Sunday, dogs and horses grouped together with smiling grooms. All the photographs were crowded together in the acceptable fashionable manner, as were the silver-framed photographs of royalty on the piano in the music room to which they had retired the night before.

Trilby's eyes wandered slowly over the

photographs, and she picked some up as she moved along the side of the table. She always loved to imagine the reality of the people behind the stilled images, wondering how they must have sounded, what they were truly like, whether she would have enjoyed their company. Finally, at the very back of the table, out of reach of Trilby's curious fingers, was a really rather arresting photograph of a woman in a beautiful white dress. Trilby stared at her for some time, wondering who she might be. After a while, so arresting was the photograph, it seemed to Trilby that, in a curious way, the young woman was staring right back at Trilby. Refusing to be put off, Trilby continued to stare, but unable from such a distance to distinguish any family likeness she went on to the next table, also crowded with objects and photographs, again some old and some really quite new, including photographs of Lewis with film stars and sporting personalities, Lewis standing grouped or smiling with people whose faces even Trilby recognised.

'Goodness, you really have had a very exciting life so far, Mr Lewis James,' Trilby said out loud, and as she did so the library door quietly opened.

'You rang, Mrs James?'

Trilby stepped back away from the table, surprised. 'Well, actually I didn't ring, Paine, but now you are here, perhaps we should discuss dinner tonight?'

'Mr James has already discussed dinner with Cook, Mrs James.'

'Oh—good.'

Trilby felt fractionally disappointed. She had really rather looked forward to discussing menus with Cook herself, but if Lewis had already done so there was really nothing she could do. It would only upset things if she changed his orders.

'I was just beginning to feel like someone in a film,' she confided to the butler. 'So, if there is nothing to be done with the menu, I wonder what I can do? Go on feeling like someone in a film?'

Paine hesitated. 'There is always the *placement*,' he told her, tactfully. 'We will be sitting down twenty tonight, only a small dinner, but perhaps you would like to see the *placement* folder?'

Trilby nodded, suddenly silent. '*Placement*' sounded really very solemn, like confirmation, or marriage vows, particularly since Paine had said it in the French manner, making it sound most particularly serious, in fact making it sound positively grim.

'Tell me, Paine. *Placement* is all about seating people in the right way so that they are amused by each other, and not getting on each other's nerves, isn't it? And all about getting their nearness to the host and hostess right, so that the important people are on the right of the host and hostess—or the left ... which is it, Paine? I am afraid I don't know.'

'Allow me, Mrs James.'

Trilby sat down again on the large Knole sofa, and the butler carefully placed a large, double-sided porcelain folder, very heavy and beautifully decorated, on her lap. When she opened it Trilby could see, attached to the pleated grosgrain on both sides of what must have once been an old letter writing folder, tiny cards, all with Lewis's crest printed at the top, and each one now carefully annotated with a guest's name.

'You will see from this that you are one end of the table, and Mr James the other, and down each side, here and here, we put the names of the guests. When we are quite happy with the *placement* we take it to the dining room and we place each card above the setting of each guest. Then we take the folder and we duplicate the place settings on a large gold plate on the hall table, so that each guest, as he or she comes in, realises where they are to be seated, and beside whom.'

'I see.' Trilby stared down at the beautifully written names, some of which were already familiar to her, like Henri and Lola de Ribes. Thank heavens there were already a few people on the cards that she had met several times.

'The protocol is that we turn to the right during the first course, and to the left during the second course, so that each person in turn is talked to, no-one is left out. Then, at a signal from you, Mrs James, the ladies leave to powder their noses, and the gentlemen take port and join the ladies after their coffee. Cigarettes and cigars may be smoked at this point.'

'Goodness.' Trilby looked up at Paine. 'And to think I used to think that having dinner was fun!'

Paine smiled encouragingly at his young mistress, but his words were not so encouraging.

'Oh no, Mrs James, I think that you will find that dinner here is not expected to be "fun", as you put it. No, dinner here is a formality, a way of going on, it is about politics and power and influence. Fun is for the lower orders.'

Trilby pulled a glum face. 'Oh dear, Paine, perhaps I could join you for dinner?'

Paine smiled as if he had not heard what she said. 'You will find everything here usually goes along quite smoothly, Mrs James,' he told her.

'Very little need concern you.'

* * *

That night Mrs Woo dressed Trilby in a black and white dress chosen for her mistress by Marion Holton. It had been part of Trilby's trousseau, a black wool sheath with a white ermine bib. As she dressed her Mrs Woo made little panting sounds. Half were gasps of admiration at the beauty of the dress and the jewellery she was handling, and half the panting sounds that anyone as small and round as Mrs Woo would make, what with the stretching and the bending that dressing someone else entails.

Eventually everything was completed, and Trilby stood in front of her maid, turning her beautifully coiffured head from side to side so that the light caught the long chandelier-style diamond earrings that Lewis had given her as part of her wedding present.

'Mrs James is looking more beautiful than any other of Mr James's ladies.'

Trilby stared down at her maid, and for the first time since meeting Lewis she felt a darting stab of jealousy. 'Did you dress any of Mr James's other ladies, Mrs Woo?'

'Oh yes, madame. Mr James always used me, and my mother, for all his ladies. He say, "The Woos are part of my wooing."' Mrs Woo burst into a small fit of laughter, holding a tiny finger under her nose as she did so, as if she was afraid that she would sneeze.

'Goodness, that is funny,' said Trilby, not smiling.

Mrs Woo did not seem to understand light

119

sarcasm but continued to laugh inordinately, before stopping abruptly and picking up her mistress's evening gloves and handbag and handing them to her.

'Not gloves in my own home, surely?'

'Other ladies always wore.' Mrs Woo looked up at Trilby, her slanting eyes holding in them a hint of warning and at the same time a solemnity which Trilby sensed went far deeper than just gloves. The gloves were a symbol of something; they probably meant that Trilby was proper.

'Yes, but the other ladies were not the mistress of this house,' Trilby said, her voice dropping to a lower tone which anyone who knew her would identify as her *thus far and no further* level. 'I am the mistress of the house. I am *Mrs* James.'

Trilby put the gloves back on the bed. It was time to assert something, she felt, although quite what it was that she was asserting she did not know.

'Velly well, Mrs James. Velly well.'

Mrs Woo strutted across to the chest containing Trilby's new collection of over two dozen pairs of gloves. Pulling open the appropriate drawer, she replaced the evening gloves and shut the drawer smartly.

Trilby turned to go out of the bedroom. She nodded to the door. The maid, sensing that there was steel where she had not thought to find it, went slowly to the door, and opened it.

Trilby walked through it, her head held high. If the little woman slammed it, she would sack her, she thought suddenly, but the little woman did not slam it. She probably would have liked to do so, but in the end she had not dared. Trilby walked slowly down the wide staircase to the hall. She hoped she had won a battle, but she had the feeling that in reality the battle was not so much a battle as the first in a series of small skirmishes. Even so, she must win.

In the library Lewis was looking almost intolerably handsome. Immaculate in his evening dress, he had the look of a man who was about to take his just reward. The look of a man who although he had owned his house for many years now felt he had at last filled it with the right person, and that person was Trilby. He sipped his ice cold champagne and threw his cigarette into the fire. As he turned back and straightened up he saw that he had a visitor, and she was his wife.

Trilby stood framed in the doorway knowing that since she had not had the opportunity to wear the dress on their honeymoon Lewis would appreciate a theatrical entrance, albeit one that was also designed to make him laugh.

'How about that?' She lifted up her arms, very much in the mannequin style, and draped one above her head, holding the other at hip height.

'Beautiful, darling.' Lewis smiled across at her. 'Stunning, in fact; you look stunning. But darling— you have forgotten something, haven't you? You have forgotten your gloves.'

*   *   *

Trilby had spent part of the afternoon in her room memorising the names of the guests, which she had copied from the placement folder, but now that the eighteen guests were coming at her she found that she could barely remember the names she had so carefully memorised.

121

'Madame de Ribes, may I introduce Mr Norman Levington?' Paine had explained that all the more illustrious guests must have people introduced to them first, before being reintroduced to the person in question. So, now, Trilby faithfully repeated the names in reverse. 'Mr Levington—Madame de Ribes.'

Paine had explained that this meant that each guest had time to absorb the others' titles and surnames.

'There is always a method in the madness of the social whirl, Mrs James, low be it said. There is always a method, you will find. And most of all, it is about putting one's inferiors at their ease. You will find that too, as you go on. As Mr James's wife, you will find that more and more.'

Correctly gloved, and armed with the knowledge that she had effectively introduced everyone to everyone else without a slip, Trilby waited for Paine's signal to go into the dining room. Everyone was drinking the excellent vintage champagne, everyone that is except Trilby, who was determined to drink only orange juice until she was quite sure that everything was as perfectly perfect as Lewis would wish, because tonight, for the first time, she felt she was mistress in her own house.

After all, she had planned the seating with Paine, and at least they had discussed the menu, although Lewis had chosen it.

A nod from Paine at the door and Trilby prepared to walk ahead of Lewis to the dining room. Her black dress fell into a slight flare at the bottom so it made walking ahead a rather stately procedure, the dress following on just a second or two behind and trailing across the floor. Trilby

122

knew enough to make sure that her hips were pushed a little forward, to show off the dress better, and once again she felt as if she was in a film, as if she was part of something not quite real, which, given her upbringing in Glebe Street, was not really dreadfully surprising, she thought of a sudden, as Lewis followed her into the beautiful, dark-panelled room with its magnificent Charles I and Charles II silver, its paintings and its feeling of having wined and dined many people, often and well.

She went to her end of the table in the accepted manner, Lewis went to his, and the guests, all presumably having checked the placement cards on the hall table, also went to their seats.

'My dear Lewis. But . . . I mean, this is not my place. I am so sorree!'

Looking first down at the place name in front of her and then up at her host, Lola de Ribes gave a slightly shocked laugh. She had gone, as had been arranged by Paine and Trilby, to sit to the right of Lewis, only to find the name *Mrs Arturo la Motte* on the placement card. Mrs La Motte, on the other hand, having moved to a chair well down the table, now found herself about to sit at a place setting meant for *Lady Bentinck.*

Lewis looked down the table at his young wife, discomforted and trying not to be angry, his eyes nevertheless saying, 'What have you done? What on earth has happened?'

Trilby quickly looked across at Paine, who was hovering by the door. Sensing imminent social disaster the butler hurried forward to Trilby's side.

'Paine, I think something has gone sadly wrong,' Trilby said, breaking the awkward silence that had fallen in the room, for what with Lewis looking daggers down the table at her, and poor Paine's top lip breaking into a sweat, it really could not have been worse. 'I think,' Trilby went on, and she opened her eyes wide and stared round at all their guests as ingenuously as she dared, 'I really think, if we are not quite careful, this is about to turn into the Mad Hatter's tea party!'

The laugh that followed from everyone and filled the previous silence was one of relief, naturally, and Trilby quickly took advantage of it.

'I am so sorry, everyone. Something has obviously gone very, very wrong, but providing you are all happy, why not let us obey the crazy cards, and then swap places after the hors d'oeuvres? By which time we will all have forgotten where we were meant to be in the first place.'

The expression on Lewis's face as their guests willingly and happily fell in with her solution was something that Trilby would always remember. A mixture of relief and pride, and something else too. But what that was she could not have precisely said.

'Well done,' said the gentleman on her right. 'One of the maids has obviously been sacked. If there is trouble backstage they always either jam the *aunt*, change all the placement cards, or throw the silver in the dustbin, anything like that.'

Trilby stared at him. He was old, he was nice, but she had no idea who he was, so she said, 'Tell me more.'

He did not smile, but if anything looked more serious. 'Well, as you don't know, Lady Bentinck and I live in Worcestershire. We have always lived in Worcestershire, but, it has to be said, since the war there has been a great dearth of young ladies wishing or even willing to work in a house. Darling Caro, my wife, has known nothing but hell because of it. They simply won't be told, do you see? So, believe me, I know all about what they can get up to, because she tells me everything. She has to, otherwise she might go mad, with the strain of it all, do you see? And then of course there is the little matter of trinkets disappearing. Take advantage of old people? Believe me they *do*. They take advantage of us old trouts and before you can say christening mug they are off with your jewellery or your snuffboxes, and nothing to be done. At least not if you don't want your barns set on fire.'

As she listened to her guest Trilby's mind wandered, back to Mrs Woo, back to her smug expression when Trilby reappeared demanding her evening gloves. Of course, she had tried to best Mrs Woo, she would be the first to admit that, but Mrs Woo had ended up besting Trilby.

Mrs Woo had won over the evening gloves, which she had handed back to Trilby with a strange smile. Could she also, the thought of a sudden occurred to Trilby, could she also have changed all the placement cards to embarrass her mistress? As a revenge perhaps? Because Trilby had been so reluctant to be dressed by her?

'You have frightened me, Lord Bentinck.'

'No need to be frightened, my dear. Just always remember that, like the press, servants always win, there is no way round that. As to us, we're selling our house, giving up the unequal struggle. Our son is furious of course, but what can you do, there is just so much that you can take, and then you have to up stumps and sell. Let the National Trust do the worrying, I say. But, there, it's different for you,

125

Lewis has a loyal staff. Lucky fellow.'

'Until now.'

Lord Bentinck looked up from his smoked salmon and stared at Trilby. 'Oh, I see, the mix-up over the placement, you too think it was sabotage? Good luck then, my dear, you will need it.'

The rest of the dinner passed off effortlessly, as dinner will do when there are fine wines and perfectly presented food, and in due course Trilby, at a given signal from Lewis, led the ladies from the dining room and up the stairs to her bedroom where they powdered their noses, fussed over their hair, and went to the bathroom.

They were all beautifully dressed, all beautifully coiffured, and perhaps because of this, Trilby noticed, they talked of nothing except hair and clothes. Where to go for your clothes, where to go for your hair, but never, ever how much they paid for the clothes, or the hair. In fact the subject of how much their clothes and hair might have cost seemed to be taboo. That at least was the same as Glebe Street where no-one ever discussed money, for the simple reason that none of them were terribly interested by it, unless they had run out of it.

Instead of talking about money, the ladies gossiped, while Mrs Woo smiled almost possessively at the scene. Women seated on the bed, women brushing their hair, women momentarily easing their high-heeled shoes from their feet. It was obviously a familiar scene to the little Chinese woman. Mrs Woo also took the trouble to smile at Trilby every now and then, as well she might, since she had won the day, and she knew it. Trilby too took care to smile innocently back, while the thought would keep recurring: after Trilby had gone back for her gloves would the little maid have had time to dart downstairs and mix up all the placement cards?

At first she was convinced that Mrs Woo would have had easily enough time, possibly because she wanted to be convinced. Paine had been in and out of the library all during the first part of the evening, and the maids would have been in the kitchen. Except—now Trilby glanced surreptitiously at Mrs Woo—except she could not help noticing, as she was being dressed by her, how breathless the maid had been. Just bending down and picking up something from the floor had been enough to make her pant like a Pekinese on a hot day.

As the ladies prepared to move downstairs again, Trilby admitted to herself that it would surely have been impossible for the maid to dart anywhere, let alone be able to run down to the dining room and mess up the placement cards. Quite apart from anything else, she would surely be afraid of being accused of trying to steal from the table.

Now that she had convinced herself, Trilby very deliberately turned and smiled warmly at the small Oriental maid in her immaculate uniform.

'Thank you, Mrs Woo.'

This time Mrs Woo did not smile back. She merely bowed slightly, and such was the intensity of her gaze that her small, dark eyes looked almost colourful, as if she was saying to Trilby, 'You'll learn, my girl.'

*   *   *

127

Downstairs, once the guests had gone, Lewis kissed Trilby long and passionately.

'You did beautifully, darling, and you looked ravishing. No-one can talk, no-one *will* talk of anything except you in that beautiful dress for at least a week, I predict it.'

'Oh, Lewis, how could you be so nice after all that business with the placement cards?' Trilby stood back from him and shook her head.

'That was nothing—it passed off very well, you handled it all perfectly.'

'All I had to do was get the placement right, and I even got that wrong! I could not have been more of a failure, really.'

Lewis stared at her, and then put his arm around her shoulders, at once protective and loving. 'You didn't feel that, did you? A failure, you? Far from it, my darling, you were a total success. None of the men could take their eyes from you. You were a complete and utter success and I predict that you will be the toast of London within months. Whichever way, you have made me the proudest man in the world, and I am now going to take you to bed and make passionate love to you.'

Afterwards, as she lay back on her pillows, Trilby's mind turned back to the mystery of who had changed all the cards before dinner. She could not let it go because she knew that she might have been *ruined*. Worse than that, since it was her first dinner party as a married woman, she might have been totally humiliated. Worst of all, she might now have been a failure in Lewis's eyes, and that, she sensed, could make her life difficult, what with her being so much younger. He might become impatient with her.

'Men do hate to be embarrassed,' Molly admitted when Trilby went round to see her the next day for coffee and related to her the near-disaster at the dinner party. 'They do. But really, Trilby, you sound as if you have done quite well, so I should put the whole matter out of your mind, and just soldier on as normal. Really, I would.'

Trilby had noticed that from the moment she walked into Molly's house, although she looked pleased to see her, Molly kept glancing at the clock. They had not met since Trilby had come back from her honeymoon, only talked on the telephone, admittedly in quite the old way.

'You're busy, aren't you? I shouldn't have arrived without telling you.'

'Well, you know, Trilby, delightful as it is to see you, and looking so well and smart—I am expecting someone, and quite soon; a young cousin as a matter of fact, and her mother. They are coming to luncheon, and guess what? I have to lay the table, although, you may be pleased to hear, there will be no trouble with the placement!'

Although they both laughed, Trilby felt suddenly uncomfortable.

'Berry is downstairs cooking up something delicious because I have to try a little harder. They may both be coming to lodge for a few months, while the daughter does a flower arranging and cooking course, you see?'

Molly's smile was still kind, still caring, but suddenly Trilby sensed the distance between them. It was entirely normal for people in Glebe Street to take in lodgers every now and then when they were feeling a little poor, or down on their luck, but now that she was Mrs Lewis James and had a Chinese maid, and lived in a house with not just a drawing room but a library and a music room, not to mention a summer dining room in a conservatory in the garden, and an indoor staff of six, and a chauffeur, suddenly the word 'lodger' seemed like something from another language.

'Yes, of course. I perfectly understand. I'll pop across to see Aphrodite, and then—well, perhaps you could manage luncheon with me next week sometime?'

'I can't do lunch next week, duck. I have taken on a little temporary afternoon job, but Berry will be here as he always is, daubing away. The week after, perhaps . . . Goodbye, Trilby, and don't forget to keep in touch with all your news. Lovely to see you, really it is, but Cousin Millie and her mother will be here any minute, I fear. Coffee and then lunch, their trains, you know, arriving from Chester at such unsuitable times. But, take care. I am so glad to see you looking so well. I only hope that Millie will make as exciting a match as you have. What an example to your generation you have been.'

Standing on the old familiar doorstep outside Molly's house, Trilby stared across the road feeling oddly disappointed and dulled. After a minute she crossed the street and knocked lightly on Aphrodite's door, which, uncharacteristically, was locked. Eventually Aphrodite could be heard pounding up the stairs to open it. On seeing Trilby she looked, it seemed to Trilby, just for a second exactly as Molly had looked, as if she could hardly believe that it was actually Trilby standing there.

'Hallo, Trilby. Er, I wasn't expecting you.' She opened the door wider. 'Molly never said you were coming. I am just entertaining Mrs J.J. to coffee and croissants, but I expect you have eaten and drunk and all that already, haven't you?'

'No, as a matter of fact,' Trilby told her, over-brightly, 'I have not. No, actually I am starving to death. I left home so early, you see, to avoid having breakfast with Lewis.'

For a second it seemed to Trilby, perhaps unfairly, that a look of relief came into Aphrodite's eyes as she imagined that Trilby had been made miserable by her marriage to a rich, celebrated and powerful man.

'Come in, come in.' She called down to the kitchen. 'It's Trilby, she has just left Lewis James!'

Mrs Johnson Johnson appeared at Aphrodite's kitchen door smoking, as always, and wearing her familiar turban and long hostess gown in brightly patterned colours. But the brilliance of her gown and hat were as nothing to the sparkling expression in her eyes as she said, 'Left Lewis James? Surely not, Trilby, you've only been married for a few weeks!'

She sounded so excited at the thought of the possible ensuing drama that Trilby could not help smiling. 'No, no! Aphrodite's got the wrong end of the stick, Mrs J.J. I have only left Lewis *at home* because he is having breakfast with a whole lot of Americans, in the dining room, so I thought I would pop out, quite on my own, and come and see all of you here, in darling old Glebe Street.'

There was a small silence and then Aphrodite said, 'Oh, I see,' and her brightened expression changed once more to deep gloom as she realised that Trilby had not left her husband after all. 'Well, never mind, have some coffee anyway.'

131

Trilby sat down thankfully in Aphrodite's kitchen. It was so nice to be back with Aphrodite and Mrs Johnson Johnson, with the coffee brewing and Mrs J.J.'s fags stinking up the air and Aphrodite waiting, as always, with a resigned expression, for the Bomb to drop. It was so nice, so familiar, so all-embracing and warm, like a dear old much loved coat that you could pull round you, so familiar in its normality that she could have burst into tears of relief.

After a long, long pause, Mrs Johnson Johnson stubbed out her cigarette and asked her if she had enjoyed her honeymoon.

'Of course. It was lovely.'

'I suppose it was the south of France and the Duke of Westminster on his yacht and everything— all that kind of fandango?'

'No, it wasn't actually. It was Cornwall, and buckets and spades, and all *that*.'

Both the women stared at Trilby, not believing her.

'That's not what it said in the papers. In the papers,' Mrs Johnson Johnson said, almost accusingly, 'it definitely said that you were honeymooning in the south of France on Lewis James's yacht, didn't it, Aphrodite?'

Aphrodite nodded gloomily. 'Yes, that's right. It definitely said you were honeymooning in the south of France. On the yacht. And that the yacht is moored right next to that Onassis man, or Lady Docker, or someone. People like that.'

'Well, the newspapers were wrong, and I should know, I went on the honeymoon, not the newspapers, and I promise you, we went to Cornwall. Lewis took over the Buckling, it's only a

132

tiny little hotel, but it is right on the water, and we had a lovely bucket and spade sort of time. I didn't want to go abroad, not after all that excitement, and so much to get used to.'

Trilby laughed, lightly, but she could see that neither woman believed her, so that they did not join in the laughter.

'Lewis James owns the paper for goodness' sake, so he should have at least got that right,' said Mrs Johnson Johnson, after a short pause. 'He should at least have got where you went on honeymoon right.'

'It's not him that writes up that kind of thing, it's all his minions. Besides, he probably wanted to put off the rest of the reporters, from other newspapers. He was probably putting them off the scent.'

'Oh, I see.'

Aphrodite poured Trilby some coffee just the way she knew she liked it, with a generous swirl of cream, and not at all like the coffee that was always served at Lewis's mansion with hot, pale, boiled milk, milk that you could not sprinkle brown sugar on, and then watch as it sank to the bottom.

'So, obviously, you are still married after all?'

Trilby nodded. 'Yup, I am married now, and I am very happy.' They both stared at her. 'No, really, I am. Very happy.'

'We can only hope,' said Aphrodite in her gloomiest tone, before passing Trilby a plate on which she had placed a home-made croissant with apricot jam and butter to the side of the knife.

'I did thank you for that lovely wedding present, didn't I? The vase, I did thank you, for the vase, Mrs J.J.?'

Mrs Johnson Johnson's nostrils flared slightly as she breathed out yet more cigarette smoke. 'Oh, yes, Trilby, thank you, yes, you did thank me. But really, when you come to think of it—well, we all thought as a matter of fact, didn't we, Aphrodite? We all thought that whatever we sent you, it was just coals to Newcastle, wasn't it, love? I mean our poor little vase couldn't mean very much after marrying Lewis *James*, in fact it could only mean very little indeed.'

'I know that is what you must feel,' Trilby agreed, munching her way through the most delicious croissant that she had eaten in weeks. 'But as a matter of fact it was very much appreciated and I keep the vase in my room on the chest of drawers over by the window, and it reminds me of all my happy days here.'

The two women stared at her and there was a short silence as they took in the sincerity of what she had just said.

'Well, that is nice, Trilby,' said Mrs Johnson Johnson, breathing out more smoke into the kitchen. 'Really, that is very nice indeed. And shows a good unspoilt attitude.' She leaned forward suddenly and kissed Trilby on the side of her head. 'Don't you think that is nice, Aphrodite? Don't you think that is nice, about the vase?'

Aphrodite turned from her stove, oven gloves covering the cuffs of her silk blouse, her eyes creased from the steam escaping from a pot whose lid she was lifting.

'Oh, good, good. Yes,' she agreed, but within a few seconds she was reading her newest recipe out loud to herself and not listening to anything that Trilby and Mrs Johnson Johnson were saying,

134

which was probably why, noticing this, Mrs Johnson Johnson lowered her voice.

'Poor dear, Geoffrey's left her you know, just a few weeks ago. For an older woman too, such a shock at Aphrodite's age, to be left for someone of over forty, but there you are.'

'Geoffrey did rather get on her nerves.'

Mrs Johnson Johnson nodded, and lit another cigarette. 'Well, that is true, Trilby dear, but you know how it is, once someone leaves you they always appeal as having been a great deal more congenial than when they were actually with you and, as you say, getting on your nerves. At least that is what I have always found, with all three of my husbands. Still, it will give Aphrodite more time to worry about the Bomb, so that will cheer her up.'

Trilby looked across at Aphrodite. 'I expect she will find someone else soon.'

'Oh, she has already, really, although she is busy pretending that she hasn't, you know. One Jeremy Dartmouth. Tall, wears sandals and reads his poems to her while she cooks. She has always kept quite a few men on the side, our Aphrodite, she prefers to, just in case. Myself I don't know how she does it, one man in one's life is tiring enough I always say, they whack you out, men, really they do.'

Trilby, now that she was married, was able to appreciate the significance of what Mrs Johnson Johnson had just muttered to her. She looked with renewed awe at dear old Aphrodite who she now realised quite obviously had barely hidden depths.

'Thank you so much for the coffee, Aphrodite.' She managed to kiss her despite the fact that the sauce was about to burn. 'So nice to see you again.

As I say, so awfully nice to see you both again.' She kissed Mrs Johnson Johnson too, and this despite the smoke from her cigarette.

There was a long silence after Trilby left, at the end of which Mrs Johnson Johnson lit a cigarette and breathed out slowly. 'Well,' she said, 'she can't really expect us to believe that she spent her honeymoon in Cornwall, but it was jolly sweet of her to try, I thought. Jolly sweet, don't you think, Aphrodite?'

Aphrodite nodded. 'Hope she's all right, looks a bit peaky to me.'

Another silence and then Mrs Johnson Johnson said, 'Perhaps she is peaky for a reason? You know.' She made a gesture at the front of her own blossoming dress to indicate a large pregnant bulk.

'Eating too much?'

Mrs Johnson Johnson sighed. 'No, dear, preggers, you know? People do get preggers still, although you and I have both avoided it, thank God.'

Outside in the street Trilby found that although she now had a vastly more glamorous home to return to, she was oddly reluctant to leave Glebe Street. It was as if she was hoping that by hanging around she might find someone who was missing her, who wanted her back living there, and, what would be better, was prepared to say so. She decided to try out her very last welcome on Berry. Molly being busy upstairs with her expected guests, she walked round to the back of the house and knocked on his studio door.

He opened to her in quite the old way, paintbrush in hand, spectacles on the end of his nose, hair sticking out, as if he had not bothered to

136

brush it since getting out of bed.

'Trilby, pussycat, come in, come in!'

He hugged her in his usual amiable way, smelling strongly of coffee and Gauloise cigarettes, turpentine and oil paint.

As soon as she was seated in Berry's little studio Trilby ripped off her expensive hat and gloves, threw them on a bench by the wall and kicked off her high-heeled shoes. 'That's better.'

Berry stared at her solemnly. 'Yes, it is, isn't it? You were looking really rather old; almost like a dowager at the Ritz.' They both started to laugh.

'I was feeling quite old and like a dowager at the Ritz, I can tell you.'

Berry picked up his beloved but battered coffee pot. 'Stay right where you are. I am going to make you a cup of something so strong it will have you spinning round the room. Then we will call on Agnes, who I know will find out anyway if you don't, and after that we will go off for a mad hatter's shop, shall we? I love to shop with a rich woman, it has always been one of my very real delights, aside from darling Molly, of course.'

Trilby watched Berry going to the small stove through the archway that led to his kitchen. The smell of oil paints, the rain pattering on the roof above them . . . she shut her eyes for a second and swallowed away what threatened to be a lump in her throat.

It was all so comfortingly familiar, so much so that of a sudden Trilby could not remember why she had ever left Glebe Street.

*   *   *

137

'Paine!' Trilby called from the library door into the hall. The butler appeared as it always seemed to Trilby, as if from nowhere, out of the shadows, almost as if he had materialised and not just arrived from another room.

'Mrs James.'

Trilby turned on her heel and walked back into the library. 'I am sorry to bother you, Paine, but I am a bit puzzled.'

The expression on Paine's face was that of polite but only vague interest. 'Madam?'

'The photograph, Paine, here—the photograph on the table. On this table—it was at the back of this table, and now it has gone. Do you know where it has gone, Paine?'

'I do not do the dusting, madam.'

There was a short pause while Trilby turned slowly to look from the table to the butler and back again. 'No, of course, I don't suppose you do dust, Paine. Oh, well, no matter. I'll ask Mr James about it when he comes in for lunch.'

'Mr James is not in for lunch today, Mrs James. He sends to tell you that he has a long meeting, to ask you to forgive him, and he will be in for dinner at the usual time.'

Trilby nodded. 'Thank you, Paine.'

'Would Madam like some coffee sent in here?'

'As a matter of fact I would, actually, Paine.'

Despite herself Trilby could not help feeling secretly relieved that Lewis was not coming home to lunch. It would mean that she could work quietly in the library undisturbed.

She sat down, and as she always did before she started work she took off her shoes. Yesterday, after their coffee, Berry and she had gone

138

shopping, and with his encouragement Trilby had bought an absolutely outrageous outfit. It was only to be worn at home, of course, but it was such fun. A black worsted jersey top and red and white skirt quite full and belted, underneath which were worn matching houseboy pants cut to just below the knee. It made her feel gloriously mad. She had hoped to show it off to Lewis when he came in, but now, since he was not coming back for lunch, she felt it would be positively inspirational, and that work on *The Popposites* would fairly zip along after her visit to Glebe Street.

She picked up her pencil and began to draw Mrs Smokey Smokey. The first drawing showed her in all her turbaned glory, her eyes narrowed against the smoke from her cigarette holder, lecturing Miss Golly Gosh.

Now, as always happened when Trilby worked, within a few minutes she had quite forgotten where she was, or what the time was, or even to drink the coffee brought to her by Paine on a silver tray; so that when the library door was flung open a few hours later and Lewis appeared in the doorway, it seemed to Trilby that she was in a dream—except that minutes later, it was actually much more like a nightmare.

But, as always, when Trilby was suffering, part of her mind took off in another direction so that it seemed to her that the anger was not really being directed at her, that Lewis was speaking to someone else, and that he really did not wish to hurt her, but was just trying out his words, much as she herself tried out dialogue with her cartoon strip.

And his forehead was not looking ugly and

reddened and his eyes narrowed because of her, but because of someone else, someone who was standing in for her, another person, someone quite different. Someone who was immensely shy, someone with a different personality, someone whom Trilby imagined that one day soon she might get to know really rather well, someone whom Lewis could not find, however angry he became, and however livid his forehead.

CHAPTER FOUR

'Where did you get those dreadful clothes? Why are you wearing them, Trilby? Why are you looking like that, like some sort of King's Road arty slut, like some kind of cheap artist's tart? Haven't I bought you enough clothes? Haven't you enough of everything here? Why are you looking like that?'

Trilby felt as if she was being cross-examined by a policeman. 'This, well, I, er, bought it yesterday, as a matter of fact, with Berry. We went shopping and I went to that new clothes shop near Harrods—you know the one, we stopped there the other day and you quite liked the clothes, didn't you, Lewis?'

'I don't remember us stopping there?'

'You must, because we laughed about putting one of my characters in some of the clothes, because they are really rather outrageous. You must remember.'

'I do not remember any such thing.' Lewis lit a cigarette and walked down the room to the French windows.

In the pause Trilby said, 'And, much as it is lovely to see you, Lewis, Paine said you were not coming home to lunch, he quite definitely said that.'

'I was always coming home to luncheon. I was looking forward to lunching with you, alone, as we did yesterday. But not to lunching with you dressed like that, dressed in the sort of clothes that I detest.'

Against her will Trilby's heart was beginning to beat faster, so she made an effort to speak more slowly, trying to coax her husband to stop looking so grim.

'It is all just a mistake, a silly mistake. I am only dressed like this because you said you were not coming home to lunch. But now I will put it right by changing out of my dotty clothes into something respectable that you will like better.'

She turned to hurry out of the door, but Lewis caught her arm. 'Don't ever let me find you like that again, do you hear? You have ruined my day.'

Trilby looked up at him. 'As I just said, it is all easily remedied. I will quickly go and tell Paine we are in for lunch. I am sure that Cook can rustle us up something, and then I will change out of these offending clothes and into something more suitable for the dining room. Will that make *oo* happy?' she finished, challenging him not to laugh.

But the look in Lewis's eyes told Trilby that he found her profoundly unamusing. 'Please, I don't have much time.'

Having rung the hall bell for Paine and ordered smoked salmon, hard-boiled eggs, ham, *anything* that they had in the kitchen that could be served in five minutes, Trilby fled upstairs and found Mrs

141

Woo, smiling.

'Emergency, Mrs Woo, I must change, Mr James is home unexpectedly.' Trilby paused, thinking quickly. 'Choose me something, anything, while I scramble out of these, and—Mrs Woo—this time, you can dress me.'

Mrs Woo hurried away, still smiling. 'Mrs James must always listen to Mrs Woo. Mrs Woo know best.'

Trilby started to pull off the 'fun' outfit that she and Berry had so enjoyed choosing the previous day. She was slender, fit and young, but she found to her horror that at that moment she was sweating. She ran to the bathroom and started to powder herself as Mrs Woo flung open the vast cupboards that contained her new clothes.

Downstairs Lewis stared at the drawings and characters that Trilby had been working on all morning. When she reappeared he looked up and said in a cold voice, 'I have just been looking at your work, and I think you'll find these need doing again, you know, Trilby. You would not want people to think that this is your work.' He threw the drawings across the tightly buttoned velvet stool that stood in front of the fire waiting for some of Lewis's tightly buttoned guests. 'You seem to have lost what I would call your—carefree quality. Really quite laboured, these drawings, I would say.'

Of a sudden Trilby, now suited and high-heeled, knew at once what this was all about. It was about taking the '*Trilby*' out of her. At the same time her mind raced back to their honeymoon. How often Lewis had corrected her, and always now, she realised, just as she was enjoying herself—'Your button's undone, darling' or 'Your nose needs powdering, Trilby.'

It had seemed so nice, that he cared enough to want her to look her best. Not now though, not now that she thought she could hear doors all over the house not shutting, but slamming.

She would have liked to say, 'I know what you're trying to do to me, and I'm not going to let you', but Trilby had grown up with nothing but adults for company, and she had long ago learned not to show her feelings to anyone, because older people never seemed to understand your inner restlessness, not really, and sometimes not at all, and certainly not for most of the time. Now a sudden feeling of cold reality told Trilby that Lewis was not just older, he was much worse: he was grown up.

'It must be marriage,' she said, laughing lightly, in answer to his criticism. 'I must have grown serious, and so must you. You used to laugh at my *oo* jokes, they used to make you laugh.'

'I really think you can do better than this, Trilby.' Lewis seemed not to have heard and he was still not laughing.

'Oh, really. Do you think so?'

'Yes, I do. I really think you can do much, much better than this, Trilby.'

'Oh. I thought it had gone rather well. But there you are, obviously not.'

Lewis shrugged his shoulders. 'Yes, we can all be fooled, darling, all of us. Sometimes even I can be fooled.'

'Really? I can't believe that,' Trilby murmured, as she poured herself a tomato juice from the drinks tray.

Lewis looked up quickly at that, suspecting

143

sarcasm, but perhaps because Trilby still took care to smile he lit another cigarette and picked up the early edition of the evening paper.

Meanwhile Trilby carefully tore up her morning's work, first in two, then in four, and finally, with some difficulty, into eight, and threw it on the fire. She did not mind doing her drawings again, what she minded was the look in Lewis's eyes.

Of a sudden it seemed to her that he had mistaken her for someone who worked for him on one of his newspapers, and although he might think he was paying her, or even that he owned her now, it was not true, because she knew that she was still Trilby Smythson, a free spirit. So, whatever he might think of her talent's having lost its carefree quality, he himself had lost his charm.

During lunch, hastily flung together by Paine and one of the maids, Lewis said, 'By the way, who is Berry?'

Thinking that he was referring to the strip, Trilby answered, 'Oh, he's the Wiz. Remember? I told you? In the strip, he's the one with the hair that sticks up on end. He's a painter. Not in the strip, but in real life. He paints.'

She was finding unearthly difficulty in swallowing her smoked salmon. Somehow, if you were upset, smoked salmon tasted slimy and fishy in a way that it did not usually, and of course the slower she was in eating the more Lewis seemed to be intent on watching her, so that she felt that just the act of her chewing the fish so slowly was setting his nerves even more on edge, if that were possible.

'I did not mean in your *strip*, as you call it, Trilby, I meant yesterday, who or what were Berry and you

144

doing out shopping together, yesterday?'

Trilby cleared her throat and answered over-brightly, 'Well, if you remember, yesterday you were breakfasting here with all those American businessmen, so I popped out to Glebe Street, you know, just to see Molly and Berry and Aphrodite and Mrs Johnson Johnson, and generally say hallo to the rest of them. And of course after that my stepmother, because my father was at work, as usual. They are my family, you see, Lewis. I don't have any other family, just my father and stepmother and the folks in the street.'

'Folks.' Lewis repeated the word disdainfully, as if it was a swear word.

'Well, not folks, perhaps, people, people in the street.' That awful feeling of becoming flushed and confused was coming over Trilby. She picked up her glass of water as unhurriedly as possible and drank thankfully from the ice cold water in the cut glass tumbler.

Please God she did not show her nerves, most especially not to Lewis who, because he was so powerful, must see more frightened people in the course of one day than Trilby had ever met. No, whatever happened she must not seem to be quaking at the knees like the rest of his minions, she must not be seen to be frightened.

'Yes, of course, your father is your only real relative, isn't he?' The expression in Lewis's eyes was oddly opaque, as if he had put his own thoughts on hold.

'You know that, Lewis. Don't you remember? My guest list at the wedding was really rather short on relatives.'

'Did you see your stepmother yesterday?'

145

'You know I did.'

'How do I know you did?' His voice was over-patient.

'Because, Lewis, she told me herself when she rang me this morning. She said that you had telephoned her and had a nice chat, just after I had left her house to go for a mad shopping spree with Berry. You were sweet to her, she said.'

'So much on my mind, I can't be expected—'

'No, no, of course not.' Trilby smiled to make up for everything and suddenly for no reason at all Lewis too smiled, and it was his best and most beautifully warm smile, the one that Trilby realised she was gradually growing to dread.

'Let's go and make love, darling,' he whispered as he stood behind her chair, helping her up. 'Let's go and make mad, passionate love.'

*   *   *

Lewis left almost immediately for the office, so he did not see his young wife's bewildered hurt, or hear her in the bathroom squeezing out endless cold flannels to put on her eyes, or see her showering and soaping herself for minutes on end, trying to wash away her unhappiness.

Later she crept downstairs and retrieved her artist's folder from the library, pausing, she did not know why, to look once more for the photograph of the beautiful woman on the large table.

But the photograph was still absent, and so, she realised of a sudden, was her inspiration. She looked down at the green marbled cover of the folder. Normally it gave her such a thrill just to hold it, but now, staring down at its familiar cover, all she could hear was Lewis's voice saying, *You seem to have lost your carefree quality.*

'I am going to lie down, have a rest until dinner, Mrs Woo. If anyone telephones perhaps you could be kind enough to ask them to call back?'

'Yes, Mrs James.' Mrs Woo looked unsurprised. Of a sudden she reminded Trilby of the chauffeur that first evening she had been taken to dinner with Lewis. As if she too had seen it all before. Not that Trilby cared. She lay down on her bed, and in the darkened room she wondered to herself what 'love', so-called, was all about.

*   *   *

'I am going to take you shopping again, and then to the theatre tonight!'

Trilby tried to smile across the breakfast table at Lewis and at the same time looked surprised. 'I thought you had to fly to Paris?'

Some weeks had passed, weeks of returned happiness, so much so that Trilby had begun to think that the events that had followed her fateful shopping trip with Berry had never really happened.

'I was going to Paris, but I cancelled it. I shall take you to the theatre and then dinner at the Savoy. But first I am taking you shopping.'

Everywhere they went that day Trilby noticed that people bowed, and sometimes the women even seemed about to curtsy to Lewis, they were obviously in such awe of him. In the shops, in the salons, wherever they went, followed quietly but doggedly by the chauffeur-driven Rolls-Royce, people's faces changed at the sound of 'Mr and

147

Mrs Lewis James'.

It was not as if the faces took time to adjust. The fact was that people's everyday expressions disappeared within seconds, literally wiped off as with a duster over a blackboard, followed by oh my God it's *Lewis James.*

Trilby knew that Lewis was famous, rich and very powerful, but until that particular day the real impact of his fame had not come home to her. She had not truly realised that his newspaper empire was quite so powerful, not just in his and his editors' eyes, but in everyone else's eyes too. Lewis's empire with its vast readership was probably as powerful as the monarchy, or the government, Trilby thought suddenly, as she slipped into yet another evening dress and dutifully reappeared in the salon for Lewis to view her, standing hips slightly forward while he lazed in his chair talking in a desultory way with the usual clutch of women wearing black dresses and anxious expressions.

'Yes, we will take that, and the previous one, but not the red. I never want to see my wife wearing either red or orange, is that understood?'

'Yes, Mr James.'

'And she is always to wear high-heeled shoes. All the outfits—' He turned to Trilby, whose heart was sinking. She had started to hate high-heeled shoes, keeping her seams straight, suspenders, the whole paraphernalia. In Glebe Street, before she was married, she had worn Capri pants and bellbottoms, all sorts and shapes of trousers and all sorts and shapes of clothes during the day, and the high-heeled shoes and stockings were kept for high days and holidays. 'All the clothes that you wear,

148

darling,' Lewis continued, this time to Trilby, 'they must all be worn with high-heeled shoes and stockings with seams.'

Oh, those seams! The hours that Trilby would spend making sure that the seams of her stockings were straight were almost innumerable.

'I love you so much . . .' Lewis told her after they had made love, yet again, after lunch.

Trilby stared at the ceiling, not really thinking of what had just happened, but instead experiencing a feeling of dread as her thoughts strayed towards evening. She dreaded wearing the clothes they had just bought, which although beautiful seemed to look so very old. Most of all she dreaded the high-heeled shoes that made her feel like Marion Holton.

Lewis sprang out of bed singing, and shortly afterwards returned to the office. Opening her bedroom door, Trilby could hear the hall door being shut by Paine down below, far below. She crept back into her room, closed the door so gently that she imagined that not even Mrs Woo could hear it, and locked it. Then, getting down on her hands and knees, she fished two packets out from under the satin-covered bed, a large one and a small one, carefully boxed up and wrapped in tissue paper to look as if they held clothing.

Her drawings and her pens and pencils. *The Popposites*—at least she had them. She crept into her bathroom and started to spread out her things. No-one knew what she did on her own for hours in there. It was her secret.

*   *   *

149

David Micklethwaite was smiling but perhaps because his features were so small it was not a particularly heartwarming sight.

'I know it's hard, but it's bound to happen, Trilby. After so much excitement, and now when so much has been happening—I understand that you attended the masked ball in Venice last week?'

'Yes, yes, we did.'

'And according to the newspapers you were the belle of the ball?'

'Well, yes, but we could not exactly take that as read, could we? Since Lewis owns most of the newspapers!' Trilby laughed humourlessly. The masked ball in Venice had of course been spectacular, the best bit, for her, being that most of Lewis's friends were—and remained—*masked.*

'As I say,' Micklethwaite continued, 'it is only natural that your work should go off, you know, when there is so much going on in your life at the moment.'

Trilby, feeling faint, and dry-throated, nevertheless smiled, as she knew she must. 'In what way,' she asked, determinedly, her voice remaining as bright as was possible, 'in what way does the editor feel my work has *gone off*, as you call it? I mean how has it changed exactly?'

For the first time during their interview together, David Micklethwaite looked uncomfortable. He started to walk about the library, picking up things that he should not touch, valuable ornaments, photographs in silver frames, and putting them back, crooked, or without looking at them, before moving on and staring at paintings that he must have seen a thousand times. Eventually he turned back to Trilby who was seated, waiting, by the

150

fireside.

'It is just not funny any more, Trilby. Just not funny, do you see? No-one, no-one in the office, none of the staff—none of them find *The Popposites* funny any more.'

'I see.'

'That particular flair that you once had—that you *first* had rather—well, since you have been married, it's just petered out, really. It is a bit sad, but of course, given your circumstances, it is only a bit sad. I mean you are not exactly dependent on the strip, are you?'

He gave a knowing laugh and at the same time his eyes moved round the room taking in the luxurious furnishings, the great paintings, the silver, the ornaments.

Trilby was silent. It was true, of course, she was not at all dependent on *The Popposites* for her daily living. To try to insist as much, living as she now did, would be ridiculous. She was far from dependent on them, in fact she was very much the opposite, and yet—they were her life. She had been living with those characters for months and months now, and she loved them all. They were part of a world that she had once inhabited and now created. They were her friends. They made her laugh, and somehow by making her laugh they gave her hope.

She stood up. 'Thank you very much for coming. Please send my apologies to the editor and the staff, and all Lewis's other minions. How awful, and indeed how strange, that, of a sudden, since I was married, the strip is no longer funny.' She smiled, staring at Micklethwaite, realising now that she was close to him that if she was drawing him

151

she would think of a ferret. 'No, I *am*—I am sorry, really sorry, that the strip is no longer funny.'

She turned and walked away from him down the room. 'I really am very, very sorry, most of all because if there is one thing that no-one can ever prove, no creative person can ever, ever prove, that is that their work is *funny.* You can prove it is well drawn, that it has a searching or analytical quality, that it is satirical, true to life, contains pathos, is sad, and dramatic, but not *funny.* So you really must be congratulated. You and your editor have effectively killed *The Popposites.* I shall never, ever, you see, be able to sit down and draw them without hearing your voice saying what you have just said: that the strip is no longer *funny.*'

Still smiling, she picked up a small glass vase and quite suddenly let go of it. Unsurprisingly it crashed to the floor, splintering.

'Now, that,' she said to David Micklethwaite, watching his expression of astonishment, 'that, on the other hand, is very, very funny indeed.' She laughed, genuinely. 'I mean the expression on your face just then, that is very, very funny, believe me!'

David Micklethwaite left the room.

Trilby watched him from the hall window. He hurried across the road and into his fawn-coloured car, unlocking it and scrambling in as if he had just carried out a hit on her, which, it suddenly seemed to Trilby, might be exactly what he had done.

He had murdered Trilby's small talent, shot it through the head, and then hurried off back to his car.

She turned away from the window feeling ill and sick. Of course she was not bleeding to death inside—she just felt that she was. Worst of all, she was lacking gumption, feeling sorry for herself. Berry would be ashamed of her. Lacking gumption was one of Berry's worst criticisms of anyone, and she would not be an object of his pity at that moment, she would be an object of his derision.

Trilby sat down on the bottom step of the staircase and stared ahead of her.

Thank God it was Paine's afternoon off, and the house was filled with that kind of quiet that swamps the senses with relief. Thank God she knew that Mrs Woo was out shopping and the maids were all footling about somewhere well out of sight—most likely smoking and gossiping by the dustbins. Somehow, to be alone just now was so right, so reassuring. She wanted no-one around her. What was more she could think of no-one in her whole new world, her married world, who could possibly understand how she felt at that moment.

She started to laugh to herself at the thought of trying to explain her feelings to any of Lewis's friends—Lola de Ribes, say, with her stiff hair and her lightly sarcastic laugh. She imagined Lola saying in response, 'But my dear Trilby, you are married to Lewis, why would you need to draw a silly little strip?'

'Why indeed? Because—I am still Trilby.'

'In that case you should perhaps try now to forget that you are Trilby and be Madame James, my dear.'

Trilby's thoughts turned back to Berry. He was the one person in her whole life who would understand exactly how she felt, just so long as she did not appear sorry for herself. He had no time for people who felt sorry for themselves.

153

She had been sacked. She had been told she was not funny. In a bare quarter of an hour she had been creatively annihilated. She stood up and rang the bell. No-one answered and so, after some searching because she knew nothing of where anything in the house was kept, she eventually found a dustpan and brush under the stairs, and slowly brushed up the broken glass from the silly little vase.

She did not care if or when Lewis came home. She would go and see Berry. She was not a prisoner. She would go and see whoever and whatever she wished and no-one could stop her. She hurried upstairs and fetched her black Christian Dior coat with its attractively deep velvet cuffs and collar. Black was how she felt and black was how the world looked at that moment. The coat seemed to settle around her in a comforting way. She tiptoed quietly downstairs again and making sure that there was no-one about she shut the front door behind her as quietly as was humanly possible, and hurried out into the rain.

Once outside the house she started to run, and as she ran she had the oddest sensation. It was cracked, it was dotty, but she felt as if she was being followed.

She told herself that if it went on like this she would go mad, and the next minute she would start seeing pins in everything, as one of Mrs Johnson Johnson's golfing friends had once done, before they took the poor woman away to be locked up in some awful institution.

Being followed? What a ridiculous notion! She kept running down the long hill towards Kensington High Street, where she stopped and waved down a taxi cab.

'Hyde Park, once round the park, and then double back to Knightsbridge,' she told the cab driver. 'I am being followed.'

'Yes, miss,' the cab driver agreed in a disinterested voice.

'I am, I am being followed, you'll have to turn, driver, and try and lose them.'

'Very well, miss.'

Trilby stared back through the taxi window. It was true. She was being followed, by Lyons, Lewis's chauffeur, in the Rolls-Royce.

Obligingly the taxi driver increased his speed, and then doubled back down the street up which he had just driven, able to turn far more easily and swiftly than the Rolls-Royce. Once again nearing Kensington High Street he turned left and drawing away from the first set of traffic lights sped on towards Knightsbridge.

Trilby sat back and stared ahead at her own mirrored image reflected in the glass behind the driver's back, satisfied at last that there was no-one of interest to her following on behind, and yet that feeling that she was in the middle of a bad dream came to her once again.

Surely Lewis could not wish the chauffeur to follow her everywhere she went? That surely could not be true? Was Lewis so frightened for her safety that he would not even let her go for a walk in the afternoon, or take a taxi to a cinema while he was out, without making sure that she was protected by one of his staff? And if so were his feelings of protection born out of the best motives?

She gazed out of the window at the familiar sights. Sloane Street, Sloane Square, the Royal

Court Theatre, all places that she knew and had enjoyed since she was a tiny child, but in the knowledge that she was being followed by her husband's chauffeur they seemed to be tawdry, dull, even garish, for the truth was that there was nowhere now that she could go to be free, except perhaps Glebe Street.

And so, once again, Trilby found herself knocking on Berry's studio door, waiting to be let in, but this time she gazed first up the street and then down it, and then again down the street and then up it, for she was becoming convinced that any minute now she would see the dreaded sight of the famous silver flying lady belonging to Lewis's Rolls-Royce nosing her leisurely way down the side road that led past the back of their gardens and Berry's studio door.

What seemed like a clutch of minutes passed, when in fact it was probably hardly more than one before Berry stood framed in his doorway once more, hair sticking up and out, paintbrush in his mouth, paint all over his smock and his hands, one of which he now stretched out, pulling Trilby into the house and kick-shutting the door behind her.

'Trilby! Just the person I was hoping to see. Such good news. Actually, your butler just rang through to say that he thought you would be coming round here to see me, which is just as well because—wait till you hear, just wait.'

Trilby stared at Berry and as she did so she could feel her throat tightening to such a degree that she could hardly swallow, let alone speak.

'My butler . . .'

'Yes, you know, Paine, or whatever his name is. Your butler, he rang. I say, you are a grand old

156

thing getting your butler to ring, talk about get you. Coffee?' Berry waggled the familiar old coffee pot at Trilby. 'As a matter of fact it could not have been more opportune, because I have been given a bloody great commission to paint a family group in Northumberland, so by the time I get back you will probably have six children.'

'Please, please don't go to Northumberland, please, Berry, please!'

Berry stared round his kitchen door at Trilby. She stared back at him and for a second kept a straight face, before bursting into peals of laughter.

'Oh, you horror.' Berry sighed with relief. 'You really had me for a minute, and for a second or three I thought you were being *trés trés* serious, and that you did not want the Wiz to go northers. Oh, lud. Do not whatever happens ever give the Wiz such a fright again, please.'

Trilby kicked off her shoes and threw her hat on one side and sighed. 'Oh, you know me, Berry, I am without any doubt the happiest person in England. I have to be,' she continued, 'after all, if you think about it, now I am married to Lewis I can have anything I want, can't I?'

Berry looked at her. He knew her so well that he even knew when she was lying. He put down the coffee pot. 'Tell me all, Trilb, concealing nothing. You have something on your chest.'

Trilby lay down on the bench and gazed at the ceiling above her. 'Very well. I will tell you a story. Once upon a time a very stupid young girl married a great emperor, and for a while she was very happy, and then he took her up to a high tower and showed her all the kingdoms of the world, and he said I have given you all this in return for you

157

granting me one wish.'

There was a long silence.

Berry said nothing. He poured them both a coffee and topped up the coffee with cream and waited.

'And that wish was?' he asked at last, quite unable to bear the suspense.

'That wish was that—' Trilby sat up again. 'The emperor's wish was that she would never ever leave the tower again. She could look at the view. She could see all the people below. She could see them waving to her. She could throw flowers down to them, but she could never ever climb down to be with them again.'

'But this is terrible. Is that why you looked ghostly when I made mention of the butler ringing on the blower? Is the man in your life of unreasoning possession, Trilb?'

Trilby put down her cup of coffee. 'Look outside, Berry,' she asked him, her voice, for no reason that she could think of, now lowered. 'Just step outside and look, and tell me what you see in Tankridge Street?'

'All right, but don't scream or faint, will you? I am not up to a great deal before I hear Big Ben chime midnight.'

Trilby watched Berry's tall, lean figure striding towards the window, sliding to an abrupt halt as he obviously decided that it might be necessary to keep himself concealed, and then sliding up towards the long velvet curtains, and twitching one.

'It's all right, Trilb, there's no butler concealed anywhere with a fedora pulled down over his nose, or anything of that nature. Just the usual. Molly's bicycle against the back, that lunatic next door's

158

motor bike, and your hubby's Rolls-Royce and the chauffeur waiting for you.' He sauntered back to Trilby. 'So, there you are, all's well that end's well of a coffee o'clock.'

'But that's just it, Berry, that's just it!' Trilby clung to his hand. 'All is far from well, don't you see? I took a taxi, I did everything to lose them, to lose him, but they're back, he's back.'

'Who are back, Trilb?'

'The people who keep following me. It's either the maid, or the chauffeur, or the butler guarding the front door, or he's ringing ahead of me to find out if I am actually going where I said I was going. It's a nightmare.'

Berry stared at Trilby. She had always been highly strung, but now he was quite worried about her. She looked pale and drawn and she kept clasping and unclasping her hands.

'What is this about, Trilb? Thinking people are following one is halfway to the funny farm, voyez vous? As in not funny at all, at all, as they never say in Ireland. Surely no-one is following you? Outside is only your motor car and the very nice driver who keeps polishing it with a very clean duster. Why would one think he is following you, when it is perfectly normal for a person of one's new station to take a motor car and the chauffeur if on a visit to a friend, however humble?'

Trilby took hold of Berry's hand between her two tense ones and clung to it, her large, dark eyes making him feel intensely protective of her. Her hands told him that he was her best friend, the one person in whom she could truly confide.

'You think I am mad, don't you? You think I am going to start seeing pins in everything, and I don't

159

blame you. But it's true, I am being followed, and all the time, he will not let me out of his sight, even if he's not there, he still makes sure that someone else is. If he is not in the house, he has to know where I am, all the time. He rings up people to find out where I am, who I am with, why I am with them, and—oh, it's no good, I can't explain. But he's not just the handsome sweet person everyone thinks he is, he is someone else too. Someone I am beginning to think I really don't like very much.'

Berry sat down, and patted the seat beside him. 'Everyone is someone else too, Trilb, they really are. There is always a smile, or a large piece of charm, or just the will to entertain which being with other people brings out. But then . . .' Berry shrugged his shoulders. 'Then, once home, well, a truly vast area of human display is, as they say, left at the gate, and not just the proverbial jolly old smile. It is all too normal. And of course, since you are young, and only just a married person, it can come as a bit of a shock to discover this other person.'

But Trilby only shook her head and turned away from Berry, as if to say, '*You don't understand.*'

What she finally said out loud in a resigned voice was, 'I am so glad you got a commission, Berry, and that you are going to the country. I should just so love to be going with you.'

'Well, then, come with me, as you did when you were a tiny person! Come with me, and trip the light fantastic in the northern clime. Why ever not? Molly can't come because of too few pennies at the bank and taking in lodgers, but you could, old thing, you really could.'

Trilby stared into Berry's bespectacled face and

for a second she imagined herself as she would have been in the old days. Probably saying 'Yes, yes, yes! What a good idea! I have two weeks left of the school holidays' or 'I have two weeks' leave owed to me from the typing pool, I can come.'

And then she would have flown back to her house, informed her completely indifferent stepmother, and quickly thrown some clothes into one of their heavy old crocodile suitcases: old corduroys, climbing socks, gumboots and such like, and shortly after they would have been off to the station, leaving Molly saying, as she always did, 'Don't forget to air the bed, my dear, hired cottages can be the devil when it comes to airing.'

Once there of course she would have left Berry alone to go off and paint whoever had commissioned him, and herself wandered off each day with a packet of sandwiches and a bottle of ginger beer to climb the hillsides, or sit by the water and sketch, before going back to tea in front of some cottage fireside, and a host of anecdotes from Berry about the person or house that he was painting.

Trilby had accompanied him many times on such trips and their innocent days together had always had that sort of laissez-faire rhythm.

'Dear days, weren't they, Berry? The good days of going off with you in my school hols or whatever?'

'Come, please come with me, I'll ask your hubby for you. I mean old family friend, middle-aged and respectable, he won't mind, not for a few days. He will let you go, surely? Old friend of the family and all that, I shall stress that. Molly never minded, and still wouldn't, Molly loves her Trilby.'

Trilby shook her head, a lump coming into her throat as it always did when people were kind to her. She cast dolefully around for her hat and gloves, and the shoes with the high heels, the grown-up clothes that made you walk tall and act mature, that insisted on your being a woman, and acting like a woman, not as she would be if she was going to Northumberland with Berry—a person.

'No, Lewis would never let me, Berry. That was what I was trying to tell you. He would never, ever let me, especially not now.'

'I'll ask him, it's worth asking him.'

Trilby, once more hatted and shod, once more the perfect young lady about town, pulled on her leather gloves and said sadly, 'No, Berry, please don't, I beg of you. He would only make me pay for it in some way. It just would not be worth it. So please, as we love each other, please don't even ask him.'

Berry did not like the look of his young friend at all, but he could not say as much. He would have liked to have called Molly down, but she was out having lunch somewhere with someone or other, which she very nearly always was, for the fact was that it worried him a lot. The way Trilby had said *He would only make me pay for it* had not been at all comforting.

And then too she was looking more than usually pale. Berry always found that one of the advantages of being a professional painter was that you noticed all the small things in a person's face, particularly once you were close to them, as he was now close to Trilby. You noticed the tension in the eyes, the dryness around the lips, above all the pallor.

'I tell you what, Trilby,' he said, slowly, making time, although he could not have said why. 'I will go northers on my own, but when I return to the Holy Capital and my very own Tower of Babel I shall call you up and ask you round to Berry Towers where we will talk more on this topic, namely of Mrs Lewis James being followed. By the way, wherefore to—I meant to ask you before— wherefore to your cartoon strip? Molly says you have come to a shuddering halt. Of course Molly does not think it matters because you are now *married and settled.* I, on the other hand, as you know, would wish to see the Muse return and you to be resolutely unsettled, which is the only way to be, is it not? Filled with the divine restlessness that only Spring and Art, and sometimes Love, can bring.'

Berry paused, waiting for a reaction, but finding there was none he fell silent as Trilby stared past him, her eyes sad. 'It's all gone at the moment, Berry. I am afraid I am quite dried up, as they say. My talent has lost its freshness. It has to be faced. I was just a flash in the pan, and now I am afraid there is only the pan left, no flash.'

They both laughed, and Berry looked relieved. 'Oh, the Muse is such a tart! But she will return at any minute, you'll see. Any minute now she will come popping up. I am sure she's just gone away only until you have become used to the wall to wall carpeting and the servants and the butler and so on; all that—well, it's just put you on the wrong creative foot. Money can often have such a very adverse effect on the old artistic juices. At least that is what I have always told my Moll, the dear old darling. And that, I am afraid, is why we have remained so resolutely poor. Any other way and I would freeze up. If we became rich, the paint would dry, but will she understand? Not a bit. She will understand one day, of course, when my duchesses and actresses are hanging in the National Portrait Gallery.'

The ongoing battles about artistic integrity and lack of funds at Berry Towers, as Berry occasionally referred to their house, had once been of great amusement to Trilby, but now they just seemed sad to her, and of a sudden she could hardly see why she had once found it all so humorous.

In fact, as she kissed her hand goodbye to Berry before she bent to climb into the back of Lewis's wretched limousine, Trilby found herself wondering why she had ever found anything humorous about Berry and Molly quarrelling as they did sometimes, or Aphrodite grumbling about Geoffrey, or Mrs Johnson Johnson coming out with one of her classic remarks about life. Now, well, now they did not seem in the least bit funny, but then, at the moment, very little did.

'Mrs James?'

Trilby turned and looked at the chauffeur. 'Yes?'

The chauffeur pointed to the car. 'Wouldn't you like to step in, Mrs James?'

Trilby shook her head. 'No, thank you. I want to walk, and walk I will.'

It would have been nice to have held out and walked all the way from Glebe Street to Kensington High Street and from there up to the upper reaches, towards Holland Park. To see the Rolls threading its way, perhaps haplessly, through the traffic behind her; but after a while, due to the height of her heels, and the tightness of her skirt, and the fact that it was beginning to rain, Trilby could no longer be bothered with her pride, and she flagged the car down and climbed in.

'That could have cost me my job, Mrs James.' The chauffeur did not smile but eyed her in the driver's mirror. 'When I am sent to fetch you I must fetch you, on Mr James's orders, it is just how it is I am afraid, Mrs James. Or else, as I say, it would cost me my job, and I have a wife and two children, Mrs James. You would not know what that is like, to have dependants, but believe me, this job, with all its perks, it means everything to me.'

'Of course it does,' Trilby agreed. 'I am sorry, Lyons.'

Her eyes fell on the seat beside her. A large box, very smartly wrapped and addressed to Mrs James, occupied the far side of the passenger seating.

'That is for you, Mrs James.'

Without much enthusiasm Trilby opened the dress box. Lewis had given her so many clothes of late she had almost begun to dread seeing anything new, but now that she gazed into this box she realised that she was looking at something very, very special, something so special that even she would not be able to resist wearing it.

*   *   *

'You are so kind. The dress is beautiful.'

The dress was more than beautiful, and thank heavens Trilby did not have to act out her gratitude as she felt she had been forced to do a little too often of late.

'Will you wear it for my birthday dinner dance next week? I know everyone will adore to see you

165

in it.'

' "Everyone" being you!'

'Certainly "everyone" is undoubtedly me, your devoted husband.'

Trilby laughed. It was at these moments that she was able to forget that other side of Lewis, the side that Berry had told her was present in everyone, even people you loved, and begin once more to think that she was mistaken in him.

Or, perhaps, she told herself, because she was young and inexperienced, she was simply not able to take in her stride ways of being and thinking that the rest of the world had long ago accepted as being a normal part of marriage, as being entirely natural. She had no friends of her own age to whom she could turn, and certainly no-one that she could trust—besides Berry. And then too, Lewis was so used to being an emperor.

Lewis was king of his particular part of the jungle. He could do anything he wanted, and what was more he could have done for him whatever he might think he wished, so no wonder he had a rather unusual way of going on. It was only to be expected. Without a doubt he would change. People changed all the time. Trilby knew this from listening to Aphrodite and Mrs Johnson Johnson. They were always talking about people changing after marriage, or marriage changing people, or people trying to change people they had married when they should really have just minded their own business and not bothered. Change had been a constant topic while she was growing up.

*   *   *

'Do you think I should wear evening gloves with this?'

'Yes, madame. Evening gloves, dark evening gloves is what goes with this dress.'

Mrs Woo's tone was quite firm. Trilby looked at her in the dressing mirror. She seemed so awfully sure of what was needed this evening that Trilby thought she must have seen a picture of this particular dress in a magazine; *Vogue*, or something like that. And as it happened Trilby herself felt she had seen such a picture, so she was quite sure that Lewis must have had Marion Holton buy it for him from one of the latest collections.

Because she was feeling so much happier Trilby twirled suddenly in front of the mirror. The white silk tulle of the dress floated upwards and, seconds later, floated downwards again. It was a happy moment, but Mrs Woo did not even smile as she watched Trilby, her face quite serious. It was not so much a beautiful as a stunning dress, which was possibly why the maid was looking so serious. It was strapless but it had a high front bodice, beautifully sculptured and outlined all the way round with hand-made dark silk flowers. The bodice was very tight, and the skirt fell from a shallow vee at the front and back.

With it, Trilby, her dark hair styled in a more formal manner, wore simple black pearl earrings and a single string of black pearls around her neck.

'Mrs James looks velly, velly beautiful.'

Trilby pulled on the dark evening gloves that matched the flowers around the dress, and smiled back at Mrs Woo. Once Mrs Woo had all but won the battle to dress her they had reached an uneasy truce, and now might even be considered to be friends.

'Wish me luck, Mrs Woo!'

Mrs Woo waved her tiny hands expressively as if to say 'Be gone with you and on with the dance', but when she turned away, long after Trilby had left the room and was walking carefully down the stairs towards the hall, she sighed.

Lewis was waiting for her in the hall. He stood watching her coming down the stairs, step by step, her face wreathed in that particular sort of happiness that young girls emanate when they know that they are looking at their beautiful best, or, perhaps, have never looked better.

'I knew that dress would suit you, darling. I just knew it.'

Trilby smiled. She had never thought to look as she did tonight. She had never, ever thought of herself as being more than pretty, but tonight she most definitely was. It was only as she went ahead of Lewis into the drawing room that something came back to her. It was only fleeting, but if it had not been Lewis's birthday she felt she would have been able to give her memory, however vague, some precise identification.

*　　*　　*

'You are a very brave young woman, to have married Lewis.'

Lola de Ribes was standing with Trilby, looking out onto the dance floor that now covered the back garden, at the fairy lights, at the marquee, at the servants in their white jackets and black ties, at the maids in their long black dresses, at the moon above them.

'I hardly needed courage to marry someone as wonderful as Lewis,' Trilby told her, quietly.

'Not now, perhaps, not tonight.' Lola's expression was not one that Trilby could read. It was neither kind nor cruel.

The older woman moved off, and, the other guests having arrived, Lewis and Trilby started to greet all their mutual friends. Lola and Trilby did not see each other again all evening, which was just as well since Trilby felt that, despite being an old friend of Lewis, and obviously in possession of greater knowledge of him than she herself, Madame de Ribes had gone too far. But why had she gone out of her way to say something so sinister to Trilby, and why had the look in her eyes been one of such real pity? Trilby wondered briefly if the older woman was jealous, if she had perhaps had an affair with Lewis? But minutes later, as photographer after photographer of a sudden seemed to be focused on Trilby, she forgot all about Lola and laughed, unable to believe such attention.

'Did you invite them all?' she asked, turning to Lewis, but he only shook his head.

'I did give the nod to *one* of my editors, and I think they must all have taken it to be carte blanche for *all* of them. It has opened the flood gates, I am afraid, but you're looking so beautiful tonight, my darling, can you blame them? Can you blame them for wanting to photograph you as you are, young and lovely, and at the height of your beauty?'

Trilby would have had to have been made of stone not to have enjoyed the attention she was receiving. She smiled and waved, and they snapped

169

away. She went out of rooms and came back into them, and still the photographers seemed somehow obsessed with her.

'I feel like a trail of aniseed with hounds coming after me!' she said to one of the many young men who, it seemed, could not wait to escort her onto the dance floor. 'What have I done to deserve this?'

'That's easy, looked more beautiful than anyone else.'

They danced, he came too close, Lewis cut in. He danced with her, smiling and proud, the flash bulbs popped yet again. Lewis allowed someone else to cut in, and then he ordered the photographers away into the night.

'What a wonderful evening, darling. You looked ravishing, everyone did nothing but talk about you. I could not have been happier with you, in every way.'

Trilby floated up to bed, and for many reasons she allowed Mrs Woo to undress her. The next morning Mrs Woo brought her a breakfast tray and on it was a note from Lewis.

I was so proud of you last night, my darling. I would be with you today, but I have to fly to Paris, can't put it off any longer. Will be back with you tomorrow. L. PS The car is at your disposal all the time.

Trilby stared across at the windows. Berry was away, Lewis was away, and she was quite alone. Since it was raining it was obvious what she must do. She must explore. Up until now she had only really been in their part of the house, the part that Lewis and herself and the servants used, and since everything in the house was so well appointed there had really been no reason to go anywhere else.

170

'Mrs Woo? Mrs Woo!'

The maid appeared from Trilby's dressing room in her small, neat, dark dress. 'Yes, madame?'

'Mr Lewis is away in Paris. Take the day off! Go and see your mother and your sisters. Oh, and here. Buy yourself something nice.'

Trilby reached into her handbag and gave her a ten pound note. Mrs Woo stared at it. She knew it was a bribe, and so did Trilby, which was probably why they both fell to silence. The expression on Mrs Woo's face became very, very serious the more she stared at the large note in her hand, until eventually she bowed. As she did so Trilby remembered Berry saying long ago that in his experience the Chinese only laughed when they were embarrassed, and that when they were happy and at ease they became immensely serious.

Soon the maid was gone and Trilby was able to hop out of bed and run round the room opening cupboards and pulling at drawers as a child might, ending up this curious expression of freedom by standing on her head. As she viewed the world from upside down she exulted in the thought that she was free for a whole day to do as she wished.

She pulled her suitcase from under the bed, at the same time reaching for the familiar packages that were also hidden there—among them her newest drawings, done in secret in the bathroom, behind locked doors, after her visit to Berry. But search as she might to find them, with more and more desperation, in the end she had to come to the conclusion that they were gone.

And when she went to the cupboard and reached up for the old crocodile suitcase her father had given her long ago, that too had gone. As had her beloved black velvet dressing gown, which she had so often had cause to wear to cross the street to have breakfast with Aphrodite.

Frantically she sorted through all the other cupboards, and in the bathroom too, but there was nothing of her old life left. For some reason that she did not understand, everything that she had been used to wearing at home had been removed.

She stared around her room. It did not seem possible. She looked about her as if the beloved old items would suddenly reappear. But everything was gone.

More than that—the crazy outfit that she had bought with Berry, that too had gone. Trilby sat down on her bed, suddenly realising that it must be on Lewis's orders. He must have told the servants to take away everything from her cupboards that had anything to do with Glebe Street, or Berry, or anyone really, other than, probably, himself.

Over the previous weeks she had grown used to having no say in anything that happened in the house. The food, the flower arrangements, the running of the house, were all done for her, and only Lewis was consulted by Paine or Cook. She had even become accustomed to being followed everywhere, either by the car or by Lewis's telephone calls, to his returning at times when he had said he would not, to his ordering her to change for the theatre at a moment's notice, only to change his mind and decide to stay in after all. All that she had decided to accept, but having favourite clothes taken from her cupboard was quite different. It meant that Lewis, and it had to be Lewis, would not allow her to put on anything, at any time, that he had not bought for her.

As soon as she was dressed Trilby decided to carry through her plan to explore the rest of the house. Now she was quite determined to go where she had not been before, to rifle through dusty cupboards looking for her beloved old clothes. They must have been put somewhere. Lewis could not have burned them, surely? The idea made her feel more distressed than she would have thought possible. Old clothes after all were old clothes, when all was said and done, but not those clothes— she had made those clothes herself, carefully chosen the patterns and found old materials in junk shops. Those clothes were her—they were 'Trilby'.

'I may be married, but I am not a mouse,' she told her own reflection in the mirror and then, quite determined on her course, she walked out of her bedroom and stood in the corridor outside.

The house was very quiet, as it would be at that time of day. Downstairs, far away, behind the green baize door she could hear laughter and talk from the kitchen and pantries. There was the occasional sound of a car passing outside but she could hear nothing else. She should have been able to tell herself that it was *her* house, but that was so palpably untrue that she could not even begin to try to *think* such a lie. The place in which she now found herself living, the square, three-floored house filled with art treasures and every accoutrement of the rich, was no more hers than her father and stepmother's house in Glebe Street. Nevertheless she determined on trying to explore. She would start with Lewis's bedroom and dressing room. Paine, who acted as both valet and butler, would be having coffee and buns by now, so she had time.

She pushed open the door. Although she had been in the room before, she had never really taken it in, probably because Lewis had such a huge personality. Now, standing alone, she sensed that particular aura of masculinity that is sometimes so clearly defined in a man's rooms. A sense of apartness that made nonsense of the coming together of the sexes, a sense of dark brown masculinity, of attitudes so different from the sex to which she belonged that she found herself catching her breath. She knew now that she was more than somewhat afraid of Lewis, not in a day to day way, but in the sense that she had gradually had to come to terms with the fact that she did not really know him, that she had fallen in love with his bright white shirts, his immaculate tan, his overt charm, and good looks, all pretty perfect effects, but effects behind which Lewis himself was hiding.

She inched quietly across the dark green Victorian carpet, passing the silver brushes on the Georgian military chest, passing the green silk curtains run up from what looked like acres of material, caught up at different points and let loose at others, and opened Lewis's cupboards. Here were folded shirts made of cotton imported especially for Lewis, here were cashmere sweaters and cardigans, dinner jackets, morning dress, top hats, squashy hats, golfing caps, ties and bow ties, boxes and boxes made of leather inside which were Lewis's beautiful cufflinks and immaculate pins and collar stiffeners; everything that could possibly be required to make up the exterior of a gentleman was here.

But there were also other boxes, almost out of reach, boxes that had to be reached on a pair of library steps, boxes that cried out to Trilby *Do not touch, do not open.*

Trilby stared up at them, her heart beating faster. It would be, she somehow knew, like climbing to the top of her stepmother's cupboard and finding her own Christmas present long before the day. She would regret looking, she knew it, and yet, helpless, she could not stop herself from doing just that, opening up not one Pandora's box, but dozens of them.

And, having done so, all at once she knew that her life was never ever going to be the same again.

*   *   *

They were beautiful boxes, carefully preserved, tied neatly together with expensive gold-threaded string, and as she carefully undid the neat bows of the gold-threaded string and looked through them Trilby realised at once why the photograph of the beautiful woman in the white dress had disappeared so suddenly from the table that day. Indeed as she opened box after box it seemed to her that she now understood everything that she had in the recent past so utterly misunderstood, and dread filled her heart, and it became like a stone set in her body, and her body just water, and the stone sinking slowly to the bottom of it.

CHAPTER FIVE

Now every day when she awoke Trilby felt sick, dreading the advent of morning, and worst of all,

Lewis. And every day that she awoke and found Lewis had gone to the office early she felt less sick, almost jubilant, only to feel more sick when he returned to lunch with her and make love before returning to his office.

The truth was that she had started to dread his knock at the door and his request, 'May I come in and see you, darling?' Everything about him, up to and including his knocking so politely at her bedroom door, made her stomach turn over. She hoped that he did not notice, because a part of her still loved Lewis—it was just that she was no longer terribly sure which part. Perhaps because of this terrible uncertainty, she had started to lose weight. Mrs Woo had to send off quantities of her clothes to have the hems put up.

Sometimes Trilby stared at her reflection in the mirror and wondered at the change in herself. Her eyes had become lacklustre, and there were dark lines underneath them where there had never been any before, lines that she secretly called her 'dread lines', lines from dreading Lewis's return. And it was not just his return; the whole of him now filled her with dread. She dreaded hearing his footfall on the stairs, she dreaded the sound of his breathing, most especially when he was in bed making love to her.

For some reason too, just lately, she had even started to dread seeing his hair on her pillows, so that now it seemed to her that she did not just dread him, but a part of her must hate him, not just his body, his demands, but the very essence of him; not just his unkindness, his power over her, but everything to do with him.

His insistence on her only eating the food that

176

he liked. His inability to see worth in any of his rivals. His meagre, narrow attitudes to life. His blind support of everything conventional, his self-esteem. But most of all, and most terribly, she hated his indestructible wealth. The newspapers and magazines that were read all over the world by millions, that influenced governments; an empire that could not, it seemed to Trilby, ever be destroyed.

'People must have their news.'

Lewis often said that to her in a complacent voice, standing before the library chimneypiece, very often in a pair of tartan evening trousers and a black velvet smoking jacket that, to Trilby, made him seem even more Victorian and unyielding than ever. 'Yes, darling, people must have their news, so we will always be here, thank God, us newspapers, until the end of time. Nothing can destroy print, not now, not ever. No wonder they were so frightened of Caxton when he invented his printing press.'

Sometimes Trilby awoke in the night and in a state of sweating, nightmare-ridden half sleep she saw the whole world spread about with newspapers. In the lonely darkness of her room, it seemed to her that everywhere from the Arctic to the Sahara was covered in Lewis's newspapers, so it followed that everywhere was, in some way, covered in Lewis's thoughts, his narrow attitudes, his xenophobia, his belief in keeping women tied to the home. His worship of everything from the Family Christmas to the Empire, from the Atom Bomb to the Sanctity of Marriage. They all covered the world. Sometimes she actually found herself hurrying down to the library of a late afternoon in

177

order to delight in the sight of one of the maids setting light to one of Lewis's newspapers under the kindling and the coals.

But despite his publicly unwavering belief in the sanctity of marriage and the family, his worship of traditional values, Lewis seemed to be the only person who did not notice the change in his young wife, until he started to ask her every now and then, and a little edgily, 'Nothing to report?'

Or he would say, 'Something should have happened by now, surely?' Pretty soon it was brought home even to Trilby that he was hoping that she was pregnant, that there would be some sort of result from his afternoon visits to her bedroom.

Of course it was normal for a man to expect to impregnate a woman, even Trilby realised that. If you married you were expected to have a man's babies. But what was terrifying to her was that she was so appalled by the thought of having a child by him. At least when he made love to her he went away afterwards and she could shower herself and forget him, put him out of her mind, pretend that she had just been through something unpleasant which could now be forgotten. But if she had his baby, it would be there—it, the baby. And there would be no possible way out; nor any forgetting.

The fact was that Trilby wanted to have Lewis's baby now as much as she wanted to have her head shaved and become a nun, but naturally she could not tell him that. Instead she smiled and looked as vague as was perfectly possible in the circumstances. For weeks now she had come to realise that there was no escape from her marriage. Day after day she contemplated trying to run away

178

from this stranger who watched her so avidly; who, when he was not watching her himself, was happy in the thought that he had set someone else to watch her.

Happily, shortly after he had at last confessed to Trilby that he had high hopes of becoming a father, Lewis went away on business, leaving Trilby yet again on her own. Since Berry was not yet back from Northumberland and she had no desire to work or even to draw, she started instead to plan a way out of her present . . . existence. No-one could call it a life. She knew that the escape she planned had to be foolproof. That it had to be impressive. She also knew that she would not be able to return to Glebe Street.

It was raining, and downstairs there would be the servants and outside the car and the chauffeur, all in their own way prison guards of a sort. All of them, certainly, in Lewis's pay.

She did not want to commit suicide. Just the thought, for some reason she did not understand, made her want to laugh. Probably because she could hear Berry's voice: 'Really, Trilb, not at your age, so awfully depressing for everyone. And I mean to say, what hope for the rest of us if you feel so dank?'

Berry was now the one bright spark in her life. He was not old as were most of Lewis's friends. And he was not part of any society. Lewis could not destroy Berry because in Lewis's terms there was so little to destroy. It would be like suing a poor man. Trilby reached into her handbag to reread Berry's card to her, because just seeing Berry's beautiful, artistic handwriting made her feel more cheerful.

'Mrs Woo? Have you seen the card that I received from Northumberland a few days ago? I was sure that I put it into my handbag.'

'No, madame. No card. Mrs Woo saw no card.' The maid's dark eyes registered no emotion whatsoever.

Trilby nodded, knowing that the maid was the only person who could have taken it. It would be ridiculous to make a fuss about a postcard, but nevertheless, she turned away biting her lip. If only Berry would come back from the north and come and see her, they could make a plan. She felt sure that he would think of something to get her out of this prison into which she had so willingly consigned herself when she married Lewis.

The worst of it was that she knew that what she was fighting now was not her initial misery, but her ever-present inertia. No-one had ever told her that despair makes you inert, that you no longer care about anything. For the truth was that, inexorably, day by day, since the wretched interview with Micklethwaite, since she no longer drew or thought about drawing, she had grown dulled by the luxury in which she was now incarcerated.

Being dressed, going downstairs to breakfast, smiling at the servants, smiling at Lewis, eating some toast, drinking coffee, going to the library, reading a book, taking the Rolls to the park on sunny days. Coming home, having lunch with Lewis, and then—and this had become the worst part of her day—allowing him to make love to her, was all now so unendingly grey.

Happily after lunch he sometimes had to leave her to go back to the office on business, and then Trilby would rest before going for yet another walk, or staying in and reading yet another magazine before allowing Mrs Woo to dress her again, this time for dinner. So much had this become a routine that Trilby sometimes imagined to herself that she was a cut-out doll, and Mrs Woo merely pinning on paper dresses of different kinds.

Tonight Lewis would be back from Manchester. They would have dinner, and because he had missed lunch with her he would probably make love to her afterwards, but only after telling her, in some detail, all about his tedious day, about which Trilby would have to feign interest.

Trilby stared at herself in the mirror and allowed herself to entertain a truly shocking thought. She had never before imagined that being made love to by someone could be dull, something to ignore, something you let happen to you, as if it was happening to someone else.

She stared into her own dark eyes, getting closer and closer to the mirror. The bathroom door was locked so that not even Lewis's spy, Mrs Woo, could see her.

Alone at these eerie moments Trilby had started to address herself in the mirror in the second person. Now she whispered to her reflection, 'Tonight, Trilby, tonight Bluebeard will be here and he will not just be here in the house, he will be up here in your room, and he will be doing that thing he does to you. What are you going to do to stop it, Trilby?'

Her eyes were so close to her own image now that she could not focus on her face. Trilby started to slip down to the floor, sliding against the mirror. There was no-one to whom she could turn, no-one even in Glebe Street, now that Berry had gone

181

away, in whom she could confide. If she called on them and told them of her misery they would think that she was spoilt, they would not be sympathetic to how she felt about Lewis. Lewis, after all, in their eyes, had given her everything, and seeing as they had suffered so much during the war, and come through it, they would merely think that Trilby was lacking in gumption, that necessary quality to get you through the lumps and bumps of life. She stared at herself, pretending that she was her own best friend. She had to do something, now, something that would get her out of what was going to happen after dinner. But as it happened, it was not necessary. Something had already happened, and it would get her out of everything.

*   *   *

'My darling! Are you all right? My darling! Do answer!'

Lewis was hammering on the bathroom door, but Trilby could not answer, she was being far, far too sick. 'I shall have to fetch someone, darling, have them break down the door. If you don't answer me now I will have to get Paine to break down the door.'

'It's all right, Lewis,' Trilby finally answered, and she unlocked the door. 'Really there is no need to ask Paine for anything. There is nothing he can do for me. There is nothing anyone can do for me. Not for what is making me sick, at any rate.'

Lewis stared at her. He had been so hoping that her pallor, the listlessness . . . that it might be what he so wanted it to be.

'Can it be true? Are you perhaps—are you

182

perhaps—are you?'

Trilby nodded slowly. 'Yes, yes, yes, I am,' she acknowledged. 'I know I am. I must be. I have never felt so ill in my life before, so I must be. I feel sick so often.'

'But this is wonderful news!' Lewis hugged his young wife to him. 'You have no idea how much I have longed for this, Tally—Trilby—darling, sweetheart, I am so thrilled.'

Trilby, still clasped to him, frowned. She was used to Berry calling her every name under the sun, but Lewis was simply not like that. She pulled back from him. 'What did you nearly call me?'

Lewis turned away, but not so quickly that Trilby did not notice that his forehead was reddening. He hurried to the door with his dressing gown cord trailing, and he almost wrenched it open before turning to her and saying, 'This is such good news, Trilby, really it is.'

'Thank you, but there is some way to go yet, you know that, Lewis. We must not celebrate too soon, must we?'

'You must go to the doctor. You must go and see my doctor.'

Lewis's doctor was extremely smart, not at all like Agnes's doctor who had an agreeably large stomach, and nicotine-stained fingers. Lewis's doctor was tall and gaunt, and he had a Rolls-Royce parked outside his Harley Street premises.

'How many—ahems—have you missed?' The doctor coughed discreetly.

'One.'

'I see.'

Trilby smiled.

'Feeling a bit sick?'

'Very sick, and my tummy feels very sore, and I feel faint all the time.'

'You do look quite pale.'

'I have lost weight too, about half a stone, maybe a little more. It's feeling sick I am afraid, it puts you off your food.'

'What do you not want to eat at the moment?'

'Practically everything. And coffee—I can't stand coffee. Just the smell of it makes me sick.'

'That is normal. Nothing to worry about there, Mrs James.' Dr Mellon smiled, and then went on, 'You know, Mrs James, when a woman tells me she is pregnant, even if she has not missed ahem I always believe her. A woman knows her own body. Nature is pretty marvellous like that, I promise you.'

'And another thing, Dr Mellon.' Trilby looked at him, and leaning forward to make sure that she had his full attention she lowered her voice. 'I can't stand it with my husband.'

The doctor's expression changed at once, as she had known very well it would. After all, Lewis was one of his richest patients.

'You can't stand your husband, Mrs James. I do not quite understand what you mean by that?'

The doctor's expression was of extreme caution as Trilby sighed sadly. 'I know. I did so like it with him, you know—It—but now, since all this, it makes me feel—well, even sicker. I don't like it, not at all, at least not at the moment.'

'That's only natural, Mrs James,' said the doctor, relaxing at once and giving her a patronising smile. 'It is quite natural that you should have more tender feelings about yourself. Your body is going through a great change.'

184

'Yes, but do you see, my husband is so much older than me. It is very difficult for me to tell him how I feel. I was wondering if you would—well, I don't suppose you can, but I was wondering if you could, you know, tell him?'

'Of course, Mrs James. He will be telephoning me the moment you leave here, and I will tell him everything that we have talked about, and of course the good news. Because of course, as you might have realised, you are quite obviously pregnant.'

On the way back from Harley Street Trilby stopped off to shop for various small items. A bottle of scent, a new hairbrush, some new drawing pens, some drawing pads. She could not believe that she was pregnant. She *would* not believe that she was pregnant. Her eyes determinedly avoided any of the advertisements for baby milks or rusks, because she did not believe that she was going to have one of those. A baby.

Returning home that night Lewis fairly bounced into the room.

'My darling, I am so happy, I cannot tell you how happy I am. I spoke to Dr Mellon and he has told me all. You are to put your feet up, you are to do nothing but rest. He said I may take you away at the end of the first three months, but not before, because we must be so very careful of you.'

Lewis kissed Trilby on the mouth and since he tasted kind and sweet, almost like the old Lewis when she first met him, she smiled up at him. If she had loved him it might have been a touching moment, but as it was she did not love him any more, and so it was not touching at all.

*   *   *

185

After the great announcement, Lewis no longer bothered to come home for lunch, which was a great relief, and on doctor's orders did not visit her for lovemaking. Perhaps because of this, for a couple of weeks Trilby started to feel happier. The sessions in the bathroom stopped, and she no longer found herself making speeches to herself in the mirror. Indeed, all was well until, fatefully, one day Lewis announced that he was coming back for lunch.

Trilby looked across the breakfast table at him. 'You will be home for lunch,' she repeated.

'I just told you, Trilby, I just said I will be home for luncheon.'

It seemed to Trilby that the whole room froze at his announcement, for all the servants must know why he made such an effort to come home for luncheon. The maids, Paine, everyone must know the significance inherent in Mr James's coming home for lunch. They must all know that it was a code for *coming home for lunch and my rights as a husband.* They all must also know that Trilby had not been well, that she was pregnant, that the doctor had banned coming home for luncheon, because if Mrs Woo knew, they would all be sure to know.

'How nice, darling,' Trilby managed to say. 'I will make sure that we have one of your favourites— Omelette Arnold Bennett say?'

Happily, Trilby could not see Lewis's smile or the expression in his eyes which said, 'And that is not the only thing that I will be enjoying.'

'Good,' was all he actually said.

The omelette might have been delicious if Trilby

could have enjoyed anything, but as it was it tasted to her like warm fishy flannels. After cheese and fruit, and at the usual given moment—and how she had not missed these given moments at all!—she left the lunch table and went upstairs for her rest.

Today Lewis followed her. Trilby turned as she heard the door open and saw him coming in. 'I don't think we should, Lewis, really, I don't. Dr Mellon said not. I don't feel very well at the moment, and he definitely said not.'

'Nonsense, Dr Mellon said you should be fine by now.'

'Dr Mellon is not a woman . . .' Trilby sidestepped her husband and darted to the bathroom.

'What are you doing?'

'I must just go and brush my hair, put scent on . . .'

Lewis smiled to himself, indulging in the moment. Trilby was very fastidious. He climbed into her bed and waited for her. He could never understand men who shared bedrooms with their wives, men who enjoyed that kind of intimacy. One's wife should have her own bedroom where one visited her and then one left her. It was tidier and more aesthetic. He should hate to share a room with a woman, however much he might be in love with her, and there was no doubt that he was still passionately in love with Trilby.

Inside the bathroom Trilby stared at herself in the mirror. She was glad that she had drunk wine at lunch, because it helped her get over the fact that nowadays he revolted her, but at the same time she was also sorry, because it made it hard to think of how to get rid of him. She felt hot and dizzy. She

187

could hardly ring down for the servants and say 'Come and remove Mr James from my bedroom', but having heard Lewis undressing she knew that he was not going to remove himself. She would have to go through with It, and forget all about it afterwards.

Lewis watched his young wife climb into bed beside him, still so slender and young, so pleasing to him in every way, despite her pregnancy. Seconds later, of a sudden, he began to make violent love to her, only to be stopped by a frantic Trilby.

Downstairs Paine heard a cry which rang out in the silence of the London afternoon. It was followed by a shout and the sound of a door slamming sharply as, upstairs, Trilby staggered to the bathroom.

The butler sighed and turned away.

Poor kid! But there you were, in marrying a man like Lewis James she had taken the king's shilling, and now she was paying for it. But really, why could the wretched man not leave her alone? As if it was not enough that she was pregnant!

He went through to the kitchen and asked the maids in a dulled voice, 'Anyone know where Mrs Woo's gone?'

'Why?'

'Why do you think? Because I think she will be needed upstairs, that's why!'

But it was Dr Mellon who was needed. He came round very quickly, and stood in his black coat and pin-striped trousers at the bottom of Trilby's bed.

'Well, well, Mrs James, never mind now, eh? Soon be quite better. Miscarriages come and go— you know. Come and go. Bit of—ahem—is there?

Well, yes, there would be, but don't worry, all quite normal, especially in a young girl such as you. Hubby a bit passionate, was he? Well, that is only to be expected with someone as lovely as you, wouldn't you say?'

Trilby turned her head away. Really, she had no idea whom she found less appealing, her husband or his doctor.

'If you say so, Dr Mellon.' Having stared out of the window, she turned back and looked at the doctor. 'I would quite like it if I could be alone.'

*   *   *

Had he been the kind of man who could feel guilt Lewis might have felt remorseful when he saw how much Trilby suffered, but since he was not that kind of person, he merely thought of the whole incident as bad luck.

Merely *bad luck*.

The doctor said, comfortingly, 'There was no real reason why your wife should have miscarried. She is well of an age, at nineteen, to have a child. No, you must not feel bad about that, Mr James. She is perfectly capable of having a healthy pregnancy. And take heart, when she has recovered, she will feel much better quite soon, I am sure of it. Probably be a bit depressed for a few weeks. Keep her in bed, humour her a little, you know the kind of thing, and after that, well, you can start again. Shouldn't take too long next time, didn't take too long this time, did it?'

Of course this was just what Lewis wanted to hear so he absorbed every word, and while Trilby lay in her bedroom staring bleakly at the windows, and even more bleakly at the trays of food that Mrs Woo brought to her every day, her husband went to America on business.

*   *   *

As soon as Lewis was back from America, Trilby made sure that she was up and about to greet him. She also made sure to go out every morning, shopping, shopping and more shopping. She shopped for shoes, and dresses, and underclothes. She shopped for food and drink and magazines and books, she shopped for so much that she could see that not even the chauffeur could keep pace with what she brought back to the limousine. Which was just as well because among the many items that were debited to the account of Mrs Lewis James was a very regular, very plentiful supply of vodka.

Trilby had never drunk much, hardly at all in fact, but now she made sure to put a plentiful and regular supply of vodka in her bedside cupboard.

'My cocktail cupboard,' she called it to herself, and before luncheon and after luncheon, and during the afternoon and during teatime, and at all sorts of other times Mrs Woo heard that bedside cupboard clicking open and clicking to as Trilby took out her vodka bottle and went to the bathroom, where she locked the door.

'You're drinking too much, Trilby. And you're drinking in secret. It's not good for a woman to drink in private.'

Lewis was alone with her in the library, but not before he had gone to the library door and checked that Paine was not listening.

'Lewis! I—er—do not know what you mean,

really I don't!' Trilby smiled a little dazedly at him. 'I hardly drink at all.'

'You are drinking to comfort yourself for losing the baby, for miscarrying, but really it will do no good, drink will not bring back the baby. You must get well again soon. We must go away together, and then you will get well, and—and we can make another baby.'

Trilby hiccuped slightly. 'Don't be silly, Lewis.' She leaned forward to touch him on the cheek, but he moved away. 'I am fine. I jus' cannot go anywhere with you, really I cannot, not until I am. Better.'

'I hate to see you like this. You lose all your appeal, all your dignity. What exactly is the matter?'

'The matter if—the matter is—I have had a miscarr-idge, and I am not at all meself, myselve. Really I am not.'

Lewis went to the drink tray and although it was far too early for such things he poured himself a double Scotch.

Silly little girl was taking this miscarriage far too much to heart. Women! He sighed both inwardly and outwardly and then he said flatly, 'I think you need a nurse. I will have Dr Mellon send us a nurse for you. She will pay great attention to your needs, she will be a professional. And we will move you to the top of the house where she can watch over you, all on her own, and make sure that you are cured. You need to have an effective cure from this bad phase.'

The nurse was a large woman with heavy legs and a dark shading of hair on either side of her mouth. She must have reached some level of superiority in her profession for, as Trilby duly noted, she wore a cap with many kinds of frills, very complicated, lace-edged frills. She was a woman of few words. She was a woman who did not really like 'spoilt girls' as she continually told Trilby, as she tried to force food down her, girls who could not appreciate how lucky they were.

The doors on the top floor were now always locked, and since the rooms had once been nurseries, all the windows were barred. Once, looking down from them, Trilby thought she saw Berry in the road waving up to her, and she opened the window and waved back down, making sure it was something particularly outrageous that she waved—in this case a frilly lace bra.

Her father and stepmother had obviously been told about the miscarriage by Lewis, because shortly afterwards her father wrote to Trilby at what, for him, was some length. As she read the letter Trilby could imagine her father at his desk, cigarette in one hand, Parker pen in the other, pausing every now and then to stare out at the roses in his garden.

My dear Trilby,

I had hoped to be the happy recipient of good news about you, but I hear that things have gone sadly awry. Happily, unlike some, you have a wonderful husband. So caring and kind, and able to provide you with every degree of comfort, and all that you need. You are a very lucky girl, and when you are quite better you must come to lunch with me. Millie, Molly's lodger, is proving to be a very refreshing presence in Glebe Street. Everyone likes her and she has taken over

192

*cooking for us, while Mrs Bartlett is away, which
is a great relief to Agnes!
Well, that is all for now, I hope you recover from
your bad luck soon.*
Love Daddy xxxxx

Trilby put the letter under the pillow. Inevitably, after Lewis had visited her the following evening, when she went to reread it, the letter had disappeared. Not that Trilby was surprised. So much had disappeared. Clothes, cards, letters—not to mention her work. It was amazing to her that the laces had not been removed from her shoes, or the belts from her clothes, so much did she seem to have become a prisoner.

Of course she was getting no better. Upstairs, incarcerated on the third floor, despite the nurse and the strict regime, despite the locked doors and the barred windows, despite everything Trilby was still not cured.

Such a disappointment for Dr Mellon and Lewis, of course, but she was determined not to be cured, not for days and weeks, not until she had managed to work out what to do with her life. Until then she would drink the little bottles of vodka that she had managed to bribe the maids to bring her on the nurse's day off.

A few days later, Lewis made a special effort to leave his office early and met Dr Mellon as he came to call on his usual afternoon visit.

'I was hoping to catch you when you came in, Dr Mellon.'

'Mr James, good afternoon to you, sir.'

They both smiled at each other.

'Might you have time to talk to me?'

193

Of course Dr Mellon had time to talk to a man like Lewis James. For a private doctor with a rich practice not to have time to talk to one of his richest patients would be insanity, to say the least.

'The fact is,' Lewis began almost as soon as the doctor had shut the library door behind him, 'the fact is, Dr Mellon, that my wife is getting no better. The nurse reports that search the rooms though she may, and looking everywhere as she has, she cannot find where she is hiding the—the whatever she is drinking—but she must be hiding it. We know that, because she is no better.'

'May I sit down?'

'Of course.' Lewis indicated that the doctor should seat himself on a Knole sofa, and he too sat down, but on a chair, with a higher seat. 'We have no drink in the house, Dr Mellon, none at all, and yet my wife, every few days, is found—well, not to put too fine a point on it, she is found completely drunk. Yesterday she even attacked the nurse. She kicked her on the shins. I saw the bruises for myself. If I had not, I would not have believed it. It was quite frightening for the poor woman. My wife has gone from being this gentle patient creature to this wildcat. I can't tell you what it is doing to me to see her like this. Apart from anything else I cannot be with her all the time, even should I wish to be. I have an empire to run. Last week, it seems, she threw all her clothes out of the window, and a few days before that she was seen to be waving a piece of lingerie at passers-by.'

Dr Mellon leaned forward, his face a picture of concern. He gave a sympathetic sigh and shook his head. 'It is so puzzling with these cases, Mr James. But, if I may tell you, sir, the fact is that people

194

with your wife's condition, and we find this time and time again, they develop the most extraordinary cunning. They can find places to hide alcohol, or whatever other drug they are committed to, and none of us, and I mean it, none of us can locate where it is. It is most particularly difficult at home. In an old house like this, you can look and you can look, but you will never find the place where she has hidden the drink from you. It is just a fact.'

Lewis shook his head. It did not seem possible to marry a young girl like Trilby and the next minute to be talking to a doctor about her alcohol problems. It was a nightmare for him, and so humiliating—in every respect the sort of thing that, if it got out, if any of his rival papers got hold of the story, well, it was the sort of thing that could be very embarrassing, most particularly to him.

'What do you suggest we do, Dr Mellon?' For a second, Lewis looked and felt quite humble.

'I suggest that you remove the nurse, just let your wife be. Perhaps give her a studio to use, something of her own. A bit more freedom.'

'She has plenty of freedom.' Lewis stared frostily at Dr Mellon, thinking all at once that he might quite soon be in need of a new doctor. 'She has the run of my house, all day and every day. She is always allowed to do as she wants.'

'That is just it, Mr James.' Dr Mellon stared thoughtfully at his richest and most powerful patient.

'What is just it, Dr Mellon?'

'You just said "my" house. Your wife is living in your house. As I say, I think she needs somewhere of her own. A place where she can be herself, not

195

just Mrs James.'

'This is just psychological claptrap.' Lewis sprang out of his chair and started to walk up and down, the red flush appearing as always when he was annoyed across the top of his forehead and spreading down towards his eyes.

Dr Mellon watched him with some detachment. He had many rich clients and he always found that if he told them the truth it was such an unusual experience for them that they always came back for more. It was just a fact. Plus, of course, he could frighten them. He had only to stare at their nails, or into their eyes, and make a doubtful 'tiss, tiss' sound and sigh and turn away, and he would have them eating out of his hands.

'A studio?'

'Yes. She used to draw and so on, didn't she?'

'Yes, of course she did. That was how we met.'

'In that case, give her a little freedom, Mr James. send the nurse home, allow your wife some time to herself; somewhere, as it were, where she can spend the mornings doodling, having coffee with a girlfriend. Somewhere where she can choose the flowers, put up a sofa bed, hang her own prints, play her own music. After all, you are much older than she is.'

This last struck home as it was meant to. Lewis stared at Dr Mellon, hating him, but also afraid of the accuracy of his diagnosis of his marriage. Even he could see the truth in what he said. It could not be denied, Trilby was much younger than himself. And she was not allowed any choice of flowers, of anything at all, in his house.

'Try it. It might work. Certainly what you are doing at the moment is not working, and if you

196

want to have a happy outcome you are going to have to do something. Locking her up with a nurse has resulted in nothing but further unhappiness.'

Lewis nodded, but it was some days before he could submit to the truth of what Dr Mellon had said to him. Perhaps it was the sudden realisation that Trilby was so thin and pale, perhaps it was recognising that the loud voice and boorish way, of the nurse in whose charge he had put Trilby would be enough, in all truth, to make anyone take to drink, but he sent for David Micklethwaite, his only confidant in such matters, and asked him to find Trilby a studio.

'Somewhere where she can regain her health and happiness. Nowhere too far, but somewhere she can drive herself and set up on her own of a morning, before coming back to lunch or dinner here with me.'

'Is this wise?'

Lewis shrugged his shoulders. 'I have no idea. Really, I have no idea at all, but it is what the doctor ordered, what Dr Mellon advised, so what else can I do?'

Micklethwaite nodded, the expression on his face sober and at the same time doubtful. 'I suppose it's worth at least a try, for a while?'

'Of course it is.' Lewis became brisk, as always when he thought someone else might be about to attempt to change his mind. 'Find her a studio, and I will present it to her. Make sure it is habitable, though, and not near where she used to live. Somewhere near here, not near them, where she came from, they'll only interfere.'

As it happened David Micklethwaite had no inclination to find himself looking for studios

197

anywhere near a woman he had boffed on the orders of the boss, so he set out to search around Holland Park, and since the area had once been famed as a bohemian quarter he very soon found exactly what Lewis had ordered.

Large, Victorian, north facing, it had a courtyard in which Trilby could sit and enjoy herself on a sunny day, but the decorations were in a dreadful condition, so he sent for a firm who painted it a bland white, and stripped the floors and sealed them.

*　　　*　　　*

The nurse's exit from Trilby's life could not have been more sudden. One minute it seemed she was there, eyeing Trilby at every moment, searching for any signs of alcoholic beverages—watching the nurse watching her had become one of the few amusements in Trilby's life—the next she had packed her bag, and left.

Trilby stared at the open doors feeling as all ex-prisoners must, frightened at the sudden largeness of her world, the sudden expansion: the whole area in front of her, the stairs, the landing, the voices from below that she could hear coming up to her now.

'Trilby.'

She stared at Lewis. He was looking handsomer than ever, she had to admit, but his eyes held the kind of wariness that she had only ever seen before in her stepmother's eyes. The expression in them was of a person who was being asked to handle an animal that might, at any moment, be about to scratch or bite him.

'Are you feeling a little better, darling?'

'I think I must be, since the nurse has gone. Since Mrs Hitler went I think I must be feeling much better.'

'In that case will you come downstairs with me, and have lunch?'

Lewis normally called it 'luncheon'. For some reason Trilby found that because he did not, because he was obviously carefully dressed in slacks and a jumper, not in his normal pin-striped suit, because he was equally obviously dressed down, for her, she wanted to giggle.

She followed Lewis dutifully down the stairs. When they passed a mirror on one of the wide landings, even she was shocked to see herself. She was not just thin, she was scrawny, and her ribs seemed to be sticking not through her body, but through her face. The shadows under her eyes were deep black, and her hair hung down in an unacceptable schoolgirl fashion, she having long ago abandoned its chic feathered look. She did not know what effect her looks had on Lewis, but one glance at her reflection and she herself nearly fainted with shock.

'Right, darling, after a sandwich lunch, after our box lunch, we're going to go out for an hour or so, and we're going to show you a surprise that I have prepared for you.'

Lewis was speaking to her as if she was very far away and could not understand English very well. Again the irrepressible desire to giggle welled up in Trilby, and had to be suppressed. She remembered grown-ups talking to her just like that when she was a child and wondering why they thought they had to speak to children as if they were daft.

'Goodness, how exciting.'

She must have sounded almost too like her old self, because Lewis, having trodden carefully ahead of her into the drawing room, suddenly looked sharply back at her.

'Yes, it is exciting.' He took hold of one of her hands and slipped it under his arm. 'I want so much for you to get better, Trilby, really I do. I want to see you back, the old you, my darling vital little Trilby. I want so much for her to come back to me.'

'I am back, Lewis, really I am. I feel so much better now the nurse has gone. Really, I do.'

Lewis stared down into her pale face. She still looked terrible, but she did actually sound a little better.

Trilby herself, hearing such sincerity in Lewis's voice, felt a sudden and awful guilt at what she had put the poor man through. Her hatred for him now seemed somehow a distant thing, as if it was someone else she had hated, not the man who stood holding her hand and looking so concerned.

'I want nothing more of you than that you get better, Trilby, that is all I want.'

Again the sincerity in his voice and face convinced Trilby that she had been all wrong about Lewis. He was so kind, so kind and so handsome, a hero of a man, really, someone upon whom she could metaphorically lean, as she was now physically leaning on him.

'I am so sorry for what I have put you through, Lewis.'

'It's all right, darling. Dr Mellon has explained everything to me. He has explained the awful effects that a miscarriage can have on a woman, and how they can even turn a woman's mind, so much harm do they cause. But now we are not even going to mention any of that any more. We are going to look only towards the future. And as soon as we have eaten our box lunch, you will see my surprise for you.'

Never had food tasted so good to Trilby as it did then, not even when she had fled Mrs Bartlett's frightful cooking and on a cold evening climbed down into Aphrodite's kitchen to wolf a plate of casserole and parsley potatoes.

'Very well, I am ready.'

Lewis beamed. He loved giving people surprises. It was one of the few things that rich people could really enjoy. After all, it was very difficult to surprise a rich man with anything that he did not already have.

On Dr Mellon's orders Lewis had removed all traces of his former safeguards. So as they stepped out of the house now there was no waiting chauffeur with Rolls-Royce, only a small black Morris Minor, the passenger door of which Lewis opened for Trilby. He could see that she was at first bewildered, and then pleasantly surprised by this. He went round to the driver's door and slipped in beside her.

'It's dinky, isn't it?'

Trilby nodded. The whole thing was so un-Lewis-like that she could not find any words to say what she thought it was, so she merely nodded in agreement. 'I love Morrises. Such chunky cars.' She sighed happily.

'So do I,' Lewis lied, and started up the engine.

'And their motors always sound just like sewing machines, don't they?'

He happened to have found out through

Micklethwaite that the one car after which Trilby had always hankered was a Morris Minor, which was why he had bought it for her.

'Now for your next present.'

'Present?'

'Yes, darling. Your next present. This is yours, this car is for you. Not for me!' Lewis laughed. 'Yes, your next present is what you must see next, but you must close your eyes when I tell you.'

Trilby sank back in her seat, thanking God and Berry that she had passed her driving test in Berry's old van long ago. It was unbelievable. To be sitting beside Lewis in a Morris Minor with the winter sun shining briefly above them, and not a chauffeur in sight, did not seem possibly possible after the misery of the past weeks.

'You are now going to have to shut your eyes Trilby.'

Lewis sprang out of the car and went round to her door. Trilby climbed out onto the pavement and dutifully shut her eyes, and Lewis took his silk neck scarf from around his neck and blindfolded them. They both started to laugh as she took teetering steps towards him on the pavement. He took hold of her hand, and carefully led her up a flight of steps.

'Slowly, slowly, up we go.'

Trilby laughed. 'This better be good,' she joked, 'or else I shall have suffered for nothing.'

Lewis held on to her as he opened the door and then one by one lifted her feet over the threshold.

They now stood in a small hall, although Trilby would not have known it except for the sudden cessation of the sound of traffic from the street out side, and the slight musty smell.

202

Again Lewis put a key in a lock, and again turned it. This time there were no steps, so he did not have to lift her feet but led her carefully through this second door into what Trilby imagined must be a large room, because it instantly felt cold despite its being a warm winter day. On the other hand it did not smell musty like the previous place. This smelt of fresh paint, and Lewis's voice echoed slightly as he spoke.

'I have bought this for you. No-one need know about it, except you. I will never come here, unless you ask me. This is your place, to do as you like, and you can come here whenever you want.' He knew he should add 'and with whoever you want' but he could not bring himself to do so.

He tried to say the words as he unwrapped the scarf from Trilby's eyes, but still they refused to come out. Dr Mellon had told him to say them, he knew he should say them, but there was no way at all that they would come out. Instead he stared around him, as Trilby was staring around her, and he marvelled at his own generosity. It was a marvellous room. He almost felt jealous of its air of freedom, its marvellous light, its very whiteness. He would like a room like this for himself. But then he remembered, as always, that he was the person giving the surprise, he was the giver, not the receiver. No-one ever gave to Lewis. He was, after all, rich, and powerful, the Great Provider. No-one ever gave anything to him.

'Lewis.' Trilby walked around the studio room looking into cupboards and peering through to a small kitchen and bathroom, opening a door into a courtyard garden, gazing up at the high north-facing windows above them. 'Lewis, I can't believe

203

this.'

Neither could Lewis, but he could not say so.

'I asked Micklethwaite to find it for me, and he did, within a few days, as a matter of fact. And it is yours, my darling, my darling Trilby's own room, to come to whenever she wants, but I hope not too often, or I shall miss her.'

If she had been feeling more attractive Trilby would have kissed her husband, but as she was feeling, and judging from her reflection in the mirror on the landing also looking, like a piece of chewed string, she kissed her fingers to him, and turned back to the studio room.

Lewis had ordered easels, and a table for her pencils and pads, and a chest whose pulled drawers displayed a vast amount of oil paints and coloured chalks; in fact everything that she, or anyone else for that matter, could want.

Lewis stared at her. He desperately wanted her to kiss him with her former passion, but he knew from Dr Mellon that for some reason this would not yet be possible. Women went off that kind of thing after miscarriages, the doctor had said. Lewis had to bide his time. It was just a fact. You could not argue with it. He turned away. He had to wait. Or did he? The thought occurred and would not go away—perhaps Micklethwaite could oblige him with someone, fix him up with someone discreet just for the interim, just until his wife, his darling Trilby, was better.

PART TWO

The way that lovers use is this;
They bow, catch hands, with never a word,
And their lips meet, and they do kiss,
—So I have heard.

Rupert Brooke, *The Way That Lovers Use*

CHAPTER SIX

Piers stared at himself in the mirror. The one good thing about going to see his Aunt Laura in London was that his mirror reflected a more sophisticated image than his usual everyday appearance. Today, once the mud and the dust had been soaped off, he might even be described as vaguely pleasant-looking, he told himself, staring at his face in his shaving mirror.

Tall, fair curly hair, slim, lightly tanned, he might not be God's gift to anyone, but at least, thanks to the West Country, he had the bonny outdoor look of a man brought up on good dairy produce, home-made bread and the roast beef of Old England.

'Come on, Topsie,' he called, whistling to his black retriever bitch, who promptly climbed out of Piers's still unmade bed, stretched, and wandered downstairs after him. 'Look after Topsie, will you, Mabel?' he called through to his cowman's wife in the kitchen.

Mabel hurried into the hall, her crisply aproned body presenting a reassuring sight as she walked through the old, worn, green-painted door.

'You going on, are you, Mr Piers? Well then, on you go, and enjoy yourself in London, and that.'

Piers touched the top of his dog's head. 'And you look after Mabel, Tops, and don't do anything that I would not do, at least not while I am in London.'

'You take care of yourself in London, Mr Piers. You know what them's like up there, take the skin off of your back, they will, in London. Take the skin off of your back.'

Piers paused and smiled at Mabel. It was an accepted part of their relationship that neither of them questioned Mabel's profound knowledge of London, although neither Mabel nor Harold had ever been there, not even passing through on a train, which was not that surprising since neither of them had even been on a train.

'I shall be very careful, Mabel. I always am. I keep in mind everything you tell me, believe me.'

'Well just as well, Mr Piers, just as well. Them's all thieves and robbers up there, I tell you.'

'I know. Mabel. So you keep saying, and so you have said for the past week or so.'

'And it bears repeating, like onion, Mr Piers. It bears repeating. That London's full of thieves and robbers, and worse. Them could be out for you, seeing you are a Montague. Them's got folk there that can have their knives in high-ups like you. And worse.'

Piers could never imagine what might be 'worse' when Mabel was in this kind of mood. This morning, probably because for once he was not in a hurry, he asked her. 'I say, Mabel, what is worse?'

'I beg your pardon, Mr Piers?'

'I was just wondering what could be worse than thieves and robbers and people with their knives out?'

Mabel looked at him balefully. There was no other word for it. Whenever Mabel regarded Piers balefully she reminded him of Eva, the worst-tempered of his cows.

'What is worse, Mr Piers, is fancy women.' Mabel turned away. 'Because they don't just take your money, they take your brains too, specially like when they know you are a Montague!'

208

Piers laughed and picked up his suitcase. 'Much chance I have of meeting a fancy woman in my Aunt Laura's house, Mabel. About as much chance as I have of winning the Derby with Lullabelle.'

'That Lullabelle, she's got to you has that cow. Never known anything like it.'

Mabel went back to the kitchen and Piers picked up his suitcase and wandered off past the empty stables, past the fields where his two hunters were turned out, and towards the old hay barn where his sports car was housed, realising with a feeling of almost shocking delight that it was probably going to be sunny enough to have the roof down for his long drive to London.

He glanced down at his grandfather's old wristwatch, working out that it would probably take him six or seven hours to reach London from Somerset, with a good stop for lunch. He hoped that Harold had remembered to start the car up for him every week, and to charge her battery, for it had been months since he had been able to afford the time to leave the farm for more than a few hours, such were the demands of farming life.

'Come on, old girl.' He patted the MG's dark green shining body. 'Time to go for a spin, eh?'

The car must have heard him for without too much ado she started up and Piers, having let her have a few joyous revs, rather like the way he allowed his hunter to give a few joyous, good-natured bucks of a morning, backed her out of the hay barn, avoiding the chickens that were wandering about outside its tall, wooden doors.

' 'Bye, Mr Piers.' Harold came up to the car window, his face as always a picture of misery when Piers left for his annual trip to see his Aunt Laura

209

in London.

'You take care of yourself, Mr Piers. You know how it is in London, it's full of no goods, and young women with mischief on their minds.'

'So Mabel has just reminded me, Harold. Very kind of you to do the same.'

'Well.' Harold stood back from the car, scratching at his sparse hair under his cap. 'Well, that is how it is, Mr Piers. It's full of no goods is a city like London, and we want you to come back to Somerset in one piece, that's what we want.'

'I shall do my best, Harold.' Piers smiled up at him from the MG.

'You do that.' Harold took off his cap, and waved it. 'You come back safe to us, Mr Piers.'

Piers watched him in his mirror as he manoeuvred his way slowly down the potholed drive.

The country lanes were frequently potholed and so, even after he had left his own short drive, Piers felt a great deal of the rough road surface through his car seat as he drove towards Bath and so to London, but no-one needed to tell him that summer was on its way, for not only was the blossom well over, and the primroses in the hedgerows jostling with bluebells, but the fresh sap green of the trees seemed, like the dawn chorus of the morning, to have suddenly burst upon him. The whole suggestion of summer's long-awaited glories that emanated from the countryside around him was entirely divorced from his usual perceptions of nature, and it seemed to him that he might well have just come back from abroad, so different did the world of a sudden appear to a young man temporarily freed from his responsibilities.

Indeed the weather, usually a matter for anguished debate between himself and Harold, had now become, like so much when a normal day has turned to holiday, a delight, and he found that he no longer cared whether or not it was about to turn, or whether it would mean feast or famine for the farm by autumn, only that it was *there*. The sun was shining and for once he was part of everything: the sun, the sky, the verdant, the celadon, the cyprus and the bice; he was part of every shade of every little glorious and varied green inch of the day.

'La donna è mobile!' he sang as he put his foot down on the accelerator. 'Blah blah blab blahbity, la dee dee dee-ee, blah blab blah blah-ah . . .'

He would stop for lunch on the way, and make sure that it was a decent one at that, no undressed lettuce leaves, no tomatoes with a sunken look accompanying a piece of fatty ham.

*   *   *

The sign outside declared it to be a pub, but inside it was indeed what it proclaimed itself to be, the Cricketers Inn, and it was full of the reassuring Englishness that a countryman travelling from his own safe environs to an inviting lunch wishes for himself.

First of all it had an old brass handle on the half-glassed door, then it had a step or two down, and no unobliging receptionist, but just a flagged stone floor which led to a large square hall that boasted a grandfather clock and a large glass cupboard full of cricketing trophies, not to mention photographs of pre-war teams, and mementoes from old matches.

Piers turned away from this welcoming sight to follow signs to a low-ceilinged bar hung about with fishing trophies, always such a reassurance to a country sportsman. And then, after a good pint of much needed beer, to the dining room where stiff white tablecloths and napkins were not the only signs of the good table kept by Mine Host; there was also a covered sideboard displaying fruit and cheeses, cream crackers and bottles of every kind.

As he sat down Piers smiled at the sunlight, the bright displays, the waiters, but most of all at the thought that he was in safe hands—and that was before he tasted the roast lamb, the home-made mint sauce, or the lemon meringue pie.

Some few hours later found him parking outside his aunt's house in Trevor Square. Indulging in this newest and most carefree of moods Piers left the MG's hood down, and strolled up to Aunt Laura's front door, carrying his hat and suitcase and smiling for no really good reason that he could think of at that moment.

'Maria!'

'Master Piers!'

He and his aunt's maid always greeted each other as if each had not seen the other for a year and a day. It was a pleasant sort of ritual. Piers then handed her his hat and suitcase. Maria took his hat and hung it reverentially in the downstairs cloakroom, but left the suitcase for the undermaid whom his aunt also employed, for Aunt Laura still liked to think that she, and perhaps she alone, kept up pre-war standards.

'Piers.'

'Aunt Laura.'

Because he knew she liked it, Piers bent over her

hand, in the manner of a foreign diplomat, nearly kissing it, and then kissed her cheek.

'Piers, may I introduce Mrs Lola de Ribes? She is an interior decorator. She is helping me with the drawing room. She is very talented. I may say, in my opinion she has the *eye*, you know?'

Inwardly Piers sighed. He knew that Aunt Laura never did let a week go by without selling a picture or buying a new one, buying some new Meissen or selling some old silver, repainting or refurbishing a room. He knew that it was her way of keeping busy, and of course it was innocent enough, but today he suspected more. He suspected that she had intentions, and said so, as he shook Lola de Ribes's hand.

'You are not here for nothing, you are here to exert undue influence on me, are you not, Mrs de Ribes? I know before the hour is out Aunt Laura is going to strongarm me into using your services, isn't she?'

Lola de Ribes smiled. 'I only decorate for friends, you know,' she announced.

'Lola has just had me made the most perfect curtains for my bedroom . . .'

But Piers was not interested in the perfection of Aunt Laura's bedroom curtains. Despite his satisfying lunch at the Cricketers Inn, he found that all he could think of, all he could look forward to, was Maria's cooking. He hoped that she was going to serve them her famous fish pie of prawns, hard boiled eggs and white fish in a glistening parsley and lemon sauce, and the softest topping of pureed potato mixed with a light cheese. Frankly, he was now so hungry it did not bear thinking about.

After a polite interval, he left the two women

and went to his room to bathe, rest and refresh before changing into the required post-war black dinner jacket, and bow tie, despite the fact that they were dining alone.

*　　*　　*

Later, Aunt Laura smiled down the dinner table at him. 'You were quite right, I did ask Lola de Ribes here for a reason, well, several reasons, really. And one of them is that I do think that you need help at the farm, I mean not with the farming,' she added quickly, 'but with the interior. You need to be made more comfy, with squashy sofas, and nice colours. You've done nothing with it since I handed it over to you, you know. And really it would be nice if you did, because apart from anything else you could ask your crusty old aunt down to stay for a few days and be sure to make her comfortable.'

Piers smiled ruefully. 'I haven't really had the time, what with the farm and everything.'

'Of course you haven't really had the time. How could a farmer like you have time for such things as interiors? But it would make a difference if you could have someone who would do it for you. Most especially important to be comfortable in winter, d'you see? If you came into a cosy house what a difference it would make. Lola really *could* help you there. She's very good at advising, and only does it for friends.'

'Of course. Have you ever met an interior decorator who did it for money?'

'Oh, touché, quite so,' Laura agreed. 'This will amuse you, then! Lola told me that there are so many divorced women who have taken to interior

214

decorating to earn a dollar or two in New York that a divorcée is now referred to as an "interior decorator". It seems rather than announce you are divorcing nowadays you say, "We are in the middle of redecorating."' They both laughed. 'Have you anything planned, do you think, for your week in London?'

Piers shook his head. 'Nothing that I can think of, just seeing you, and so on. Would you rather I had?'

His aunt smiled. This was typical of Piers. Always ready to accommodate someone else, no matter what. In that respect he was what one read about and hardly ever came across, the perfect gentleman.

'It is funny, isn't it?' She paused. 'Coming to London to relax!'

'I know, but you know farming, up at four thirty, bed at nine, what time is there to enjoy yourself?'

'I know. And one does need more than a game of cards on a Saturday night.'

Piers looked thoughtful. He enjoyed the company of his farming neighbours, games of nap on a Saturday night, but the truth was that despite his active life he was lonely, and sometimes, worse than that, he knew it.

'Tomorrow morning I am going round to see a young friend of mine. Well, she's not a friend of mine, she's a friend of Lola de Ribes. She's had a bit of a bad time of it lately, some kind of mental breakdown, and the doctor has ordered painting as a way of getting better. We met at a party at the de Ribes' house, and apparently, for some ridiculous reason, she took it into her head that she wanted to paint me. She used to be a cartoonist, something

215

like that, but that's gone, with this nervous breakdown, apparently, so now she has started to paint portraits, just for friends of course, nothing else.'

On hearing this Piers could not prevent his heart from sinking. There was nothing, frankly, that he wanted less than to accompany his aunt to the studio of some loopy artist who had suffered a nervous breakdown. Tomorrow morning sounded as if it was going to be about as exciting as having his hunter standing on his foot on a numbingly cold frosty morning.

'I don't know why this young lady should want to paint me, I am sure I don't.'

'I do. Because you are a beautiful woman, that is why.'

His aunt blushed, although not so heartily as another woman of her age might have blushed, because the truth was that she was beautiful and she knew it. She had lovely long white hair that she wore in a stylish French plait, a pink and white Dresden china skin, blue-grey eyes and a perfect profile, which she herself always pronounced *profeel*.

She had not only kept her figure, she had never lost it, even temporarily, so that she was still wearing some of the same classic evening clothes that she had worn on her honeymoon in India some—heaven only knew how many—years before. Although she was now a widow, and had no children, she was never lonely, having a plentiful supply of friends who liked to come and stay and be cosseted by her. Generally speaking she spent her life in London enjoying herself in a fashion that someone a great deal younger might find tiring.

216

Tonight, however, by tacit consent, they both retired to bed early, neither wanting to keep the other up too late. Besides, as Aunt Laura explained to Piers, she had been to a dance the night before, had not returned until the early hours, and now felt she ought to catch up on her beauty sleep.

Breakfast the next morning was so perfectly served and held so many culinary delights that Piers found himself accompanying his aunt to her young friend's studio with less dread than he would have expected. Perhaps the fresh look to London on a warm spring day with the ladies all wearing some form or another of smart grey suiting lifted his spirits, or perhaps it was just that London after so many, many months away had a foreign look, and the people the same, so different were they from those that he normally passed in Somerset.

'Ah, here we are.' Aunt Laura leaned forward and knocked on the taxi window with the curved ivory handle of her silk umbrella. 'Cabbie! We are here,' she trilled. 'Just there.' The umbrella pointed vaguely towards a side entrance approached by a small flight of steps. 'You may get out before me, Piers, and hand me out.'

Piers did so, and so it was that, with all the grace of a young woman who had never wanted for a dancing partner in her life, Aunt Laura alighted from the taxi, and stood while Piers paid it off.

It was a pleasant custom between them that Piers paid for everything, and a few weeks later Aunt Laura sent him a cheque for 'something needed on the farm'. Needless to say the cheque was always for the precise amount that Piers had spent on them both during his London visit, never less and never more. Of course Piers always wrote and thanked Aunt Laura, protesting that she was 'far too generous', and so the little charade ended. It did however have its charm, for it meant that Aunt Laura was made to feel feminine by her much younger nephew, and Piers was prevented from feeling patronised.

Aunt Laura stared up at the house. 'Yes, yes, this is it.' She smiled excitedly and the tone of her voice was almost girlish. 'Such an excitement I always think, going to a painter's studio, lovely smells of oil paint and canvases stacked against walls, coffee and drinks at all hours. If I had remarried I should have loved to have married a painter, except I hear tell that they are always running off with their models, so perhaps I should not have liked it at all!'

She climbed up the steps towards the smartly painted plum-coloured door and knocked on it with the black-painted doorknocker. For a few seconds they both found themselves staring at that door knocker. It was a strange confection for such a serviceable object, a smiling dolphin, obviously hand made and something of an *objet d'art*, as Aunt Laura remarked while they waited for the door to open. For some reason, too, it made both the visitors realise at once that the person inside the studio was, like the door knocker, going to be out of the ordinary. It was a curtain raiser, as it were, to whoever opened the door. Certainly, of a sudden, it sharpened Piers's awareness of the day, the street, the clear springtime light, and long before the door opened and their hostess stood before them, Piers found himself feeling oddly excited.

It was as if the door's opening was more than just a physical act of great ordinariness; it was as if it might be beckoning him into something

218

dangerous and exciting, something that he had not experienced before. In the split second between the door's opening and his looking up he found himself willing this to be so, and at the same time preparing himself not to be too cast down if it were not to be the case.

*   *   *

Trilby opened the door to her visitors wearing a mustard-coloured shirt and purple velvet pageboy trousers that ended halfway down her slim legs in a row of small, black silk bobbles. With this what Aunt Laura subsequently referred to as 'very outré' outfit she wore black velvet slippers, and her hair was once more cut in the elfin style that she thought suited her best.

Aunt Laura, probably because she had met Trilby before, seemed quite accepting of this slightly outrageous-looking elf. Smiling happily and calling 'Hallo, hallo,' she promptly stepped over the threshold into the small hall that led to the second door.

'This is my nephew Piers, Trilby dear, I do not think you have met.' Aunt Laura waved a vague land towards Piers who smiled, and shook Trilby's hand.

'How do you do?'

Trilby too smiled and shook the slim, slightly roughened male hand held out to her. 'Hallo. Come in, come in.'

But it was too late. Ever eager to join bohemia Aunt Laura had already pushed open the second door, and so the younger people followed her and her inimitable umbrella—a brolly that Piers always thought had a quite separate personality of its own—into the wider, instantly cooler interior of the studio.

It was such a bright early summer day that at that moment the studio's interior seemed lighter and more spring-like than anywhere else that either of the Montagues had yet been in London. The light also had the effect of making Trilby's appearance seem more outrageous and dashing than it might have done in a darker room. To Piers she seemed to have stepped out of some seventeenth-century painting, and he half expected to see her turn and rest a slim, white hand on the top of the head of a large dog, while the other hand rested on a dark oak table as in some painting by Van Dyck.

It was her very boyishness, Piers realised in an instant, that made her seem so feminine, probably because she was so slender. Almost too thin—as if she had been very ill, which perhaps she must have been if she had, as Aunt Laura had asserted suffered some kind of mental breakdown.

'I expect you would like some coffee?'

She took a tray of coffee from the top of an old oak chest of drawers, and then hurried to a small side kitchen from where she eventually emerged with a very plain French-style coffee pot, which she expertly tipped from top to bottom to allow the hot water to filter through the coffee grounds.

'You are kind to come,' she said conversationally to Aunt Laura, as she set out small Parisian-style coffee cups, poured coffee and offered sugar and milk, knowing of course, as she must, that Aunt Laura was actually quite flattered to be asked to sit to her.

'Not kind at all, love this sort of thing, always have, always will.'

Aunt Laura smiled conspiratorially from Trilby to Piers and back again. Her look, of a sudden said, 'This is our secret,' and without realising it Trilby and Piers smiled in the same way, but at each other, and Piers found that instead of wandering off in search of some new shirts, or the fountain pen that he so badly needed, he took a chair, and stayed for the rest of the morning.

His aunt Laura sat impressively still while Trilby first quickly sketched and then started to paint. Piers found himself resting, tranquilly, like some great tropical fish in a pool of sunshine by the French windows which looked out onto the back courtyard. The conversation between sitter and painter was desultory, but sporadically interesting and he listened in to them as if they were a programme on the wireless, himself feeling more relaxed than he had for years.

After a few hours Trilby, to no-one's surprise, refused to let them leave, but instead made them all a light lunch of salad Niçoise, hot French bread and, eventually, a perfectly ripe French cheese followed by large, sweet white grapes.

As soon as he saw her choice of food Piers knew exactly what sort of person Aunt Laura was sitting to. He had always, quite privately, maintained that you could tell everything about women from the kind of food they liked. Whatever their choices on a menu Piers always knew at once exactly the kind of person they were. Now it seemed to him that Trilby was as exciting as her clothes.

* * *

In the days that followed so swiftly, one after the other, as if they were cards being played far too quickly on a table that was his holiday, Piers found that it became more and more difficult, indeed impossible, to keep away from Trilby's small studio. Instead of inventing some excuse to accompany Aunt Laura, he merely went along with her, as if it was part of their accepted routine, and perhaps as a consequence of this Aunt Laura accepted it as such, and neither his aunt nor Trilby seemed to expect him not to accompany her for her daily sittings.

Of course Trilby would not let them see the work in progress, because, she joked, if she did, neither of them would ever come back, least of all, in all probability, Aunt Laura. Her sitter, who had been painted many times before, expressed no interest in how she was being depicted in the painting, but plenty of interest in the painter.

'She married this Lewis James man, you know the one I mean? The one with all the newspapers? And not long after it seems she had this nervous breakdown, which was very painful to all concerned, because mental illness is always taken so badly by families. I mean, her family have not come near her since, I heard from Lola de Ribes. Of course they feel she is just indulging herself in this depression thing, which must be very painful for her. After all, the poor little girl, she has surely enough to contend with without feeling that she has let them down in some terrible way. Lola says that all Agnes, her stepmother, keeps saying is "It's not hereditary", which really does not help. Anyway, the painting, and the studio, it's all part of what the doctors have ordered, to keep her mind off her sadness, and I really rather agree with it myself. Although why she should wish to paint old ladies like me, heaven only knows, and only heaven! But there you are, if it makes her feel better we must go along with it, wouldn't you say?'

Piers could only agree. He found himself, day after day, not going to a film or theatre matinee as had been his wont when he was in London, no shopping for much needed luxuries never found in the wilds of Somerset, but waiting with mounting impatience for the taxi to arrive, for Aunt Laura to climb in ahead of him; always waiting, it seemed to him, for that moment, which sometimes seemed to him to take more than a million minutes, when the door would open to the dolphin's knock, and Trilby would be standing there.

Every day that she opened the door, to his secret delight, she appeared before them in yet another outrageous outfit, her strange elusive personality somehow always evading him, disappearing at moments when he expected it to appear, and reappearing again from nowhere when he quite thought it had disappeared.

'Oh, Trilby is a typical artistic type,' Aunt Laura said once or twice when they discussed her over dinner at night. 'Very defined, and yet as elusive as smoke. That is the artistic temperament, Piers dear. But how she came to marry this Lewis James man the Lord alone knows, and only He *does* know. Because it must be oil and water at home, really it must. Lewis James is not a man to cross, men like that truly never are. They cannot be what we would call soulmates.'

Lewis still came home for lunch, as he now called it, but instead of staying in his suit, as had been his habit, in an effort to please Trilby should she, as he hoped, come home for lunch he now went upstairs and changed into more informal clothes.

Every day, day after day, after day, he waited in his carefully chosen informal clothes, hoping that Trilby would appear. But despite this, to him, great concession to her youth, day after day, after day, she did not come home for lunch with him, but chose to stay, as he thought alone, in her studio.

He could see that Paine, his butler, and the maids, in fact his whole staff, thought that he had taken leave of his senses, as week after week he insisted that they lay a place opposite him for Trilby, that they cook a three-course lunch for two, only to find that they had no-one to serve, and half the food had to be set aside to feed whoever in the kitchen quarters did not mind its being reheated.

Sometimes he imagined Trilby sitting opposite him, and looked up from his first or second course to smile at her. Sometimes he hoped that he heard her footfall on the polished floor outside the dining room and the door opening to reveal her smiling mischievously, but when he turned it would always be Paine or one of the maids coming in, never Trilby.

Dinner was different, of course. At dinner she would join him, looking, day by day, increasingly happier and healthier, and artlessly confiding in him news from her studio, news of people who were sitting to her, news of everything that she must realise that he knew nothing about, and quite frankly, had less interest in. Compared to his world hers was such a little place, with no great decisions, no powerful people, nothing but ordinariness, an ordinariness which, for some reason he could not understand, fascinated Trilby.

That was what, among many things, Lewis found so difficult.

But he found that his irritation at her preoccupation with light, or some other nonsense, was nothing compared to his growing frustration at not knowing where she was at any time of the day. He had to accept that from the moment she left the house and stepped into either her Morris or his Rolls-Royce, he knew nothing of what she was doing. He had to trust her not to be doing anything he might not want, and although he knew he *must* do so, on Dr Mellon's orders, it was still an agony for him.

Worse, he felt a growing resentment that she should *want* to be away painting some old woman here, someone's child there, when she could be waiting at home for *him*. Waiting for him where *he* wanted her. At home. In his house. It was intolerable, and yet the proof of the efficacy of Dr Melton's prescription for Trilby's mental recovery was that, gradually, bit by bit, she was beginning to look as she had when he had first married her, and he had imagined that they were happy.

Although she still would not kiss him on the lips.

She smiled, she laughed, she entertained him, she looked beautiful, but her pretty lips, at times pink, at others red with freshly applied lipstick, would not meet his—any more than any other part of her seemed willing to do.

But Lewis was very much a man. He needed a

225

woman, regularly. Married though he was he had already started to take other women, but for no reason that he could name, other women, however beautiful, now seemed of a sudden boring and dull compared to Trilby, perhaps because they represented no challenge to him. He had liked to make love to Trilby, and he had made love to her, in every way, and he had got her pregnant, full of his baby, something he certainly could not do to another woman, however willing. He wanted to make Trilby pregnant again, but not if it meant her returning to her former, terrible state. He did not want to have to hire nurses again, go through all that humiliation, everyone, including the servants, knowing that his young wife, despite everything that he had given her, and continued to give her, was quite out of control, a semi-lunatic, a mental case.

So he had to wait. And it was that waiting, symbolised by the waiting for her to return at lunch, that ate into him, made him feel morose and sorry for himself, emotions to which he was not at all accustomed.

And, too, his inability to control his life in this small area now seemed to him to be spilling over into every aspect of his life, so that each time he summoned Micklethwaite, or some other minion, to his presence, it seemed to Lewis that he could see mockery in their eyes, and that everything they said to him had some other meaning.

They might say 'Yes, sir' or they might say 'Of course, Mr James' but nowadays it seemed to Lewis that they did not mean it. They meant it about as much as Trilby meant to come home for lunch. Or perhaps as much as she meant, ever, to let Lewis touch her again.

He longed to say that one word 'When?' but he could not. He longed to feel her body against his again, to hear her sigh and whisper as he made love to her, or watch her run off to the bathroom, her slim figure disappearing as soon as he had finished with her, and perhaps it was this very longing that led him to make new plans to re-establish himself in her life.

Following on a particularly intense feeling of hopelessness, he began to call for her, every now and then, at her studio, telling himself all the time that he was not reverting to his old pattern, but making sure that she was all right. That was all; he just wanted to know that she was all right. After all, she had been very ill. She was, most likely, not quite better yet. He would just call, unexpectedly, not suspiciously, of course not, just as a surprise, just every now and then, without warning. She would probably be grateful. She would probably be quite happy that he was still taking an interest.

What he soon realised was that she would never let him actually go in no matter how unexpected his arrival. She would never let him inside. It was always, 'Oh Lewis, there you are. Just wait, would you?'

And then the door would close and Lewis would stand looking and feeling embarrassed, half smiling down at his chauffeur standing by the car, sometimes shrugging his shoulders at him as if to say, 'Well, you know women!' Until, eventually, Trilby would reappear wearing her coat, firmly shutting the outer door behind her and pocketing the key.

But calling for her every now and then soon

turned into offering to drop her off at the studio in the morning, and then ringing her once or twice during the day, just to make sure that she was all right, until finally she said, putting a friendly hand on his arm, 'Lewis, I am at the *studio* all day. I don't go anywhere else. Except to the shops to buy coffee or something for lunch. You really must stop telephoning. I mean if I trust you are at the office, you must trust that I am painting at the studio, otherwise there is no point in being married.'

'That is just it—' Lewis began, the *When?* once more raising its unhappy question mark in his mind, but then he stopped. 'That is just it. I am married to you, so every now and then I like to hear your voice,' he ended, quietly.

'I understand.' Trilby put her hand over his and he kissed it quickly, and in return she touched the top of his head lightly, looking for a second just the way Piers had seen her that first morning.

That lightest of touches was fatal, of course, for it once more gave Lewis hope. It took only those few seconds and he was once again alight with the hope that Trilby would come back to him, be with him in the same way that she had been with him before, never realising that it would never be possible, that now—fatally—she felt sorry for him.

He did not know either that she could not bring herself to tell him that with her unexpected discovery of those carefully wrapped boxes in the cupboards of his bedroom all memories of any happiness they had enjoyed together had quite disappeared, as if they had been chalked on a board and were now wiped off, leaving no trace whatsoever.

Nor could she tell him that she had fallen in love

with Piers Montague.

*   *   *

Of course Trilby had not meant to fall in love, very few people do. They might have some vague idea when they wake up in the morning that today could be different, or that they might meet someone who will change their lives for ever, but generally speaking most people just get up and get on with their day. Trilby knew this, because that was what had happened to her. The day that she had met Piers for the first time, she had just got up as usual, dressed herself—poor Mrs Woo having long ago left for a more conventional post—and insisted on driving herself to the studio, saying, jokingly, 'Lewis, if you don't let me use the Morris, it really is going to rust up, you know! And what is more, if I keep being driven everywhere I will forget how to drive it at all.'

Lewis had looked humble at this, and laughed lightly, but the next day he still offered to give her a lift, as if he had quite forgotten what she had said, and Trilby, because for some reason she could not quite yet name she felt guilty at always refusing to go with him for at least part of his journey, gave in and climbed into the car beside him, realising as she did so, her heart sinking with the knowledge that Lewis would never change. Very soon, it would not just be the occasional lift to and from the studio, or telephone calls from the office during her painting hours, but demands to meet him somewhere at lunchtime, or orders to return home quickly because he had invited sixteen people to dinner and he needed her to be there in good time.

But worse than the realisation that Lewis would never change was the acceptance of the fact that from the moment that she had met Piers, even sitting beside Lewis was torture. It was trying to keep her eyes from sparkling, trying to keep her body from tensing with excitement at the notion that she might be going to see Laura Montague's nephew again, that made it so difficult for Trilby to sit beside her husband. Lewis was no fool. No man who employs hundreds of people can afford to be. He would, Trilby knew, notice the slightest change in her, particularly for the better. After all, and this was something they both knew, he wanted to be back in her bedroom. Any sign of returning health would be acted upon immediately.

The truth was that Piers was more than a shock to Trilby, more than a total surprise, he was a tidal sweep coming towards her, at a time when she could least do with it. She never wanted to even think that she was in love, ever again. She never wanted to be surprised by love again. Indeed in the last grim weeks she had imagined that she never, ever wanted to love again.

But that had changed the moment she met Piers. As soon as she shook his hand she knew at once that the emotions she felt were as unlike those she had felt for Lewis as was perfectly possible.

These new emotions were not a ladder down which she could thankfully escape from her father's sad, accepting misery and her stepmother's viperish ways. No, Piers, she realised to her astonishment, as he stood smiling diffidently down at her, was not a way out, but a ladder up to somewhere, up to some heaven that she had not yet enjoyed, to some paradise, some arcadia that she had never yet glimpsed.

Happily, since she was nevertheless determined to avoid what was happening to her, Trilby had Laura Montague and her portrait on which to concentrate. Unhappily, though, it was simply not possible to avoid the realisation that Piers too must be aware of the thunder clouds gathering, the lightning threatening, since rather than leave his aunt alone with Trilby in her studio he did not just accompany her of a morning, he stayed with them all day.

And he did not just stay to do nothing but read the newspaper and talk, he stayed to become part of their morning, going willingly to make coffee for them all, or to buy lunch. And he bought the kind of lunch that he did not just arrange on a plate, but cooked himself, telling her gaily that being a bachelor he had been forced to learn to cook as well as he liked to eat.

Meanwhile Aunt Laura, as the old so enjoy doing, sat and watched, and realising just what was unfolding around her she mentally smiled and shrugged her shoulders, because that is all an older person can do. They can smile, and watch, but there is nothing they can do about what is going on around them except perhaps sigh a little, and sometimes enjoy what is happening, while all the time hoping that the outcome will not be as cataclysmic as common sense suggests that it must be.

By the time the end of that first week arrived, London was just beginning to look a little tired, with too many pieces of paper flitting about the streets, and too many people walking too slowly and too aimlessly. Piers was due to leave for the country that morning, but having said farewell to his aunt in Trevor Square he did not head for Somerset, as Aunt Laura guessed he would not.

They both knew that he would drive straight to Trilby's studio.

* * *

'I am leaving for the country, but I had to see you before I left.'

Piers was still tall, and still tanned, but looking across at Trilby he felt quite the opposite. Worse than that, he felt as if he was not just pale and insignificant in every way, but perhaps actually ill. He felt trammelled by what to him now seemed like the endless mornings and afternoons of that week when he had stood where he was now standing and not said anything to her, just looked at her, longed for her, and yet said nothing. And now, when he was leaving, he had to say something, but the truth was that he did not know how, because the simple fact was that Trilby was a married woman. Trilby was forbidden ground, a person who had made a union that no man could put asunder.

Finally she made the running, saying quietly, 'It's all right, Piers, I do actually know why you are here!'

As soon as she finished speaking they were in each other's arms, and they were making love as Trilby had never yet made love, so that she was nowhere near earth but transported to some other world, and neither of them said 'We shouldn't, we mustn't'.

After all, they had held back for seven long days, and seven days for lovers is for ever.

CHAPTER SEVEN

'What are we going to do?'

It was the eternal lovers' question and it was Piers who asked it, as Trilby sat and stared at him out of large, panda eyes.

'Nothing. We can't do anything. I am married, and you, thank God, live in the country, in Somerset, far away from everything, most of all me.'

'I can't leave you, not now.'

'You will have to,' Trilby told him calmly. 'You will have to leave me, you know very well you will. You're a farmer, and I am married.'

'I could stay another week. I can telephone to Harold, my cowman, he will hold the fort until I go back.'

Trilby shook her head and jumped to her feet and walked down the room, talking as she went. 'Look, you have to understand, Piers. I am married to Lewis James. There is not a hope in hell that he will give me up. He is just not that kind of person. In fact he will kill me if he even suspects what I have just done, I promise you.'

'That would be a bad thing to do,' Piers said, flippantly, and then as Trilby looked hurt he added, 'because it means that I would be in mourning for the rest of my life.'

'Don't fool yourself. I am not just any married woman, Piers. I am a very, very, very married woman. I am married to Lewis James. He can do anything. Not just because he is rich either, but because he owns—what does he call it—oh yes, he possesses *the most powerful weapon on earth: newspapers.* He chews up politicians for dinner, and lunch, and sometimes if he is bored for tea too. He is not a king, he is an emperor. I'm afraid we're quite up a gum tree without a paddle!'

They both started to laugh at her ridiculously mixed metaphor, and as soon as they did they started to kiss and kissing led to more love, which was interrupted by the telephone ringing.

'My God.' Trilby stared at the telephone, instantly losing colour, as if the instrument was a person.

'It's him, isn't it? It's your husband?' Piers said, lowering his voice for no reason that he could understand.

Trilby nodded silently, and then, clearing her throat several times, and switching on the wireless as she passed it, she went to the old-fashioned telephone and picked it up, humming artlessly to the music playing on the radio as she did so.

'Hallo. Lewis. Darling. Sorry, yes, I'll just turn down the wireless, if you could just hold on for a minute.'

Piers gazed silently at Trilby as she acted out her telephone call to Lewis, and when she replaced the receiver he stared at it for a few seconds after she had carefully put it back on its cradle. 'I really hope that you never have cause to deceive me, Trilby,' he murmured, and as Trilby turned and looked at him he went on, by way of explanation, 'you're far too good at it.'

Trilby nodded in agreement and sighed. It was true. She was good at deceiving people. It was living with Agnes. She had learned to lie at an early age, out of fear, and to get out of being punished, which was ridiculous because Agnes always punished her anyway. She had also learned not just to deceive but to act.

She had learned to act gratitude, and say, 'No, of course not, I would love to go to the Victoria and Albert Museum,' when she had already been that morning. She had learned to smile and say 'That was delicious' when it was quite the opposite, and to wear clothes that she loathed and pretend that they made her feel pretty when in fact they made her itch and feel frumpy. She had learned to behave as though she did not miss having a dog, that she thought the vicar's sermon was brilliant, and to eat up pork fat which made her feel sick, because to do otherwise meant that Agnes punished her.

'You must go,' she told Piers. 'Really. I know Lewis. He will suspect something, and soon. He suspects me anyway, I mean he always has. He has always been violently possessive, but now—well, now he really does have something to be suspicious about.' She looked sombre. 'I hate to think what he will do.'

'Aren't you being a bit melodramatic?'

'No,' Trilby said flatly, and the look in her eyes was so opaque as she said it that Piers found that he believed her. Despite the heat of the studio, the warmth of the day, and their lovemaking, he felt, of a sudden, lowered and sad.

'You don't know what he's like.'

'Tell me.'

Trilby shook her head. 'I couldn't, really, I couldn't.' Again she stared past him. 'We must say goodbye.'

'I can't. I just can't,' Piers said simply, and

clearly, because it was the truth.

'You must.' Trilby did not add any passion to those two words. It was not the moment to be passionate, and they both knew it. 'And what is more you must go now.'

She reached up to kiss him briefly on the lips, realising at once that his lips were as cold as hers. They had both become chilled standing still, agonising in the darkening studio.

'It's not your fault, Piers. It's my fault. I am sorry. I led you on. We should never have made love as we have done, but we have, and no more to be said about it.'

'Don't say that.'

'What else is there to say?'

'Of course we should never have made love, but now that we have there is no going back, you know that. I know that.'

Trilby smiled. 'Of course. But whoever knows it, either one or the other, must also know that you must go, and now. And I mean now.' She glanced at her watch. 'Please. Lewis has a habit of suddenly coming back when you least expect him. And what with Mrs Montague not being here, and you *being* here, believe me, it will not be nice if he finds you alone with me. He has suspected me before, in the past.'

'How do you mean, in the past? Have there been others, I mean besides me, other men, here, with you?'

Trilby shook her head, looking suddenly cross and impatient at the very idea. 'No, no of course not. Now, please go. Please. You just don't know what he's like.'

'When shall I see you again?'

'I don't know. Now please, just go.'

No matter how fast he drove the endless miles down to Somerset, those words of Trilby's echoed around Piers' head. *You just don't know what he's like.* They were ordinary, everyday grim words at the best of times, but when you had just fallen in love with someone they held a million implications, implications that made him wonder at just how courageous Trilby was being. Made him wonder, over and over again, what Lewis James was really like.

*   *   *

A little later, after Piers had driven off, Trilby drove herself back to the house in her Morris Minor. During the short journey, she concentrated hard on pretending to herself that none of what had just happened had actually occurred. She indoctrinated herself. She interrogated herself. She forced herself to believe her own lies.

She had not made love with someone not her husband. She had not deceived anyone. Piers was not her lover. He was just an occurrence. And what was more Piers was no longer part of her life, and would never now be so.

She had to make herself believe everything that she now told herself for many reasons, but most of all because she knew that if she did not, Lewis, attuned as he was to the slightest difference in her behaviour, would guess. Trilby thought she was brave, she imagined that she was brave, until she thought of what Lewis might do to her if he ever discovered that she had just committed adultery.

It was such a large word somehow. Adultery. It

bit into the mind with all the unrelenting, narrow cruelty of the Inquisition. It had none of the soft, sly sensuousness of a word like 'deception' or the gaiety of a word such as 'affair', it was a stark, unforgiving word with dark implications. A woman taken in adultery was a slut, a betrayer, a thief of purity.

She told herself all this as she drove back to Lewis's house with its great grand glass-canopied entrance. She told herself that she could, only an hour or two before, have been taken in adultery, that she had taken a risk beyond any imagining in allowing Piers to make love to her. A risk so great that it now seemed almost unbelievable.

As she drove slowly back to her marital home she reminded herself that she had just sinned against her marriage, against Lewis, against her upbringing, against everything that she should have held dear, if she had the remotest morality or loyalty to anyone or anything. But the real truth was that by the time she was parking the Morris in its mews garage behind the house, the repetition of these self-accusations had done no real good at all. Rather, they had served only to enhance her memories of the short period of joy she had just experienced, making it glow all the brighter, making what had passed between her and Lewis seem worse, and the secret that she nurtured about his past a thousand times more awful, and the very thought of his making love to her again a million times more degrading.

'Your parents are coming to dinner tonight, remember?'

In the excitement of the past week Trilby had quite forgotten that she even had parents. And now that she was reminded they seemed strangely distant from her present predicament, nothing to do with her real life, something out of some previous fiction, like a story that she had once read and easily forgotten.

Indeed, since meeting Piers, if she had thought of her father and stepmother at all, it had been in the same way that she had thought of Lewis: as tall, remote figures that cast great shadows over where she had once stood through force of a whole set of circumstances that she could now only vaguely remember.

Once Piers had come into her life, stepping over the threshold into her studio, smiling, handsome, diffident, of a sudden it seemed to Trilby that she had stepped out from under the shadow of those great dark silhouettes, of father, stepmother and husband, into a paradise of warmth and sunshine.

'Goodness, I *had* forgotten! Yes, of course, my parents are coming to dinner. How ridiculous to forget. Quite silly. Sorry, Lewis.' Trilby turned on the second step of the great oak staircase and smiled absently down at Lewis. She was acting for all she was worth, acting vague, and also just a little strange, so that he would not follow her upstairs and try to make love to her, which every evening and every morning during the previous weeks she had dreaded that he might—but never more than this evening.

If Lewis followed her up the stairs and tried to make love to her he would be sure to guess that she had already enjoyed another man, if not at once, then soon, because she feared that she would be unable to conceal from him how repulsive she now found him, and from that inability might follow a confession.

Of a sudden she saw herself perhaps sobbing, perhaps white-faced and begging forgiveness, certainly, in the heat of the moment, unable to keep her deception from him.

The Woman Taken In Adultery. There must have been a thousand paintings on the subject, or at any rate hundreds, and yet as she smiled distantly back down at her husband Trilby could not remember one, certainly not one that accurately conveyed the dryness of tongue, the beating heart, the slight sweat to the palm that she was feeling at that moment.

'Darling.'

She could not have been acting vague and strange enough, because Lewis, she was horrified to see, not yet changed for dinner into his customary evening jacket, now came to the bottom step and held up his hand to her. He was looking, as he always did, tall, tanned, immaculate, and handsome, and yet Trilby could not have felt more repelled by him.

'Yes, Lewis?' She managed to smile down at him, acting out the affectionate if still slightly mad wife.

'Trilby.' He began again. 'Darling, I wonder if I might come and see you now, you know?'

If Trilby could have sat down at that moment and put her head in her hands and sobbed with fear, she would have done.

'It might be all right, Lewis. Yes.'

She saw hope in his eyes as he stepped closer to her, and she could hear him breathing a little faster, perhaps preparing himself for the excitement he imagined was about to be his, because after all, although he was much older than her, Lewis was fit and well.

'Oh good, darling, I do so love to come and see you.'

Trilby had always wanted to tell Lewis that she hated the way that he always said 'Can I come and see you?' before making love, but never more than now. 'Can I come and see you?' was so arch somehow, and at the same time negative, reducing making love to the banality of a dull social visit, taking away every kind of spontaneity, pushing the kind of passionate encounter that she had just enjoyed into the realms of unreality. Suddenly it was as if she had never known Piers, never met him, because there was Lewis, still wanting to see her, and there was she still standing on the second step of his great, grand oak staircase, looking down at him, her husband, still his wife.

'Yes, do come up.' She smiled and he started to follow her up to her suite of rooms, until she reached the doorway when she turned and said, 'Except I have just remembered I, er, have . . . you know. Goodness, I am getting vague, aren't I?' As Lewis stared at her, at first not quite understanding, Trilby went on in a rush, 'Goodness, I am sorry, Lewis. How silly, I should have remembered. It must be painting, makes me so preoccupied, I hardly know the time of day, let alone the time of the *month* nowadays.'

Lewis's forehead started to redden as he slowly took in the implication of her words, and her emphasis on the word *month*.

He hated to be thwarted at any time, and just at that moment he loathed it. But he realised at once that there was nothing to be done, and if Trilby had become a little vague in that respect then it was not to be wondered at. At least she had not turned him down, which, given the hiccup of the past weeks, he had begun to suspect might easily have happened, forcing him into a situation which could risk sending her back to take refuge in alcoholism and heaven only knew what.

'Well, if it is not to be, it is not to be.'

'Soon, Lewis.'

He nodded, turning away and going back down the wide corridor to his own rooms. 'I quite understand.' He kissed a fingertip to her, and let himself into his own suite.

As he did so Trilby thought she could almost hear him swearing, and as she turned to go into her own rooms she thought she could also hear him thinking, 'Well, well, in a few days' time, then, it will be all right. Just give her a few days, and then I will be back in her bed again!'

Trilby lay against her shut bedroom door, her mouth still dry, her pulse still beating faster, it seemed to her, than it had ever beaten in her life, and stared ahead of her.

She realised at once, given the danger just past, that she could not keep up this barrier against going back to having a husband in the fullest sense of the word for more than a few days, which meant that in a very little time Lewis would be back in her bed, visiting her every afternoon after lunch, and then again in the evenings sometimes, intent on getting her pregnant for the second time. As nausea threatened to overcome her, not at the idea of another pregnancy but at just the thought of Lewis touching her, let along making love to her, she fled to her bathroom and put her head over the basin, at the same time splashing her face with cold water.

What was she to do? Soon, and it would not be long, Lewis would once more be staring at her over lunch or dinner, and following her up the stairs, wanting her to have his babies, wanting her back in the clothes that he so liked her to wear, reducing her, daily, to being his amatory servant, never once thinking that she had a mind of her own.

As Trilby dressed she quite put out of her mind any possibility that she might not stay with Lewis any more. To even think of escape was too liberating. Besides, she might, without realising, just by imagining such an eventuality, let her eyes glow unnaturally, or she might look suddenly carefree or, worst of all, in love.

Trilby had learned many things from her relationship with her father, but most of all she had learned never to underestimate the male mind. Men had women's intuition too.

What was more, they could recognise the slightest change in the colour of someone's skin, the look in their eyes, their tone of voice. Remembering this, a lesson sometimes learned the hard way when living in her father's house, Trilby powdered her face with a pale powder, darkened her eyes a little, and left off her lipstick. After all, she had to act out what she had just implied to Lewis. Not to do so would mean certain discovery.

Having bathed and changed, and wearing a dress bought for her only recently by Lewis, Trilby descended the stairs to the hall. Paine came forward.

'You look very nice tonight, Mrs James, if you don't mind me saying so,' he murmured as he went to open the library door for her.

Trilby smiled gratefully. Paine and she had become friends the first day she had arrived for luncheon in Lewis's house, when he had advised her to keep her borrowed coat with the lining that matched her borrowed dress.

'Thank you, Paine.' Trilby listened to the sound her voice made and then, realising it did not sound quite as it should, quite as low in tone, quite as full of suffering as might be necessary, she said again, 'Thank you.'

Satisfied that she had hit a better note she walked towards her father and stepmother, her hands out in welcome.

Her stepmother inclined her head towards Trilby, as she always did, giving her stepdaughter the impression that if she could get away with not kissing her she would, but since she could not, she would give in gracelessly and allow Trilby to peck her on the cheek. Her father on the other hand gave her a quick, loving embrace, and sat down again.

'Trilby's still looking a bit peaky, isn't she, Lewis? She's still looking a bit thin and pale, to my mind.'

Lewis looked momentarily awkward. For a second it seemed that his father-in-law might hold him responsible for the whitened state of his daughter's outward demeanour.

'Only to be expected.'

'Yes, I suppose so.' Michael Smythson turned the lighted end of his cigarette towards himself, studying its fiery tip with simulated interest.

'She's much better than she was,' Lewis murmured.

But it seemed that Michael would not let the matter rest, because he continued staring at Trilby. 'I thought you would look a bit better than this by now, Trilby, really I did. You should get this husband of yours to take you away for a big change, really you should. Get him to take you somewhere exotic. After all, he can afford it, can't he!'

Trilby must have looked astonished, because her father gave a sudden grunt of laughter. It was not like her father to mention money, let alone Lewis's money, nor to shout with laughter in that sudden way. He had quite obviously drunk too many martinis before leaving Glebe Street, but, worse than that, it seemed that he did not care who knew it.

'Michael. Please.'

Agnes looked beautiful, sour, and solemn, all at the same time. Money was a very serious subject as far as Agnes was concerned, probably because, Trilby thought, she always felt that she had never had quite enough.

Michael Smythson must definitely have had too many cocktails before leaving home, or perhaps he simply did not care any more what Lewis, or Agnes, or Trilby or indeed the hovering Paine might think, because he continued inexorably, 'Yes, this husband of yours, Trilby, he can afford to take you away somewhere exotic, somewhere you can eat good food, build up a tan, put this whole pregnancy thing behind you. Because that's what you need, believe me. I know because I need it too. We both need a great big change. You need to get away from this stuffy old house, and everyone in it, and I need to get away from my stuffy old house and everyone in it too.'

To fill the astonished pause that followed this outburst, Trilby said quickly, 'Lewis has been very kind, he has bought me a studio.'

'A studio is not a holiday, Trilby.' Her father put a heavy arm across Trilby's slender shoulders, weighing her down as if determined to din into her the thought that she was in dire need of a holiday. 'You need to get away from all the bad memories of this place, get away from this dratted old husband of yours, get away from everything and everybody. Really, you do. I know I do!'

No-one knew this more than Trilby, but looking up into her father's eyes she saw a desperate despair that she had never seen before, and she knew at once that for some reason he was trying to help her escape Lewis, trying to free her from this luxurious cage in which she was now incarcerated, but most of all perhaps trying to help her escape in a way that he would like to escape Agnes.

As always, Paine came to the rescue. 'Dinner is served, madam.'

Trilby nodded her thanks to Paine, but as she stood up and walked ahead of them all in to dinner, she wondered, how did Michael *know*? Or rather what did he know? Was he aware of her misery? He could not know about Piers. Certainly Agnes could not know about Piers, not that she would care if she did. After all, if there was one virtue in Agnes's egomania it was that she was without the slightest interest in anyone except herself.

*   *   *

'That was a perfectly terrible evening.'

Lewis stared across at Trilby. Her parents had

left early, she and Lewis were alone, and he was staring at her as if she was totally responsible for the whole debacle. Agnes, beautifully dressed in a pale green strapless satin evening dress and matching coat, her swept back dark hair coiffured to within an inch of its life, had sat for most of the evening in frozen silence. Michael on the other hand had sat holding on to a bottle of wine and drinking it all by himself, before trying to do the same to the port, while either end of the table Lewis quite obviously seethed and Trilby, bit by little bit, started to work out a plan of escape. It had to be soon, it had to be now, delay was impossible. Somehow what her father had said to her about getting away, everything that he had, admittedly drunkenly, stated, had served to panic her into realising that she did have to leave Lewis, immediately.

Lewis was still grumbling vociferously. Dutifully, Trilby focused her attention on him.

'I know. I am sorry, Lewis. I have never, ever seen my father like that before. He never loses control. I don't know what has happened to him, to make him like that. He must be terribly unhappy, or have had bad news, something like that.'

'It is none of your father's *business* whether I care to take you away on holiday, or not. None of his business!'

'I know. I agree. But he was only being concerned. He is my father, and like any father, I suppose, he worries.'

'He was boring and boorish tonight, not to mention hanging on to my wine like that. The manners! And in front of the servants. Behaving like that in front of Paine, the maids, everyone. In future, Trilby, you will do us both a favour by going to see your parents in their house, and not inviting them here.'

'Very well.' Trilby knew it was more than likely that Paine would be listening outside the door. 'I wonder if you could lower your voice a little, Lewis? I mean, you know, it would be less embarrassing for both of us.'

'No, I will not. I will shout if I like. And I do like. I have never known behaviour like it. The man is a lout. He will never be asked again.' Lewis lit up a cigarette and started to walk about the room. 'You really should have asked other people with them. It is quite hopeless asking a couple like that on their own. They are just not interesting enough. If you had asked other people with them your father would not have dared to be so impolite to me, and in front of the servants too. On and on he went. I thought he would never stop.'

'He's not usually like that, really, he isn't.'

But Lewis was not listening. He continued to pace up and down, talking more to himself than to her. 'You should have learned how to entertain by now, Trilby, but you quite obviously have not. I always remember the first evening we had a dinner here, remember?'

'Yes.' Trilby's voice had grown, if it were possible, duller at the realisation of what he was on the point of reminding her about. 'Yes, I remember.'

This did not stop Lewis. 'You did all the placement wrong. You embarrassed everyone with the wrong cards, everyone seated in the wrong places.'

'One of the staff did that, Lewis. Apparently it is

248

par for the course, when you are new to a place.'

Lewis did not hear her. 'It was perfectly terrible. Happily for you everyone I had invited, every single person, had been before, or they might never have come again.'

'Would that have mattered? After all they were all quite boring, Lewis. All your friends are really quite heartbreakingly boring. They only know how to talk about clothes or the servant problem, and their answer to world problems is just to drop an atom bomb on everyone.'

But Lewis did not seem to hear this either, or else he chose, momentarily, to ignore Trilby, because he went on, 'I shall never forget that. It was then that I realised just how much I would have to take you in hand, how far I had to go before you would understand what was required of you . . . What was that you said?'

Trilby stood up and moved swiftly towards the door. She had no idea why she had suddenly said what she had, but since she had she wrenched open the door, inwardly sighing with relief when she saw Paine straightening up in the hall outside.

Thank heavens for Paine and his nosy ways. Indeed, thank heavens for having servants, for at such moments they acted as a protection.

'Good night, Paine. And thank you. Everything was perfect.'

Trilby tried to smile at him and failed. They both knew that whatever the quality of the dinner the company had been everything except perfect.

Perhaps Paine noticed the sudden unwanted tears in Trilby's eyes as she turned away, because he whispered, sotto voce, 'Don't worry, Mrs James, really, it's just his way. Mr James likes to put people in the wrong, even me, madam, and I've been here over ten years. Gets some kind of a kick out of it, I always think.'

Trilby was just about to answer when the library door started to open again. The butler quickly grabbed the handle from the other side and once more assumed his most austere expression as he solemnly reopened it, and Trilby ran up the stairs to her bedroom suite quickly and quietly locked the door behind her.

She lay down on her bed in the dark and stared at her mistakes, at her marriage, at her own shortcomings, examining what she could have done, and what she should do now.

She had been too long in leaving Lewis. She should have left him after the miscarriage. Staying with him in the hope that he would somehow change had been, and still could be, a disaster.

Hearing a footfall outside in the corridor she half sat up, staring at her bedroom door. Lewis, along with her father, had drunk too much at dinner and most especially after dinner, and that might encourage him to think that he could *come and see* her. Stealthily she switched on her pink-shaded bedroom light and found herself watching the bedroom door handle with fascinated eyes. It was turning, slowly, so slowly. Quickly she shut off the light and lay back, her heart beating. Thank God she had locked the door.

*   *   *

She packed nothing except an overnight bag, knowing that whatever she took might be a clue to where she was going, and besides, Lewis had chosen all the clothes in the wardrobe for her, and she wanted none of them.

Morning seemed to be a century in coming, as it always is when you wait for it, but at last, little by little, Trilby saw the light coming up over London and heard first the milk float and then the newspaper boy, and eventually a number of taxis picking up and dropping early risers, or perhaps people only just going to bed.

From high above Trilby was intent on watching for only one thing and that was Lewis's car picking up Lewis and driving him away from the house, driving him away for long enough for Trilby to escape him.

At last there it was, and the chauffeur was busy polishing its already very polished exterior and waiting to open the door for Lewis, which he did some twenty minutes later, Lewis handing him his briefcase to put on the front seat.

As soon as the car started on its way, Trilby ran towards her bedroom door dressed in travelling clothes and carrying only a small suitcase. She sprang down the stairs two or three at a time. She had locked the door behind her, stuffing the keyhole with paper, and left the radio on in the hope that it would sound as if she was still inside her suite. She knew that the chances were that Lewis would come back, that he would make some excuse and return, because he was like that, and sure enough, no sooner had she crossed the street to the other side than she saw the famous flying lady on the front of the Rolls-Royce returning. She crouched down behind a parked car and watched with frightened eyes as Lewis got out of the car again and stood looking up at the house to her bedroom window, but, perhaps because she had taken care to leave her curtains drawn, he remained for only a minute or so before stepping back into the Rolls again, and being driven off once more.

Minutes went by, but since he had not returned Trilby dared to double back to the mews where she garaged her Morris. Getting in, starting up, threading her way from Holland Park towards Richmond, the open road and freedom, seemed to take for ever. In Trilby's mind it actually took a century before at last the road in front of her was open, and she was able to stop and stare at a map, and wonder where on earth she was, and why.

She had money, but she knew money was not what would protect her from Lewis. The only possible way of protecting herself from Lewis would be to hide away somewhere so remote that he would not be able to find her, and to hide away in such a fashion that she could not be recognised by anyone.

She had left Lewis a letter explaining that she no longer loved him, that she had not had enough time before marrying him to get to know him, and that now she had she was unable to stay, as they were quite obviously not suited, and that she wanted nothing from him, just peace of mind. This would, she imagined, be enough to put an end to most marriages, but not she knew to hers. Nothing would stop Lewis from coming after her. He did not have the mentality to give up. Anyone as violently possessive as Lewis would never give up chasing after someone he imagined he now owned, and once he caught up with her there was no knowing what he would do. She realised now that he must be, in many ways, what a more normal person would call—mad. He was possessed by possession, he had to dominate everyone and everything, and he would not, perhaps could not, ever change.

Stopping at traffic lights Trilby stared at herself momentarily in her driving mirror. What she needed now, more than anything, and urgently, was a complete change. She parked outside a chemist's shop near Berry's studio in Tankridge Street, and quickly made some purchases.

*   *   *

'Titian is as Titian does,' said Berry, staring at Trilby, 'but lud, Trilby ducks, I think it's quite good. I may yet be a challenge to your old friend André of Mayfair.'

It seemed to Berry that he had hardly unpacked all his precious paints and travelling easel from Northumberland before he found Trilby standing outside the studio door, just like the old days, looking half waif and half stray, and wholly miserable.

Of course he had pulled her inside, shut the door and made them both some very strong coffee before setting about helping her with her transformation. Colour shampoo, change of make-up, some art student clothes from the old days that he managed to find at the back of his dressing up box, which always came in so handy for sitters, and voilà, she no longer looked twenty going on thirty, but quite twenty again.

Trilby stared at herself in the old studio mirror. Thanks to Berry's efforts on her behalf her hair

253

was now quite definitely red, and what was more, with the help of the really wonderfully weird clothes that Berry had fished out of his precious studio box for her, not even her own stepmother would know her.

'Now, Trilb, no messing about, I am afraid. If you are intent on running off from the great man, you should take care not to be found. So where are we going?'

Trilby stared at Berry. They had always been so close. He must know that she would never run away to nowhere; that, in a way, she was too sensible to do that, just as she had been quite clear in her letter to Lewis that she would not be coming back to him, and wanted nothing from him.

'I am going to Somerset.'

Berry stared at her. 'Somerset?'

He smiled for the first time. 'Well, not even Sherlock Holmes will find you there, old love. Somerset, the land of Doones, the faraway place of hidden depths with its Levels and its mysteries, the undiscovered, forgotten county. And who, may I ask, is "Somerset"?'

'Piers Montague. I painted his aunt.'

'Oh. Well, I expect he's very nice, people with aunts generally are very nice. I always slightly suspect anyone without an aunt. Even I have an aunt or two, so, finally, I am not suspect. However, none of this is getting us anywhere at all, and you, if you are to go to Somerset, have to be got somewhere pretty damn quick. What I suggest is that having transformed you, abracadabra, we now swop cars. You take my old jalopy, because no-one will truly look for you in a van, old thing, will they? And I will take your Morris, and if anyone comes after me, I will just say you came here in a rush, and left it and la di da di da, yes?'

Trilby nodded, her heart sinking.

'I think you're getting the better of the deal,' she said when they hurried outside and she climbed into Berry's battered jalopy.

'So do I, and don't I look smug? Listen, we can swop again when you've unmuddled yourself, but take care, and don't talk to anyone, no-one, until you get where you're meant to be, in the next century, if you're lucky, in that thing.'

He leaned forward and kissed her quickly and tenderly on her cheek. 'Quick, quick, and no looking back. You can only be doing the right thing. We all knew you were miserable, just had to let you find out for yourself.'

He waved briefly and went back into his studio, shutting the door quickly as if he did not want to say goodbye, but knew that it was for the best.

*　　　*　　　*

It was more than late, it was the early hours of the morning when Trilby eventually arrived at the farm, Berry's old van eventually creeping, lights dimmed, quietly up towards the house. Trilby could not see the pale stone of the old farmhouse, or take in more than a dark outline of the aged staddle stones set about the short carriage drive, or the old walnut tree that stood at the entrance by the old iron gate, but she could, nevertheless, sense the countryside all around her. There was a light smell of newly mown grass, as if someone had just given the front lawn its first cut of the summer. And distantly she could hear a cow mooing and see, by the light of the bright moon, first an owl swooping and then bats, the light fleetingly catching their strange little faces and winged bodies.

She climbed stiffly out of the van and stood quite still. She had taken for ever to arrive at Charlton House Farm, driving by small back lanes and minor roads, criss-crossing the West Country, map in one hand, steering wheel in the other. Piers knew she was coming, because she had telephoned him and they had exchanged brief words, Trilby too emotional to say more than 'Expect me', but since a glance at her watch told her it was half past one in the morning she imagined that he would have been in bed hours ago, until she saw that several of the lights were still on in the house, one of them spilling onto the gravelled driveway on which she stood. She closed the van door, carefully, and stole as quietly as she could, overnight bag in hand, up to the front door, and rang the bell.

If she had imagined that Piers might have changed from the last time she saw him Trilby knew, as soon as she saw his face coming towards the half glass of the old doors from out of the low lighting of the hall, that he had not changed at all. He was still Piers, tall, handsome, curly-haired and diffident. What she *had* quite forgotten, however, was that she had changed.

'Trilby?'

He stared at her. Trilby stared back up at him, and then down at herself, and then up at him again, and then she covered her mouth with her hand and exploded with laughter.

As soon as she laughed Piers knew that it was quite safe for him to laugh too. Bent double with laughter Trilby stepped into the hall and into

Piers's arms.

'You look—you look—' Piers began again, removing one hand from around Trilby to wipe his eyes and standing back to look at her again. 'You look like—' He started to laugh again. 'You look like a little red bantam! If I hadn't known it was you, I would have put you in the hen house.'

'I had to, you know, change my appearance as soon as I could, because Lewis gets back at lunchtime, and you know how it is, he will go straight to my room and demand to see me.'

A few minutes later Piers glanced across at Trilby as he put down a cup of hot chocolate in front of her. 'Drink up, young Trilby, and then off to bed with you. Mabel has prepared the back room, so you will not be disturbed when I creep off at four thirty in the morning.'

Trilby glanced guiltily at the old school clock over the old, cream-coloured pre-war Aga, realising for the first time that her arrival must have deprived Piers of most of his night's sleep.

'I won't keep you.'

'We'll talk when we meet at lunchtime.'

She nodded, already half asleep. It was as if she had come home at last, to a real home. Not to her stepmother's house, not to her husband's house, where she had always felt herself to be a lodger, but to somewhere that was familiar in some strange way, somewhere she had known before, yet she could not have said when. The feeling was so new to her, and so warming, that she hardly dared to give it recognition.

Piers went ahead of her up the shallow, polished wooden stairs, carrying her overnight bag. Pushing open a door, he led the way into a large sparsely furnished whitewashed bedroom whose near bleakness was relieved by red Irish wool curtains and tufted Swedish rugs.

'Don't look round,' he begged her. 'This is badly in need of the feminine touch, I'm afraid.'

Trilby looked round nevertheless, but said nothing, waiting for him to say more, which he did not, and finding eventually that she felt a strange little frisson of both relief and disappointment when Piers went on, 'My room is down there, your bathroom opposite.'

He pointed vaguely down the passage, and then having kissed her in a brotherly fashion he shut the door and she listened to the sound of his retreating steps.

Hardly able to move from the stiffness of her drive, and hardly able to keep her tired eyes open, she unpacked her few possessions, cleaned her teeth in the clean but spartan bathroom across the passage, and climbed thankfully in between the carefully darned sheets and wool blankets on her bed, settling the flowered eiderdown over her feet. Seconds later, she turned out the small bedside light with its old-fashioned lampshade set about with bobble fringes, and fell asleep.

*   *   *

To wake up to the sound of a cock crowing outside your window, to hear the sound of the dawn chorus, and smell the scent of lavender on your pillow, to feel cool, crisp old linen sheets covering your tired body and to know that somehow you were at last free, was unimaginable. Trilby lay staring at the white-painted ceiling above her head and tried to overcome the feeling of unreality. In front of her was a picture of a small boy in a Victorian costume making a cricket stroke. Beside her, across the old wooden floor was another single bed covered with an old worn patchwork quilt. On the white-painted table between was a bunch of flowers with their buds just opening, set in a painted jug. It was all so real and so beautiful after the claustrophobia of Lewis's house, where the flowers were all hot-house blooms with large heads and too much scent, where there was always too much fruit in too many brightly polished silver bowls set out on too many tables, fruit that Trilby used to find depressing, knowing, as she did, that it was changed religiously every day, and only ever eaten by the servants.

Here it seemed to Trilby was simplicity, and therefore purity. Every item stood out from the others, every cast of light from the brightly curtained windows picked out something clean and shining: a jug and bowl, a newly painted chest, a bright coloured rug. Nothing too much, and yet everything somehow calming and peaceful.

'I am going back to sleep again, just in order to wake up once more to the bliss of knowing that I have escaped from Lewis, that I am free,' she told herself, and turning over she did fall asleep again, and almost immediately.

Later she drew the rough tweed curtains back and opened the bedroom windows, and, fixing the catches on them, leaned out. There were climbing roses growing directly outside, roses that had the promise of summer in every leaf, so that it seemed suddenly to Trilby as if the outdoors was pulling her by the arms, tugging at her like some overjoyed

259

friend, urging her to come outside to join in its mad dance towards summer.

The earth must be already good and warm, because there were cowslips in the grass by the fence and a mass of bright blue periwinkle under a neighbouring silver birch tree whose leaning branches were catching at the lush West Country grass, and although they were still bare they too seemed to be longing to compete with the buds and leaves already present on the other trees. Outside her window, Trilby could sense that May was about to burst upon them, leaping centre stage, refusing to be left waiting in the wings for one more tiny second.

Knowing that it would be some time before Piers returned from the fields for his lunch, she crossed once more from her bedroom to the old bathroom opposite.

It was large, and, like the rest of the farmhouse, most probably dated back to the nineteenth century. Its aura was not one of luxury but one of cleanliness next to godliness. The bath was old and iron, the taps the same, and such was the change in her circumstances after Lewis's plush bathrooms with their American taps, shining modern tiles and countless mirrors that the filling of the old bath with steaming, vaguely russet-coloured water took on an extraordinary significance. By the time the tub was filled, and Trilby was walking up the two wooden steps built to the side of it and lowering herself into the soft water, it seemed to her that such was the intensity of her pleasure that this bath might well have been her first, which in many ways it was. It was her first bath after leaving Lewis, and with every stroke of her flannel and every bubble from the Coal Tar soap she way washing him away.

Lewis. Just the thought of his name was awful, She imagined that he would have read her letter by now, that he would be setting out to find her, making enquiries, unleashing his hounds to chase after her. But would even Lewis be able to track her to this remote Somerset farmhouse surrounded by hundreds of acres of farmland? Here, Piers had told her during his week in London, not even the postman bothered to call, sending what letters there were up with the milkman who picked up the farm milk for the delivery rounds at five in the morning.

'Hallooa! Is anyone there, my dear? My dear, is anyone there?' a voice called, followed swiftly by the welcoming sound of a spoon rattling against china.

Wrapping herself in an old, clean thick white towel with the faded initial M embroidered in the corner, Trilby opened the door with some caution, the steam having damped her hair so that it was more a little red cap than a style.

'My dear.' A pretty, cheerful face set above a clean cotton pinafore beamed at Trilby through the door.

'Good morning.'

'That's it, my dear. And a very good one it is too. I'm Mabel Burlap and I have brought you up some breakfast, my dear, seeing that Mr Piers is out on the farm and you wouldn't know where to put your hand to anything, I brought you up some breakfast all done and ready.'

Trilby smiled at Mabel Burlap but her eyes strayed at once, and with some gratitude, to a heaped breakfast tray. 'That looks delicious. Thank

261

you so much.'

'It's a pleasure, miss. I always did like to think that Mr Piers would have more friends here when he took over the farm, that way I should have more to do, but as it is you are the first to stay since he came back from his National Service, aside from his children that is.'

Trilby concentrated on the faded flowers on the china, on Mabel's cheerful face, rather than allow herself to show the slightest emotion.

Of course, there had to be a catch, there was always a catch. Piers had children. That was the catch.

'I brought the tray up to you, seeing that you must be tired after your long journey, and I shall put it in your room, under the window, so that you have sight of all the lovely fields and the grass outside, sight of the cows too, if you're lucky. Ever seen a cow before, miss?'

'Well, yes,' Trilby called as she quickly pulled on her dressing gown and reopened the bathroom door. 'Yes, I have seen a cow before.'

'More than our evacuees in the war had ever done, my dear,' Mabel told her comfortably, preceding her into her bedroom.

Such was the confusion of her emotions that Trilby would have dearly liked to refuse breakfast, repack her overnight case and sweep out of the farm, but she could not for many reasons, the first of which and almost the most important to her at that moment, being that she was so hungry, and it had to be said that Mabel's breakfast, which she was placing in the window, looked too enticing for words.

Porridge, cooked, she told Trilby proudly,

overnight in the Aga, and served with dark brown sugar and thick West Country cream, made from their own cows' milk. After that, grilled bacon, tomatoes and sausage under a covered dish, everything cooked to perfection and mouthwatering both to look at and, Trilby discovered thankfully before long, to eat.

Mabel sat down on Trilby's bed, facing her back, and sighed contentedly as she watched her tuck into her cooking. Obviously feeling that she must be in need of company, she went on comfortably, 'Mr Piers is such a good cook that I am only ever allowed to do the breakfast and tea and suchlike for him. He's that much the lord of his own kitchen. He keeps us all up to the mark, does Mr Piers. And when the children come here, of a Sunday sometimes from school, he keeps them down one end, never lets them near him, not while he's cooking.'

His children again! Oh well, so what if Piers had children? It would not be so very surprising, considering. After all, if Trilby had a husband, why shouldn't Piers have a wife? But—children?

Trilby stared out of the window at the beauty of the early summer day. Did she honestly have to care at that moment? Having finished both the porridge and the bacon and sausage, not to mention home-made bread with home-made marmalade and a couple of delicious cups of tea, Trilby decided that at that moment, and perhaps really rather unsurprisingly on such a beautiful morning, she could not bring herself to care if Piers Montague had a dozen children.

'Mr Piers's wife, does she, er, come out with the children?'

Mabel looked flabbergasted. 'Lord bless you, my dear, Mr Piers has no wife! Lord bless you, what would he be doing having you to stay if he had a wife?'

Mabel's large, innocent face coloured and she patted the back of her cottage bun hairstyle as if to make sure that it was still there, which it was, to her obvious relief.

'No, Mr Piers has no wife. I have a husband, mind. My Harold, he is Mr Piers's cowman, and I come in and help him in the house, and I do the chickens, and the ducks. Would you like to see the chickens? Jerseys, Suffolks, Sussex, we have a right old mix here, you know. And as for the ducks, well, Mr Piers is so fond of them he won't rightly eat one, not one. I don't mind eating duck, not so long as I don't know its name, but Mr Piers, he won't have that. They're his friends, he says. Not to mention all the other wildlife that he likes to have around him. Just as well he's a dairy farmer, my Harold always says.'

With her back conveniently turned to Mabel, Trilby had now changed from her cotton dressing gown into a yellow cotton dress, one of two cheap cotton dresses she had purchased in the small suburban town where she had so effectively transformed herself into what Piers had called a little red bantam. Now she smoothed the dress down with her hands as, taking her courage into both hands and attempting to look appropriately nonchalant, she asked, 'So if Mr Piers has no wife, um, how come he has, er, children, Mrs Burlap?'

For the second time since their meeting Mabel Burlap blushed to the roots of her cottage loaf hairstyle.

'Why, Lord bless you, miss, er, why Lord bless you, them's never Mr Piers's children.' She recovered from her shock and started to laugh. 'Why Lord bless you, no! No, the children aren't of Mr Piers's, no, them's his mother's children.'

Mabel continued to laugh while Trilby brushed out her short, now auburn hair into its customary impish style and at the same time smiled at her laughter. 'Oh, I see.'

'Mrs Montague, senior, that is, not that there is a junior, but Mrs Montague, she lived abroad a lot when she was younger, and as a consequence—tropical heat very likely, my Harold puts it down to that more'n anythin'—she had children by a number of husbands, and not always husbands, as I understand it. Well, their grandparents, they sent for them, once they realised they was all growin' up as little savages, and they put them all in school over here, and Mr Piers, he takes them out on Sundays sometimes. They run about the place, and he cooks for them to beat the band, roast beef, Yorkshire pudding, mounds of roast potatoes, and any amount of puddings—I'm allowed to help with them—lemon meringue pie, fruit crumble, blackberry and apple pie with my butter pastry, that's the kind of thing we like to give them, and then back they go to their schools, but at least we know they've put back enough to keep them going till the next time, poor little devils, because they don't feed them at these boarding schools, you know.'

'Please. I know I've only just had breakfast, but you're making me feel hungry all over again!'

Mabel Burlap gave her comfortable laugh, and before picking up Trilby's breakfast tray she squeezed her arm with a hand that bore the thinnest of gold wedding rings.

'I am very glad you've come to stay with us, my dear. Mr Piers, he spends too much time on his own, really he does, and that being so it's good for him to have someone his own age around the place. I expect you'll be wanting to change things, too, and that will be no bad thing neither. He may be a cook, Mr Piers, but he has no eye to comfort, really he doesn't. So long as he has the radio, and a sofa, and a place to leave his boots and his dog, he says he's as happy as the day is long, but I know better. Now come and see the hens.'

From the moment that she followed Mabel out into the farmyard Trilby was entranced by the variety of animal life that abounded around and beyond it. Not just hens pecking about the yard, or ducks swimming on the large pond, or doves circling the old stable yard, but any amount of other life: the dipping of house martins and swallows over the water troughs, the brown and white cows in the fields beyond, the garden filled with small birds of every kind, a kingfisher making a sudden appearance, the brightness of its turquoise back providing a momentary flash of tropical colour before it disappeared into the green of the trees.

For a second, as she watched Mabel throwing maize and corn for the chickens, and observed the wildness and variety of the life around her, the ceaseless movement, the precision of design of each piece of flora or fauna, the tiny white dove feathers scattered over the stable roofs, the buds on the rose bushes, and the brightness of the cockerel's head, Trilby imagined Lewis in Holland

Park, the dryness of his life, the ironed newspapers, the breakfast in silver tureens, the maids hovering, no sense of divine and beautiful disorder such as she saw here, only the lifeless outlines of great wealth.

And still Piers was not yet back. The moment he was she imagined that they would run upstairs together and make love.

What she did not know was that Piers's tractor had broken down in the middle of Hundred Acre Field, and that as he walked off to find help neither love nor lunch was uppermost in his mind.

Mabel, who was well used to the disappearance of men for hours at a time, laughed when she looked at the clock and saw, much later, that it was well past two o'clock. 'That's farmers.'

Trilby nodded, trying to conceal her disappointment, and a few seconds later she heard the unmistakable sound of male feet on the gravel outside. 'There he is!'

Mabel nodded at Piers' rough-coated retriever who always preceded him into the house. 'You've got a rival here, in Topsie, miss. I must warn you, she's been mistress of this house for far too long, and no mistake. Now, I'll be going along. Mr Piers, he never does like if I'm around when he's having his lunch and listening to the Archers and that.'

*   *   *

'May is the most perfect month. Wherever you are, if you ask people what is the best time to visit, they will always say, "Oh, you must come back, but next time come in May!"'

Piers and Trilby were sitting talking after their

267

late lunch of chicken mayonnaise, new potatoes, tomato salad and lemon mousse, when Trilby stood up suddenly.

'What are you doing?'

'You cooked for me, so now I am going to wash up for *you*.'

'No, don't, really.'

'No, do really. I love washing up. Soapy water, rolled-up sleeves, I have always loved washing up.'

'Well, all right, but only because I don't suppose Mabel will be coming in again until tomorrow.' Piers patted the top of the retriever's head as Trilby turned back momentarily from the old-fashioned butler's sink. As Trilby went to say something, Piers quickly added, trying to look serious and not quite succeeding, 'Topsie does not I am afraid approve of female persons living in the house.'

'I shall be doing your washing up until I go, and that's final. It's the least I can do. Besides, I've missed it. I've missed all those everyday things.'

'Topsie is not against you personally,' Piers went on, trying to ignore the feeling of searing disappointment that had shot through him. 'It was my own fault really.' He stood, and picking up a tea towel he started drying up. 'I am afraid I went through a bit of a phase, after National Service in Africa, fighting Mau Mau, and after my parents died. Well, that's my excuse. Came back to England, but after Aunt Laura handed over the farm to me, I went a bit mad with the opposite sex. And then—' He stopped.

'And then?'

'And then, of a sudden, I realised I was behaving really rather mindlessly. And so, I stopped. But it all left a bit of a scar on poor old Topsie here. I mean I told her you were only coming here for a little while, but once she'd seen how pretty you were, I am afraid I don't think she quite believed me.'

'Did *you*?'

'What?'

'Did *you* believe you?' Trilby looked at Piers who stared at her for a moment.

'Isn't there a poem called "Trilby Kissed Me"? Yes, I am sure there is a poem called "Trilby Kissed Me".'

'Why? Are you thinking of reading it to me?'

This time Piers caught both her wrists. 'No, I am not thinking of *reading* to you, no, reading was not what I had in mind at this moment, far from it, I am afraid!'

Seconds later they were running upstairs to the first floor together, whispering and laughing, closely followed by the retriever.

Outside his bedroom Piers opened the door. Topsie promptly and obligingly leaped from the door to the bed, at which her master equally promptly closed the door and snatching at Trilby's hand whispered, 'Right, now that we have Tops fixed up, I am afraid we'll have to retire to your room for your bedtime story!'

They tiptoed down the corridor, and into Trilby's room where they drew the curtains to shut out the bright sunlight. By the light that was filtering through the curtains Trilby looked to Piers both beautiful and ethereal, and the moment to which he had been so looking forward arrived, and he was able to start unbuttoning her yellow dress. In fact, at once, and in unspoken agreement, they

269

undressed each other by turn, slowly and carefully, as lovers-to-be so often do, and fell into bed together, unaccountably still whispering. It was as if they were afraid that someone was listening to them, that there was someone outside the half-open window, which, of course, in the country, there always is.

CHAPTER EIGHT

'Trilby.'

Sometimes he stopped and said her name out loud. It was such a pretty name. In fact to him it was actually the prettiest name he had ever known, just as she was the prettiest girl he had ever known, and her way of being the most engaging, the most delightful, the most enchanting. She was the depth and the height, the ultimate in complete happiness, and without her, it seemed to him now, he would surely not wish to live.

Having leaned back against the wall and sighed over the subject of his thoughts Piers's eyes fell on the calendar. Against next Sunday he had written the words *The children for lunch!* After which in less sophisticated writing was scribbled *Steak and kidney and chocolate mousse please, please, please, please! And don't forget!*

Piers smiled. The children liked to know where they were as far as their culinary delights were concerned and so they had taken to scribbling their favourite, longed-for dishes in his diary. He picked the calendar off the wall and put it in the centre of the kitchen table.

When she came in later, Trilby could not help seeing what was written large by next Sunday, which she was meant to do, but for a second it seemed to Piers that she looked disappointed.

'Of course, the children.'

Piers pointed to the calendar. 'These are not *my* children, in fact knowing how my mother went on after my father divorced her, I very much doubt if any of them have the same father. In fact I am quite sure they haven't, but there you are, since our mother died, a few years ago, they've all been living under the same roof, with their maternal grandparents at Wake Park in Dorset, not far from here, only about fifty minutes, as a matter of fact.'

'They must be quite a handful for a bachelor, even one who cooks.'

Piers did not answer at first, continuing with his train of thought as if the children were something that he had at some time had to learn to talk about, yet still found a little difficult.

'The children come and see their much older half-brother—that's me—every few weeks, well, fortnightly, really. But don't be too moved by their devotion, please, they only really come here to be fed by Mabel and me. Granny and Grandad's board is not up to much, not exactly groaning with goodies. You know how it is—older people seem to be able to live on air. *You want another piece of toast? But do you realise that means that you have eaten two today, Millicent!*'—he finished, mimicking an indignant old lady's voice. 'So, no, these are not my children, they are my mother's children.'

Trilby looked at him, and for the first time since he had met her it seemed to him that he had no hint of an idea of what she was thinking or feeling.

'I have to take them out. They look forward to it so much.'

'Of course, but I can't stay while they're here. I must go. I can't have them meet me. It could risk everything, if they meet me and they know someone I know, they would be sure to tell, they wouldn't mean to, it would just come out.'

'Oh no, have no fear, I promise you they will not concern themselves with anything except playing table tennis and cricket and eating, that's their fortnightly treat, coming here and being allowed to behave like children instead of little old people, which they have to do at their grandparents' house.'

'Well, just so long as you stick to not telling them anything more than they have to know and remember my surname is now "Ardisonne". That's what I told Mabel.'

'Very well, Miss Ardisonne. I say, that rather suits you.'

Trilby smiled. 'It's nice to feel single again, believe me.'

Piers looked momentarily hurt but said, 'Yes, I suppose it must be nice.'

'Love and marriage do not go together like a horse and carriage,' Trilby sang, ruthlessly but gaily, adding, 'Don't think I will stick around too long, Piers. I promise you, like the swallows I am only here for the summer.'

Piers nodded, not believing her, only wondering if they had time to make love once more before he had to go outside again.

*　　　*　　　*

The next few days were filled with idyllic sunshine, so much so that with the early morning sun flooding their bedroom it was difficult for them to stay in bed too long, but then again it was difficult for them to stay out of it too long too. In short it was difficult for either of them to do anything except make love. Indeed, Piers was so besotted with Trilby that he told the redoubtable Harold that for the next few days Harold must consider Piers to be on holiday.

'Satan can disguise himself in many ways, you know that, Mr Montague?' Harold told Piers with undisguised gloom. 'Most especially in the form of a woman. Satan dearly loves, as I understand it, to appear to a man in the form of a woman who will seem to be all things to him, but will lead him down the path to hell.'

But Piers had neither listened to him nor heard him, as Harold soon realised. He had fled back to the house, to the garden where Mabel had told Harold that she knew that they danced, under the cover of darkness and beneath the bright stars, while during the day they hung the wireless outside one of the bedrooms on a hook and once again danced, or lazed about under the old apple tree eating picnics and drinking wine.

'He's very keen on this one, Harold. Deserves a bit of time with her,' Mabel declared.

Harold knew very well that his wife kept in touch with Miss Laura in London, and that Mrs Montague liked to hear from Mabel what exactly was going on at the farm, so that when her nephew went up to stay with her once or twice a year the old lady could be quite sure that she was completely up to date. Although he knew all this, and put all the shenanigans down to women and their wicked ways, nevertheless a part of Harold hoped that Mabel would not keep Miss Laura in touch with what was happening now, because, it had to be faced, Miss Laura, who had lived at Charlton as a child, might not approve. Old ladies were like that, Harold had found; they liked to have a young man to themselves. And what was more Harold doubted very much that she would approve of Mr Piers having carnal relations.

'Now, Mabel, not a word to Miss Laura, like, not a word, do you hear? Mr Piers might be ensnared with the devil and all his works, but it's none of our business if he is, and we don't want Miss Laura coming here and making trouble. Might affect us. After all, when all's said and done, Miss Laura she buys us a lot of this new-fangled machinery. 'Member when harvest was bad two years back, and she came in to help out with animal fodder and the new milking parlour? She's a rich woman, is Miss Laura, and you don't fangle with rich women, Mabel, you don't at all. You treat 'em like the bees' nest in the roof, you leave 'em to sort out theirselves, and that, you do really.'

'What does you mean, Harold? I don't know what you are talking about, I don't really. What does you mean? I am sure I don't know.'

'I've warned Mr Piers already, I've warned him that the devil is a woman, and that's all I can do. You know good and well what I'm on about right now, I mean none of your tittle-tattle down the village. As far as we're concerned this girl, she's not here, doesn't exist, Mabel. Not if we know what's good for us.'

'Your last word is not my last word, Harold.

Same as all the rest. I know that this Miss Ardisonne is a good girl.'

'How do you know that?'

'Because I do. Besides, you've not been near the house since she arrived, you don't even know her, you don't, she's a little darling she is.'

'I been emptying the rubbish bins, haven't I, and this is what I found.'

Harold held up a bottle and Mabel took it and frowned, trying not to look shocked. 'She's not natural then, Harold?'

'She's not natural at all, Mabel. But never mind what she is, don't you go telling Miss Laura nothing when she rings you. I don't want the old lady upset, Mabel, really I don't. I don't want her boat rocked. So long as she's happy I know I can go and get me some new overalls. Or ask Mr Piers for a new harvester when needed, or anything I want, like. But if she starts getting restless, stands to reason she'll find another way to spend her money, and we don't want that, girl, do we?'

Mabel swallowed and turned away. 'I dare say you're wrong, Harold, I dare say you are. She seemed such a nice little thing, first off. From the moment that she arrived I thought she was ever such a nice little thing, nice manners, and that, not to mention pretty ways with her, always opening the door for me, and helping with the dishes as willing as you could wish.'

But the grim evidence was still in Mabel's hand, and they both knew nice girls never dyed their hair, that was just not what nice girls did, everyone in Somerset knew that. The only girls that dyed their hair during the war were the kind that went off with American airmen, and were never heard of

275

again.

'*Gone to London*' it was known as in Somerset. The only trouble was that this girl, from what Mabel could gather, she'd *come* from London, so there was no hope of her going back, she supposed, at least not for a while.

'We seen it all before, Mabel, that's why we have to be so careful like—at our last place, remember? It were all right, winter and summer, rain or shine, we were right as trivets at our last place, until when? Until when a few years had gone by and the young man found himself a new wife.'

Mabel nodded. It was true. She picked up her coat, and turned away. 'I'm off to W.I. market. It'll take me an hour to walk there in this rain.'

Harold watched her for a few seconds and then he called, 'You take care of yourself then, do you hear, Mabel?'

In his heart of hearts he hoped that he was wrong about this Miss Ardisonne or whatever she called herself, but somehow, since he had found that bottle of hair dye, he very much doubted it.

*   *   *

'Piers?'

'Hallo, Aunt Laura.'

Piers tried to sound like his old self, but it was difficult. It was so hard to keep *it* under cover, remember not to let *it* affect his voice, the *it* bit of him that kept bubbling up and spilling over, and not caring who knew that he was in love.

'Have you seen Mrs James lately—you know, the artist, Trilby Smythson? Has she telephoned to you, perhaps?'

276

Piers knew at once that Laura knew, and this was her way of telling him. 'No, I haven't, Aunt Laura. Why?'

'No good reason, it's just that I have rung her studio a couple of times and no-one answers. I have Lola de Ribes and her husband coming to lunch and I rather wanted to ask her too. Never mind, I expect that newspaper man has dragged her off to somewhere exotic at the last moment and she just forgot to let me know. By the way, should I tell Lola that you are happy for her to come down to the farm? To come and see what could be done to the interior?'

'No.'

They both knew that Piers had said 'No' far too quickly.

'How's everything else?'

'Thriving.'

'Good. Keep in touch, Piers. And do take care of yourself.'

Laura replaced the telephone without another word, and Piers was left, as he sometimes had been in the past, staring at the old black receiver that partnered the old black telephone that sat on a wobbly table beside the old blackened inglenook fireplace in the old nineteenth-century kitchen.

'Oh dear,' he told Topsie. 'Aunt Laura is worried.'

But almost immediately Piers heard a sound coming from his snug next door to the drawing room, the place where he kept his wireless, his papers, his farm bills, and his only other telephone.

For a second he thought it was the wireless playing, so sweet was the singing, but as he and Topsie strolled towards the source of the sound he

277

realised it was nothing more than Trilby singing, and so he found himself quickening his pace until he arrived in the small, sunny room, sliding to a halt in front of Trilby's stepladder.

'No, no, shut your eyes.' She ran across the room in her ballet-style shoes and covered his eyes. 'No, shut your eyes,' she repeated. 'I haven't quite finished yet. I wanted so much to surprise you.'

Standing in the middle of the room with Topsie leaning against his legs, and the smell of Trilby's scent vaguely in the air, Piers sighed with gratitude for the day, the hour, and the moment, the matter of Aunt Laura and her obviously troubled state already quite forgotten.

He had a surprise for Trilby too. That was why he had gone to Wells, to come back with something to surprise her, something that he felt sure she would love.

'Very well, now you can open them—open your eyes.'

He looked round and was duly, if unsurprisingly, and gratifyingly astonished. 'Now, let me see,' he teased her, looking round, 'there's something different here, isn't there?' A touchingly vulnerable look in her eyes told him not to go on being facetious. 'It is really clever. My chairs, my curtains—everything is the same, only different. You know, you are really very clever, I can see why Aunt Laura dotes on you.'

'I love this modern turquoise in informal rooms, don't you? I mean for cushions and things.'

'Absolutely, and I love you for doing all this.'

Piers caught her up in his arms and kissed her, because one glance told him that everything, books, bills, farming ledger, was where he wanted

278

it, in other words still where it had been, but everything was smarter, tidier.

'I found this rug, would you believe, in one of the *barns*?'

'Of course.' Piers assumed his most pompous expression, and proceeded to speak in a sermonising vicar's voice. 'It is a well known fact that where there are barns in the country there will, necessarily, be found to be furniture. Sometimes even the odd, usually very odd family portrait, sometimes the most valuable rugs, and sometimes even a Ming vase which the cowman has found to be most useful for keeping his various treasured instruments out of harm's way—gelding irons, calving scissors, docking knife, they will all have inevitably found their way, you may be sure, into the old Ming vase standing in the corner of the feed room.'

'Ugh, don't go on, I shall probably faint into a heap.'

'Now it's my turn to tell you to shut your eyes.'

Piers disappeared towards the hall, returning a minute or so later with a large parcel which he placed in Trilby's hands. He could not wait to see her face when she undid the parcel. It had taken him for ever to find, and when he had, he just knew that it was going to be the perfect present for her.

'All right, you can open your eyes now.'

Trilby stared at the parcel, smiling, but without understanding why she found her heart sinking.

'Go on, open it.'

She nodded obediently and putting it on the old chintz sofa she cut the string with Piers's pocket knife and tore off the brown paper.

The box was large and white, quite large enough,

in fact quite vast enough, to contain anything. She lifted the lid hoping against hope that it would be velvet for curtains, or silk for a bedroom, because it was quite obviously heavy, but it was not. It was pink, and it was tulle, and it was a dress.

'I took your measurements from your cotton dress upstairs,' Piers told her proudly. 'And there are shoes to match.' He peered into the box. 'Shoes. Look,' he repeated. He put them on the floor, and, taking the dress out of its tissue paper, he held it against her. 'I don't think you can do better than redheads in pink, my uncle, Aunt Laura's husband, always said.' Piers sighed with satisfaction. 'It is just—so—good. So good. I say, you are going to be stunning in this.'

Trilby nodded, wordlessly, and then, to their mutual horror, tears started to fall down her face. Piers' face paled. He had searched and searched, telephoned to shops all over the place, and at last, in Wells of all places, he had found her the perfect dress, and now—she was crying.

'You don't like it?'

'No, I do, I do. It is just so kind of you.' She put up her arms and kissed him. 'So, so kind!'

Later he said, 'You don't have to wear it if you don't feel like it, but on Saturday, I thought we could have a party.' Seeing her face fall, he added, 'Just the two of us, that kind of party, you know? We can put candles all over the back garden, and you know, I always think, a dress like this—well, as soon as I saw it, I thought that's a dress to wear outside, on one of our special evenings. You know I really can't wait to dance with you, wearing that. We will tear up the lawn together—me Fred Astaire, you Ginger Rogers.' He pounded his chest, gorilla-style.

'It'll ruin these shoes. Dancing outside, it will ruin them.'

Piers nodded happily. 'You bet.'

'What is the party for?'

Piers sighed this time. 'Trilby, Trilby—how can you be like that?' he asked her reproachfully. 'How can you? There is never a good reason for a really good party, not a really special party. A good party is always only for two, and it must never, ever be for any other reason than love and laughter, or there is no point.'

But first they had to prepare the food.

Trilby made vol au vents, and fried chicken legs, and Piers made mayonnaise which seemed to take hours and hours, but was well worth it once it was done.

Trilby stood back. 'I can't wait for dinner,' she said longingly, surveying their efforts.

'You've really changed, do you know that? When I knew you in London you only picked at your food.'

'I don't think that's true.'

'It is.'

Piers looked at her. He had green eyes, not blue, and on such a sunny evening as this it seemed to Trilby, momentarily, that he looked a little as if he had come from the woods, a mythical figure who might even have pipes to play which would make her dance too fast until she dropped, or follow him into the deep darkness of the forest from where she would never return.

'You are really the Piper at the Gates of Dawn, aren't you?' she said. 'That's who you are.'

He looked at her. 'I might be.'

A few minutes later, after washing up rather too quickly, they were making love, and not long after that running a bath, and each washing the other's hair, laughing and talking, when the front doorbell rang.

Trilby, who was still in the bath, her hair clinging damply to her head, busy squeezing a large sponge over a body that she noticed with surprise was already turning brown, bit by little bit, stopped and looked up at Piers.

'I'll go.' Piers wrapped a large, rough white bath towel around his waist and went downstairs. He opened the front door to discover Mabel standing in the old stone porch.

'Mr Piers.' She looked momentarily embarrassed. 'Mr Piers, I thought I ought to call, well, that is, I am here to tell you that I find I shall be unable to come back to work on account—on account of the *gallivanting.*'

'I gathered that, Mabel.'

'I did not want too much water to flow under the bridge without coming and telling you that it is on account of my conscience and nothing else that I am not returning.'

'Good, Mabel, so now that is off your chest—'

'Which it is, it is off of my chest now—'

'Good—' Piers went to shut the door. 'Now if you don't mind I am feeling a trifle cold in only my towel.'

'But while I am here,' Mabel put a large foot in the door, and wedged it firmly, her face still sticking through the opening, 'while I am still here, I thought you would like to see this what was left in the dustbin and found by Harold, Mr Piers. It might be of some considerable interest to you, I

282

thought.'

Piers took the proffered bottle, looked at it, and then promptly gave it back to her.

'I don't need this, Mabel, not yet anyway, as you can see.' He touched his hair briefly. 'No doubt quite soon, however, if you go on pestering me like this, so, if you don't mind, perhaps you would like to go?' He shut the door and locked it, loudly and firmly.

'What was that?' Trilby too was now out of the bathroom wrapped only in a towel.

Piers shook his head, and picking up his dressing gown from the bed he said, 'Oh, nothing, just Mabel suddenly being a pest.'

'Oh.'

Piers stopped by the bathroom door and told Trilby about the bottle and they both started to laugh.

'In the country,' Piers said, eventually, 'to dye your hair is as much as to declare that you are a prostitute.'

'So, no more Mabel?'

'Oh, don't worry about Mabel, or Harold, they get like this every so often. Once they didn't come to the house for a week because I used their lawnmower on a Sunday. It all blows over. Now come on, time to get dressed.'

*　　　*　　　*

To appear at the top of some set of stairs and stun the audience below with your glamour and your beauty is always gratifying, but to be dressed by the man who loves you, slowly, carefully, and with love, to see yourself mirrored in his eyes, must be, it seemed to Piers, for a woman to know true sensuality.

'Why are you trembling?'

'I—er, I—have never been dressed by a man before. And you? Why are *you* trembling?'

'Because I have never dressed a woman before. Before, other women, they always sent me away, never wanted me to see them making themselves up, or . . .' He kissed each of Trilby's feet before slowly pulling up the new nylon stockings he had bought for her, snapping her suspenders to the frail and precious nylon tops, 'or pulling on their stockings. If I could only tell you how I feel about each part of you, but I can't, so I am dressing each part instead.'

'Piers. I can't lie to you—'

He was holding the dress up, still on its hanger.

'I am not trembling for the same reason as you.' Trilby's teeth had started to chatter. 'In fact I am trembling for quite a different reason.'

'You're cold—' He walked towards her with the dress.

'No.' She backed away from him down the room. 'No, I am trembling because—because I am so afraid.'

Piers frowned. 'You are afraid of—of what are you afraid?'

'I am afraid of you doing this, to me, it's giving me a sort of claustrophobia, or a vertigo, I can't explain properly. I just know that I'm—I am afraid of wearing a dress like this, and shoes like those.' She pointed at them, still in their smart box. 'I am so frightened, but because I love you—I know, I mean I know I must wear them, for your sake, for your sake I must wear them.'

'You *must*?' Piers stared at her, astonished, and Trilby realised at that moment just how utterly nice Piers must be, for he did not say, as other men would, 'Do you realise how much this dress cost?' or 'Do you realise how difficult it was to find this dress?' He just stood holding up the dress, and laughed, before going on to say quietly, 'That is why I love you, Trilby. I know now, why I love you, even if I didn't know before. It is because only you can have a fit about a beautiful new dress!'

'It's not that I don't love it. It's beautiful and it's—it's everything that I want, but I feel it's something else too, a sort of binding thing, and I don't want to be bound, not to anything, not ever again.'

'Tell you what, Trilby.' Piers put the dress on the bed and kneeling on the floor beside her he put his hands around hers. 'Tell you what,' he said again, 'put on the dress only if you want, put on the shoes only if you want, put on what you would like. If you want to come to our party wearing only your underwear that is perfectly fine too. Everyone must feel happy in their clothes at a party, really, everyone. I know because my mother once sent me to a party wearing a grey shirt, and I never recovered from the embarrassment. I should hate anyone else to feel as I did that day. So. I'll leave it to you.'

Piers's reward was that Trilby flung her arms around his neck and hugged him, and in the event she came downstairs in the short, pink, silk tulle dress, her new Titian hair combed out in a more formal way.

Piers, on the other hand, as if to demonstrate his point in full, namely that each of them should

285

choose to wear exactly what they wished, waited for her at the bottom of the stairs wearing his late uncle's old, faded maroon smoking jacket and a silk shirt and no tie or cravat, while on his legs he wore knee breeches and white stockings. The whole outfit was completed by a pair of faded tennis shoes, and his second reward was to see Trilby bursting into fits of laughter.

Finally they both sat down, side by side on the bare wooden stairs, unable to stop laughing at the success of it all.

As for Trilby, she went barefoot that night so that Piers promptly dubbed her 'Henny Penny' because he said she was just like the hen in Beatrix Potter who lost her stockings and went 'barefoot, barefoot'. They dined and danced, not this time to the sound of the wireless hung precariously outside the bedroom window, but to an old wind-up gramophone that Piers had found and put under the apple tree. It did not matter that most of the records were old seventy-eights from before the war, they danced to them, round and round the apple tree and under the stars, until finally they crept up to bed, leaving the dishes and the glasses spread about the lawn, and Mabel and Harold with all their suspicions thoroughly confirmed.

Except, as Piers had predicted, when they went down the next morning they found that for some reason best known to herself, Mabel had cleared up all the dishes on the lawn, washed them up, and left their breakfast laid and ready to be cooked.

On the table propped against the blue and white teapot there was a note: *I will come in to make the tea. MB.*

Trilby picked it up and showed it to Piers, who

286

hardly glanced at it.

'Mabel gives in her notice for religious reasons at least once a week,' he said airily, flinging some bacon into a frying pan. 'It's a hobby with the Burlaps, you'll find.'

Trilby put the note back on the table feeling absurdly envious. Piers it seemed had everything. A beautiful house, people who looked after him, a healthy outdoor life; everything that anyone sane would long for, Piers already had. She on the other hand sensed that she had only a few weeks.

CHAPTER NINE

When Lewis read the short note Trilby left for him on the mantelpiece of her bedroom he felt only relief that he was not still employing a maid for her. He had always hated the servants to know too much of his life, and while it was true that they always did know something of what was happening to him, to his certain knowledge none of them had yet known everything.

He took the letter to his own room and burned it. He did this at a terrified, panic-struck speed. It was as if he had murdered Trilby, not simply driven her away. And this despite the fact that her letter had stated that it was her fault, not his. *I should never have married you. It's my fault, not yours.*

Those words made Lewis more angry than ever. He found himself staring at them until, if his eyes had been a magnifying glass and his soul the rays of the sun, the sentences would have been burned out of the paper on which they were so carefully

287

written in Trilby's sloping Italianate handwriting with its beautiful loops and tails.

Once he had calmed himself a little, which took a great deal of pacing up and down with his teeth grinding with fury and his fists clenching and reclenching themselves, he sank down on his own bed, his mind searching, coldly as always, for the best way to handle this piece of news.

The way forward came to him after many minutes. He would handle Trilby's desertion, her betrayal (for that was how he was gradually coming to see it), in exactly the same way that he would handle *any* piece of news: he would sit and consider what to do. He would not be panicked, as he had just been panicked into a furious, angry reaction, he would sit and consider this news, Trilby's news, as if it was just any news, as if it was an item brought to his attention by one of his staff. He would try to be detached. He must remain calm.

After a while he cleared his throat, and, wiping his palms on a white silk handkerchief, he picked up the telephone by his bedside and ordered David Micklethwaite to come round to the house as soon as possible. He made sure that his voice was calm and controlled, because you never quite knew who would listen in, and newspaper staff were not only trained to pick up every nuance, every possibility that might turn into the smallest scrap of news, they were adept at it. As Lewis knew all too well, rumour was the coursing blood of Fleet Street feeding the sinews of fact.

Micklethwaite sounded surprised, and as if he was particularly busy, and therefore more than a little reluctant to leave his desk, which was a good cover, Lewis thought. Naturally, however, because

288

it was Lewis who was asking for him, he agreed to come round as soon as possible. Lewis, of course, made it clear that he wanted to see Micklethwaite on a matter of some urgency, but not of a personal urgency; that could wait until he saw Micklethwaite in person.

'Come into the garden.'

They always talked in the garden, no matter what the weather; it was the only place where they could guarantee each other total security. Micklethwaite therefore followed Lewis past the perfectly planted early summer borders to the middle of the large expanse of lawn that made up the greater part of Lewis's London garden.

On the drive over, Micklethwaite had tried to pre-empt what it was that Lewis needed to tell him. He imagined that Lewis, as sometimes happened, must have become excited about some new piece of scandal, wanted to confide in him some government failure, or give him the true version of a spicy story concerning royalty and an actress, or even just an actress. He was therefore wholly unprepared for the look on Lewis's face when he turned round to confront him for the first time.

Nor did he think that he had ever seen Lewis with tears in his eyes before.

'She's left me, David. Trilby, she has only gone and left me!'

Micklethwaite leaned forward, the expression on his face one of amazement, but not, he realised much later, of surprise. He himself had never approved of Lewis's marriage to someone so much younger, with so little experience of the world, and more particularly of men. Micklethwaite, during his boss's long drawn-out bachelor days, had kept

Lewis fixed up with many a pretty, sophisticated girl. Indeed he had often prided himself that he always knew Lewis's type.

Lewis did not like prostitutes, preferring a more discriminating companion, but she had also, Micklethwaite knew, to be someone who would shrug off whatever he chose to do to her. He knew this so well that as soon as Lewis produced this new girl, at that first print party for her, or whatever it was meant to be—the party at the Savoy in her honour—Micklethwaite knew that she was going to prove to be different, but not at all what he himself would choose. He knew what was right for Lewis James, and Trilby Smythson was definitely not the tough little middle-class girl with her eye on the main chance that had always, until then, fitted the bill. This other type of girl would have taken her chance, taken her payment, taken her leave, and then gone on her way, putting out of her mind both Lewis and the experience, looking only to the fattening of her bank balance.

From the first Trilby Smythson had struck Micklethwaite as being too highly strung to stand the pressure of Lewis's personality, of his meticulous attitudes, of his imperious ways. No-one knew Lewis better than David Micklethwaite. In many ways he was more married to Lewis James than any wife. He knew the pressures, the covert egoism, the sublimated sadism, and such had been his conviction that Lewis was taking a wrong turning with this girl that, now that it seemed he had been proved right, of a sudden there was very little he could think of to say.

However, he had to begin somewhere, and the dim and distant past was certainly not the place.

'You have been having a little bit of trouble with her anyway, haven't you, sir?'

Lewis turned away, nodding, avoiding Micklethwaite's eyes and staring at nothing in particular. 'Of course I was having trouble with her,' he agreed. 'About as much trouble as you can possibly imagine. It was all because she lost the baby we were expecting. It drove her to drink, you know. She became a different person. One minute she was fine, and the next—really quite, well, mad, really.'

'Women do tend to take those things so seriously.'

'You're preaching to the converted, David. I had to hire a nurse to—well, you know. You know what it was like for me, I had to hire a nurse to look after her. She was mad after all! I tell you, she was, she was mad! And after all that, now she's left me. Bloody gone and left me. She is mad, of course. We must accept that now—her madness is probably not just a passing pregnancy baby madness, it is probably insanity, true insanity.'

Lewis's forehead was scarlet with fury. Micklethwaite thought that he had never seen it so vivid, not even when one of Lewis's editors married one of his ex-mistresses and defected to another newspaper group.

'It's a bit awkward, isn't it, sir? I mean, looking at it from an objective rather than a subjective point of view, it is a bit awkward, wouldn't you say?'

'A bit!' Lewis savaged both words. 'A bit! I'll say! It is just about as awkward as it can be.'

If he was not so much the accomplished courtier, in view of the unending service that was required of him in every way, twenty-four hours a day sometimes, David Micklethwaite might have enjoyed this moment more, but as it was he could only enjoy his master's vulnerability fleetingly, to his regret. Even so there was, as always, a frisson of enjoyment at the spectacle of such a powerful man as Lewis looking and sounding so discomforted.

'We must keep quite calm, not be panicked into anything, not be wrong-footed. But it is awkward, especially after last time.'

Micklethwaite made sure to make his words sound soothing, but at the same time he was at pains not to suggest anything which could rebound at his feet. He wanted no part of his boss's marital guilt.

'*Especially* after last time.' Lewis took up the cry. 'But couple this with the fact that my enemies, of whom doubtless you are aware I have quite a few— my enemies will be sure to try to nose around this part of my personal life, and then who knows what might not happen? In fact, the more we think about it, David, the more we must realise that this must not get out, not at any cost, not for any reason. We will have to come up with some valid explanation for why she is not presently with me, and then we can make a plan. We must make a plan that will let us *out* of this potential scandal. I can't afford a scandal, not at any price, you understand?'

'We will make a plan now, sir.' Micklethwaite's voice was at its most soothing as his mind went back to the top-secret files at the office.

It had all happened a long time ago, but it was none the less a fact, if only at the office, filed away in a safe. The code numbers needed to open that safe had, as always with Lewis, not been written down. They were stored in a very safe place—David Micklethwaite's head. It had all been covered up of course, the true story never coming to light, but both Micklethwaite and Dr Mellon knew what had happened, and the fact that they were the only people who did made the whole matter even more important—for them. That knowledge alone was the power that kept them where they were, and their lifestyles what Micklethwaite would call 'very nicely thank you'.

She too, like Trilby Smythson, had been young, and innocent. Well, as innocent as any girls were nowadays. Hardly Queen Victoria but nevertheless Talia—what had been her surname—oh yes, Talia Fisherton. Nice little thing, not as pretty as the new one, but very, very sweet, and although not from the top drawer that had not mattered in the least, because if you marry someone as rich as Lewis that kind of thing, the class thing, really did not show up, not when you had the clothes, the lifestyle, above all the servants to cover for you.

Lewis had met her in Canada during the war, and they had married out there, and he had brought her back to England, given her everything, more than everything, more than any girl could dream of, and she had repaid him by committing suicide, taking her own life only weeks after marrying him.

What more terrible condemnation for a man could there be, Micklethwaite had often wondered, most particularly for a man who could give a woman anything she wanted. To be a multi-millionaire with access to everything that should make a woman happy, and then to find her dead from an overdose of sleeping tablets, must be not like a slap in the face, it must be like a karate blow to the throat. To go in to your young wife, a beautiful young girl whom you loved passionately, and to find her dead, surrounded by the trappings of extreme luxury—it was more than insulting, it was degrading.

It was as if Talia had been saying, 'You can give me everything but not even that is enough when it comes to living with you.'

Lewis James had gone into the most terrible mourning. So Lewis's father had singled out Micklethwaite, being more or less the same age as Lewis although only new to his staff at that moment, to deal with him. Then of course the father had only upped and died, just at that most awkward of moments, and Lewis, being in the state he was, had been quite unable to cope with his new responsibilities.

Day after day Micklethwaite had called round to his house to find him sitting crying and stroking all the clothes he had bought for her, all her trousseau. He had just sat about stroking every item of her wardrobe, wandering about her bedroom like a mad person. Of course Dr Mellon, the eponymous family doctor, the ever reliable spectre at the feast, had smoothed over what was always decorously referred to as 'the arrangements' and the poor girl was immediately taken away, whisked back to Canada, and buried in discreet circumstances, and no more to be said.

Finally, on Dr Mellon's advice, Micklethwaite had sailed to South Africa with Lewis for an extended holiday, and eventually, very eventually, they had come back to England, and Lewis had taken up his responsibilities and returned to a full social life. The matter was never referred to again, until now.

'It's a bit difficult to know how to go about tackling this problem, isn't it, sir? You say she left a note? I wonder if I might read it? See if it had any, er, inclinations in it—any depressive signs—that sort of thing?'

This was the nearest that Micklethwaite dared to come to referring to the previous tragedy. Indeed, they were both well aware that he could not trust himself to say any more. Even Micklethwaite, who had never been famed for his sensitivity, understood only too clearly that if it had to be recorded that there had been two suicides in two marriages, Lewis would start to be looked upon as having achieved some sort of ghoulish marital record.

Apart from anything else, Micklethwaite shuddered to think of the implications as far as rival newspapers were concerned. And then there was the political side to it. Doors to ministers that had always remained permanently open to them might shut if a newspaper proprietor was made out to be some sort of monster. Doubtless they would put about rumours of sadism, or unacceptable sexual practices. All this ran through Micklethwaite's mind as he waited for Lewis to tell him what he had done with Trilby's letter.

'I threw it on the fire. I threw Trilby's letter on the fire.'

If he had not been talking to Lewis James, David Micklethwaite would have said, 'Not a very clever thing to do, was it?' but as it was he merely nodded. He knew Lewis had many minor obsessions, one of them being that he insisted on the servants lighting

295

the fires in every room, winter and summer, simply because he liked the smell of wood burning. Another was his preoccupation with covering his tracks, a natural consequence perhaps following the tragic failure of his first marriage.

'If you can remember the wording, sir, it would help. I mean,' he went on more boldly, 'I mean there was no hint of—er—no sort of finality in the tone of the letter, was there? If you don't mind me asking?'

Lewis shook his head. 'Far from it, the tone was almost cheerful. Crisp, in fact. Yes, that is how I would describe it—crisp.'

'Crisp.'

'Yes, crisp. She merely stated that she was very unhappy with me, and she no longer wanted to live under the same roof as me, and that she was leaving without taking anything more than her toothbrush and an overnight case, and I could keep everything that I had ever given her, and she wished me happiness in the future.'

Lewis sat down very suddenly on a nearby bench. The reality hitting him once again had made him feel quite faint. It was true. He suddenly realised just how true it was.

Trilby was gone. She was his and yet she was gone. He felt as if someone had cut off both his arms. He felt more than bereft, he felt suicidal, and at the same time insane with fury, so much so that he felt like shredding himself into little pieces. No-one but no-one treated him like this.

Except—and again the realisation hit him in a strangely fresh way, as if it too had only just happened—except someone else had, and she had escaped from him for ever, to the grave.

He looked up at Micklethwaite. 'In view of my past bad luck in this area you realise that we have to treat this situation with kid gloves, David? I can't afford a second wife committing suicide, can I?'

David Micklethwaite shook his head slowly.

'Well, then, David, you've got a double first from Cambridge—'

'Not me, no, sir. That was Edmund Harrap, your other assistant, the one that left—I am afraid I am not the clever one, sir.'

But Lewis did not seem to hear. 'We must view this whole matter in the coldest manner possible. First, we must not let her *family* know what has happened. They will not suspect at first, because they take very little interest in her, really. Though the father behaved very oddly last time they were here, seemed very drunk I thought.'

The mention of Trilby's family made Micklethwaite colour. He was not a man with a very tender conscience, but seducing Agnes Smythson on a chilly British beach was one of the less proud moments of his life.

'I agree, that seems a good idea, to keep it from them. For the time being at any rate.'

Lewis must have noticed Micklethwaite colouring because he said, 'Of course, you seduced Agnes. You did seduce her on that ridiculous seaside holiday, didn't you?'

Micklethwaite nodded slowly. 'Yes, sir, yes, I did.'

'In the circumstances, David, when we come to think of it, that could prove to be very useful.'

Lewis hardly ever called him 'David' but when he did, he did it so often that it became horribly noticeable, and for no reason that he could

297

understand it always made Micklethwaite shiver inwardly. Lewis's usage of his Christian name appealed to him as being a little like a torturer being kind to you before pulling out your toenails.

'I don't understand what you mean, sir?'

Of course Micklethwaite understood exactly what Lewis meant. He could see from the look in his eye exactly what he meant by its being 'very useful'.

'You could do it again, couldn't you, David? You could seduce Agnes again, she's a very good-looking woman, it won't be much of a sacrifice, I wouldn't have thought, and that would put us in the catbird seat, wouldn't it? A terrifically strong position, that. You could hold it against her, promise not to tell her husband about you, thereby securing her loyalty about her stepdaughter. You could do that, couldn't you?'

Lewis looked excited at the notion. It was as if he had found a new and original line on things and was feeling buoyantly creative as a result.

'And then, then you could find out from her, she must know, you could find out from her, surely, where her stepdaughter is hiding? And then we could rescue Trilby from her fit of insanity, because obviously she has gone mad, must have gone mad, to up and leave just when she was getting so much better?' Lewis was looking more and more cheerful. 'And we could put her into Dr Mellon's hands, make her realise she needs treatment. He has that new clinic near Ascot, we made a large donation to it—remember?'

'Yes, of course. He's pioneering something or other there, isn't he?'

Lewis did not seem to hear. 'We must make

ourselves responsible, after all, for rescuing this poor girl's mind, mustn't we, David?'

'Yes, sir.'

David Micklethwaite sighed inwardly. He disliked becoming too personally involved in Lewis's affairs, and tried, as much as possible, to keep them at arm's length, fixing him up with women when needed, but not more, not after the first marital fiasco. Business affairs were much more his field. Although, of course, it was because of the first marriage and the potential scandal, because of Micklethwaite's discreet handling of it, that he had secured the confidence of Lewis James to such an extent that there was some information, some financial information in particular, that was stored *only* in David Micklethwaite's head, and nowhere else. This information, more perhaps than any personal details, was so valuable to the conduct of Lewis's business that Micklethwaite knew it would never be safe for it to be written down.

No accountant, no employee, could *ever* be entirely trusted, he and Lewis James had agreed that years ago. If anything happened to David, Lewis had often joked to Trilby, part of his empire would wither, because there were certain investment details that only Micklethwaite knew. In return for all this, Micklethwaite had been able to pursue a lifestyle which to someone less privileged might seem to be almost on a parallel to that of his boss. He had a town house, and a country house—not of the same value, of course, but very plush—and he had a bank account in Switzerland, tax free, that was building up annually, so the returns for his loyalty were 110 per cent. He just hoped that he would be able to remember all

299

this when faced with seducing Mrs Smythson again. Not that she was not beautiful, but really—there were certain activities which he felt were now beneath him, and seducing women to keep his boss in wives should, he felt, be one of them.

'Good. Well, that is at least a start.'

As Micklethwaite's heart sank at the prospect before him, Lewis's own feelings of despair started to abate. He had made a plan. He always felt better for making a plan.

'You will make sure to seduce Mrs Smythson, David, now won't you?'

'If necessary, sir.'

'I think it is very necessary, David. It is far too long since you last seduced her, that moment will have lost its power, I should have thought. Ring her today, make a date with her, and let me know how you get on.'

'And you, sir?'

'I am going to go to my wife's studio and search for clues as to where she could have gone, and then I am going to use my trusted friends the de Ribes to help me. They are the only friends that I know I can trust. The only ones that I know will stand by me and remain discreet.'

They both knew that Lewis paid both Henri and Lola de Ribes a small fortune to spy on the upper echelons of Society. There was not a duke, or a countess, not an impoverished honourable anywhere who could count on their privacy when the de Ribes were around.

The de Ribes knew everyone, and of course everyone knew them. But the de Ribes went one better than just knowing the aristocrats, the members of the European royal families, and the international set, they knew *about* everyone, every single aspect of their servant problems, their illnesses—access to Dr Mellon's medical records was most useful in this respect—their love affairs, their problems with their children, drugs, drink: whatever happened the de Ribes were always the first to know.

Between them they had set up a network of spies second to none, and needing none other than the people they fed off they never really had to use much influence, for the truth was that most people were betrayed by their own friends and families, willingly, with malice aforethought, and without a single telephone call having to be made. Envy being the father and mother of all gossip and malice being the child, there was never a chance that anyone in whom the de Ribes might be interested would not, at some time, be betrayed.

'I am not sure that Mrs Smythson is not away, sir.'

'Then find her, David, find her, and do your stuff. She's a beautiful woman, and you're a man, aren't you?'

Micklethwaite had to agree with this, but the fact of the matter was that, although Agnes Smythson was a very attractive woman, he could not find it in himself to like her. He could not even pretend to like her, and that made it difficult for him. He always preferred to be able to convince himself that he at least liked a woman before he took her to bed. It was probably a bit of a boyish thing, some lurking sentimentality, but there it was. He did not feel he could ever like Agnes Smythson. She was undoubtedly a beautiful woman, but so hard.

'I hope I am a man, yes, sir. However. If I can't

301

locate Mrs Smythson, I'll be back to you in twenty-four hours.'

'Good.'

Lewis was beginning to feel better, much better in fact. He would find Trilby whatever happened, one way or another. But despite having set his personal servant on the trail, he nevertheless determined to start to make his own investigations. He would begin by going to Trilby's studio at once.

*   *   *

In fact, as helpless in practical matters as rich men so often are, Lewis found himself outside his wife's studio door before he remembered that she was the only person who possessed a key.

'What now?' he asked his chauffeur, more than a little aware that he was looking a fool and that his chauffeur was all too aware of the fact.

'I think I know someone who can pick locks, sir.'

The chauffeur bent down to the keyhole of the studio door while Lewis stared at the door knocker. The face of the dolphin, for some reason that he could not name, reminded him of Trilby. Perhaps it was because she so loved dolphins, always looking for them when they were in Cornwall on their honeymoon. The memory of their delightful honeymoon being so painful, he turned his eyes from the door knocker to the chauffeur.

'Come on, man, hurry up. Where do we go next?'

The chauffeur remained phlegmatic, as he always did when he was dealing with Lewis. 'We don't go anywhere, sir.'

Lewis frowned as his driver returned to the

Rolls-Royce waiting by the pavement, and opening the boot of the car removed from it a grey cloth roll the inside of which, some seconds later, revealed itself to be filled with keys of different sorts and sizes.

'Very useful, sir. I always keep this, for emergencies. After all, you never know, do you, sir?'

The chauffeur straightened up. Lewis stared at him, realising in an instant that if his driver could open Trilby's studio door with such ease, he could open many another door too. Doors that Lewis had thought inviolable were available to Lyons. It was at these moments that he found he was grateful to David Micklethwaite. No-one, after all, could possibly use a key to open his memory. There at least, in Micklethwaite's head, was the safest of safes, the safe that had no key.

Lewis stepped into the small hallway, and perhaps because he had obtained entry by such a devious method he quite forgot to leave the chauffeur outside, which meant that Lyons stepped in after him.

'Stay there, Lyons, will you? I mean, guard the door. I don't want my wife coming back and finding us—particularly me—here. She doesn't like me coming in, you know.'

'Yes, sir.'

'It is ridiculous, but it seems she has some sort of bee in her bonnet about my seeing her paintings. You know what women are like, don't you, Lyons?'

'Yes, sir. She was very highly strung, wasn't she?'

Lewis turned at that 'was'. 'She *is* very highly strung, Lyons, very, that is why I have to come here to examine her paintings. They may well prove to be—you know—a guide to her state of mind. Show up her—well—her unbalanced approach to life.'

'I don't think Mrs James was unbalanced, if you don't mind my saying, sir. She never struck me as being unbalanced at any time, if you will forgive me saying so, sir.'

Again Lewis turned. He would have liked to have said, 'What the hell business is it of yours, what she was, or is?' But they both knew he could not for the simple reason that they had both just broken into what was to all intents and purposes private property.

'Oh, don't you, Lyons? That is interesting.'

He meant quite the opposite. Lewis did not find Lyons's opinion at all interesting. In fact, he suddenly realised that he had probably never before heard an opinion from Lyons the whole time Lyons had been working for him, thank God.

'Mrs James was, or is, just a modern young woman, sir. She did not understand being caged. That does not mean that she was insane, if you don't mind me saying, sir, it just means that she was not the old-fashioned sort. Not the kind to have her feet bound like a Chinee. I drove her so often I should know. She was a nice young woman. Nothing mad about her, or insane, sir, if that is of any comfort. And I grew to know her quite well, really I did. She might have been a bit highly strung, but that is all.'

'Dr Mellon thinks that losing our baby accounts, probably more than anything else, for her recent erratic behaviour. That is Dr Mellon's private opinion and his medical one too.'

Lewis was now bored with his chauffeur and his opinions, so he wandered off down the big room in

304

search of some clues as to Trilby's exit from his life, where she could have gone, and with whom.

Lewis had never had any interest in Trilby's painting, any more than he had much interest in her as an individual, once they were married. Women were not, to Lewis's mind, individuals; being a newspaper man he did not think of the opposite sex in that way. As far as he was concerned women were either the kind that were prepared to wear black lace underwear for the fashion columns, or the ones who posed for the Society pages in a cashmere twinset and a string of pearls. They were either two-faced or faithful, divorced or happily married. All in all they were either good girls or bad women, faithful wives or naughty mistresses, all of the types reflected on some page or other of the hundreds of pages of his publications. What they were not, at any time, and he could never bring himself to think of them as such, it was too complicated and somehow irritating—what women were not, at any time, were people. Men were people, not women.

So it was with a sense of shock bordering on panic that he now viewed Trilby's paintings, noticing with a mounting, unreasonable anger that she had even signed them *Trilby Smythson*, not *Trilby James*.

At work here was not the young innocent girl that he had met and married, the creator of the amusing little cartoon series that he had put out for a few weeks under the pseudonym *Jerry*. Here was not the young woman who had so decoratively occupied the seat at the other end of Lewis's dining table or graced his drawing room, here was not the innocent girl who had made love to him, or sat silently admiring him as he aired his views and entertained his friends, here was an individual with a strong and passionate sense of the world, a love affair with colour, and a vigorous style all of her own.

Many of the paintings, for some reason he could not understand, were of the tropics, but they were not the travel posters of most people's depiction but splashes of brilliantly coloured and exotic plants, and beaches filled with happy natives wearing nothing at all.

Of course Trilby being Trilby had given many of the paintings humorous titles, such as *Ascot Hats* for a painting depicting African ladies with red and yellow bandannas around their heads, and absolutely nothing else on their bodies except broad, happy smiles.

Aside from the exotic there were paintings of what Lewis's papers always referred to as 'ordinary decent people'. A railway man standing outside the closed gates of an Underground line. A flock of ducks on the Serpentine being fed by a nanny and child, an old lady with white hair seated on a chair, staring out with calm eyes at the world that she knew she might, quite soon, be leaving.

All the paintings were meticulously notated and framed, with the exception of the old lady who, Lewis could see when he grew closer, was not yet finished. This must therefore be the last painting she had been working on. Mentally Lewis turned away from the words 'last painting', dreading that it might be true.

He might hate Trilby at that moment, he might be hoping that she was mad (after all only a madwoman would leave Lewis James, wouldn't they?) but he definitely did not want her dead. He could not afford to have two wives who died on him. It could destroy him in the eyes of the world. They would think that there was something wrong with *him*!

It was an appalling thought and one that had haunted him for the past hours. His editors, his staff, his servants, all with accusations in their eyes, all imagining him to be some kind of Bluebeard, some kind of monster, a man whose wives so hated him that they had both taken their own lives rather than carry on living with him.

'You have dropped my wife here quite often, Lyons, haven't you? Do you, by any chance, know this woman?'

Lyons, his chauffeur's cockaded hat under his arm, came up to the canvas, and stared up at it. He knew very well who the lady was, but he was not prepared to tell Mr James. He liked Mrs James too much. Besides, it was none of his business. Moreover—he looked at Mr James, standing there in his expensive Savile Row suit, his valet-ironed shirt, his gold cufflinks showing at just the required length on his shirt cuff—he had never thought that the governor treated his poor little wife as he should.

Always sending Lyons chasing after her, spying on her, as if she was a bloody Nazi agent, not a young woman with a will of her own. Time after time Lyons had been reduced to feeling like a private detective sent on some sleazy surveillance mission, following the poor girl to some innocent place—the art shop where she purchased her paints, the café where she bought herself sandwiches at lunchtime, the hairdressers where

307

she had her hair trimmed into its modish elfin style.

'I knew she was painting an old lady, lately that is, the friend of a friend, I think, but I never did ask her name or anything, Mr James. After all, we were not meant to communicate too much with Mrs James, were we, sir?'

'Why not?'

'As I remember it, sir, it was on your orders.'

Ordinarily, Lyons would have smiled at this palpable hit, but not with Mr James. If he had dared to smile at such a dig Mr James would have noticed, and sacked him. Instead he stared at one of the paintings as intently as any prospective buyer.

'On my orders was it, Lyons? Oh, yes of course, I suppose, it must have been, now I come to think of it.'

Lewis had the feeling that he was getting nowhere with his chauffeur and it was making him unnaturally humble.

'Yes, sir,' Lyons continued with some relish. 'If you remember, sir, it was on your orders, to all the staff at all times, that we were asked not to talk to Mrs James more than was *absolutely necessary*.' He was flinging the words back in his employer's face, and enjoying it too. 'That, sir, is why I would not know who Mrs James was painting, or why she spent so much time at her studio rather than at home. I knew it was your orders that I was to mind my own business, so I left it at that, at minding my own business. Left it to her who she was painting. None of my business, really, as I say, on your orders. I dropped Mrs James off, and I picked her up, sometimes, if you remember, sir, with you, and other than that I just followed your orders, but I

308

never knew what she was painting—sir. That would not have been right, not after you had made it so clear that we were not to communicate with her more than was strictly necessary—sir.'

Lewis now had the very definite feeling that his chauffeur was cheeking him, but he was damned if he knew what to do about it. It was a fact that no matter what he said to Lyons just lately he always had that same feeling, that Lyons felt himself to be superior to Lewis in some way. Trouble was he was a damned good driver, which made it difficult to get rid of him. And what was more, Lewis knew that other people had been after Lyons over the years, but Lyons had remained loyal to Lewis, and that after all was something.

'Oh well, I'll soon find out, no doubt someone else knows who this old bag is. I'll ask Madame de Ribes, she knows everyone. She will no doubt be able to identify the old lady for me.'

Lyons nodded, his face as inscrutable as Mrs Woo's, as it always was when he was being made privy to information that he knew would probably be his and his alone.

'Yes, sir. Madame de Ribes should be able to help you, she usually can, can't she, sir?' He turned on his heel as if that was an end to the matter, but his mind was working overtime, as it usually was when it came to Mr James. He did not like his employer. He liked his employer's little wife. He did not want the poor little thing found, not, that is, if she did not want to be found.

*　　　*　　　*

Piers was talking to Trilby. His subject, not really

309

surprisingly in the circumstances, was her husband,
Lewis.

'I think you will find that Lewis probably no
longer cares where you are by now. I mean, once
he found your letter saying you don't want to be
married to him any more, that would be more or
less that, I should have thought.'

'I wish I could believe you.'

'There's been nothing in the news, and none of
his reporters have been sent after you. If his people
cannot find you, he will probably wipe your name
from the slate, and that will be that. Besides, you
must remember, you have rights. No-one but no-
one should be forced to continue in a marriage
where they are desperately unhappy.'

Trilby leaned forward. Despite the fact that Piers
was older than herself, despite the fact that he had
fought the Mau Mau, he was naïve.

'Remember when you were in the army, Piers?'

'Yes, of course.'

'You had rights then, didn't you?'

'Yes.'

'Remember what they amounted to?'

'Yes.'

'Go on.'

'They amounted to what my corporal would call
"diddly squat".'

Trilby smiled. 'Exactly. Well, it's the same with
wives. We have *diddly squat* when it comes to rights.
That is the reality, whatever anyone tells you.
Besides, by leaving I know I will have dented the
pride of the great Lewis James, and he won't like
that. You see, what is difficult to understand is that
he can do anything he wants. I have sat at his
dinner parties and heard him and his friends

discussing ordinary people. They—we—are gnats on their windscreens, probably less than gnats, really. To him, and people like him, we are entirely disposable. And besides, even should he divorce me—what then? I shall be a pariah. In England getting divorced is still the one sin you do not commit, even nowadays.'

'I think you are exaggerating out of fear.'

'I wish I was, but I know that, one way or another, Lewis will find me, he will track me down, wherever I am.'

'This is the 1950s. Not even the great Lewis James can behave like Hitler, Trilby.'

'He can and he will. More than that, he has spies, everywhere. I haven't a chance of not being found, and then—well, I don't really know. After all—' Trilby stopped suddenly.

'After all?'

'They have only just repealed the act that allows a husband to put his wife into an asylum if she can't answer six questions put to her by his doctors! Look at poor Mrs Eliot—the poet's wife—he had *her* locked up.' She smiled. 'Heaven only knows, I would never have got past the first question, let alone six!'

'Lewis will have to get past me, remember? Think of me as your knight in patched-up armour.'

Trilby smiled at Piers as he raised his elbow and displayed his patched jumper, and then she gazed out of the wide open kitchen window.

It was well past midnight, the night sky was a myriad of beautiful stars, the chorus line accompanying the biggest star of all—the moon. Lewis would be somewhere out there, under some portion of that same sky, but not as yet near. For

311

now it was enough to listen to the hooting of the owls, to hear the night breeze rustling through the thickets and wonder idly when she went outside for their last walk of the evening if she would see a flash of pale emerald that would signal the eyes of a hunting fox staring out of some hidden hedgerow. Of a sudden it seemed to her that she was just part of that same natural world that lay beyond the kitchen window, one of the hunted, always waiting, daily, nightly, pushing away the thought that one of these days, when she turned round, there would be Lewis, the fox, behind her.

*   *   *

David Micklethwaite had booked the top suite of a hotel not far from Glebe Street. He knew the form very well. He should, after all he had been through it many times, if not with Mrs Smythson with many another married or divorced woman. But they, happily for him, had been of his own choosing, while this woman, although undoubtedly beautiful, was quite definitely not.

He tried not to think of this as he waited for her in the downstairs bar drinking a glass of champagne a little too quickly, constantly checking his tie in the mirror behind the bar.

'Ah, there you are.'

He had not remembered her as being quite so good-looking. He turned and smiled at her, hoping that he was looking as sincere in his welcome as he had ever done when meeting some aspiring young journalist who was all too prepared to do anything with him, or for him, but again his imagination failed him.

312

She was wearing a black beaded top with a tight black skirt, itself decorated around the hem with tiny beads. It was beautifully cut, he could appreciate that, and he liked black. Her clothes were expensive, and her jewellery was expensive. He liked that too. He liked a woman to look expensive. He did not know why, because really the time could not matter less, but he found himself glancing down at his own expensive Rolex watch as if he had a train to catch, which was ridiculous, because he had a driver and a car on tap whenever he wanted them.

'Shall we go straight in to dinner?' Meeting her eyes, Micklethwaite saw with some guilt that she looked suddenly vulnerable, as if she knew that he did not want to waste too much time on her.

'Yes, of course.' Her voice, which had been cheerful and optimistic when she greeted him, was now dulled and subdued.

'We can order champagne in the dining room. You like champagne, don't you?'

'As long as it's vintage,' she said, not smiling. 'I don't want shop girl's champagne, if that is what you mean.' She laughed suddenly.

How dreary hotel dining rooms were, it seemed to Micklethwaite, when you were, as he was, constantly in them out of obligation. When you were in them out of dire necessity, out of penal duty, they were worse than dreary, they seemed to be full of the damned, eating, eating, eating. Fat people eating to make themselves fatter, thin people eating and staying thin and greedy. No-one really needing or enjoying what they were swallowing, no-one staying cheered by what they were drinking.

'You're not in love with me, are you, David?' Agnes looked across the table at him.

They had eaten and they had drunk, and pretty soon they would have to—at least he would have to—make love.

'No, I am not in love with you. Did you imagine that I was?'

She was not stupid, so it would have been incredibly foolish to even attempt to lie to her. She was a woman of the world. She would not tolerate a romantic lie. Any woman who looked as she did, and gave that short, sharp, cold little laugh, would not have believed him had he attempted to deceive her.

'No, I did not imagine that you were.' Again the cold little laugh, followed by a sip of her coffee, and another of her brandy. 'No, I just wanted to make sure that we both felt the same.'

'Which is?'

'Real.'

'Oh, I think we both feel real, all right?' For the first time Micklethwaite gave a genuine laugh.

'Good. Because I enjoy sex with you, but I would hate you to think that I was in love with you, or worse, that I thought you were in love with me.'

'This is tough talking.'

He smiled, and for some reason he did not understand he started, for the first time, to find this hard woman terribly attractive. It had never occurred to him before that a woman would go to bed with him for the same reasons that he would go to bed with a woman, for the plain enjoyment of sex, and nothing to do with love. He always thought that women were romantic enough to at least persuade themselves that they were in love with a

314

man. That here was a woman who seemed to have no such requirement was, to say the least, intriguing. He was, of a sudden, very glad that he had booked the best suite, and his earlier fears now seemed groundless. It might be possible that he could have a good time, and, what was more, accomplish his mission of blackmailing her. It was going to be nothing but a pleasure to take her to bed, and remembering Lewis's dismissive attitude he even found himself feeling sympathetic towards her. He just wished that he did not have to blackmail her too.

But here again he was to be surprised.

There was no need to blackmail Agnes Smythson. He had no need to threaten her with telling her husband of their dalliance, or anything else, for that matter. She was far too practical.

'Now.' She sat with her back against the satin bedhead and smiled across at him. Her hair was slightly tousled, as it would be after lovemaking, and she was now wrapped in a black satin dressing gown, and smoking a cigarette, which made her look pleasantly decadent. There was a slight look to her of a courtesan painted by some minor French artist, and, with her dark hair hanging over her shallow forehead, at the same time an attractively raffish air.

'Yes?'

'Yes. Now, down to business, because that is why you are here, is it not, *Mr Micklethwaite*?' she said, coyly teasing. 'Here to do business for some reason that I am dying to know!'

She smiled, but Micklethwaite did not return her smile. The matter was too delicate, too important. 'Very well, to begin at the beginning. How fond are

315

you of your stepdaughter?'

There was a long silence before Agnes Smythson started to laugh. 'Fond of her? She has been a thorn in my side, and her wedding day the happiest day of my life, although I have to say that I certainly did not realise it at the time. I can't tell you, getting that creature off my hands and out of our house was the best thing that has happened to me in years. Her and her father, peas in a pod, two of them in one house, it was enough to drive you dotty.'

'Then you can help me?'

'David. You know I will help you. Any time, anywhere!' She laughed, but this time it was a rich laugh and one that seemed to ricochet off the walls and around Micklethwaite's head, a laugh that belonged to a woman who enjoyed sex, but did not understand love.

'She has left Lewis. He is distraught. We need you to help us to find her, if you will.'

There was a long silence while Agnes took this in, and then she scrambled off the bed, stubbing out her cigarette in the ashtray on the way, and pulling her black satin robe around her.

'My God, but this could mean that I'll have her back with me, at Glebe Street. I certainly hope it doesn't mean that. Where is she? She must be found and sent back to her husband at once. We must find her.'

Micklethwaite nodded in agreement, feeling only gratitude that they were as one in their ideas. They must find the little bitch and send her back to her husband, his boss, and pronto, chop, chop.

'Exactly, we must. The only trouble is . . .' Micklethwaite looked at Agnes and shrugged his

316

shoulders. 'The only trouble is that we do not know where to look for her. Don't even know where to begin. And Lewis, being Lewis, and being in the position he is in, and having so many enemies, a man in his position, and so on, and not being able to afford bad publicity, is, as I say, distraught. In fact he has told no-one except, so far, myself. He has to throw himself on your mercy. You have to help him find her.'

Agnes stared at Micklethwaite. He did not know, as why should he, that he was not the only man with whom she had enjoyed sex over the past months, so the last thing she needed was for some nosy stepdaughter to come back home to live with her. The very last thing that she needed, was someone else around the house spying on her, wanting to know where she was going.

Looking at it dispassionately, Agnes had known for some years now that her marriage was a sham. Michael was too distant, too inhibited for her more exuberant personality. He never wanted to socialise, as she did, never wanted to take her anywhere, except to the occasional restaurant on an equally occasional day of celebration. Yet, conventional as she was, the idea of infidelity only crept up on Agnes very gradually, after she had returned from Bognor of all places, following the brief fling she had enjoyed with David. The whole deceit of it was thrilling. Lying to Michael, watching his seeming indifference, was all part of a thrilling adventure, and one to which she had become extraordinarily addicted.

'Do you know the expression "Follow the man home"?'

Micklethwaite watched Agnes Smythson with

some fascination as she paced the floor, his admiration for her increasing. She was something that he admired, a hard woman. He had met many hard women in the course of working for Lewis James, but they were really not hard enough underneath to be intriguing. They all had turned out to have some sort of soft centre. Some well-hidden weakness for their dogs, or their children, or an old boyfriend, something. But this woman was different. She was truly hard, and she did not bother to conceal it. More than that, she enjoyed being hard. She had, obviously, every reason not to want her stepdaughter to leave Lewis James, but, surprisingly, it was not to do with money.

'I do know the expression. Follow the man home and you will know everything about him, all his reasons for acting as he does in business.'

'We must find out why. Why would Trilby want to leave him? She had everything, didn't she?' The expression on Agnes's face became dreamy as she thought of her stepdaughter's clothes, her jewellery, her large house in a fashionable area, the holidays that she could take when and if she wanted them; of Lewis James's yacht, the paintings in the dining room, the priceless furniture. 'How could she walk out on so much?'

'No reason that we know of, yet. There was nothing, no reason that we can find, as yet,' Micklethwaite continued. 'Lewis had given her everything that she wanted, after her—you know—after her illness. Bought her a studio, and everything in it. And what is more, he handed it over to her to do what she wanted in it, when she wanted. He has been more than generous, more than reasonable, in fact he has been, to my mind, quite, quite saintlike.'

'Of course.' Agnes had stopped her pacing and was standing in front of David. 'Lewis *has* been perfect. He has been a perfect husband. We all know that. She knows that. She is just spoilt, just a spoilt brat. Her father always indulged her, she could always twist her father around her finger. The moment I was out of the door, he took her side, indulged her, and this is the result. But now, not even her father could find her, I don't suppose.'

'No, not her father, but you could. You see, the day that she left she had been in the middle of painting some old lady. But we don't know who, and as it is we can't ask. The matter has to be kept so secret. As you can appreciate, the moment we lift the telephone and start asking questions, well, the cat will be out of the bag.'

'I see that.'

'Which is where you come in.'

Agnes had turned away to the mirror and was applying a thick, red lipstick to her full lips. As soon as she was satisfied that they were glowing and carmine, she eyed Micklethwaite through the mirror, her own eyes narrowed, before brushing her hair, then powdering her nose.

She was such a good-looking woman that Micklethwaite began to feel proud that he had pleased a woman of her undoubted attraction and beauty. A little hint of the more mature film star, a soupçon of the gracious beauty, and more than a dash of the risqué made Agnes Smythson immensely desirable. If he was not otherwise engaged with another equally attractive woman, he would have liked to repeat his experience with her, but as it was, he had done his duty to Lewis James,

319

and it was over, although not to be forgotten.

Nor could he now remember why he had been so reluctant to take her to bed before. Perhaps it had been because of Trilby? Down by the seaside with Trilby dashing about the beach, braving the waves in all weathers, standing on her head in the sand, Agnes Smythson had seemed all too tarnished compared to her slender, innocent stepdaughter.

'Very well. Carry on, quickly. There is obviously no time to lose. Tell me what I can do to help you and Lewis?'

'Well, I thought if you came with me now, we could go to her studio, and you could identify the woman in the painting, the one that she was painting, and you could tell us, perhaps, who she was? And since she was the last person to see Trilby, as far as we know, at any rate, it would hurry things up so much. We could go straight round to her.'

Agnes was now dressing herself with all the speed of an actress in a fashionable revue with only half a minute to spare before she had to go back on stage to perform in another sketch.

'I'll come with you straight away,' she told Micklethwaite. 'What about the hotel? What did you tell them?'

'The hotel?' Micklethwaite looked surprised. 'What did I tell them? Why—nothing.' He smiled. 'I didn't have to. We own it.'

Agnes laughed, impressed. She liked the kind of style that went with vast unseen wealth. In fact she liked everything about the Lewis James organisation, and she could no longer remember why she had been against Trilby marrying him. She dimly remembered it was because she had found that Trilby acted as a distraction for her husband, Michael. Her stepdaughter's comings and goings had been a really rather good cover-up for Agnes. As long as Trilby was dashing in and out of the neighbours' houses, Agnes could come and go as she pleased, seeing friends, shopping, going to events that she considered important, such as fashion shows and jewellery exhibitions, staring at so much that she wanted and so little that she could have.

Hastening round to the studio, on foot so as not to attract any attention, Micklethwaite and Agnes laughed and talked all the way, both of them sure that the painting of the old lady must, without doubt, lead them to the person who had last seen and talked to Trilby. It was bound to, they persuaded themselves; it could not fail to, they told each other. They were both buoyant with the idea of catching up with the little bitch and returning her to her rightful owner.

'She did not leave a suicide note, nothing like that,' Micklethwaite reassured Agnes, but Agnes, who was nothing if not a flinty-heart, merely shrugged her shoulders as if to say *So what if she had?* 'In fact the note that she left was really quite realistic, almost matter of fact, apparently, in tone. So we do think, we almost know, that we could swear to the fact that she is alive. The question is— where?'

Lewis had given Micklethwaite Trilby's spare key to the studio, which he had found in the tiny kitchen when he broke in with Lyons, and this Micklethwaite now inserted quietly into the lock of the outer door. The side street in which the studio stood was as quiet as any country lane at night, and the slightest sound would, he feared, serve to attract the attention of someone who knew Trilby and would wonder what they were doing there. Perhaps some neighbour walking a dog, or some other painter—for there were a number of other studios in the street—returning from the small local pub where mildly bohemian folk liked to meet and exchange mildly left wing views.

'Right, good. Now for the second door.'

Agnes had not even known that Lewis had given Trilby a studio in which to paint. And even if she had she would have been less than interested, for the truth was that Agnes was never even vaguely curious about anyone else, unless they were interfering, or, as in this case, threatening to interfere, with her pleasures.

David Micklethwaite switched on the lights and looked round the suddenly big, light room with blinking eyes. It was after midnight, and he knew that just the lights going on could attract unwanted attention.

'So this is where she was painting?'

He nodded as Agnes stared around her.

'And what else was she doing here?'

'Else?'

Agnes started to laugh at Micklethwaite's expression. 'Don't be naïve, David. A girl like Trilby married to an older man, coming here every day, you don't suppose she was *just* painting, do you?'

'Oh yes, I think she was, I don't think that Trilby is promiscuous in any way. In fact I happen to know that she was not, absolutely not promiscuous, she was, is, just not that sort of girl. I would stake my life on it. Besides, Lewis being Lewis, she would not have had any opportunity. He always had her watched, or so he said.'

Micklethwaite surprised himself by the shock in his voice. He had never been aware of feeling loyal to Trilby in any way, but now he realised that he did feel loyal to her. At least, he felt loyal enough to defend her, or to defend the person he imagined she was. Indeed there were times, knowing what he knew about Lewis, when he had, albeit fleetingly, even felt a little sorry for her.

'Oh, well, if you choose to take that line, I can't stop you. But believe you me, if a girl ups and runs off, it is hardly ever with no-one. In fact, if you care to take a bet, I will lay you ten pounds that we will find that my stepdaughter has a lover.'

Micklethwaite, again for no reason that he could name, felt shocked by the very notion of an innocent, fresh young girl like Trilby being an adulteress. He surprised himself by his deep-seated desire that she should always remain as she had been when he had first met her. He knew it was impossible that she could, yet he hoped, illogically, that she had.

'We had better find this painting before someone finds us.' He nodded up at the skylights above them. 'People in these narrow London streets are always so nosy. If some neighbour sees these on, they might call the police.'

'We'll be all right.'

'Not for long we won't, she never ever works here at night. Lewis likes Trilby home at six, on the dot, when he gets back, and there would be all hell to pay if she stayed any later, I know that.'

Micklethwaite walked down the room and started to sort through the various canvases stacked

323

against the wall, picking them up and staring at them uncritically, searching for a painting of an old woman. Until he remembered that Lewis had told him that the relevant painting was the one that was still on the easel at the very back of the studio.

He went at once to the easel, and stared up at it. It was indeed a portrait of an old lady—the hands, the frock, the shoes told him that—but the face, the hair, the neck had all been blacked out. He stared at it, mesmerised. Like everything disfigured by desecration, by graffiti, the once innocent canvas now looked shockingly obscene.

And yet a blacked-out canvas can become mesmerising, asking, as it does, why? What lay behind it? Suppression lends importance, and at that moment nothing was more fascinating to Micklethwaite, and even to Agnes, than that blacked-out canvas.

CHAPTER TEN

The Sunday following the start of Trilby's summer sojourn, having watched Piers cook more food than, she imagined, could possibly be eaten even by a bunch of hungry youngsters, she set off with Piers to collect 'Mum's brood' from Wake Park.

The winding narrow lanes of Dorset were lined with bright fresh green grass full of early summer flowers. As they drove with the windows down, the dawn chorus, always so noisy in early morning, had turned from choral work to duets and solos, so that every now and then, when they stopped to allow another car through, or sat while a farmer moved his cows from one pasture to another, Piers would put his head on one side and say 'Listen—a nightingale'. Or 'Ah, my friends the blackbirds', and Trilby, who really did not know one bird's song from another, would also put her head to one side and strain to hear what Piers could hear—the innocent differences of nature carolling into the pure, clear Dorset air.

Wake Park was originally Jacobean, Piers had told her, but had been added to over the centuries by different owners, long before the Society for the Preservation of Ancient Buildings came into being. The end result, in the twentieth century, was a house that presented itself in as unplanned a manner as a woman who has somewhat carelessly chosen her clothes from many different designers, but ended up with a surprisingly harmonious effect. Wake Park was therefore revealed to be a little grand to the front, a little informal to the side, and a little surprising everywhere.

As soon as the housekeeper brought the children downstairs, the old dark wood-panelled hall rang with shouts and laughter, and the whole feeling of the interior of the house became one of informal gaiety. Solemnly Piers introduced each child to Trilby, and Trilby, equally seriously, shook their hands, before heading back with Piers to the old Land Rover in which the children were ferried to and from their grandparents' home.

As one person, and obviously knowing what to expect, the children jumped into the old capacious jalopy with its muddy exterior and worn seat which Piers had made more comfortable with old horse rugs. Upon these the four of them now sat, chattering non-stop to each other, and to Piers, interrupting each other, their conversations happily inconsequential, words and laughter a carousel of sound that went round and round, rising above the noise of the old engine, spiralling towards the early summer day outside.

Climbing last of all back into the Land Rover Trilby sat down beside Piers, but she had hardly settled herself into her seat before he started to sing and the children behind him, on cue, joined in.

They sang all the way from Wake Park to the farm, and the children, obviously knowing what was expected of them, gave of their best without a pause. They sang old songs and new songs, they sang songs they had heard on the wireless, and songs they had learned at school, or in church, and they did not cease singing until the Land Rover finally drew up in front of the old farmhouse. Then they all, with one joyous shout, jumped from the old farm vehicle and ran into the house, talking and laughing at the tops of their voices.

'Are you tired already?' Piers asked, raising his voice above the din, and as Trilby shook her head he went on, 'Well, you soon will be, I can promise you!'

The children obviously knew the Sunday routine, because armed with jugs of lemonade and packets of crisps they left Piers and Trilby alone to finish off cooking lunch while they streamed back out of the front door to the barn, where table tennis and other amusements were waiting for them. Meanwhile in the kitchen Piers set about identifying each child in more detail to Trilby.

'Minette is the tall one, she had a Trinidadian father. Lindsey is the boy with the reddish curly hair, his father was Governor of—well, never mind, but anyway he was a governor. Then there's Jonathan and Millie, both blond and English-looking—they share the same father. He was a major killed in Singapore, I think, something like that. So, that's the lot of us, except me of course. I was Mum's first, before she did a bolt to the West Indies, for some reason best known to herself.'

He smiled briefly at nothing in particular and poured the Yorkshire pudding mixture into a baking tin. Trilby went on scraping carrots, not saying anything, knowing that if she did, and it was the wrong thing, it might turn out in some way or other to be wounding.

'My mother was very beautiful,' Piers said, straightening up from the Aga. 'Men just adored her. If they liked red hair, that is. She was red-haired like Lindsey, which is probably why he is such a handsome boy. Still, much as I loved Mum, God forbid he should turn out like her, really.' He smiled. 'Not that I would not want him to have her charm, but you know how it is, she was one of those wild creatures that are always at odds with the world, and I really would not want that for Lindsey. My grandparents disowned my mother. They still say they have no idea where she came from, so unlike was she to the rest of their really rather staid family. Perhaps she was conceived on some wild night when the moon was red. At any rate she went from bad to worse, and back again, never once staying still, not once. Every few months, we moved, myself, Mum, and this ever growing family. When we were in the West Indies, we island-hopped all the time. She took me away from school so that we could move around quicker. That was how and why I learned to cook, because if one of us

327

didn't, we should all have starved. My childhood memories are always of being in a kitchen trying to keep Mum's ever growing tribe of love-children from passing out from no victuals! Finally, once they could dress and wash themselves and tell the doctor where the tummy pain was, my grandparents took them all over, and I went into the army, and my uncle died and Aunt Laura reverted to her maiden name and, for reasons I never have found out, made over Charlton to me. So, here I am, busy, busy, busy, as you see, and still cooking for them, the little devils.'

Having finished chopping the vegetables, Trilby sat down on one of the kitchen chairs. Putting her chin on her hand, she sighed happily. 'You have just made me feel so, well—so lightweight, really.'

'How about these for pies?' Piers held out one of two perfectly cooked steak and kidney pies, with their decorative pastry animals cooked to a golden brown to match the underlying crust.

'Perfection. But I have never seen so much food. Roast beef, Yorkshire pudding, roast lamb, and pies! It doesn't seem possible!'

'Oh, it's always the same, every fortnight. They all long for something different, you see, and seeing that I am their father and mother replacement I cook it all, and that makes them realise that I love them all quite equally. Can't have any favouritism.'

'A friend of mine used to say that you could always tell a really loving mother because she cooked Yorkshire pudding not just with roast beef, but with roast lamb too!'

Trilby sighed again, just as happily, but also nostalgically. Moments like these, kitchen moments full of warmth and sunshine, reminded her of days long ago. After a minute or two she went on, 'As a matter of fact I always thought that men like you, army men, that they wouldn't cook, or anything like that. I thought that certain kinds of people never did those kind of things, that they only really liked hunting, shooting and fishing and that sort of thing.'

Piers turned briefly from his Aga and smiled. 'We all grow up with preconceived notions about each other. It is just how it is.' He threw what looked like half a pound of farm butter into a vast saucepan of soft parsley potatoes and started to mash them energetically. 'It is quite wrong, really. And dull. I mean, I have known generals who could do tapestry better than their wives, and cut out dress patterns better than their sisters. I have known colonels who could draw and paint well enough to be hung in the Royal Academy. Good Lord, Rex Whistler went into battle with his drawing pad fixed to the side of his tank. And every time there was a pause in battle proceedings, he would sketch. It is only other people who put us all into little pigeonholes. It is just mental laziness, really, and it can be rather cruel. Saying which, it is now time to call in the troops.'

Trilby said little over lunch, not because she felt shy, but because she was too interested in what Piers's half-brothers and sisters had to say. As a result she quickly discovered that although the children might not have too many fathers in common, they certainly shared the same sense of ridicule. By the time they were satiated with Piers's chocolate mousse, they had painted a picture of their life and the people who dominated it which was so clearly defined that Trilby felt she could have sat down and sketched all the characters involved.

'Their sense of humour,' Piers told her, as they washed up together, 'is their way of surviving. They know they are a minority, and that out there, beyond the gates of either Wake Park or Charlton House Farm, they are illegitimate, sometimes even "bastards". So their response to this is to put up a humorous flak, a very effective barrage, and hide behind it. Making jokes about everything is their safety valve, and a very good and effective one it is too. Stops people getting at them, because they, as it were, get at themselves first.'

'Lindsey told me he wants to join the Navy, go to Dartmouth.'

Lindsey came into the kitchen at that moment, so Piers, obviously following a much loved routine, immediately whistled a hornpipe, followed by the high-low sound which traditionally pipes an officer on board, at which Lindsey immediately executed a perfect naval officer's salute. After which, with a shy grin at Trilby, he darted back outside with the jug of lemonade that he had called in for.

'They're playing Charlton House Farm Cricket. It's lethal.' Piers nodded towards the window, an expression of modest pride on his face. 'I made it up, ages ago, one rainy afternoon. They take it very, very seriously, I have to tell you. Want to come and watch?'

It was one of those warm, sunny Sunday afternoons when England seems absurdly over-English, what with the trees in full leaf, and the sound of cricket ball on cricket bat, and children's cheers ringing out in support of every run scored.

Four o'clock tea, and the return to their grandparents' house, came far too soon, and not just for the children.

As he stood outside the old house in Dorset, and the evening light began to replace that of the afternoon, Piers took care to embrace each of the children in turn, ruffling heads and making encouraging noises, pretending not to notice that the moment their feet had touched the gravel they had all assumed determinedly cheerful expressions, quickly hugging and kissing their tall, fair-haired half-brother, while he said something different to each one. Reminding Millie to try harder at her maths, Jonathan to let him know if some senior boy was still bullying him. Minette was told not to worry about her Monday history test, and Lindsey wished good luck in his coming house cricket match. All the usual admonitions and encouragements that a good father would make, Piers made.

In return the children all listened to him, bravely, gravely, attentively, for all the world as if he truly was their father, which, as far as they were concerned, he must have seemed to be in every way, except fact.

Trilby tried not to be touched by their courage as they turned towards the tall old house where their grandparents tolerated them in circumstances which had long ago slipped from their control. Where the servants palmed them off with food that was either half cooked or overcooked, and where the sun must, she supposed, seem to shine much less brightly than when they were with Piers at Charlton House Farm, playing cricket and dashing about with the kind of careless energy of which the

331

old are incapable.

'The two weeks until they see you again will seem so long, won't it?'

Piers glanced sideways at Trilby as they drove back to the farm. She was wearing one of his old summer gardening hats, and had slipped down in her seat, her feet propped up on the space at the bottom of the old windscreen.

'Let's sing again,' he suggested, avoiding the question.

Trilby squinted up at him from under his old straw hat and nodded. 'Very well. You start and I will follow, pretty approximately, I am afraid.'

They must have sung exactly the same songs as they had when the old jalopy had been filled with cheerful children, with one exception. As the Land Rover nosed its way towards the farm, Piers, pretending to keep a straight face, sang a solo, at the top of his voice. 'People Will Say We're In Love!'

Despite knowing both the words and the tune, Trilby did not join in the song at any point, but stared straight ahead of her, pulling the hat down lower on her nose, and pretending to take no notice as to its import.

*   *   *

When David Micklethwaite reported back to Lewis that the painting of the old lady had been blacked out by a person or persons unknown, Lewis started to feel that particular sense of threat that afflicts those who are in the privileged position of employing numbers of people

'Who would do such a thing?'

332

'I have no idea, sir,' Micklethwaite said with some degree of sincerity, principally because it was true. He did have no idea. 'I went there with the stepmother, it must have been after midnight. We were there for about a quarter of an hour, and that is when we discovered it. Of course she could not identify the old lady, unless, that is, it is a very black lady that we are looking for!' he ended, half jokingly, trying to relieve the grim atmosphere.

'I was there with Lyons at six o'clock. Myself, and the chauffeur, we were there. You know Lyons, David, he is very loyal. Loyal Lyons, we call him here. He has been with me for about—well, must be over ten years. I doubt that he would do such a thing. In fact I doubt that there would be anyone else who would do such a thing, excepting perhaps Trilby herself.'

They were walking up and down the garden once more, and had reached the point, by the wall, where they always turned. They did so now, and Lewis was at once seized with an idea.

Supposing that Trilby had returned to the studio, after he and Lyons had gone? Supposing that she, and she alone, had returned and defaced her own painting, to stop Lewis finding her?

'She must be in London, David. It must have been her who sneaked back to daub out the painting. No-one else would do such a thing, would they? I mean who else would bother?'

'Surely not?' Micklethwaite stared at his boss. Not just his forehead, but his whole face was now flushed. It was the terrible strain, of course, but even so, Micklethwaite worried for him, knowing as he did, from previous times, just how much emotional upsets affected his health and behaviour.

'Why *surely not?*' Lewis frowned even more furiously.

'Well, because, logically, if I may say so, sir, logically speaking if a girl wants to leave her husband, if she is, let us say, either unhinged, or over-emotional, or plain unhappy, she will, I should have thought, put as much distance between her and her husband as is possibly possible, I should have thought, sir.'

'Yes, but you are not taking into account the fact that Trilby is, was—is—a very talented painter. If she returned to the studio to daub out the old lady, it may be because she was filled with some hatred for her work, that she truly loathed what she was doing, and that being so, well, don't you see, David, she could still be nearby! She could be over this wall, at this minute, watching me coming in and out, and enjoying every moment of my anxiety, like a naughty child. That is what she could be doing.'

In the face of what he considered must be total fantasy, Micklethwaite felt that the best option open to him was to pause, and pretend to be thinking deeply, which he certainly was not. It seemed perfectly obvious to him that it must have been the chauffeur who blacked out the canvas. Trilby might have paid him off, or he might have some misguided sense of loyalty to a young girl he had been paid to spy on for most of her short marriage. Or he might have been in love with her. But it was useless even hinting that this might be so, because like so many rich, powerful men, Lewis found the idea that one of his most trusted servants could be disloyal to him unthinkable. His whole world would start to crumble even more than it already had. Inwardly Micklethwaite sighed to himself. The rich were, in so many ways, so awfully pathetic.

'I understand, from Dr Mellon, that on his last visit she had seemed to be much better, she had seemed to be recovering from the overwhelming sadness which led to her alcoholism. It is a terrible experience, apparently, sir, losing a baby is a terrible experience.'

Lewis burst into a sudden and violent storm of tears.

It was so sudden and so unexpected that Micklethwaite had no time to feel embarrassed either for his employer or for himself. To his extreme surprise he felt only pity and compassion. The sound of Lewis crying, the sound of his deep down hurt, cut into Micklethwaite, and if he had not been so much in Lewis's pocket, if he had not been so much his hireling, he would have put his arm round him, and patted him on the back. As it was, he did not, but only stood looking on helplessly, unable to be of any assistance to the man who was in thrall to such sudden and terrible grief.

'If you had only known how much, just how much, I was looking forward to that baby. How much I longed to hold a child of my own in my arms, and to see her, Trilby, who I adore and worship, holding that child. There is nothing, believe me nothing, David, so beautiful to its parents as the unborn baby. It is more beautiful that any angel that comes closest to the heart of God.'

Again the tears started to pour down Lewis's cheeks and Micklethwaite, the bought man, the hired hand, the employee who was being paid to stand where he was standing, could only look on. Denuded of any friendship as their relationship was, in this moment of extremity it was exposed as being as barren as, in effect, it had always been.

'I am sorry.' Lewis turned away, hating himself for giving way, and then, seconds later, hating Trilby, hating everything and everyone to do with her.

After a minute he straightened his shoulders. Hatred was always an easier emotion for him, and never more than at a moment when he had shown himself to be as human as the next person.

'Don't be sorry, sir, it is only natural. You have, after all, had a bad shock.'

'Shock.' Lewis stared around him as if he had been parachuted into his own garden. 'Yes, I have had a bad shock, you are right. It has been very bad, but now, now I must do something about it.'

Lewis's mouth, never very full lipped at the best of times, now looked to Micklethwaite to be somehow smaller than ever as he cast about him to make a plan, to send someone somewhere on his behalf, always such a relief to a powerful man.

'Yes. The shock has been very bad,' he agreed, playing for time. 'Now, I want you to do something for me, David. I want you to . . .' He paused. 'I want you to go round to—yes, I think you should go round to Henri de Ribes and *talk* to him. He must know *something*. He always does.'

'Is that wise, sir? The de Ribes, well, they are very useful to the newspaper group, I agree, but gossip only, sir, that is their field. I mean, I will agree, sir, that he and his wife are unendingly useful for our gossip columns, but not much more I should have thought. Besides, I should also have

336

thought that it would be better, sir, as we have been saying all along, not to tell too many people. If we tell too many people, well, the cat might very well be out of the bag and no putting him back again.'

Lewis inhaled a great tranche of air, and breathed out noisily. He hated everyone at that moment, but most of all, next to Trilby, he hated David Micklethwaite.

'Look, Micklethwaite, how much do we pay the de Ribes? How much do we pay them annually? Ten thousand—pounds that is, not dollars. And how much does the average man get paid—about twenty pounds a week?'

'I would have to look the precise sum up—'

'Never mind the sums, we pay them a bloody fortune, and what is the end result? A few desultory items every week in a few boring little gossip columns. Well, that being so, I suggest, without any due modesty, since I sign the cheques, or you do on my behalf, I suggest that you get off your backside and go round to their bloody house and you extract from them a few thousand pounds of their time and labour, which is a great deal more than they have contributed so far to the success of my newspapers. And if they fail, I want you to tell them they can kiss goodbye to any more money from me. Again, if the point has not already struck home, you may lead them to understand that by the time I have finished curtailing their money they will be lucky to get to Monte Carlo on a bus, let alone in a chauffeur-driven car! And what is more I will personally make sure that the only member of the international set they will be meeting will be in a fish queue. Now get along. Get cracking, or else.'

No Roman emperor could have been more

337

commanding. But they both knew, Micklethwaite and Lewis, that his sudden volte face, his anger, his bitterness now directed towards the hapless de Ribes, was in fact fury at himself for showing weakness. He had cried in front of his hireling and Lewis, proud man that he was, knew that Micklethwaite would always remember him like that, crying, weak, despairing. The fact that he had seen him in as terrible a state before, over Talia Fisherton, only made matters worse.

When Talia had been found dead, however many years ago it was now, leaning on Micklethwaite had cost Lewis dear. And however rich you may be, and however rich you may think you are, money is still money, and being skinned alive hurt. And it was nothing to do with how much you were being taken for, or because you could not afford it, but because you did not like being taken. No-one liked the feeling that they were being taken, least of all Lewis.

*   *   *

Lola and Henri de Ribes lived in an extraordinarily expensive house. Micklethwaite called on them there, without preamble, knowing as he did that he could secure their attention at once. Moreover, familiar as he was with their invariable habits, he knew that they would be in, changed into evening dress and sipping dry martinis prior to going to the theatre, or out to dinner.

He was well acquainted with the extreme luxury of their house, because he signed the rental on it annually. He had also signed the cheque that paid the interior decorators to stuff it with elaborate chintzes, flowered materials, and copies of ancestors that were no relation whatsoever to either Lola or Henri, but nevertheless hung at decorative moments on silk-lined walls every step of the way up to their first floor drawing room.

The maid announced Micklethwaite in a strangled Spanish accent, and he was left standing staring at a scene that he had already envisaged.

There was Henri in immaculate evening dress, his shoes shining, his thin silk evening socks displaying an equally thin ankle, his gold and enamel lapis lazuli cufflinks catching the fading evening light, the matching signet ring on the smallest finger of his left hand bending around the stem of a slender martini glass.

But if Henri de Ribes seemed to Micklethwaite to be part of some tired déjà vu, some previous dream or old reality, his wife, although lacking the natural beauty of Agnes Smythson, was breathtaking in her fashionable elegance, even to Micklethwaite who had, after all, signed the bills for her clothes. She might be middle-aged, but Lola de Ribes always looked not ten times the part that she played with such dedication, but a hundred times the part. One glance would satisfy almost anyone that she belonged to the upper echelons of European Society, and better than that, that she revelled in it.

But of course there was a flaw, a flaw which, Micklethwaite observed to himself, many of her kind did not appreciate. For, having been born on the edge of the world in which she now occupied the position of a queen in her own right, Lola de Ribes had become more aristocratic in demeanour than any patrician would ever dare to be. That being so, it was still discernible, although admittedly only to a very few, that she was not what she pretended.

Tonight she was wearing what Micklethwaite, with his intimate knowledge of her bills and accounts, knew must be a Norman Hartnell dress. Hartnell's famed embroidery, the intricacy of the work that he commissioned for his designs, was recognisable even to Micklethwaite.

The dress was of cream satin with pink beaded floral motifs, strapless to show off a pair of white, powdered, sloping shoulders. It was tightly waisted and fell in two side pleats from the bodice to a three-quarter length. With it she wore matching satin shoes and—presumably since the dress was so lavishly embroidered with stones—no other jewellery besides a few heavy rings whose edgings of small diamonds, like her husband's cufflinks, caught and played with the gentle London light, throwing it towards the ornate furnishings of the room as she raised both her hands in welcome.

It was unsurprising given the elegance of the scene that Micklethwaite, despite his own wealth, felt dowdy, inelegant, and worst of all somehow inferior. In fact the scene before him could not have been calculated to have annoyed him more. He wanted to stamp on it. He wanted to deface it. And, which was more than satisfying to a man like himself, he knew without any doubt that he could. More than that, he had been given the authority to do so. He could threaten the exquisite scene which now affronted his eyes, he could tear it down, sack the actors and replace them with others.

'I think we had better go into the garden.'

The de Ribes both knew, at once, as spies and

340

agents always do, that this was a signal for important news. Their help was needed urgently.

Lola de Ribes's stiffly blackened eyes slid sideways to her husband. They were meant to be going to dinner with the French ambassador in twenty minutes. She did hope that whatever it was that Micklethwaite wanted to tell them would not take long, but of course she could not say so, any more than she could make it plain that going into the garden in satin evening shoes and a satin evening dress and matching coat was not what she considered a lady should have to do before going out to dinner.

However, since the wretched Micklethwaite was a top man in the organisation that kept them in a luxury that neither of them had ever previously enjoyed, she dutifully went to her bedroom and collected a change of shoes from her maid, not to mention a silk rain cape and an umbrella, because she was not going to risk a sudden change in the weather, not even for Lewis James, or the beastly little man he paid to do his dirty work for him.

Out in the garden Micklethwaite communicated to the de Ribes what he had just learned from his master, insisting of course on the need for secrecy. Then he firmly placed the responsibility for finding the second Mrs James squarely in their hands.

'But where should we begin? How do we know where she could be?' Lola de Ribes looked indignant. The situation was serious, but if she had known just how serious it was, for her and her husband, Micklethwaite thought smugly, she would not have looked indignant, she would have looked frightened.

'You know everyone, ma'am. Lewis is counting

on you.'

'I will ring Lewis and explain. We can't possibly be asked to take this on. We know nothing about the girl, not really. She has not been his wife for long enough. The doctor knows more. Dr Mellon knows more than we do, why not enlist his help?'

'This is an order.'

'How do you mean?'

Lola de Ribes knew at once, in two seconds flat, what was meant, but Henri was too slow to catch on to the implications immediately.

'I mean . . .' Micklethwaite stood back and gazed at the outside of their immensely expensive house, the newly laid London garden with its use of back mirror on the wall and its careful sense of colour, its elegant eighteenth-century lead statue, its brickpaved paths, and its small fountain. 'I mean, if you cannot be of any help to us, we will not, in the future, be able to be of any help to you.' His eyes ran over the de Ribes in their finery, his meaning quite overt.

This time even Henri cottoned on to what the horrid little man might mean, as Lola caught her breath and stared at Micklethwaite. 'You are holding a gun to our heads, Micklethwaite.'

'Yes.' Micklethwaite smiled and nodded.

'How long have we got?'

'Twenty-four hours, at most forty-eight, I should have thought. Twenty-four hours to come up with something that will lead to Lewis finding her.'

'But she might be dead.'

There was a pause as Micklethwaite considered this.

Dead. Once again he contemplated the idea that Trilby could actually have committed suicide. After all, he had only Lewis's word that the note that she had left had not contained a hint of ending her own life. Supposing he had thrown the letter away to cover up the fact that she had actually wanted to take her own life? Supposing Lewis did have some strange proclivity which drove women to kill themselves? Being a man himself, he would not necessarily know it. Anyway, who knew anything of anyone, when it came to the bedroom? Who understood what made up the human psyche? Not Micklethwaite, certainly. Women were just women to him, even if Agnes Smythson had pleasantly surprised him with her open attitudes.

The strange thing was, in light of Lewis's assertion that the tone of Trilby's letter had been cheerful, Micklethwaite had barely considered the idea that they might find Trilby James dead. Now that the thought had for the first time become a real possibility, he was horrified. He could hardly bring himself to think of the consequences of such a reality, not just for Lewis, but for himself as well, not to mention the two over-dressed phonies standing in front of him.

Because of course the de Ribes were no more 'de Ribes' than he was King Kong. They were, originally, not French aristocrats or even Swiss millionaires, they were not even perhaps Ruritanian. Having apparently got to know Lewis in Canada they had eventually followed him to England, although they were certainly not Canadian either. What they were originally, Micklethwaite had never had any idea, and, until now, very little interest. As far as he was concerned they might as well have been Mongolian goat herders. The only possible reason for him to have any contact with them was for business purposes. Lewis had found them useful to him, that was all Micklethwaite needed to know. And while Micklethwaite had nothing but admiration for anyone who pulled themselves up by their boot straps and changed themselves into languid post-war twentieth-century aristocrats with haughty ways and a large bank balance, the truth was that every now and then, despite their undoubted use to Lewis and his organisation, they got on Micklethwaite's nerves. So for them to look not just mildly indignant but positively affronted at being asked to carry out a small piece of detection for the large amount of money they were being paid was positively hypocritical.

'I don't think that she is dead. You can find her, though, I am sure.' He nodded brusquely, and a few minutes later he was back in his car, being driven off in another direction altogether.

'How I hate that man!'

Lola de Ribes had torn off her silk cape and flung it on one of the over-plump sofas. She also kicked off her outdoor shoes, and went to stare at herself in the gilded and moulded drawing room mirror that dominated the mantelpiece.

'There is no point in wasting emotion, my dear. We must get to grips with our problem.'

'No.' Lola turned. 'No. You go to the dinner. You go to the embassy dinner and I will start to get to grips with our problem, as you call it.'

For no reason that her husband could think of she started to pull off her large, expensive rings, so that what with her stockinged feet and her overwrought expression she gave the impression of a woman returned from a bad dinner, rather than

344

someone who had not yet graced anything but her own drawing room.

'But you are expected, my dear. The ambassador so particularly loves you to sit on his table, to be near him.'

'He should do! I have supplied him with enough information about our fashion industry and manufacturing to keep the French trade figures buoyant for years to come. No, I will not go. You go, and make my apologies. Tell them that, most regrettably, I have a violent migraine. Which, by the time I catch up with this wretched young wife of Lewis's, I undoubtedly will have. I told you that this marriage would be a mistake. No innocent young girl can cope with a man like Lewis James. You know that, I know that, it is just such a pity that the wretched man himself does not realise it.'

'Yes, yes,' Henri agreed, not wanting to remember. 'The man is uncivilised, I agree. But really, I think you should accompany me tonight.'

'No, Henri. Go. I will stay. I have to find out from someone—there must be someone to whom I could link this whole silly episode. I am sure that I can find her, but only if you leave me alone.'

Obediently Henri went alone to the dinner at the French embassy, and his wife sat down and went slowly through all her address books. Addresses were the stuff of life to someone like Lola de Ribes. She had at least twenty address books, none of which were ever discarded. People were her industry, contacts her bread and butter. She had long ago decided never to let her set of contacts from any one of her worlds, and she had many, know that she knew the others. Hence the multiplicity of her filing systems.

Once she had thought about Trilby, concentrating on all the aspects of her personality, Lola took down her 'odds and sods' book. This book of names and addresses, unlike the rest, was constantly changing. It was also full of names that were useful to her in her decorating venture, an enterprise which was only a sideline to her real business of supplying gossip, but a valuable sideline nevertheless, and not one to be despised. There was many a detail of some poor innocent's life that had been absorbed by Lola while that lady was pretending to measure for curtains or covers, or standing with colour cards helping some inane Society hostess choose the exact shade for her drawing room walls.

'Very well, now we have to think of old ladies, do we not?' she asked her Siamese cat, who had just wandered into the room. 'If Micklethwaite is right, and the painting has been blacked out, then that means that whoever sat to her in the weeks before she disappeared is likely to be able to lead me to her side. She will know more about her than anyone else.'

She frowned. Everyone she knew was always sitting to someone, particularly during the London Season, when it passed the time of day, and made a pleasant hobby. Even so, there were not many old ladies who sat to amateur painters, and not many amateur painters who were the wives of men as rich as Lewis James.

She turned the pages of the gold-embossed blue leather volume, calmed now by the idea that she was narrowing the field, and also by stroking the cat, who, purring in the enjoyment of the attention and the warmth of the room, always soothed any

346

unexpectedly ruffled feelings that she might be experiencing. She knew that she could find Trilby James, just by concentrating on the names that she was staring at so intently. It was as if she was a witch and the addresses the entrails of animals, as if she could see in an address a picture that no-one else could see, a picture of a person. More than that, she was allowing her mind to rest, to relax, to remember every thread of every conversation that she had recently enjoyed. Such was her concentration, it was hardly surprising that within a short time Lola had seized on the right name.

'How stupid of me,' she told her cat. 'How stupid of me to forget such a thing! Gracious, it must be the London Season that does it, too many buffet luncheons, too many cocktail parties, too much of everything, and of a sudden such a conversation goes out of one's mind! Of *course*! How ridiculous to have forgotten.'

She stood up and smoothed down her satin evening dress in the excitement of the realisation that the name in her address book would lead her to Trilby James as surely as a trail of aniseed would attract a pack of hounds. She glanced at the ormolu clock that stood in front of the mirror. It was still only half past eight, so she picked up her white telephone with its Belgravia number and dialled.

The old lady invited her round at once, but it was only when Lola had replaced the telephone that she realised that Laura Montague had not sounded in the least bit surprised by the urgent nature of her call.

*   *   *

347

'There has to be another man, doesn't there, Laura?'

Laura nodded slowly. 'Yes, I agree there does have to be someone else in the picture, as it were. But I simply do not understand who would have blacked out that lovely painting she was doing of me. The dear little thing, she is really quite talented, you know.'

Lola de Ribes was not in the least bit interested in Trilby James's talent, only in Trilby James herself.

'Who called at the studio when you were there? Do you remember the men that called to see her? She must have had callers, surely?'

'No, no-one really, not that I remember. I mean, very well . . . no, I lie.'

Lola leaned forward expectantly, her expensive scent making Laura feel a little queasy because she always wore too much.

'Yes, you're right. The chauffeur would call from time to time to pick her up. So, yes, she did have callers.'

'Is he personable, is he good-looking?'

'I have no idea, it's always very difficult to tell with chauffeurs. It must be the cockades on the front of their hats, they can give one such a false impression, I always think.'

Lola frowned, trying to remember Lewis's chauffeur and failing as heartily as Laura. It was true. It was difficult to make out the exact nature of a chauffeur's face under those cockaded hats.

'What about your nephew, Piers Montague? What about him?'

Laura looked sad. 'Yes, that would have been quite the thing, I would have said. They would have been so suited, I agree. Except, no, I am afraid not.'

'Why ever not?'

Laura shook her head, her expression even sadder. 'Oh, no, I am afraid not. You see, my nephew is—ahem—a, er, a confirmed bachelor and always has been, if you understand me? We always knew, everyone in the family knew, he was born that way. Nothing to be done. But he is very charming.'

There was a long silence while the import of Laura's words sank into Lola's head. She knew exactly what the euphemism 'confirmed bachelor' implied in pleasant society. It meant that the man mentioned could never possibly find himself attracted to the opposite sex.

'Piers is very attractive, I grant you,' Laura went on, and a sweet, proud look came into her eyes. 'He is very tall and handsome, but he just does not like the opposite sex in that way. He likes older ladies, which is probably why he comes to stay with me from time to time, but he has never been known to take out a young lady whilst here, I am afraid.'

'But you were talking about sending me down to decorate his house, weren't you? I remember you said that I could help him with his farmhouse, or some such, didn't you?'

'Yes, I thought you could, but the reason I did not get back in touch with you was because—well, apparently he has a little friend who is going to do it for him, now, someone he has known for quite a long time, I believe. So really there was no need to worry you, was there?'

Laura managed to look innocent and vague at

349

the same time. For some reason that Lola could not understand, she blew on the tops of her lace-mittened fingers.

'Just give me your nephew's address, Laura, and I will sort out the rest.'

'There is no real point in giving you his address, I mean Piers's address in Somerset, Lola dear, because I happen to know from a friend—whom I cannot of course name—that she has in fact gone north. Mrs James has gone north. She wanted to get on with some painting, and my friend was taking her to his studio there, to paint the Yorkshire Dales, I think he said. At any rate, she is definitely not in Somerset.'

'The Yorkshire Dales, you say,' Lola stared at Laura Montague. She was too much the innocent old lady for her liking. She was too cute for words, what with her old-fashioned, pre-war black silk frock and her black lace Whistler's Mother type mittens, and her immaculate white hair. 'How do you know, from this friend,' she asked, suddenly suspicious. 'How do you know that Trilby has gone north?'

'Because,' Laura told her, sweetly anxious to help, 'he is a neighbour of her parents, also a painter. I bought something from him only the other day. You know Chelsea, ten painters to every yard!' She gave a light laugh, one mittened hand going up to her mouth as she did so.

Lola stood up, her face flushed from the heat of the old lady's fire. 'So where is this place, this place where your friend has a studio, in the north, where is it?'

Laura told her, and then, having done so, she said, 'You'll never find it, though. I went last summer and it was impossible to find. It is one of those addresses that, quite frankly, no-one can find, a post office conundrum. You know, like saying you live in say Leeds, when in fact you are four miles to the north. Besides which, my friend has gone there with her, so really, you can appreciate, it might well be impossible for you to find the place. And, too, it might be a waste of time. Trilby might have left once you get there.'

By now Lola could have screamed, what with the heat of the room and the overwhelming, almost patronising patience of the old woman, but instead of screaming she said, 'If you could just give me the address I am sure I will find it.'

'Of course. I should be delighted.'

Lola almost ran out to her car again. Her heart was singing at the idea of catching up with Trilby, and probably exactly within the twenty-four hours that Micklethwaite had so sadistically set. She felt clever beyond words, and, not only that, but oddly excited. She liked a drama, and she imagined that whatever else the next twenty-four hours would bring it would certainly bring that.

*   *   *

The face was appearing, slowly, a ferret, and looking like a ferret, but with David Micklethwaite's character. Next to him appeared another animal, a field mouse, looking oddly like Trilby herself, and beside her a dapper-looking hare with more than a passing resemblance to Piers. And then the telephone rang, and, as if she was in a train arriving at a station she did not recognise, Trilby realised what it was almost too late. It was the phone, and it was ringing. Reluctantly she picked it up, coming to her senses, taking in the newly painted sitting room in which she sat, with its bright rugs and books, and the small fire burning in the grate because the farmhouse rooms were still damp, even in summer, and Piers liked to light the fire for her.

A woman's voice greeted her, and Trilby's face brightened. Finally she said, 'Yes, thank you, thank you so much. No, I understand. Yes, that would be lovely.'

She replaced the telephone, and then stared at it, wondering why on earth she had said yes to the unknown voice at the other end. She had been too deep in her drawing, in another world, and now someone who had announced herself as an old friend of Piers was coming round.

Trilby stood up and went to the old mirror hanging on the wall by the fireside and stared at herself. Would anyone who had ever known her know her now, she wondered? Even with her red hair, and her light tan, would they know this Trilby, in her cheap cotton dress and sandalled feet, as the old Trilby James who wore real women's clothes and attended dinner parties every evening, and went to the opera and played obedient hostess to her husband, who was a powerful man of whom it was said that he could, if he wished, help to bring down governments?

Trilby leaned closer to the mirror. Her own answer to her image had to be no; she herself would not know her new self. But really it had nothing to do with the clothes, or the hair colour, but everything to do with being rounded and happy, with not living in fear of Lewis. Everything

352

perhaps to do with being in the country—enjoying the freedom, the lack of restraint, the sense of being able to be herself, not someone that someone else wanted her to be: 'Mrs Lewis James' in tailored suits and dresses, in high-heeled shoes and stockings that needed straight seams and nails that must always be varnished.

But now there was to be a visitor, and what was worrying was that, now that Trilby had remembered what she had said, she seemed to know who Trilby was, and wanted to come round as a result. To put her off could have roused suspicions, but on the other hand, now that she was coming to the farm, she might become too curious. Trilby turned from the mirror. Whatever happened she must act normally. She would say she was just staying with Piers, for a few days, until she had finished some sketching, that kind of thing.

It seemed that only a few minutes had passed when there was a ring of the old iron bell outside the front door. Mabel answered it, and Trilby heard her say, 'Well, I'll have to go and ask Miss Ardisonne.'

Mabel now stood at the sitting room door, her innocent presence as reassuring as a plateful of home-made scones. 'There's Mrs Marston, an old friend of Mr Piers, at the front door, says she's come to see you, and she rang a few minutes ago. Says I told her to call, although I can't remember any such conversation, really I can't,' she added.

'Thank you, Mabel, yes, show her in.'

'Ah, there you are.' The visitor was a large woman in an over-bright mackintosh and matching hat. She cut a colourful figure in the newly decorated sitting room, which Trilby and Piers had

353

painted over a number of happy evenings. As soon as she saw her visitor Trilby smiled. It was difficult not to, for everything about the woman spoke of jollity and good nature. Not just her bright clothes, but the correspondingly bright expression in her eyes, and the bright lipstick that matched her hat and seemed to be spread across the white surface of her face like jam on top of a rice pudding. 'So you're Miss Ardisonne, is that right?'

'That's right.'

'Where's Piers, the old devil?'

'Out in the fields. He will be home at six, or near enough. Not so long now, if you want to stay and see him?'

'Not a bit, I have no intention of staying and seeing him, by no means. No, my dear, I came to see you. I had such a need to see a civilised face. Really, I did. My name is Mary Louise—always known as Marilu. But, you know, you can call me what you like. Goodness, it is good to see someone vaguely civilised. I heard about you from Mabel in the village shop, so I plucked up the courage to come up to the farm and introduce myself. You don't mind, do you, Miss Ardisonne?'

'No, of course I don't mind. It's very nice.'

'Hallo.' They shook hands briefly and Trilby smiled. 'I like to think that I like country life, but moving here—Somerset, it is in the depths of beyond, isn't it? I mean to say, if you're not a cow, if you'll forgive the expression, or an excuse me sheep, if you're not an excuse me hen or a duck, you might as well just hang up your hat around these parts, that is how interested Somerset is in people. If they can't shear it, or kill it, if they can't wring its neck, smoke it, or ride it, they simply

354

don't want to know. Mind if I smoke?'

'Of course not, please. Do sit down.'

Mary Louise sank down into one of Piers's old leather armchairs and lit an untipped cigarette with a slim gold lighter with the expertise of a woman who had been waiting to smoke for at least ten long minutes. She exhaled thankfully, and at the same time carefully removed a piece of tobacco from the tip of her tongue.

'I hate to think of you having to go through what I have had to go through these last ten years, my dear.'

Trilby looked interested by this statement, but not startled. 'Has it been very tough?'

'Tough. My dear, can you imagine? Not a shop that sells anything except lisle stockings, not a hairdresser that knows how to cut anything except the Windsor Bob, and worst of all nothing to eat but game or rabbit, game or rabbit, or just for a change venison, venison or—venison! Really, I promise you, if my husband can't shoot it personally, he won't eat it, I swear. He needs to have seen it die and hung it himself in his very own game larder before a morsel will pass his lips.'

She paused, breathing out smoke smoothly and without any outward emotion, only the tight grip on her cigarette hinting at inward feelings, feelings that Trilby could only guess at.

'Not that I don't love Charlie, because of course I do, but he is only happy when he is up to his thighs in squelch, or sitting on a horse which is also up to its thighs in squelch, and really when you have been born within a quarter of a mile of Woollands and Harvey Nichols, not to mention Harrods and Peter Jones, when you have been born with the heavenly sound of tissue paper ringing in your ears, and the smell of Chanel Number Five floating in your nostrils, when you have been used to not walking more than ten yards to take a taxi, or twenty yards to spend money, when you have been used to silk underwear, and silk stockings, and flowers that are arranged for you, life in Somerset is about as appealing as a long spell in hospital.'

'Oh dear, and it seems so lovely, I mean to me, I'm only here on a visit. Oh dear, how horrid that you hate it so. Oh dear.'

'Oh dear indeedy, my dear. Oh dear, fourteen hundred times over. Yes, you may well say oh dear! Of course, it is all my fault. I am entirely to blame. Because although I love Charlie, I am about as suitable as a wife for him as Mrs Simpson was for the Duke of Windsor. I can't ride, and I hate horses, except to look at from a reasonable distance when they can look very pretty and decorative. I loathe shooting, I would far rather shoot myself than some poor bird that can hardly fly and half the time is too fat to take off. No, I am a personal disaster, which is why I am here, really, because I was really rather hoping that you might be too?'

Trilby, aware that she had not offered her visitor any refreshment, went quickly to the drinks tray and poured her a small glass of sherry, it being after five thirty, which she judged to be not too early for a small something, but not late enough for a gin or a whisky.

'Let's say "Cheers", shall we?'

'Why not?' They both laughed.

'I have no idea why it is vulgar to say "Cheers", or "Bottoms up" for that matter,' Mary Louise confided. 'Such a cheerful custom, it always seems to me.'

Seeing that they were still out on the table Trilby quickly collected up her drawings and put them away, placing them in a magazine rack to the side of the fire. Mary Louise watched her, making no comment, only smiling at her.

'So, you are here for rest, and holiday, and that sort of thing?'

'That sort of thing.' They both smiled once more at each other, slightly at a loss.

'Would you like to come over and see Charlie and myself? We should love it. And I promise you not to give you game. In fact I will cook you something from my Constance Spry book, or similar, something special, not game, not venison, I promise! Saturday night? This Saturday?'

Trilby nodded and smiled, but as she did so she had a sinking feeling that Mary Louise might be on to her, that she might know who she really was. 'Of course. I should love it.'

Later, Piers made light of her anxieties. He came in from the fields with all the bonny outdoor look of a man who has been toiling all day in a good and hearty fashion and cannot wait to have a beer and eat a good dinner.

'Of course we will go.'

'You don't think she might . . .'

He picked up Trilby's unspoken suspicion and shook his head. 'No, absolutely not. Charlie and Mary Louise never see anyone but themselves, they live in total seclusion—farm nearly eight hundred acres, and if you can't shoot it or ride it, believe me, Charlie won't be interested. And he only reads the *Daily Telegraph*.'

'Oh dear,' Trilby said, for perhaps the tenth time, and then wondered fleetingly why it was that for some reason she felt as if the summer idyll, her undiluted happiness with Piers, was over.

'Don't worry,' Piers reassured her, 'Charlie will love you.'

*　　　*　　　*

Trilby wore a black silk dress embroidered with tiny white flowers around the bodice. It was strapless, showing off her fine, slim shoulders, and tightly waisted, showing off her fine, slim waist, and Piers, having chosen the dress, felt justifiably proud. He had still no idea why Trilby had seemed so upset the first time he had given her a dress, but whatever the reason she now seemed to have got over that particular emotional hurdle and stepped ahead of him out of the front door looking happy and relaxed.

Of course, as he had predicted, Charlie fell in love with Trilby at first sight, and the evening was a great success. The food, cooked by Mary Louise, was delicious, sophisticated and of many courses accompanied by vintage wines. The house was undoubtedly very large. Tall and square, it was of seventeenth-century origin, and made to seem even larger by the fact that only four of them dined, waited on by an old lady who tended to present dishes at a frightening angle, and to whom Mary Louise spoke in low and conciliatory tones.

'Been with us for more years than I care to think. There was a time when she ran the place, but now she just runs me.'

Mary Louise had filled the four endless floors of

358

Merrilands with furniture of all kinds, many large cabinets filled with old china, and vast flower arrangements, not to mention ornaments of every description. Indeed everywhere that Trilby looked she could see signs of her new friend's struggle to make her house as feminine and welcoming as possible, but as she showed Trilby round she seemed to indicate that she felt she had lost the endless battle to make the place homely.

'You know how it is.' She smiled, a little helplessly, at Trilby. 'With these places, the house usually wins. Are you thinking of staying on at Charlton?'

Trilby smiled. 'No. I can't, not really. I shall have to go soon.'

'Oh, that is a pity. It is such a lovely house, and so easy to manage.' She looked genuinely regretful. 'I could do with a friend in the neighbourhood, too. I mean, not that Charlie is not a friend, but you know how it is with farmers, they are always outside. And I could see that you had already added the much needed feminine touch to the sitting room. I was hoping to help you with the rest of the house. Knowing what I know, it can be for ever before you find a decent curtain-maker or someone who will upholster a chair.'

'No, I can't stay. I love Somerset, but I have to go soon.'

Trilby dropped her eyes. She knew that despite being deep in conversation with Charlie, Piers would have heard everything she had just said, as lovers always do, and that quite suddenly the party would not seem such fun any more.

He said nothing on the way home, and neither did they sing, but both went to bed feeling more sober than they would have thought possible after such a convivial evening.

*   *   *

'Harold is going to show me how to milk a herd of cows.'

For once Trilby was awake at the same time as Piers, and, what was more, dressed.

'Is there much point in learning how to milk a cow, if you are not going to stay on in Somerset?' Piers looked across at her, the expression in his eyes and his tone of voice as flat as Trilby had ever known them.

'Oh, I think so. After all you never know when you might need to milk a cow—terribly useful I should have thought.'

'Be careful not to get leaned on, cows are great leaners.'

But Trilby had not heard. She was already halfway down the stairs ahead of Piers, and whistling.

Every morning when the milkman came by with his pony and cart, through the open windows giving on to the lane that ran by the old house she heard him whistling, perfectly in tune, every note reproduced as thrillingly as any bird. Sometimes it was 'Foggy Day', sometimes it was 'Bye Bye Blackbird', at others 'I'll See You Again'. All the popular hits were aired at some time or another, except on Sundays, when, Piers had pointed out to her, in deference to its being the Lord's day the milkman would only whistle a hymn.

It seemed he was famed in the villages for the perfection of his whistling, and had even been

360

written up in the local paper. Now, Trilby was determined that it was not just the whistling that she would appreciate, but the milk that went from the churns into the bottles on the back of the whistler's cart.

It was five o'clock in the morning and it was raining, but Piers had bought her a pair of Wellington boots and a thick, serviceable mackintosh, such as cowmen wear. The boots were a little big, but she had borrowed a couple of pairs of Piers's socks, and what with some newspaper in the bottom they were now a snug fit, for which, seeing how wet the milking sheds were going to be, she could only be grateful.

'Very well, my dear,' Harold said, affably, 'follow me. You like milk, do you?'

Trilby found this innocent question difficult to answer. She looked up into Harold's dark brown eyes, noting his West Country complexion, like that of a healthy baby, round, smooth, pink and white and fresh as a daisy just opening in the summer sunshine. What could she say? She actually hated milk, and the idea of drinking it warm from a cow was purgatory to her. Now she realised that, long before breakfast, she was about to watch gallons and gallons of the sacred liquid being taken from the cows and along the airlines into containers.

'I love butter and cream, and frothy milk in coffee,' she told him, carefully sidestepping the issue.

Happily, despite having asked the question, Harold did not seem at all interested in what Trilby liked, but strode ahead of her a little, his own long boots making a firm impact on the path that led up to the sheds.

'We have a mixed herd here, with some Ayrshires added which Mr Piers goes to Scotland to buy, as many folk in Somerset do, you will find. Ayrshires are less rich in their milk, see, better for babies and children, the doctors say. Mr Piers, he goes regularly to Scotland for them, and as you see'—having arrived in the sheds Harold was able to pat the rump of one of the cows, the look on his face one of fleeting affection—'they are a fine and neat cow. Now this is Katie. She is an Ayrshire, with nice udders, kept well off the ground. They don't trail, so that is why Mr Piers and I, we particularly like her type, it's her neatness, do you see?' Harold gave the cow another affectionate pat and it turned a dreamy gaze on him. 'Now cows, Miss Trilby, are a nice sort of creature, but they can never be taken for granted.'

Harold paused and lit an acrid-smelling self-rolled cigarette, and for a second Trilby and he watched the smoke rising from it with brief interest.

'Yes, they are a nice sort of creature, but you can never, ever take a cow for granted, Miss Trilby,' he repeated. 'Not ever. See Pauline over there, well her ways are her own, I will tell you that. Of a morning, if you don't take care of yourself, Pauline will lean on you hard with her rump—might be against you, or it might be against your hand, but she will always be looking out for you, won't you, my dear? Now, let's start, shall we, Miss Trilby? First, watch me now, you smear the cows' quarters with salve, then you fix each of these'—he held up the rubber teats attached to the milking lines—'you fix 'em to their quarters, and then you wait for the milk to fill up there.' He pointed to a vast clear

362

vat on the wall.

Milk, milk and more milk! And what with four teats to an udder, and the fact that when she tried to fix them on the cows' quarters, as Harold called them, the rubber teats seemed quite determined to pop off, by the end of helping to milk eighty cows Trilby could have willingly climbed back into bed and fallen asleep.

But that was only the beginning, for the next task, for which they were joined by Mabel and her sister, was to fill all the milk bottles by hand, each bottle having to be stopped, also by hand, with cardboard stoppers, not to mention a whole set of different sized bottles for the school milk round.

Because, as Harold said, 'No-one asked us farmers when they decided that they would give a third of a pint of free milk to the children. They looked at the cost, but not at the inconvenience to the farmer, didn't they? No-one thought that the milk bottles for school would be a different size to the rest, so it would take half the amount of time again to fill them and stop them! But then the government only gave us tractors when the war came and they suddenly realised that if they didn't the country would starve! War's about the only time that politicians appreciate farmers, and that's the truth.'

'I reckon we beat the Nazis single-handed we did,' Mabel went on, taking up the story. 'How we did it, us farmers, I will never know. We worked twenty-four hours out of twenty-four, doubled our output, we did, but now the war's over, you watch—they'll soon find a reason to forget all that.'

'I hope not,' Trilby said, standing back and eyeing the rows of filled milk bottles with some satisfaction. 'An island people is lost without farming, I should have thought.'

All at once, the monumental task of milking every cow in the herd was over, and in the thankful pause that followed Harold cocked his head, and smiled suddenly, his large brown eyes taking on a satisfied look. 'There he is, Mother!'

And sure enough in the quiet of the still-early morning could be heard, in the far, far distance, not just the sound of a pony's hooves on the old country road and the rattle of a cart, but soaring above that sound, over and above the noise of the rain falling over the milking sheds, a clear, piping whistle.

'What's it this morning, Mabel?'

' 'Bye Bye Blackbird',' Mabel said with some satisfaction. 'He always does it justice, I will say that for him. Better'n a recording on the wireless.'

Shortly after the impromptu solo, round the corner came a pony and cart driven by a handsome, middle-aged man, cap on straight, pony in shining harness, the cart behind him empty. The whistle continued until the moment he pulled the pony up in front of the farm buildings, at which point Harold and Mabel hurried forward as he began to back the pony in the direction of the milking sheds.

'Good morning, Jack,' Mabel called.

'Morning, my dear. And a right good morning it's turning out to be.'

The rain having stopped, he climbed down from the cart and shook himself, his outer clothing shedding the wet as satisfyingly as a dog's coat.

They loaded up the cart with the milk bottles and those of the milk churns that were to be left at the station for the train, and Trilby, having thanked

Harold for her lesson, walked happily back to the house, breakfast foremost in her mind.

'No wonder Harold and Mabel have always laughed at me for being a Londoner—until this morning I had no idea of the awful effort that went into a jug of milk! I shall never look at one again without seeing it for what it is, a truly great achievement.'

Piers smiled, and turning from the Aga placed a plate of bacon and eggs in front of her. 'And that is all before we turn to keeping hens and pigs,' he said, gaily waving the wire basket that made such perfect Aga toast to accompany a strong cup of coffee.

After two hours in the milking sheds Trilby's breakfast tasted like a meal in a million. Just as she was pushing her toast around her plate, mopping up the last of the perfectly fried egg, the telephone rang.

They both stared first at it and then at each other. Half past seven in the morning was not a time when the telephone at Charlton normally rang, unless Piers had had to ring the vet and was waiting for him to ring back with his time of arrival. He had not rung the vet, and they both knew it. Cautiously Piers picked up the old black pre-war telephone.

It was Aunt Laura. Piers looked across at Trilby as they both registered her voice piping down the line from London, knowing at once that it had to be—as Trilby had predicted to Mary Louise the night before—time for her to move on.

CHAPTER ELEVEN

Trilby had always known that Lewis would catch up with her, that very soon the sinking feeling that accompanied just the thought of his name would become part of a much larger emotion. She also knew that she should have left Charlton days before. That she had not was because she had found herself to be truly happy for the first time in her life.

Of course Aunt Laura, having done what she could to distract Lola de Ribes, sending her on some wild goose chase to Berry and Molly's hideout in the Yorkshire Dales, could not be counted on to do any more than she had done. Now it was up to Trilby herself to disappear. But where could she go?

'You're not going abroad.' Piers looked at her, the expression on his face unusually adamant.

'Why not?'

'For the good reason that if you go abroad you will be more—let us say *vulnerable* in every way. About the only place people can hide effectively is Africa, or South America, and even then a white woman, particularly one as pretty as you, soon becomes the talk of the village, and the cat is well and truly out of the bag. No, the place to hide a book is in a library. You are an English girl. You must hide in England until we can sort something out.'

'You must understand that Lewis, being Lewis, really does feel that he can do what he wants with his wife. I keep telling you—you have no idea what he is like. If he finds me, I know he will try and make me go back to him.'

Piers was on the point of asking the one question that he had wanted to ask all along when Mabel, having barely knocked on the sitting room door, ambled into the room. Piers let go of Trilby's hands, and Trilby herself sought refuge in the window, suddenly embarrassed for them both. Where before she had felt no embarrassment at being in love with Piers, at loving him quite openly, now, in the realisation that she was going to have to leave him and Charlton, that their short idyll was over, the fact that she was a married woman and he was a bachelor, that they were in effect living in sin, seemed stark and real, and somehow tawdry.

'Mr Piers.' Mabel looked sympathetically at them both, knowing that their situation was not as it had been, but obviously not quite knowing why. 'Mr Piers, there is a man at the door. Quite smart he is, I will say that. He, well, he looks to me like he might be the new vet come to introduce himself, but I think you should see for yourself.'

Piers went into the hall, assuming as casual an expression as he could and opened one of the pair of half-glassed front doors.

'Mr Montague?'

'Yes.'

'You don't know me, sir, but I am a friend of David Micklethwaite's. He sent me to see you. On behalf of Mr James. Wanted to know if Mrs James might be about? Or at least whether you might know of her whereabouts?'

'I am sorry, could you repeat that question?'

'Mrs James, sir. Might she be available?'

'I don't know a Mrs James. I know a Mrs

367

Jameson. I know Mrs Lynda Jameson, great point-to-point rider, won the ladies' race last year. I had a fiver on her as a matter of fact.'

'No, sir. This is Mrs Lewis James, sir.'

'Jimmy James, know him. Lives near Frome, used to be a printer, but he's retired now. Oh, by the way, if you don't mind me asking, why did you announce yourself as the vet?'

'I didn't, sir. It was your housekeeper. She said, "Oh, you'll be the new vet." I never said anything.'

'Well, since you're not the new vet, and I don't know of any Mrs James, I don't expect you'll mind going away, old love, and leaving me to cook my breakfast?'

Piers went to close the front door but the man stopped it with his foot. 'If you don't know Mrs James, how about Miss Smythson, sir, Miss Trilby Smythson?'

'Oh yes indeed, yes, of course. I met Miss Smythson in London. Yes, I know her. But she is in Yorkshire, I believe. My aunt rang me this morning, as a matter of fact, and said Miss Smythson was in Yorkshire with friends. You can give her a ring.' Piers scribbled Aunt Laura's number down on a piece of paper. 'I would know if Miss Smythson was here, I think.'

'No-one staying here, then, sir?'

The man's eyes travelled to the flowers with which Trilby had filled the hall the day before. To the sewing basket, left out on one of the hall chairs, and to a pair of unmistakably feminine shoes tucked underneath it.

'Oh, yes. Miss Ardisonne, an interior decorator, is staying here for a few days. Why? Are you in need of one, or should I ask is Mrs, er, in need of one? She's very good is our Miss Ardisonne, a dab hand at finding the old antiques and suchlike. Yes, and as for colour, her eye—well, she really does have the eye, does Miss Ardisonne. I'll call her if you like. Fancy her doing up your sitting room, do you?'

Trilby could hear Piers sounding more and more flippant and effeminate. They had after all hugely enjoyed it when Aunt Laura had proudly revealed that she thought she had put Lewis's people off by telling them that Piers was a confirmed bachelor.

'No, no, thank you, sir. I am only a reporter from the local paper, owned by the James Group. Can hardly afford a pot of paint on my salary, let alone an interior decorator.' It was his turn to give a short cynical laugh, and at the same time he turned away, obviously put off by the squire of Charlton's suddenly open, warm and far from masculine manner. He backed off down the drive.

Piers called after him, 'If I can be of any help in the future please don't hesitate to call me, I would love to put you two in touch. Miss Ardisonne really does have the eye.' He watched him climb into a pre-war Riley and chug off down the drive, and then he shut the front door and turned towards the sitting room. Trilby must leave now, without any question, and of a sudden he knew exactly where she should go.

'Go and pack a suitcase as quick as you can,' he told her. 'I am going to load up the horse box, drive it round the back, and back it up to the old garden gate by the wall, you know where I mean?'

Trilby nodded, silent. She had heard everything of the conversation in the hall, and knew as well as Piers that she had to leave at that moment,

369

immediately, and even now it might be too late.

To lend credulity to the whole operation Piers quickly loaded up his old hunter and his companion goat. Harold helped him.

'Trouble, eh, Mr Piers?' Harold looked sympathetic.

'Like you've never known,' Piers agreed, and jumping into the driver's seat he drove round to the back gate that led to the road. He beckoned to Trilby, who shot into the horse box and crouched down beside the goat. For a second both animals turned to look at her, but then perhaps because they knew her, they soon turned back to their hay and continued to munch at it, looking pleasantly surprised by the undoubted bonus of an extra feed.

'Off we go,' Piers called back to her.

Trilby wanted to call back 'Where?' but the sound of the horse box was too noisy and she was afraid that she might frighten the animals.

Her dread of the past days had become an awful reality, and when at last the horse box stopped, and Piers climbed down to let her out of the back, she found that she was shivering, not from the breeze that was moving the old trees amongst which they stood, but from fear.

'I thought I had a bit more esprit de corps than this,' she lamented as, clutching her suitcase, teeth chattering from the suddenness of the whole operation, she followed Piers up to a small, tumbledown cottage. 'Where are we, by the way?'

She looked around briefly. From the number of trees that surrounded the small clearing she imagined that this out of the way dwelling must be a wood burner's cottage, or that of a forestry worker of some kind.

'You are right in the middle of Charlie's land,' Piers told her, and as he looked down at Trilby his heart turned over because of a sudden she looked so young and so vulnerable.

He tried not to remember her dancing on the lawn in the dress that he had bought her, tried not to remember her drawing by the fireside in the evening. He tried not to remember trying to teach her to play nap, the farmer's favourite Saturday night card game—a game whose rules seemed to change by the minute, once Trilby took it up. He tried not to remember any of those things as he pushed open the old oak front door that had neither lock nor key.

'You'll be all right here,' he told her, but even he knew that he did not sound as convincing as he would have liked.

If only they had had more time to think. If only they had not been so in love, so intent on their own happiness. He should have taken her abroad. He should have run off with her days before.

'Charlie and Mary Louise will come and see you. And here—I am leaving you my old air rifle, just in case. So comforting. I will come and see you this evening.'

Piers walked ahead of Trilby into the cottage, pushing open the front door by merely turning the handle. The whole place smelt of damp, and there were cobwebs hanging from the light.

'It's not on anything like mains or electricity. But we can make up a bed for you.'

Trilby nodded. 'It will be fine.'

But Piers could hear from her voice that he was not the only person who needed convincing.

'Remember you are quite alone in the middle of

371

eight hundred acres. No-one comes this way, except the hunt, and then only occasionally. No-one comes near this cottage, and has not done so for years.'

He kissed her briefly, casually, hoping that by doing so he was reassuring her that she was in no real danger now, just as by giving a brief but cheerful wave he was hoping to give the same impression.

Trilby waved back to Piers, and then, taking the old air rifle that Piers had left propped against the front door, she went back into the cottage and stood staring around her, unsure of what to do next.

Piers had not been gone long before she heard twigs snapping with what seemed in the silence to be a deafening report behind the old stone cottage. Trilby straightened her shoulders and looked around for Piers's old rifle once more. Then she crept across the old brick-lined floor and flung open the weathered oak door.

'My dear!' Mary Louise put up her hands in mock surrender. 'Don't shoot me until I have unwrapped the picnic, will you?'

'Oh, Marilu, thank God, it's you.'

'You're a poet though you don't know it,' Mary Louise trilled, walking past Trilby into the dim, dark cottage with its strong smell of damp and its aura of total neglect. 'My dear! What a dreadful little place. I've only ever ridden by here, never come in, and now I can see why. Now sit down while I unwrap all my goodies and pour us both something very strong, because I know you have lots to tell me.'

Trilby nodded. It was true. She had.

Micklethwaite sighed. The de Ribes had been completely useless, which, when he came to think about it, really, they could always have been counted on to be. It seemed that, on the recommendation of the old lady—whom, give them their due, they had at least found—Lola de Ribes had gone tearing off up to the Yorkshire Dales, only to draw a blank. After which she had come tearing down from the Yorkshire Dales and deposited herself back at her Belgravia address, where she had sat in a sulk ever since.

Knowing that something like this might be on the cards, Micklethwaite had gone back to what was known in newspaper circles as his 'source', namely Agnes Smythson.

Happily for both of them they were now able to meet for lunch without feeling that there was an emotional apple cart to upset. In fact that particular morning Micklethwaite, having left the office in good time, found himself positively looking forward to seeing Agnes Smythson again.

'Ah, there you are.'

Agnes was looking exquisitely pretty in a turquoise silk blouse and fashionable pale grey coat and skirt, which she wore with peep-toed snakeskin shoes and a matching handbag.

'Yes, here I am.' She smiled at him as if he was an old friend, which, considering their previous intimacies, he realised of a sudden that he must seem to her to be.

They ordered dry martinis, ate a hearty lunch, and then settled down to business.

'We can't find her anywhere. Tried all kinds of places, to no avail.'

'I told you, David. She must have a lover. No girl runs off and leaves a man like Lewis without having been induced to do so by an unsuitable boyfriend of some sort.' Agnes blew out a couple of perfect smoke rings and Micklethwaite watched them drifting out into the main arena.

'I've always wanted to do that.' He looked at her with sudden boyish enthusiasm.

'I'll teach you,' Agnes promised without even a trace of coquettishness, which somehow turned the whole idea into something vaguely sinister, as if by teaching Micklethwaite to blow smoke rings she was teaching him some sort of lethal self-defence.

'Please. Now. My problem. You know what it is?'

'Yes, of course. And I have the solution.'

'Which is?'

'Set a trap. Trap the silly girl, and send her back to Lewis. That will teach her.'

Micklethwaite looked at her with fascination. He could see that she was enjoying the moment, that she was looking forward to trapping her stepdaughter as eagerly as Lewis was looking forward to regaining possession of his wife.

'And how would we do that?'

'Leave it to me.'

'But surely you will need to know where she is?'

'It will take a few days. Here's to trapping the little wretch, soon, sooner, soonest.'

'Here's to finding her.'

Micklethwaite could not contemplate the idea that they would not find Trilby. As it was, the whole idea of having to put Lewis's emotional house in order yet again was not something to which he was looking forward.

The following day, on Agnes's instruction, Micklethwaite planted a piece about Michael Smythson's health giving cause for anxiety. He planted it in one of the more upmarket columns of one of their more upmarket newspapers, the one he knew to have the biggest female readership, and then he sat back and waited.

*   *   *

'Coo-ee!'

Despite the snapping of the twigs, Mary Louise's arrival still meant that Trilby grabbed Piers's old air gun, just in case.

'My dear! I've brought you breakfast, been awake half the night worrying about you, as a matter of fact. Worrying my little bedsocks off, wondering if you would be all right here.'

'Oh, I'm fine,' Trilby lied, adding, 'but if you could bring me an eiderdown next time you come, I should be ever so grateful.'

'Course.'

Mary Louise, her ample back view busy at the cottage window, now set out a breakfast to warm the heart of the most forlorn prisoner.

Fresh home-made bread, farm butter, crisp-cooked bacon that could be eaten with fingers, sausages still warm from the Aga, fruit, hot coffee in a Thermos flask, all delicious, and all so welcome that Trilby could only smile up at her dazedly as she ate.

'Goodness, that was good!' She sighed with satisfaction. 'No, it was more than good, it was perfect.'

Of a sudden she remembered the good old days in Glebe Street when Aphrodite or Berry and Molly gave her late breakfasts, or early suppers, or shared a midnight feast when they came in from a party. She sighed.

'It's beastly here,' Mary Louise agreed, noting the depth of the sigh. 'But we'll soon have you out. It's just a question of who we can trust until we get your separation and divorce and all that sorted out.'

'I can't divorce Lewis, Mary Louise,' Trilby told her, sadly.

'Why not, bless you?'

'Because he won't let me.'

'You may have to wait, but you can divorce him, bless you, really you can. Why even men like Lewis give in in the end, my love. Really, they do.' She shook out the paper she had been reading while Trilby ate her breakfast. 'Yes, even men like Lewis James have to give in some day or another.'

'He'll crucify me, you know that, don't you?'

Her new friend nodded, and then folding the paper she said suddenly, 'I say, this is such a toshy newspaper, nothing in it worth reading, so I am going to make it into twists. Fetch us some kindling from outside the door. And look, here, miracle of miracles, here are some dry logs.'

Mary Louise quickly took the newspaper and started to tear it into strips, laying the kindling that Trilby collected on top of it, followed by the logs, and then she set fire to it all, with a feeling of overwhelming relief. She did not know what she was going to do next to help Trilby, but she did at least know that no good was going to come of her reading in one of her husband's newspapers that her father had been taken ill.

*   *   *

'It was a plant. The piece was a plant, I am sure of it. They have planted it to make Trilby worried, bring her to her father's bedside.'

Piers nodded. He did not take a newspaper, other than a local one at the weekends, not having time to read it during his long, farming day. But he knew that Mary Louise was an intelligent woman, and that she understood the newspaper she read to be lightweight and female-orientated. He also knew from her that half of what was placed there was either highly organised propaganda, adhering faithfully to Lewis's stated policies, or used for purposes other than those the constant reader might believe.

'There is no need to tell Trilby, I agree,' he said. 'After all, if her father was really unwell, her stepmother would let her know, I should have thought. I mean she would find a way of telling her, but not like this. Not through a newspaper, no-one would do that, not to their family. No, this is Lewis at work, and very subtle too, when you think about it. Drink?'

Mary Louise nodded, and they both drank more than a little thankfully of the generous gin and tonics that he had poured.

'The thing is, Piers, she can't stay in that ghastly little cottage indefinitely, can she? I mean the aunt doesn't work, and there is no heating, and autumn will all too soon be upon us, not to mention winter, and then she very definitely will have to move on. So we must think of our next move, I mean really.

377

What could be her next move? Where can she go?'

'I know she has a friend with a cottage and studio in the Yorkshire Dales. I was thinking of letting him know that she is with me, and taking her there. Frankly, the sooner we get her out of Somerset the better.'

'The Yorkshire Dales in winter, my God, the poor girl.'

'I know, but since they have already drawn a blank there, they're unlikely to look there again. We can move her at night. Even the reporter that they have put on our trail must go to sleep at night.'

'Charlie says he has been sniffing round all the local pubs. Went into the Red Lion last night, played darts and bought everyone countless rounds of ale. But you know Somerset, they have only to know that you are trying to find something or someone to send you in the other direction! Same thing happened in the village.' Mary Louise laughed. 'Sniff, sniff, sniff went Mr Wolf around the place, and as soon as they realised, the post office and everyone sent him packing in the opposite direction. Round and round Somerset he went. It was the laugh of the county this morning.'

'Yes, but that's what I mean. How long until someone guesses that Trilby Ardisonne is Mrs Lewis James?'

'Too late for that,' Mary Louise said. 'I am afraid they have already guessed that. Even Mabel and Harold are on to it. Course everyone's on your side. Course they are, but really, it means we should get on with moving Trilby now, before we have her hubby here hotfoot and breathing fire and brimstone.'

Naturally Trilby was unaware of the well laid plans being made for her, but she knew an overwhelming relief when she saw Piers arriving that night carrying yet another suitcase filled with all the things that he had given her, and with Topsie on a lead.

'I am going to take you to your friend Berry's cottage in the Yorkshire Dales,' he told her cheerfully. 'Since that is where Aunt Laura sent them on a wild goose chase before, there is very little likelihood that they will go back.'

Trilby clung to Piers, suddenly cast down lower than she ever remembered being before, even when she was locked up at the top of Lewis's house with the dreadful nurse.

'I am such a nuisance, aren't I? I am so, so sorry.'

Piers hugged her tightly in return. 'We must be on our way, I am afraid.' He looked at his watch. 'We have such a bloody great drive ahead, and really we should try to be there before anyone is up and about, I mean in Yorkshire. Don't want you being spotted arriving and thereby arousing the attention of the neighbours, all two of them, or whatever there is there.'

'Will there be neighbours?'

'Apparently not, not according to Berry, but those that there are will be sure to be interested, he says. Other than that, well, you won't need a car because apparently the postman will bring you stuff from the village shop, anything you want, and all you have to do is line his pocket a little, explain that you are not well, and need utter peace and quiet, etc. I wish to God all this wasn't necessary, but I am afraid it is.'

Trilby nodded. 'I think it is a jolly good plan, brilliant really, I mean they aren't likely to look in the same place twice, like sardines when you were little, don't you think?'

'Just like sardines,' Piers agreed, smiling. 'There is actually very little else we can do, at the moment. I mean Mary Louise and Charlie have a very good lawyer, and all that, we can get things going this end, but other than that, the best thing is for you to hide out until your wretched husband realises that you are very definitely not going back to him. Because you're not, are you?'

Trilby shook her head. 'No, I am not. Not ever.'

The thought of it was so terrible that she could not even begin to contemplate it. After living with Piers, really, Lewis would be the sort of hell that made you realise why people took an overdose. If life was that bad, why stay?

'You're sure?'

'Sure? I have told you before I would rather kill myself.'

*   *   *

The morning that Trilby arrived in Yorkshire was also the morning that she waved goodbye to Piers, a part of her wondering if she would ever see him again.

However, happily, as soon as his car disappeared down the long, winding road, and she turned once more towards her temporary home, she realised that things could have been much worse. And what

380

was more the weather was mild and sunny, so that all the wild flowers that blew about in the thick grass seemed more than anxious to cheer her with their pale and beautiful colours, and their air of tough fragility.

But again, the moment passed, and seconds later Trilby had blotted out any of the beauty that surrounded her, of a sudden seeing only her situation, which was more stark and real than she cared to contemplate. More real than the moor that was encouraging the warm breeze that ruffled her reddened hair. She saw only too well that she might not see Piers again, that he might be driving off and leaving her, and who could blame him? What was more, it was highly likely that, given the mighty organisation that he had behind him, Lewis would track Trilby down, and he would finally win.

She turned back to what Berry had described to Piers on the telephone as his 'little gingham telephone box'. With unimaginable generosity Piers had decided to leave Topsie with her. Trilby looked down at the dog, now her firm friend, and patted the silky fur on the top of her dear old black head. 'We are just going to have to get used to being each other's best friend, Tops,' she told the dog. 'And before long, who knows, we probably won't want to know about anyone else. We'll become a right couple of old spinsters, happy in each other's company, and quite able to let the rest of the world go by, eh?'

Topsie looked less than convinced, until Trilby opened a tin of her food and set it down in the tiny gingham kitchen, at which, like the sensible soul that she was, Topsie immediately ate up, and, Trilby having lit the fire in the sitting room, before long they had both fallen asleep.

* * *

She awoke to the sound of heavy knocking at the door. The fire was out, and the room had become cold. Outside the sky was leaden and grey. Trilby stared around her for a few seconds, and as Topsie started to bark she took up Piers's air gun, and placed it carefully to the side of the cottage door. Once she opened the door, it would be hidden from the view of any visitor.

And as Piers always said, 'Any man who isn't frightened by the sight of a woman with a gun at her shoulder is in my opinion either mad or not a man!'

'There thou is!' A red face peered out at Trilby from under a General Post Office issue cap. 'I have been knocking that long I'd have said that thou art a ghost, I would! But seeing that thou aren't, I would like to introduce myself. I am Fred your postman, and anything you might feel that thou wants, you tell me.' He pointed cheerfully towards his old motor car. 'My car here, she takes me everywhere, and when she doesn't then I takes t'wife's pony and trap, so thou must not think thou will ever be lonely, thou must not, not when Fred is here to see to things!'

'Oh, goodness, how kind of you,' said Trilby, firmly planting herself across the threshold to prevent Topsie from pushing her way through to the postman. She smiled, and in a curiously childlike gesture she ran her hands down her front and breathed out. 'What lovely air, isn't it?' she asked, for want of something better to say.

'Yorkshire air is t'best in t'world, t'best, all right, very best. My missus always says that if all th' world breathed in th' same air as us, t'd be no need for pills, and that is t'truth.'

'I think your missus is right,' Trilby agreed. 'She must be a very clever woman.'

There was a short silence, and then Fred nodded. 'She's that clever that I always think she could have passed into anything she chose, if she hadn't have been a woman, that is—but there we are. She makes t'lightest scones and pastry in t'county, and she's not afraid of no-one. You must come and have tea with us, you must, young lady, if thou likes thy victuals, that is. No good coming to our house if thou don't like a good meal. And bring thy dog too,' he added, hospitably.

'I should love that. Thank you.'

'Goodbye for now, then, Miss . . .'

'Ardisonne.'

'And don't forget, anything that's wanting, thou must just tell Fred.'

Trilby turned back to the fire, to Topsie, to the gingham curtains, and what now seemed to her to be going to be very much less of a very long sojourn.

She looked down at Topsie, a thought suddenly occurring. 'I say, maybe now's the time for me to start to grow out this awful hair colour, stop looking like a little red bantam! Goodness knows there is enough time for it goodness knows, Tops!'

Tops shifted her head on her paws. It would be time for her biscuits soon, that was all that was interesting her at that moment. Meanwhile, she was happy to feel Trilby's hand stroking her head, and the warmth of the fire.

Piers too was happier than he had ever been about Trilby's situation. He had seen for himself that the little stone cottage was convenient and comfortable and as far from so-called civilisation as it was possible to be. He missed Trilby, but he did not regret what he had done, and while he rose at his usual time of four thirty, milked his cows, let out his hens, and contemplated buying another dog, he felt happier than he had for some time, for to his mind Trilby was now safe. She was somewhere where her husband would never find her.

They had agreed not to write to each other, and since there was no telephone in the cottage, he had to hope for the best that she would stay well. And yet every time he heard the milk cart approaching, and the sound of the beauteous whistle that accompanied it, he became filled with that particular melancholy that attaches itself to a happy memory, because Trilby and he had always stopped to listen to the whistle, making a happy competition out of being the first to recognise the tune.

Soon enough he knew snow would fill the lanes around the farms, and Mabel and Mary Louise would be grumbling about their streaming colds. The winds would be whistling through the old farmhouse, and when the fire was lit at teatime he would find himself in front of the fire remembering their magical summer together, their lovemaking and their happiness. But most of all he would remember that Trilby was no longer with him.

*   *   *

Trilby was sitting drawing by the fireside. Outside the weather had turned mild and slushy, although, according to the weather forecast from the old kitchen wireless, snow was once more imminent.

She and Topsie had settled into a sensible routine of eating, sleeping, working, walking on the moors when possible, and looking forward to seeing Fred the postman bringing shopping from the village, every now and then, when he was able to get through to them.

And it *was* only every now and then, because they had already been snowed in twice, although admittedly for only a few days at a time. But with the larder stacked up with tins and every imaginable comestible, and a good recipe book, a cheerful acceptance of their situation had settled over both Trilby and Topsie.

Now Fred stood at the door stamping his feet and blowing on his mittened hands.

'It's not snowing but might as well be, miss, might as well be. Eee, but this is the longest winter, intit, 'bout as long as the one we had last year!' He handed Trilby out some shopping bags from the back of his car.

'Would you like to come in for a cup of tea, Fred?'

' 'Aye, I would that.'

Fred stood in front of the small cottage fire looking round the tiny sitting room. 'You've made this place right homely you have, miss, really you have.'

'I love it here, I feel so safe.'

Trilby brought in tea on a tray, prettily laid with odd pieces of pottery and china, reminding her of all the other odd pieces of pottery and china she had used for tea and coffee in Berry's studio in Tankridge Street.

'And dropped scones, I have made some dropped scones.'

Fred took one, ignored the proffered plate, and bit into it appreciatively. After eating it in silence, he looked at Trilby.

'They're not as good as my missus's scones, but they're coming on, I will say that, they're coming on. Thou will never have quite the knack of a Yorkshire woman, but enough to please I'd say.'

He took another one and stared at the jam piled onto it. 'And thou's generous with the jam, I'll say that for thee.'

Fred now drained his tea, and placed the cup and saucer back on the tray. Trilby, as was their ritual now, filled the cup once more to the brim, and he once more took it up.

'Thou knows that Christmas is coming, does thou?'

Trilby nodded. 'Yes. I heard it on the wireless.'

They both laughed, and then there was a long silence while Trilby stroked the top of Topsie's head.

'And thou knows about Christmas being a time to share what thou hast?'

'Well, yes, I heard that on the wireless too, and as a matter of fact I plan to share a chicken with Tops.'

'Nowt else thou can do, is there?' asked Fred, reasonably.

'Nowt else,' Trilby agreed, smiling.

'Well, my missus and I, we have no family like this year, so we were wondering, at least she was, if thou and Topsie here would like to share our meal

386

with us? Would thou like that, Tops?' To take the embarrassment out of the invitation he bent down to Topsie and this time it was he who patted the dog.

'Goodness, that's awfully kind of you and your missus, Fred. We would love to, wouldn't we Tops?'

Fred nodded, serious. 'Yes, thou can bring the dog, like I said, Trilby, and no more said.'

Trilby looked up, startled. Fred had never called her Trilby before, and having drawn a great deal of money from the bank before leaving London she had taken care to pay him cash for her weekly shopping.

He smiled at her. 'Thy name's on thy drawing pad—see?'

Trilby stared down, and sure enough she had signed her name at the bottom of her latest drawing. *Trilby Ardisonne.* Funny how habits like that died hard. She smiled across at Fred.

'I am afraid you will probably have a rather unoriginal present, you and Mrs Fred, because of not getting to a shop.'

'Something thou makes thyself is better'n anything from a shop. And missus's name is Hilda. Fred and Hilda, that's us. We'll have a slap-up day, we will, just you wait.'

Fred grinned suddenly, and replacing his cap on his head he strode off to his car. Trilby watched him from the door. The only time that she ever felt isolated was when Fred drove off. For those few minutes, standing alone at the cottage door, her isolation in the middle of the Yorkshire Dales became all too real.

She must have fallen asleep in front of the fire because she was awoken, she did not know how much later, by another knock. It took a few seconds to come to and realise that she was still alone, still in the cottage, and that outside it was getting dark, and there was no telephone.

As soon as the knock had reverberated around the little sitting room Topsie barked while Trilby waited, not feeling in the least bit anxious to open the door. The curtains were not drawn, but thanks to the low ceilings and strange geography of the old cottage she knew that it was impossible to see into the front room. Even so, it could be anyone, and she was, after all, more alone than the sheep that grazed outside on the moors. And Fred had called only hours before, so logically it could not be him.

Again, another knock, while Topsie continued to bark, running up and down the small room, deftly avoiding the furniture.

'Open up, open up! It's the landlord.'

Trilby flung herself against the door, and not thinking what she was doing she wrenched it open and stared out into the already darkening countryside outside. There was no-one there, and for a second her heartbeat accelerated frighteningly. Panic-struck, thinking that she had in some way been tricked, with one hand on Topsie's collar and the other on the door, she started to slam it shut again.

'Boo!'

'Oh my God, oh my God, it is you! Oh, Berry, I could kill you, really I could.' She flung her arms round him and hugged his dear silly old spectacled face, while Topsie ran round them both, still barking.

'I don't know who you are,' Berry said, looking round a few seconds later when they all stood

388

inside, 'but I am here to tell you that it says in the lease no dogs at Gingham Cottage, not for all the tea in China. Talking of which, ducks, my tongue is as swollen as if I had come across the Sahara. Make me a cup of the best Yorkshire brew, would you, while I take off my boots. Where's my van, by the way?'

'It conked out, Berry. I am sorry. I left it in Somerset. Piers brought me here. He was worried about someone spotting it, the police, or someone, or something, you know, number plates and things, and the fact that you painted it yourself, it makes it really rather distinguishable, Piers thought. You know, in case Lewis put my going . . . out on . . . the news . . . or something silly. And also, it would take twice as long as his, your van would, I mean.'

'Very sensible.' Berry took the cup of tea, and collapsed in one of his own armchairs as Trilby heaped up the fire again. 'I left yours back outside your hubbies house, and bought something else for myself. A Ford, I think. I think it's a Ford, anyway, it goes.' He looked around the cottage, the fire burning, the little homely touches, and sighed with content. 'I say, wonderful to be here. Do you know, ducks, I feel like Captain Scott and all the other people in his expedition rolled into one? What a jay for journey! It's taken me the best part of a day I should think, stopping for refreshment on the way, that is.'

Now that he was sprawled all over an armchair sipping at his tea Trilby wanted to ask Berry *why* he was there, but since it was his cottage it did not seem quite right. After all he had the right to arrive at his own cottage any time that he liked, so instead of questioning him, which she thought might be impertinent, she went upstairs and started to make up the spare bedroom with fresh sheets for herself, and put more of the same for Berry on the double bed that she had been using.

From downstairs she could smell Berry's cigarette, and hear him coughing intermittently as he sometimes did, Gauloises being so strong.

Helping him set about unpacking, trotting backwards and forwards between the kitchen and the sitting room with parcels of food and packets of what he called 'goodies' and heaven only knew what else, it occurred to Trilby that Berry was so generous that he could well have come all the way from London just to bring her food and presents, a tree and everything else, because that was the kind of person Berry was.

But as it happened, she could not have been further from the truth.

*   *   *

'I was afraid of Lewis, Berry, that is why I ran away from him in the summer.'

'Yes, that fact had rather come to my notice, ducks. After all, one does not up sticks and run off because one is wildly happy, does one? I was ever so glad, as it happens, you know.' Berry's hair seemed to be sticking up a little bit more than usual, and he lit another of his Gauloises and breathed out the smoke, traces of half-removed oil paint on his fingers giving the gesture an odd kind of bohemian insouciance. 'As a matter of fact Lewis always struck me as being peculiar. No, more than peculiar, he always struck me as being quaint to the point of insanity. I mean I know that he had given

390

you everything that this world could offer, but I always felt that he behaved as if he had seen you and bought you at auction, the way he buys everything. See it, want it, take it.'

'Well I thought he was just the bee's knees. I didn't really think about much else except that he was tall, handsome and fun to be with. But you're probably right.' Trilby paused. 'The true story of Lewis is, however, far from being that, I am afraid. He *is* tall and handsome, but once you're married to him—well, the story changes. And, you see, Berry—I didn't know that he had been married before, years ago, in Canada. That he had a first wife and that she killed herself, after only a few weeks of being married to him.'

Berry stared at her and after lighting another cigarette he shook his head in disbelief, and as always coughed a little. 'I say, Trilb, all just a tiny bit Bluebeard, isn't it?'

Trilby nodded. 'You bet. I only found out by chance. Well.' As Berry stared at her, Trilby found herself having to be honest. 'No, it wasn't by chance, I was snooping in his room, as a matter of fact. And let's face it, if you look, well, you will nearly always find something that you shouldn't, and I did, I mean both looked and found something that I wished I hadn't, namely all this other girl's clothes, her trousseau, everything, the account of their wedding in Canada, her death certificate . . .'

'Pretty upsetting, ducks.' Berry looked sympathetic and tapped his cigarette on the side of the pottery ashtray.

'But I didn't just find her clothes, I found all *my* clothes! All these clothes that had been designed

391

for me—at the top of his cupboard.'

'Maybe the maid put them in the wrong cupboard, love, maybe she was worse for wear and you know—'

'No, no, not the clothes I was *wearing*, I still had all my clothes. No, Berry, everything that he had bought for me, all my trousseau, every dress, every suit, every coat—they were all stored up there in boxes, duplicated, for heaven's sake. What I had thought was just the old-fashioned, grown-up taste of an older man was in fact this—this other girl's clothes. With the exception of my wedding dress, every single thing of hers had been duplicated again, and again, and reproduced for my trousseau. I mean I must say—I did always wonder why Lewis had taken such a close interest in my wardrobe, but again I just thought it was an older man's way. But it wasn't. It seemed he was determined to try to make me turn back into his first wife. There must have been something about me that was similar I suppose. Or just the fact that I was young and inexperienced, someone he could mould. I don't know, something anyway. Right from the start when I went round to lunch with him that time, I must have represented for Lewis another opportunity to be married to this other girl who had killed herself. That is why he was so obsessed with me. In his imagination I was this first wife, this girl who had died, but now with me wearing her clothes he must have been able to pretend to himself that she had come back to him, that she had never killed herself, that she was still with him.'

'I have heard of this before, now you mention it—men putting women in their dead wives' clothes—but, oh lud, it must be—well, Trilby love, it just must be a mite, a tiny wee bit spookalorium, I should have thought.'

'Once we were back from honeymoon, I suppose he just thought of me as *her* come back to life. That is why he had me followed all the time. That is why he came back unexpectedly at odd times of day, to keep me under his thumb, make me powerless. In some way he must have seen it as another chance for him to prevent me from being taken from him, from dying, as she had done. Just imagine, after I had found all those clothes, all her trousseau, every time he made love to me, every time he looked at me, I knew that in reality he was not making love to me, not speaking or looking at me, but at someone else, a dead girl. Until in the end, well, in the end, I felt I might as well have been wearing Talia Fisherton's shroud.'

Berry stared at Trilby, before giving in to a short bout of coughing. She was looking much better than when she had fled Lewis James's house and come round to his studio in such a fuss, but nevertheless, going over old ground the way she was now doing, had made her tense and upset.

'Yes, but, in that case why didn't you face him with it, old love? You know, have the kind of conversation that begins *I have been meaning to talk to you about something*?'

'I know, I should have done, but I just couldn't.' Of a sudden Trilby reached out and took one of Berry's cigarettes for herself and lit it, and then she too coughed, but neither of them smiled, because she had after all, in the dim and distant past, smoked with Berry before, but only when she was upset about Agnes or something. 'Yes, I should have, as you say, I should have.' Almost immediately she hated the taste of the cigarette but did not care, because smoking it was somehow justifiable in the circumstances. 'Yes, I kept telling myself that I should, you know, face him down with it, but you see, Berry, I had snooped in his cupboards, and you know when you snoop you keep feeling that it's your fault if you find something. And then I got pregnant, and miscarried, and all that.' She stubbed out the cigarette in the ashtray, and stared at its strange snakelike outline as it fell into the ash. 'And he was so much older than me. You know, everyone that I have ever really known has always been so much older than me, and I never realised it, until now. All the time I was growing up, I was always with older people. And sometimes it seemed as if there was some secret that they all knew, that they were all going around with, locked up in their heads, some secret about life that they were not telling me, so I stayed hanging around these much older people, always hoping that I might find out what the secret was, but now I realise there was no secret, just—they were older.'

'It's always been a tiny bit awkward for you, old love, with Agnes being how she is and your dad a trifle stifled, to say the least. But don't let's talk about it any more. I don't believe in chewing the cud about anything that is not pleasant. What's the point-ski? Makes one so mizzy, and then it gets to one's tum and one can't chew one's food or appreciate the gorgeous things of this world, which is a shame. So, let us bury the old miseries with the old year?'

'No, you're right, there is no point in going over old ground. But I had to tell someone, and you're

394

the only person I could tell. I couldn't tell Piers. In so many ways we have got past that point, you know—in too deep. Anyway he is such a happy person, like you, always seeing the best in everything, I wouldn't want to pull him down.'

Berry looked at Trilby as he saw her face soften at Piers's name. 'It's quite a thing, that you waited to tell me, ducks, really it is. Kind of flattering too, to be able to confide in old Berry, really. In fact more than kind of, positively squishy making. It could even be a weepy moment, couldn't it?' He smiled suddenly as Trilby stared at him not quite registering what he meant. 'Don't you remember, that's what you used to say when you were knee high and trudging after me with your Warners junior easel and paint box? *Oh dear, Berry, weepy moment.* Dead rabbit to be buried, knock-out sunset, all that, always the same *I think this is a weepy moment, Berry.*' He reached out and stroked Topsie's head. 'So, where from here, do you think?'

'I don't know. I mean the good thing is that Lewis has not called out the police and gone mad searching for me, so perhaps he really has accepted that I have left him and perhaps is even now trying to divorce me and find some other poor soul to dress up in Talia Fisherton's clothes.'

'He hasn't been faithful, you know, if it's of any interest to you. Molly found that out, you know.'

Trilby stared at Berry, feeling strangely thrilled at this news. It meant that she was of a sudden completely free now in a way that she had not thought she would ever be again. She sighed. 'Oh, but Berry, that is wonderful. How simply terrific, and how dear of Molly to go to the trouble of finding out.'

'Yes, I suppose it was rather dear of her. She is dear, in many ways, she really is, although sad to relate she just doesn't like living with me now, which of course doesn't stop her being dear, but does mean I rather miss her, now that she has gone off with Aphrodite's old lover Geoffrey.'

Trilby went to say something and then stopped because as always she thought it better not to say anything at all rather than say something that was out of place. She remembered Aphrodite saying that Molly had always fancied Geoffrey, what now seemed like a hundred years ago.

Seeming to understand her silence, Berry continued, 'Molly always was in a fret, a sort of underneath fret about me not bringing home the bacon, or at least not quite enough of the stuff, and quite frankly she's still a good-looking woman, looks chic, kept her figure, and so on. And as you know, he was always coming round to the house since the year dot.' Berry sighed. 'But then you know Glebe Street, no-one ever stays in their own house, doors are always open, that sort of thing. The va et vien of life, cocktails and laughter, ha, ha, ha, that sort of thing.' He lit another cigarette and breathed out the smoke. 'And then, lately, they kept meeting at your stepmum's house, more and more cocktails and laughter—and what comes after *everyone* knows. And I have spent so much time away daubing duchesses; I think she thought she ought to jump ship while there was another ship on which to jump. Et voilà. Nothing much more to say. Molly has left me and Glebe Strasse, and gone to live with Geoffrey in downtown Kensington, but you know she will have all the things that she has always wanted, and that I have never given her, and no more lodgers and all that. The truth is, finally, I got her down, but the other truth is—I loved her. I failed her, but I did love her.'

Trilby stared at Berry. She felt selfish going on about Lewis and all that, which was after all quite old news now, whereas Berry's sudden arrival and Molly's sudden departure were new news, and therefore, for Berry, all too fresh pain.

'What will you do?'

Berry stared into the fire, still stroking Topsie's head. 'Oh, just carry on as if she was there. I mean I always did all the cooking, so that's no trouble. Moll never cooked, it just was not her, to cook. I don't expect any of my duchesses and debutantes will notice that I have no wife, so the daubing will go on, until eventually I go to the great studio in the sky in the hope that I will meet Titian and Ingres, to mention but a few. I have always imagined that the mansion in heaven that houses the painters will be most especially special, that they will all be busy painting Paradise, and that God will visit in the evenings and tell them how beautifully they have done, and they will be so happy, because there will be no imperfections in their work, it will all be quite, quite perfect. Here we see only tiny echoes of that perfection, don't you think—there, perfection will be just one long reality.'

Trilby smiled. There was nothing to add, so she changed the subject. 'I say, Berry, I don't know about you, but I am starving.'

Berry was on his feet a second after she had finished speaking. 'Imagine me, and I too am starving. I know just what I shall cook for you, Trilb, old love, I will cook that chicken pie that you

397

always used to like so much—with the lemon pastry. My luggage is all food, you will be glad to hear, and only three pairs of jeans, like the Chinese, one on, one in the wash, and one to spare. Tallyho, and away we go.' He rubbed his hands together, and they both started to unpack the mounds of foodstuffs on to the cold shelf in the little kitchen larder.

Later, as she watched Berry cooking and laughing, and as they both drank wine, one of many bottles that he had thoughtfully brought up to Yorkshire, it seemed to Trilby that she was once more in safe hands. Nothing terrible could happen to her while her old childhood friend was around.

'There is one other thing, Berry, though.' She had carefully chosen to tell him the one other thing while he was equally carefully lifting his pastry onto its pie dish. 'Hilda and Fred, the postman, have asked us to Christmas lunch with them.'

'Couldn't be better,' was all Berry said. 'Couldn't be better, a real Yorkshire Christmas,' and he prepared to cut out the little fish and stars with which he always decorated his pies. 'I like Fred. Good sort.'

*   *   *

Snow had threatened on Christmas Eve, but by the morning it became clear that in fact threaten was all that it had done, so that as Berry and Trilby climbed into Berry's car, with Topsie, and set off towards the village it seemed to both of them that God must indeed have come down to earth as a little baby at midnight, and that He really had lain in the manger with the oxen and the ass, because everywhere the landscape sparkled and shone with that particularly pure glow that comes from winter sunshine bathing and drying an uncluttered landscape with its clear light.

'God really has come down to earth this morning, Trilb,' Berry called out to her over the sound of the car engine pulling up the ancient countryroads. 'I can feel that He truly has come down and now He is with us, bringing us hope eternal.'

Trilby, to whom God was a reality but not a formality, nodded happily. She had always believed in a loving God, but never realised until now quite the extent to which Berry did too. It was not something either of them had ever touched on, which was strange.

'You have to believe in God, because there are times, particularly when the going is hard, when you can actually feel that He believes in you, and that's what's keeping you going, that's my point,' Berry went on. They were entering the village, and he was pulling up the flying flaps on his old flying hat as if he had just landed a Spitfire and so was now able to relax a little. 'Where now Fred and Hilda, Trilb? I am ashamed to say I've forgotten.'

'Carry on over the old packhorse bridge ahead of us, and then you'll see the village straight ahead and the post office to the right. They live at the back of the post office, apparently,' Trilby read out from Fred's precise instructions left with them the day before.

Given the peace of all around them, the church bells that had now stopped ringing, the sun that was shining, the gifts for Fred and Hilda which were on the back seat, Trilby would have been in a happy mood anyway, but she was in a most particularly happy mood since she had, the day before, received a Christmas card from Piers. In the letter that accompanied it he described the new puppy, which had just arrived to comfort him in Topsie's absence, as well as Charlie and Mary Louise, Harold and Mabel, the cows, the hens, the doves, and every other thing on the farm, as sending their love and missing her. Most of all him, of course. The children were coming to spend Christmas with him so he would have his hands full, but his heart would be empty without her. He loved her now, today, as much as he had yesterday and the day before, but not as much as he would tomorrow, as the French saying went. He enclosed a snap of the new puppy, Steve, himself holding it, and another of Harold and Mabel outside the milking sheds making a V for Victory sign for no reason that Piers, as he said, could imagine. It was just something that they always did every time he snapped them.

Of course Piers would not know about Berry coming up to Yorkshire, but she knew that he would not mind, because he was well aware, from everything that Trilby had told him of Glebe Street, that Berry was like a much older brother to her.

With her woollen muffler wrapped up round her, and her gloves and fur-lined boots keeping her warm, Trilby smiled. She could not wait to write to Piers about her change in fortunes. No longer alone, with both Topsie and Berry for company, she could last out the winter, and pretty soon Lewis would be like the melted snow on the village road, a grey memory of something now gone for ever.

Fred and Hilda were at the door of the post

office, in mufti. Well, Fred was in mufti, in other words his Sunday suit, but Hilda was in a silk frock with a flowered pinny over it. Trilby had soon realised that Fred really liked Berry, because he now handed him one of his cigarettes before he led the way back into the cottage.

'That is such a favour,' Trilby said, impressed. 'Fred never gives anyone a roll-your-own unless he really likes them, he told me so himself, a few weeks ago. It's from being in the war, cigarettes so precious, and all that. They used to queue for one, you know, he told me that. Just one roll-your-own.'

Now Hilda led the way into the back parlour. It was lit with a tremendous fire which instantly brought a flush to both Trilby's and Berry's faces, after the cold outside. Mulled wine was on a hob in the kitchen and mugs were produced, and their flushes got deeper as they sipped at the sweet, cinnamon-flavoured concoction.

The small house was most interesting, the most interesting in the village, Fred told them, because it was made not just from old local stone, but parts of it from an old theatre which had once played host to the great Victorian actor, Henry Irving, and many another famous thespian. Much of the wooden flooring came from the old playhouse, and they might even now be treading the boards that those famous feet had once trod.

'Shall we begin the great feast with a Yorkshire pudding, do you think?' Berry asked Trilby when, in answer to her call, Fred had hurried out to help Hilda in the kitchen.

'Oh, I expect so.' Trilby rolled her eyes. 'Fred says they always start with Yorkshire pudding and then good old roast beef of Old England, and so on to more pudding, and so on. Keeps them well tucked up against the weather, Fred says.'

But, perhaps in deference to the foreigners from the south they were entertaining, Fred and Hilda produced a Christmas lunch which had no Yorkshire pudding either to start or to accompany. Theirs was a Christmas lunch in the best tradition. The bread sauce had a rich, buttery, glossy, creamy taste and look to it, and the stuffing was so redolent of the herb garden that it would have been difficult to believe that the parsley and sage had not been picked minutes before they sat down. The sausages were home-made, and the turkey grown for the table, and as for the Christmas pudding it was as delicate and special as any that either of them had ever tasted, as was the lightest of pastry that went to make up the mince pies. The mincemeat itself was so filled with currants and raisins, with spices and brandy, that these last were almost a bridge too far.

But only almost, because as Berry said, in the dreamy voice of a man who had finally to admit defeat, 'There is not a spare inch now, Mrs Fred, not a spare half an inch, but every mouthful will stay in my memory for ever.'

Berry had come into his own with Hilda when he was revealed by Trilby to be a cook in a million, although Berry had naturally added quickly, 'But not a patch on you, Mrs Fred.'

Hilda smiled. 'We'll have a pastry competition one of these days, see if we won't, Mr Berry, and soon see who's who, won't we?'

'Hilda will win. She wins everything round here. Can't go in for nowt now though, can you, love, not now thou's won everything, makes for bad feeling.'

'I shall play Father Christmas now,' Berry announced, and handed out the parcels they had brought in for their hosts, parcels that revealed presents of a grandeur that was not out of keeping. A pair of Fair Isle gloves for their hostess, together with matching scarf, and a bottle of brandy and matching glasses for mine host.

'How did you know these were things that they would like, that they are perfect for them?' Trilby had asked Berry when they wrapped them the night before.

'Because,' Berry had said, a mysterious look to his eyes, 'I know that wherever you go these are the presents that are always acceptable to both sexes, presents that everyone likes, and no-one dislikes, it is just a fact.'

Trilby had done them both a drawing. One of Topsie, of course, for Fred, and one of Fred, of course, for Hilda. After that they talked about the village, and all the people who had lived there once. Folk like the mad vicar who had set light to himself one dark winter's day because he thought, the theory went, that Satan had come for him, so he might as well send himself to hell as wait. The girl who was ravished by the local squire and found hanging from a branch of one of the old yew trees in the graveyard. The maid in the great house, who fell in love with a nobleman thinking he was the gardener, married him and lived happily ever after. The usual tales of haunted cottages and ghost riders in tricorn hats passing over the packhorse bridge, not to mention ladies in white dresses who passed through walls just when someone had stopped to speak to them.

'That was just about the best Christmas lunch we

have ever enjoyed, either of us, wouldn't you say?'

They had waved goodbye to their hosts and were driving back in the gathering dark with snowflakes beginning to fall. Topsie who had been feasted almost as well as themselves was snoring on the back seat, and Berry who had the flaps of his flying hat down once more was shouting as people always do when they cannot hear themselves.

'Wouldn't you say, that was just about the best, ever?'

Trilby shouted, 'You bet!' while taking care not to take her eyes off the road, because Berry and Fred had shared not one but a couple of brandies, and as the snow was coming down more and more thickly she was starting to wonder if they would lose sight not just of the road, but of the cottage, so quickly, as she had discovered in the previous weeks, could the landscape change in just half an hour.

'Left here, Berry, no, left!'

Berry gave a great hoot of laughter. 'That is not my favourite word at the minute, Trilb—*left* is not my favourite word, as you may well imagine!' He gave another shout of laughter, and still speaking at top volume he went on, 'Never hear anyone say "Do you know so-and-so's *right* him", do you? Unlucky word, left. *Sinister* in Latin. The place where bad news always enters from—the left.'

'Berry, you are going off the road, you are nearly on the verge!'

Gaily, if slowly, Berry continued, fecklessly and carelessly in what Trilby prayed was still the right direction, because they had long ago left the village and there are few landmarks on the moors.

She knew that they had no spade or rug in the

404

boot, for which she cursed herself roundly. Neither did they have a map, and there were no telephones within miles, and what with the snow piling up ahead and the snow piling up behind them, she had good reason to know that she was only being realistic when she realised that she was beginning to feel frightened.

At last there they were, and the cottage within sight, just in time, and Berry with a rich laugh, pulling on the brake, was saying, 'You were beginning to take fright, weren't you, Trilb? Thought we were lost. I knew where we were, even if you didn't.'

Trilby, who had not drunk any brandy, did not mind anything now that she could see the comforting old stone of the welcoming frontage. She did not mind the snow piling down the back of her collar, nor the bitter little wind that had got up and was whipping round the side of the cottage, first taking care to take a bite out of her face. They were home at last, and that was all that mattered.

'You were a scaredy-cat, Trilb, you were, weren't you, go on, admit it!' Berry opened the back door of the car and Topsie, who was now wide awake, at once jumped out and past him, her lead trailing along the ground.

'Berry! Catch her lead! Quick, step on it!'

Too late Berry cantered tipsily after the dog, but snow or no snow, Topsie was in her element. Sensing the freedom that the leap from the car had given her, she was now darting off past the little cottage, on up the now invisible road and on and on into the snowy banks against which her black coat stood out boldly, but more and more remotely.

Berry, in hot pursuit, soon lost sight of her,

leaving Trilby watching in freezing horror as she realised that, what with the snow and the growing dark, it was very likely that they had lost Topsie to the moors. If the snow continued, she would not have a hope of being found for days and days.

'Oh my God, oh my God! Topsie!'

As Trilby too started after the dog, Berry turned back and shouted, 'No, you go back, stay by the car, I will go after her. One of us has to stay by the car, in case she makes a circle.' Trilby could see the logic of this, and so ran quickly back to the car and waited.

A lost dog is like any lost person to those who wait at home for it. Its whole personality, its divine characteristics revisit its owner more tenderly, more colourfully, more beautifully, so that its probable loss becomes wholly tragic, and so it was with Trilby, who had become as devoted to Topsie as her master. As she stood in the freezing snow stamping her feet and calling for her above the sound of the wind and into the growing darkness, it seemed to her that there was no dog, would never be any dog, as good or as beautiful as Topsie, and her heart ached for a sight of her.

Berry was gone for what seemed like hours, but of course was not, although it was so dark that Trilby had at least had the sense to put the car lights on, something for which she became only too grateful when she saw both Berry and Topsie returning, Topsie's eyes glittering greeny-yellow and sparkling in the headlights, and Berry exhausted, panting as much as the dog, the ears on his battered airman's helmet flapping against the side of his face, making him look for all the world like a mad spaniel.

'You should have gone in, you should have gone in!' he whimpered, gasping. 'Go in now, while I catch my breath.' He coughed suddenly and horribly, leaning against the side of the car. 'Oh my! What a dreadful thing to happen. We nearly lost her, supposing we had lost her?'

In front of the fire Topsie quickly thawed out, leaving puddles around her paws, while Berry, his teeth chattering, coughed, grew flushed, drank tea, and then fell asleep.

Outside the snow fell, and silence, that great thick silence that only snow can bestow around a small house, fell too. The fire, now blazing once more, crackled and spat in the cosy quiet. Topsie and Berry were both asleep, and so was Trilby, which was just as well. For quite soon that state of happy rest that associates itself with danger now well passed was about to be shattered.

PART THREE

Bacterial pneumonia . . . the patient is taken suddenly ill with a headache, severe pain on one side of chest, shortness of breath, panting, dry lips . . . the patient has a high colour, lips tinged with blue, accompanied by *delirium* at night, temperature ranges 103–104.

CHAPTER TWELVE

It was the unreality of it all that Trilby would remember, how unreal it had all felt at the time, the feeling of being in a situation in which she could do nothing, in which she was totally helpless, because by the time she realised what was happening, that it was not just a fever or influenza, it was too late to try to call help, too late to try to remember if Berry might have had something more than a cough and a bit of a high colour when he had arrived in Yorkshire, whether he might have been braving it out, pretending that he felt all right, when in reality he was already ill.

The bald facts were that she had heard him waking in the quiet of Christmas night coughing and complaining of a pain in his side, but then he had fallen into a feverish sleep, so she had left him and gone back to her own bed, hoping against hope that he would sleep it off, whatever it was, and that she could go for a doctor in the morning. But then she was woken again, and going in to him she realised that he must actually have become delirious, because he kept calling out names of people that Trilby did not know. Realising that he must now be very ill, she flew downstairs, collected up some hand towels, and started to fill a bowl with cold water in which to soak them before putting them on his forehead and chest. This she kept on doing though the night, but with no effect. Berry remained delirious.

By the time morning came the snow around the cottage was so thick she could not even open the door to let Topsie out, and the sky was black, as skies so often seem to be in the early hours of the morning; as black and dark as the night that had just passed. And all she could hear was Berry breathing, short little breaths that came in painful spasms and made her stand by his bedside to watch and listen, thinking that he must already be dying, so short were the breaths, so painful their passage. She knew she had to get help, but there was no telephone in the cottage, and it would surely take a tractor, not a car, to get into the village.

That was when the feeling of unreality had become so acute. Upstairs Berry as ill as she had ever seen anyone, downstairs only herself and the dog.

She switched on the wireless, softly, afraid that it might wake Berry, and listened to the news. It confirmed that the whole country was blanketed with snow and that there was nothing anyone could do, but said that if it went on for days more there were government plans to drop food parcels to outlying areas.

'If *we're* not an outlying area, who is?' she asked Topsie.

She switched the wireless off again, unable to bear the cheery tones of *Music While You Work*, or *Housewife's Choice*. They would sound so inappropriate at that moment, like raised voices in a sick room.

She rinsed out yet another bowl of cold water and yet another flannel and went up the steep wooden stairs of the cottage again, Topsie at her heels.

'Sorry, Trilb, such a nuisance.' Berry's gentle voice, thick in tone, coughing, but reassuringly still

412

alive, came from the bed.

Trilby smiled, and inwardly sighed with huge relief. It must, after all, just be some sort of fever, a fever brought on by running after Topsie perhaps? Or caught in London and now, as bad luck would have it, come to horrible fruition just when Berry was out of reach of a doctor and medicine.

'It's just a fever, you'll be better soon.' She rinsed out the flannel and laid it on his burning hot forehead. 'I could keep warm just standing by you,' she joked. 'No need of a fire.' Nevertheless, she stoked up the logs in the bedroom grate, and heaped yet more of her own blankets onto his bed.

She wished that she had learned first aid or something similarly practical. Why had she not asked Berry if he was all right when he first arrived? If his cough was hurting him? Why had she just taken him for granted, good old Berry, the bringer of laughter and happiness? Everyone always took him for granted.

Molly leaving him like that, perhaps that had brought on the fever? People became ill after a shock, their system depleted, Mrs Johnson Johnson had often told Trilby. Heartbreak too could bring on illness. Sometimes people died of a broken heart, it was not unknown. Molly leaving him like that could have broken his heart. He was being so brave. From the moment he arrived he had been at pains to appear so nonchalant. Whatever it was that was wrong with him, she knew from the shortness of his breath and the heat of his forehead that it must be serious, but having no medicine, no antibiotics, not even an aspirin in the cottage, she could only sit by helplessly.

If it went on, when the light became better she

413

would have to try to go to the village on foot, struggle through the snow. Struggle through the snow. Yes, she told herself, that was what she would do, she would struggle through the snow, and somehow she would get to the village. She would get to a doctor and come back with medicines, everything that Berry needed.

*   *   *

It took her hours. Hours and days in her own mind, but how long it had actually been in cold reality did not seem to matter, because when she eventually reached the village again, this time on foot, and flung herself against the door of the doctor's house, the doctor was out, and Fred whose house she ran to next seemed to know more about where he was than his own housekeeper or secretary, or whatever she was.

'Delivering a baby somewhere, my missus Hilda says. Twins 'pparently. Or something like.'

For a second Trilby found herself looking up at Fred and wondering what *something like* twins could be, if not twins, and imagined herself telling Berry what Fred had said, and how Berry would laugh.

'I best be getting back now, Fred. If you could tell the doctor, tell him to please come out, it will have to be on skis or a tractor or something if he's to get through, but he must come out, because poor Berry is very, very ill.'

'Soon as doctor comes, I'll tell him, Trilby.'

Fred looked momentarily worried, but then turned back to his own life and concerns. He had a post office to run, things to see to. Besides, if someone could tell him the good that worry did he would worry, but as it was they could not, so he would not, he would just keep a sharp eye out for the doctor.

'You take care going back now, and don't forget to dose him up with my Hilda's aspirin,' he called after Trilby.

Aspirin would do nothing for Berry, and they knew it, but somehow, like so much that is useless when someone you love is in danger, it was nevertheless a comfort.

When Trilby eventually reached the cottage once more she could only inch her way through the front door, but inch her way she did, and then quietly up the stairs, followed by the ever faithful Topsie. Pushing open the door her eyes concentrated at once on the figure in the bed with the heaped-up blankets.

His hand was hanging down by the side of the bed, and she somehow knew at once from that oddly artistic, dear, familiar hand that if he had any fight left in him it was now going, and that the disease, the pneumonia or whatever it was from which Berry was suffering, was winning hands down.

She moved quickly to his bedside and slid her arm under his head, sitting up beside him by his pillows.

'Come on, Berry,' she said softly, 'you've got to make it for me, you know. After all, I can't do without you, you've got to make it, there'll be no-one to laugh with if you go, you can't go.'

His lips, now blue at the edges and cracked, moved slightly, and Trilby bent her head to listen.

At first she could not hear. 'What did you say?'

Eventually, after seconds of effort, his words became as clear to her as her own.

'Could be going to be one of your weepy moments I'm afraid, Trilb.'

*   *   *

Trilby had always thought that if she shouted hard enough at the future, at the fates, if she willed something hard and long enough, it would happen; that she could actually prevent something terrible happening by this huge effort of her will. Now she found that she could not.

She saw that no matter how hard she willed now, life was ebbing out of Berry as surely as the stream at the bottom of the garden was starting to trickle once more in the afternoon sunshine.

The doctor finally came out, but as soon as he saw Berry's condition he shook his head. He intimated quietly that there was nothing he could do, and within a few minutes he was proved to be right. He closed Berry's eyes to the sound of Trilby's sobbing.

Berry had been her best friend, the first person to whom she could talk, the person she ran round the back to see, always greeted with the same kind of words: 'Ah, my favourite person. Lud, but you look in need of something, ducks, sit down.'

Now, kneeling down beside him, Trilby called to him in her head. *'Why did you have to leave me so suddenly?'*

But even as she did she knew that she could hear Berry's voice, laughing at her.

'Good a time as any I should have thought, Trilb. You know, Trilb, take your leave after a

416

cracking day out. Lovely times, short weepy moment, and then off to Paradise, to paint the heavens with brushes made from moonbeams dipped in clouds of magic. Looking forward to God coming visiting of an evening, you know, *"Well done, kid, good stuff"*, that's what it's all about, wouldn't you say, Trilb? Painting a little bit of Paradise. Not just the tiny bits we see here, but the whole shoot. Something to look forward to, ducks, really, something to which to look forward.'

EPILOGUE

Finally, after a great deal of persuasion from everyone, most of all David Micklethwaite, who by now was completely bored with the subject, Lewis had come to and realised that Trilby was not coming back to him. As a consequence he divorced her in Mexico, and to put the icing on the ex-marital cake, as is the way with the rich, managed to annul the marriage in America.

As it happened this actually seemed to bring him luck, and proved to be a great relief not just to Trilby but to him too, for within a short space of time he remarried for the second time, yet another young girl, but one who was obviously more temperamentally suited to him, for within months of this event she bore him not one son and heir but two, and became a popular subject for all his newspapers and magazines, opining on the glories of motherhood, the Empire, and the joy that her twin boys had brought her husband, and being pictured busy at her tapestry seated beside the fire into which Trilby had once thrown her drawings with such a sense of despairing futility.

Molly too had remarried, Aphrodite's old lover Geoffrey, but only after a graceful period of mourning. Whether or not she felt guilty at what she had done to Berry no-one but Molly herself would ever know, and as Berry himself would have said, 'Well, if that's not where angels fear to tread, Trilb, where is?'

Far from having a traumatic effect upon Trilby herself, the discovery that Glebe Street was quite as

419

fallible as Lewis's world meant that Trilby no longer looked back to those dear days of crossing the street for breakfast with the same sense of romantic longing. As far as she was concerned Glebe Street was now closed, never to open again, and although the people who had lived around her father and stepmother were no longer 'grownups', with that particular sense of mystery that older people seem to hold, but just human beings, they did not become less in her memory for all that.

As if in recognition of a chapter's having closed, Michael and Agnes had sold their house and moved to Marbella, where, in the warmth of the Spanish sun, and the absence of a stepdaughter to irritate Agnes, their marriage seemed not just to revive, but to thrive. About this too Trilby knew that Berry would say, paint on his fingers, his hair sticking up, coffee pot in one hand, cigarette in the other, 'Ours not to reason why, thank heavens, Trilby love!'

Now that everyone and everything seemed more settled, Trilby and Piers had finally plucked up the courage to send out invitations to their July wedding. It would be a small affair, with the reception to be held at Charlton. Nothing too grand, but nothing too dull either. For the reception Trilby was to wear a three-quarter-length tulle dress and simple flowers in her hair, as far from the kind of bride she had been to Lewis as was perfectly possible. Piers was to wear knee breeches and his favourite old jacket with a silk flowered waistcoat, but old-fashioned evening pumps, not tennis shoes, as on the night of their first party together.

Lindsey was to be Piers's best man, and the rest

420

of their young either bridesmaids or attendants according to their sex, but all dressed in festive rural style, and set about with wild flowers as behoved the bucolic theme.

For the great day, the cow byres, having been re-tarmacked by Harold especially for the occasion, were washed down by the boys with extra zest and Piers's favourite cows scrubbed and garlanded, before the children turned their attention to the hen house and every other place that could be found.

Mabel had made Topsie and Steve—still known as 'the new puppy' for all that he was now over two years old—special white satin collars, and herself a new floral dress, not to mention a floral waistcoat for Harold.

On the morning of the wedding Charlie and Mary Louise were to be found busy in the kitchen making a wine cup that they kept reassuring everyone would have them all ending up with the hens and the dogs, under the trestle tables that were already being dressed and laid on the front lawns.

But Berry was not forgotten, because his van was cleaned out and lined with rugs and Trilby driven to the church in it by Mrs Johnson Johnson. Happily for both the bride and Mrs J.J. the chapel was only half a mile away, because any more would have asked too much of the old jalopy.

By the time the wedding party returned, the summer sun was high in the sky, the cows grazing peacefully, most of them having eaten their garlands, and the hens as always running about under the tables and chairs. With a good harvest forecast, all boded beautifully well under an

English sky in a small part of what was still an English heaven.

Only Aphrodite, looking stunning in a pink hat and dress, was, as usual, filled with that sense of melancholy which is so particular to certain personalities, owing to their insistence on trying to see into the future, instead of leaving it to take care of itself.

'Too much on my mind, Trilby dear, you know. Just too much on my mind. Have you read this— about the end of the world? Very good, Trilby, really very good. You see the thing is, Trilby, tomorrow might never happen, that's my point. And you will see what I mean when you read it. Tomorrow might never happen.'

'Exactly Aphrodite, tomorrow *may* never happen.'

'No, Trilby, no. Please, you must understand.'

Aphrodite tapped the paperback book she had taken from her handbag. 'What I mean is, it might never come. Very good pâté, though!'

Trilby smiled and looked around her at the happy guests gathered down the length of the table, or walking about under the apple trees with glasses in hand, surrounded by laughter, talk, sunshine, blue sky, colour.

All that mattered to her was that yesterday had finally been defeated. Living with Piers at Charlton she had found that she no longer looked back, and although she did sometimes catch herself of an early summer morning imagining that she could hear her mother's voice coming across the years to her, singing 'I'll Gather Lilacs in the Spring Again', or the joyful bark of the dog that she had so loved as a child, she recognised that this was because,

422

with Piers at Charlton, she had returned to the very life that she had once so enjoyed as a child.

For the most part, though, all she actually heard in the early morning, besides the dawn chorus, was the sound of the pony's hooves on the country road, and the milkman's whistle borne on the clear air, piping out a song from his youth—except of course on Sundays—when in a perfectly fitting manner, the clear sound of that exquisite whistle turned to that of a hymn giving praise for all that lay around them.

Chivers Large Print Direct

If you have enjoyed this Large Print book and would like to build up your own collection of Large Print books and have them delivered direct to your door, please contact **Chivers Large Print Direct.**

Chivers Large Print Direct offers you a full service:

* ☆ **Created to support your local library**
* ☆ **Delivery direct to your door**
* ☆ **Easy-to-read type and attractively bound**
* ☆ **The very best authors**
* ☆ **Special low prices**

For further details either call Customer Services on 01225 443400 or write to us at

Chivers Large Print Direct
FREEPOST (BA 1686/1)
Bath
BA1 3QZ